The Peregrine Memorandum

The Peregrine Memorandum

John W. Dowdle

Writer's Showcase presented by *Writer's Digest*
San Jose New York Lincoln Shanghai

The Peregrine Memorandum

All Rights Reserved © 2000 by John W. Dowdle

No part of this book may be reproduced or transmitted in any form or by any means, graphic, electronic, or mechanical, including photocopying, recording, taping, or by any information storage or retrieval system, without the permission in writing from the publisher.

Published by Writer's Showcase presented by *Writer's Digest* an imprint of iUniverse.com, Inc.

For information address:
iUniverse.com, Inc.
620 North 48th Street
Suite 201
Lincoln, NE 68504-3467
www.iuniverse.com

ISBN: 0-595-00576-4

Printed in the United States of America

To my wife, Virginia, who suffered graciously through many rewrites, even though she hates spy novels.

Epigraph

This (our nuclear arsenal) would be a deterrent—but if the contest to maintain this relative position should have to continue indefinitely, the cost would either drive us to war, or into some form of dictatorial government. In such circumstances, we would be forced to consider whether or not our duty to future generations did not require us to *initiate* war at the most propitious moment that we could designate.

Dwight D. Eisenhower,
President of the United States, in a September, 1953
memorandum to Secretary of State John Foster Dulles.

Acknowledgements

Over the years there have been may people who have helped me with this manuscript, and I wish to thank them all. In particular I wish to thank

W. A. Armfield, for his unfailing efforts in critiquing the many versions

Frank K. Sloan, for providing insight into the inner workings of the defense establishment

Vernon Tom Hyman, whose editorial expertise contributed greatly to a tighter story.

I

Prologue

In 1977 the Soviet Union, under the leadership of General Secretary Leonid Brezhnev, began deployment of their new generation, highly sophisticated SS-20 intermediate range nuclear missile in Eastern Europe. NATO, already at a conventional forces disadvantage, believed this put the alliance at a theater nuclear forces disadvantage, as well. Helmut Schmidt, Chancellor of West Germany, expressed the fears of many that without corresponding theater nuclear forces, Western Europe would be vulnerable to Soviet aggression. This was based on a concern that since the main US deterrent to a Soviet attack on Western Europe were ICBMs based on American soil, which if used would invite direct retaliation against the US, America might not honor its commitment to protect its NATO partners in a limited engagement.

In 1979, after negotiations with the Soviets to remove the SS-20 failed, NATO made the decision to deploy the US built Pershing II IRBM and land based cruise missiles in Western Europe when they became available in 1983.

In November 1982, two days after the death of Brezhnev, Yury Vladimirovich Andropov, then a member of the Politboro and head of the KGB, became general secretary. He subsequently consolidated his power by also taking the positions of chairman of the Presidium of the Supreme Soviet, president, and chairman of the Defense Council. He continued Brezhnev's massive arms build-up, as well as his policy of refusing to negotiate removal of the SS-20 unless NATO reversed its decision to deploy the Pershing II and cruise missiles.

On March 8, 1983, President Reagan addressed a group of young people at Walt Disney's EPCOT Center where he denounced the Soviet Union as an "evil empire". This was followed on March 23 by an address during which he revealed some recently declassified information about the Soviet Union's extensive modernization and deployment of nuclear weapons, including ICBMs, and made public his decision to proceed with the Strategic Defense Initiative, later dubbed "Star Wars".

On May 17, 1983, George Kennan, who had begun his foreign service career in Moscow under President Roosevelt, and had more personal experience with US-Soviet diplomacy than any other American, stated that relations between the two countries were "in a dreadful and dangerous condition". He declared that the antagonism, suspicion and militarization of thought between Washington and Moscow "are familiar characteristics, the unfailing characteristics of a march toward war-that and nothing else."

On July 11, 1983, President Reagan sent a handwritten note to Andropov assuring him that the people of the United States were dedicated to the cause of peace and the elimination of nuclear weapons. He suggested direct communication to resolve issues relating to such things as arms control. Andropov responded by letter dated August 4, 1985, that "So long as the United States has not begun deploying its missiles in Europe, an agreement is still possible." Paul Nitze, chief arms negotiator for the US, advised the president that the Soviets would not budge on removing the SS-20 until the US deployed its own missiles, and on August 24 Reagan informed Andropov that unless negotiations on removal of the SS-20 made it unnecessary, deployment of the Pershing II and cruise missiles would begin in early December.

During the night of August 31, 1983, a Soviet military plane shot down South Korean Flight 007, a 747 airliner, killing 269 passengers including a US Congressman and sixty other Americans. Outraged over the use of deadly force against an unarmed passenger aircraft which appeared simply to have strayed off course Secretary of State George Shultz denounced the action as "barbaric". And, even though the US had recorded and made public the conversation between the Soviet pilot and his ground controllers, including the report that two missiles had been fired and the target was destroyed, the Soviet government denied responsibility until September 6 when it admitted responsibility, but took the position that the aircraft was on a spy mission for the US.

On September 7, 1983, Secretary Shultz met Soviet Foreign Minister Gromyko in Madrid at a meeting originally scheduled to improve US-Soviet relations, and to invite Gromyko to the White House to explore a possible Reagan-Andropov summit meeting. Instead, in the bitter aftermath of the KAL 007 shoot down, the meeting turned into an acrimonious exchange. The chill which then developed between Washington and Moscow, lead Pope John Paul II to warn three days later that the world might be moving from the post war era to "a new prewar phase."

On October 23, 1983, the US invaded Grenada to oust the Cubans who, as surrogates of the Soviets, had taken control of the government and were engaged in building a landing strip capable of handling Soviet intercontinental bombers and fighter planes.

On October 30, 1983, the Washington Post reported that the Soviet leadership had begun to prepare its civilian population for a crisis with the US.

During the period November 2-11, 1983, the US and its NATO allies conducted Operation Able Archer, a nuclear release exercise based on the US Single Integrated Operation Plan (SIOP), and designed to test communications and command procedures in the event of a nuclear war. In doubt as to the US and NATO intentions, the Soviet Union placed its armed forces on a higher state of alert, and placed nuclear-armed fighter planes stationed in East Germany on immediate alert.

On November 14, 1983, the first ground launched US cruise missiles arrived in Great Britain. Also, before the end of the month both the West German and Italian parliaments voted to accept US missiles on their soil. As deployment began, Soviet negotiators walked out of both the intermediate nuclear forces, INF, and the Geneva arms control talks.

On November 24, 1983, Andropov officially confirmed the break-off of negotiations, and announced military countermeasures including the deployment of more SS-20 missiles in Eastern Europe, and the deployment of nuclear-armed submarines closer to US coastlines.

To many observers, the waning days of 1983 seemed to foreshadow an inexorable drift toward nuclear war.

1

The Ministry of Defense, Moscow, USSR.
0800, Saturday December 3, 1983

Outside the ministry, with a harsh, sub-zero wind blowing sheets of snow across Red Square, the day was as grim as the face of the Minister of Defense, Marshal of the Soviet Union, Dimitri Ustinov.

Today was the day Operation Maskirovka would be presented to the Politburo. With all of the meticulous planning that had gone into the operation, it should proceed like clockwork, but whether it did would make no difference. The leadership had committed to the operation in early April.

The lean figure in military uniform who stood at attention in front of the minister's desk appeared more Aryan than Russian. Arkady Maxsimov's career had begun as had many others with his entry into the General Alexandr V. Suvorov Junior Military School, the choice of those wishing a career in the officer corps of the Red Army.

His time at the school was distinguished only by his excellent academic record which paved the way for his entry into the Mikhail V. Frunze Military Academy in Moscow, the Soviet equivalent of West Point. His career had taken a giant step forward during his first assignment outside the Soviet Union as a military attaché when he prevented a senior officer from defecting to the West. The incident brought him to the attention of Ustinov, and in addition to being promoted to full colonel, he became the Marshal's protégé. Now, as his aide, his future seemed assured.

Turning from the window of his cold, sparsely furnished office, Ustinov said grimly, "Good Morning, Comrade Colonel."

"Good morning, Comrade Marshal." Maxsimov used Ustinov's military rank because he knew that Ustinov considered it the more prestigious of his two titles.

Seating himself at his desk, Ustinov asked, "What is the status of *Maskirovka*? "

Still at attention, Maxsimov began his recital. "Everything is proceeding on schedule, Comrade. Complete plans for mobilization and deployment of troops has been signed off on by Chief of Staff, Marshal Ogarkov. Preparations for mobilization of Warsaw Pact troops will begin in one week with general mobilization of all armed forces to begin on seventeen December. Redeployment of the ships and aircraft needed to transport the occupation troops, except those which will be deployed from Cuba, is slated to begin immediately upon receipt of your order. Marshal Ogarkov cautioned that unless we begin at once, he cannot guarantee we will meet the deadline."

"I'm aware of that," Ustinov broke in brusquely. "He will have the authority to proceed later this morning. What about Peregrine?"

"Viktor reports that it is in place, and has been tested. Also, the three supplementary transmission stations together with their phased array radar tracking facilities are in place. All components have been tested and declared operational."

"The satellites?"

"All twelve are in place on heavy lift boosters and prepared for launch. The first two are scheduled to lift off on the twelfth, with two following every day until they are all in orbit."

"And the ultimatum?"

"Comrade Foreign Minister Gromyko had it transmitted to ambassador Dobrynin yesterday. It was sealed in a separate pouch with instructions that it was 'eyes only' for the ambassador, that he take personal charge of it and not open it until December twenty-third."

Maxsimov remained at attention, his eyes fixed on a spot one foot above the Marshal's head.

"There is something else?"

"Yes, Comrade Marshal." Maxsimov hesitated.

"Well, what is it?" Ustinov made no attempt to hide his impatience.

"I feel I should report to you that some of the staff generals do not believe the occupation of the US can be maintained even if it is successfully implemented."

Ustinov's frown deepened and his eyes became slits. *Could he tell his young protégé that the generals were correct—that he had been convinced from the beginning that an occupation of the US could not be sustained? Could he tell him that it became a part of Maskirovka only because without it the operation would not have been approved either by Andropov or the Politburo? Could he tell him of his real plan—that once the ultimatum was issued, he would find a way to launch the preemptive nuclear strike which would forever eliminate the US as a military and industrial power? No!*

"The generals are old maids." he spat out the words with disdain. "They lose their nerve because of some Afghanistan guerrillas. They do not remember the success we have had in Eastern Europe. They can be replaced."

Ustinov turned back to the window as Maxsimov withdrew.

Ustinov's journey from the Ministry of Defense to Staraya Ploshchad, the Old Square, was short. When Ustinov entered the Kremlin, he was passed by KGB guards through the metal gates of the entrance to the right wing of the building—the private domain of the general secretary and his staff. He went down a carpeted corridor partly paneled with wood, past the entrance to the secretary's office before reaching his destination. As he entered the austere conference room with its long table covered with green cloth, his misgivings remained, even though he knew the outcome of the meeting.

General Secretary Yuri Vladimirovich Andropov would not be there. With diabetes, one kidney removed and the other failing, he was almost at the point of death. His increasing dependence on a dialysis machine forced him to take up residence in a VIP suite at the Kremlin's Kuntsevo hospital. Even though his capacity for work continued to dwindle, and his power was fast slipping away, he was nevertheless still head of the Party and chairman of the Presidium of the Supreme Soviet. But, that would make no difference since he had already approved the operation.

Konstantin Ustinovich Chernenko, who would chair the meeting in Andropov's absence, had also approved the project. An old-line conservative, he had been Brezhnev's aide and confidante, and had believed himself to be in line to succeed him as general secretary. He had been surprised when Brezhnev died and he was unable to rally sufficient support quickly enough to prevent Andropov from out-maneuvering him to become Party leader. When ideology chief Mikhail Suslov died, Chernenko had become Party Ideologue, the second most powerful position within the hierarchy. This allowed him to chair the Politburo meetings when Andropov could not attend. He would make sure it went the way Ustinov desired since he hoped Ustinov would support him when the time came to replace Andropov.

The meeting Chernenko had called was not precisely an *oprosniy poryadak*, which would involve only Moscow Politburo members. But at Ustinov's insistence, candidate members were excluded.

Ustinov was the last of the ten full members, less Andropov, to arrive. When he had taken his seat, Chernenko opened the meeting.

"Comrades, this meeting was called to make you aware of a matter which is of utmost importance to the survival of the Party and the Rodina." He paused to stare pointedly at each member. "It concerns a plan called Operation *Maskirovka* which is set to go into effect on December twenty-four. This plan has the support of your leadership, and implementation has begun. However, since there are only three weeks left for all the massive preparations that still must be made, it is imperative that all of you be aware of its purpose so that you will understand what is happening."

Those members who as yet had no knowledge of *Maskirovka*, stirred restlessly as they realized they were being told the operation, whatever it was, had already been approved. This, of course, meant that Andropov, Chernenko, Ustinov, and Foreign Minister Andrei Gromyko were in favor of it, and the rest were expected to go along without question. Several of the older members exchanged glances as they recalled being informed in much the same manner of the decision to invade Afghanistan long after it had been made by the leadership.

Scowling, Chernenko waited until he again had the undivided attention of his audience. "If information about the operation reaches the West before it goes into effect, it could doom the plan. Therefore, in view of the need for absolute security, details of the operation will not be revealed at this meeting, nor will there be any discussion of it. I will now turn the meeting over to Comrade Minister Ustinov who will explain the purpose of Maskirovka."

Sensitive to his shortness of stature, Ustinov made up for it by his bellicose nature. He slowly stood up and moved behind his chair so he could look down on the other members. "Comrades, all of you know that today we face a threat which is far more dangerous to the future of our Party and the *Rodina* than all the Nazi legions which the madman Hitler threw at us. There is now another madman in power who is intent on our destruction. With its nuclear weapons the US is much more powerful than Germany ever was, and its leader, President Reagan, has the means—and, we believe, the intention—of destroying us. All that was won in the revolution and preserved at huge sacrifice in the Great Patriotic War is now in danger of being lost." He paused as a white-haired member fumbled in his coat for a pen.

"As all of you know, we have sufficient nuclear missiles in place to totally destroy the US, but, at the same time, we also know the US is similarly armed. Thus, while the first strike capability of each is more than sufficient to annihilate the other, neither has been able to use the power to advantage. Even a surprise preemptive strike can be answered by the other before his first strike capability is neutralized. As long as this situation exists neither will risk destruction by attacking the other. But, if either side were to lose the ability to respond to a preemptive first strike with a similar strike, it will immediately become vulnerable to defeat."

There was a restless shuffling as those seated around the table exchanged glances.

"Please accept my apologies, Comrades, for restating matters with which you are well familiar," Ustinov continued, with a hint of sarcasm. "But, when the US begins to put its Strategic Defense Initiative in place, which we believe will be soon, and when they finish deploying their intermediate range and land-based cruise missiles in Europe, which has already begun, they will not only have a viable defensive shield to protect their homeland from our nuclear ballistic missiles, but because of the short distance between their IRBMs and our major ICBM launch facilities, they will have a first strike capability to which we may not be able to respond.

"Make no mistake about it, Comrades, once the balance of power is tilted in favor of the Americans, we will be at their mercy; they will be able to hold us hostage to a nuclear threat against which we will have no defense. Then, even if they do not take control of and destroy our government, as we have every reason to believe their President Reagan intends, we will, nevertheless, become a second-rate nation with no power to shape our own destiny. That must not happen."

Ustinov paused to glare at the members of his audience. "Anticipating this possibility some time ago, we developed a program we have named Operation *Maskirovka*," he continued. "Its purpose is to deceive the Americans as to our capabilities, while we tilt the balance of power in our favor before the Americans have the means to tilt it in their favor."

He raised his voice almost to a shout. "By enabling us to do this, Operation *Maskirovka* offers the *final solution;* the end for all time to the threat which the bankrupt system of capitalism poses to the *Rodina* and to the Party."

After pounding the table with his fist, he continued, "The first strike nuclear weapons which the US has deployed against us fall into three categories—their so-called 'strategic triad'. They consist of their strategic air command, their land-based intercontinental ballistic missiles, and their submarine-launched ballistic missiles. The intermediate range missiles and land-based cruise missiles which they plan to deploy in Europe, are not yet a threat, but we must move before they become one.

"Since neither their B-1 nor their stealth bomber is operational, the first leg of their triad consists primarily of their aging and slow B-52s and their short range F-111s, which can be handled by our air defense systems. This leaves only their ICBMs and SLBMs as their main deterrent forces. Project Peregrine, which is the key to Operation *Maskirovka* is designed to neutralize these weapons."

Seventy-year-old Grigori Romanov, who had been Leningrad Party chief before being brought to Moscow by Brezhnev, was not intimidated either by Chernenko or Ustinov. Without waiting to be recognized, he broke in. "Comrade Minister, you will forgive my skepticism if I point out that we do not have a defensive shield in place to protect us. We are not even sure the defenses we have placed around Moscow at great cost will be effective."

Several heads nodded in agreement. Scowling heavily, Chernenko cut him off. "Comrade Romanov, you will be told all that you need to know, nothing more. Do not interrupt again."

Smugly, Ustinov continued. "Since we have the ability to destroy any missile launched by the US before it reaches its target, the balance of power has now been shifted in our favor. Accordingly, plans have been drawn up by Chief of Staff, Marshal Ogarkov, to begin mobilization of our armed forces shortly. When that is complete, and we have moved totally to a wartime footing, we will issue an ultimatum to the US on the twenty-fourth of December.

"We will inform President Reagan that we have the ability to destroy all ICBMs and SLBMs his country launches, and demand that his government capitulate and allow occupation of all major military facilities and installations, or we will launch a nuclear strike. He will have no choice but to capitulate, and when he does, we will move rapidly to take over all of their command, control and communications centers. By the time they are secure, our occupation forces will be moving into place to continue disarming their forces, and to maintain order."

His speech done, Ustinov sat down, breathing heavily from his strenuous, long-winded tirade.

Ignoring the obvious skepticism on the face of Romanov and several others, Chernenko abruptly closed the meeting.

Gorky Park, Moscow, USSR
1340, Wednesday December 7

A heavily muffled elderly man in the process of crossing the park, stopped to rest on a bench close to its center. When he left, there was a small length of black string protruding from a crack in the wooden arm rest of the bench.

Two hours passed before a younger man paused to sit on the same bench. After observing the few people passing from time to time, hurrying to get out of the cold, he felt under the arm rest and removed a small piece of cardboard stuck there. When he left a short time later, the string was no longer in the crack. After stopping at a coffee shop to make sure he was not being followed, he began a slow circuitous trip back to the US Embassy.

2

The Pentagon, Arlington, Virginia
1850 Friday, December 9, 1983—Day One

Jeff Hollis glanced at his watch. It was nearly six o'clock. Although he could not see outside from the windowless room deep in the bowels of the Pentagon, he knew that winter's dark and cold had already descended and that the snarl of weekend rush-hour traffic on Memorial Drive would be worse than normal, swollen from its usual interminable crawl to something approaching gridlock by an invading army of Christmas shoppers. He decided to wait a few more minutes. By six he should be able to get out of the Pentagon parking lot.

As he closed the file he had been examining his eyes moved automatically to his in-box. He had not checked the last mail delivery which been delivered at around four, and the item on top, a standard eight and one-half by twelve inch envelope used for inter-office mail, caught his attention.

He unwound the string that held the envelope closed and removed the contents—a one page memorandum. He was surprised almost to the point of being shocked when he saw the official DOD stamp at the top with the rectangular border which enclosed the words "TOP SECRET" and on the two lines below, "PROJECT PARTICIPANTS" followed by "EYES ONLY".

Putting his questions aside for the moment, Hollis quickly scanned the memorandum. As far as he could tell, it pertained to a research project referred to as "PEREGRINE", and appeared to be a response to a feasibility query which involved the modification of a command computer component used in ballistic missile rocket boosters. He wondered why he had never heard of an R&D project by that name.

Eight months before, Hollis had given up the opportunity to move to a high level position in CIA to become deputy undersecretary of defense in charge of internal security. Although he still had much to learn about his new job, the Department's policies concerning sensitive research and development projects was clear.

In no event would a memorandum relating to such a project and classified top secret have been sent anywhere in an unsealed, unmarked inter office envelope. Also, the requirement for compartmentalization of all information relating to such projects would mean that a conceptual memorandum, such as this was, would be available only to a relatively few high level people, yet here it was. Had someone simply been inexcusably careless or was something more involved?.

Hollis got up and stretched his arms over his head and yawned. He was not cut out to be a bureaucrat. Sitting at a desk all day always wearied him excessively. At six feet, one hundred-eighty pounds, Hollis appeared more slim than he actually was. Also, his close-cropped wavy light brown hair above a friendly face highlighted by a strong chin and pale blue eyes, gave him the appearance of an athlete much younger than his forty-two years.

He consulted his watch again. He was to be guest of honor at an anniversary party given by some of his CIA friends celebrating his last trip to Afghanistan before he left the agency. Considering the traffic situation, he decided he'd better be on his way.

He hurriedly gathered up the loose papers on his desk, including the memorandum, and put them in his brief case. He then locked the folder he had been examining in his confidential safe.

As he headed for the door, it occurred to him that maybe the envelope would provide a clue as to who had sent the memorandum to him. He retraced his steps and took the envelope out of his out-box. He was disappointed when his examination revealed that, although the envelope was designed to be reused merely by crossing the last name off and filling in the name of the new addressee below it, this one was new and his was the only name on it. Printed in block letters, it provided no clue as to who might have sent it. Also, the courier who had delivered it would be long gone by now.

It could be something as simple as someone coming across it by chance, and not knowing what else to do, sent it to him as head of security. More likely, it was something else. In either event, it would have to wait. He would be out of the office most of the following week. Then the thought occurred to him that he could get the investigation started before he returned to the office. He picked up the phone and hit the automatic dial for David Dawson, director of the Defense Investigative Service. After the fourth ring he got Dawson's recorded voice-mail message.

Hollis thought *That's unlike David. He's usually in his office later than this.* He paused briefly before hanging up. Maybe he was reading too much into the situation, but he did not want to leave information involving a top secret memorandum on an answering machine, even one as secure as Dawson's, so he simply said, "Jeff, David. I'll be out of the office until Thursday. You have my itinerary so don't hesitate to call if you need to. I'll call as soon as I'm back."

As he started the long walk across the parking lot to his car, a chill, gusty wind blew occasional snowflakes against his face. He pulled up his collar. He probably should have tracked Dawson down and gotten him started on the investigation.

3

California Route 1, North of Salmon Creek
1535 Saturday, December 10, 1983—Day Two

Hollis joined the short line of people waiting to board taxis outside the domestic terminal building of the San Francisco International Airport. He savored the mild late autumn weather. It was a welcome change from the raw wet morning he had left behind at Dulles.

The business part of his trip, which was to review the security procedures of several DOD contractors, would start on Monday. He had come early to spend some time at the family retreat of Undersecretary of Defense, Paul Montague. The invitation had come suddenly and unexpectedly, but Hollis welcomed the break.

The Montague property was situated in a remote area a hundred miles north of the city, so getting there would require a car. This would allow him to indulge his only hobby—getting behind the wheel of the closest thing to a formula racer he could rent.

His passion for high performance cars had developed when he was growing up in a small South Carolina town close to the Darlington speedway. He had spent much time on the local dirt oval, and at stock and formula events. A good amateur, he considered turning professional until his father's unexpected death left him with some hard choices. He chose the classroom. A sober, serious student, he worked his way through law school, but never lost his love for exotic cars.

Leaving the airport, Hollis directed the taxi to a rental agency which usually handled the type of equipment he sought. What he hoped to find was a Lamborghini Countach 500, a Ferrari Testarosa or 328, or even a Porsche 928S 4. What he settled for was a red Jaguar XJ-S Cabriolet.

After crossing the Golden Gate bridge Hollis pulled off the highway into an overlook and lowered the top. Even though the wind would be a little chilly, he liked the freedom of view. Moving back into traffic, he turned on to California State Highway 1, the coastal road north. This was not the shortest route to where he was going, but he wanted the driving challenge and the scenic beauty the route offered. He planned to stay on the coast road until he reached Point Arena, then turn inland to his destination.

As Hollis drove, his thoughts turned to Montague. They had first met when Paul was an Attorney in the Criminal Division of the Department of Justice. He had a reputation as a trouble shooter, and was generally given *ad hoc* assignments to prosecute federal criminal actions which were either politically sensitive or complex enough to require skills above the ordinary. It was during one of these assignments that Hollis and Montague had worked together and become close friends even though Montague was his senior by fifteen years.

At the time, Hollis headed an FBI counter-intelligence team operating out of Los Angeles. He was conducting an investigation which implicated the president of a small aerospace firm performing highly sensitive defense work in selling classified information to a foreign agent. However, the suspect had a solid record of party support, and had taken leave from his company to accept a high level political appointment. When it became obvious that criminal prosecution was likely, the sensitivity of the matter required it be given special handling, so Montague was assigned to the case.

Montague had worked closely with Hollis during the last phases of the investigation, and their combined efforts led to the decision to seek an indictment. The subsequent trial resulted in a conviction.

Shortly thereafter, Montague joined the staff of Nixon's National Security Adviser where his achievements added to his reputation. And when Ford took over as president, he was offered a high level administrative position with CIA. Then, remembering his work with Hollis, he persuaded him to leave the FBI for a position in Covert Operations. After the election, not wishing to become a casualty of Carter's partial dismemberment of the Agency, Montague joined a Washington Law firm. He was named to his current position of Undersecretary of defense for policy when Reagan came into office.

Montague's overall responsibility included security for the Pentagon's highly secret research projects, as well as advanced weapons procurement. As the initial research which led to the president's announcement of the Strategic Defense Initiative began, Montague recognized that security would take on an added dimension of importance and difficulty as the program progressed. His solution was to create an additional deputy Undersecretary position, the DOD Security Czar, as it were, to assume overall responsibility for all of the various DOD security functions. He chose Hollis for the job.

Even though the twelve-hour days Hollis and Montague were putting in prevented their getting together socially, they met frequently to discuss security activities. When Montague had called Friday and invited him up to his retreat, Hollis was surprised when Montague had said, "There are some things we need to talk about."

After turning inland to the small village of Philo, Hollis turned onto the road that led to the retreat. A short time later he pulled up to the console just outside the entrance gate, buttressed by heavy eight foot high chain link fence topped with barbed wire stretching out of sight in both directions. He pressed the intercom button. There was a low burst of static, then a voice boomed over the speaker:

"Identification, please."

"Jeff Hollis to see Paul Montague."

As the gate rolled open, the voice continued with a slight Russian accent: "You are expected. Please stay on the paved road. It will take you directly to your destination."

The mile or so drive to the house was along a two-lane paved road which followed the meandering contours of the landscape through a thick, well-maintained virgin forest with the most enormous trees Hollis had ever seen. The last hundred yards led directly to an oval drive in front of a large single story U-shaped stone house, with tennis courts and servants quarters, set off by a well-tended lawn, and manicured shrubbery.

The sudden view of the house brought with it a sharp pang of remorse and sadness. The only other time he had seen the house, Maggie had been with him. She had reacted with mock awe, and they had both chuckled as she exclaimed, "You mean *this* is Paul's little fishing shack!" referring to Montague's invitation. But, that was several years before she had left him, and filed for the divorce which had only recently become final. Hollis understood why she had left, and did not fault her for doing so. He was still as much in love with her as ever, maybe more. She had left an empty spot in his life that he was unable to fill.

As Hollis drove up to the front door, Montague emerged. "I'm glad you could make it. How was the trip?"

Hollis smiled. "Great. I always enjoy driving up the Coast highway." He opened the trunk of the Jag to get his luggage.

"This is Sergei, by the way," Montague said, nodding to a man in work clothes standing behind him. "Leave the car here, he'll take care of it. In the meantime, we'll get you settled in."

Montague led Hollis to a guest room. "After you freshen up and get into something comfortable, let's meet in the study, say around six, for a drink. There are a couple of things we need to go over before dinner."

In his room, Hollis stripped off his clothes and stepped into the shower. He was intrigued by the mystery of what Montague wanted to discuss. They had reviewed the security program in depth no more than a week ago. Well, he would find out shortly.

The study was a large room with oriental carpeting, floor to ceiling bookcases, luxurious overstuffed furniture, and a large desk holding two telephones and an oblong flat box with switches on it which he did not recognize. Montague was standing at an elaborate wet bar, pouring a Vodka Gibson over equal portions of ice and pickled pearl onions.

"Bar's open, Jeff. Help yourself."

Montague watched as Hollis put together a scotch and soda "I'm glad our trips to the Coast coincided, it gave me a chance to visit the old homestead."

Hollis nodded and held up his drink in silent toast. "It's a fantastic place." He grinned. "If it were mine, I'd retire here with a bevy of starlets who know how to play tennis and sit around a pool and drink myself into a euphoric oblivion."

Hollis knew this would get a reaction out of Montague. Known on the Washington scene as a somewhat Victorian type, happily married with two out-of-college children, Montague did not smoke and very strictly limited his alcohol intake.

Montague acknowledged the jab with a smile. "When I finish this stint with Defense, I am going to give up the Washington rat race and retire here. But I think I'll skip your 'bevy of starlets' and catch up on my trout fishing."

"You know, I've always wondered about the heavy gate and fence?" Hollis' voice took on a tone of wonderment. "That's pretty sturdy stuff for a place this far out in the boondocks. It must have cost a fortune." "My father had that done. After he retired he moved out here full time and got a little security conscious, I guess. When he died—about a year ago—he left the place to me. But I hardly ever get to use it. In fact I haven't been up here in over six months, so I let all the staff go except Sergei, who takes care of the place. His father came to work for my father from the old Russian community down the coast, and Sergei more or less grew up here. In fact, he lives over in the servant's quarters."

Montague rose and began pacing around the room, a signal that the conversation had turned to business. "I don't know precisely how much of what I'm about to tell you that you already know, Jeff."

He paused, and when he resumed, his voice had taken on a somber note. "I assume you're aware that we're about as close to war with the Soviets as we have been since the Cuban missile crisis."

Hollis nodded as Montague continued. "Ever since the president initiated SDI, the Russian military has been on a high state of alert. And they got so excited when Exercise Able Archer started, we really had to tone it down and not send all the top brass that normally would have participated. Then right after the president announced deployment of the Pershing II and the cruise missiles, they walked out of the arms negotiations and moved to an even higher state of alert. They're now at what we'd call DEFCON II. That's only one small step short of full mobilization."

"My God." Hollis didn't try to hide his shock. "Are we moving our forces to a similar alert status?"

"No. General Vessey and the joint chiefs recommended that we do so at the last National Security Council meeting, but the president vetoed it. He doesn't want to do anything at the moment which could be interpreted by the Soviets as escalating the situation."

Montague held his drink up to the light and peered at it, as if it were a crystal ball in which he could see the future. "In the meantime," he continued," the Soviets not only have intensified their efforts to sabotage SDI through disinformation, they have redoubled their efforts to access all of our research and development activities which relate to it."

Montague tasted his Vodka Gibson, then peered at it again. "Which brings us to something called Operation *Maskirovka*."

He watched Hollis' raised eyebrows with satisfaction. There was some pleasure to be had in being able to capture someone else's attention so completely. "Very few below the Undersecretary level know about it because CIA felt that until they had some idea what it was, the list of those in the know should be kept extremely limited. I'm sort of jumping the gun by telling you about it now, but I believe we know enough to assume that it could directly involve your area of responsibility."

Hollis finished his drink in a gulp and got up to make another.

"My Russian isn't very good," Montague continued, with a self-deprecating smile. "I'm told the Soviets generally use the word to connote a program of concealment and deception designed to disguise the real purpose or significance of a weapons system by showing a false picture to the enemy. And that may be precisely what they intend here, but we don't know. So far, the only thing we're sure of is that it's the Soviet's most jealously guarded secret."

"You said you thought it might involve internal security?"

"That's right," Montague responded. "But it's a lot more than that. It doesn't take much imagination to guess what could happen if the Soviets had the ability to neutralize our nuclear strike capability, and we did not have the same ability."

"No, it doesn't," Hollis agreed. "The balance of power would be altered so much in their favor that we'd find ourselves open to nuclear blackmail, or something worse. Is that *Maskirovka?*"

"We don't know for certain, but some CIA analysts are convinced that's the purpose of the operation."

Hollis looked skeptical.

"On the surface it obviously sounds pretty farfetched," Montague agreed. "Until recently, both CIA and Defense Intelligence believed we were able to follow fairly closely most of the research and development in the Soviet SDI program. And both agreed that in some of the more exotic areas, such as particle beams and lasers, the Soviets were probably making about as much progress with basic research as we are. In fact, they think it's anyone's guess as to who is ahead. But in the high technology areas they believed that we were far ahead of them. Now they're not sure."

Montague regretfully shook the remains of ice and pearl onions in the bottom of his glass. "One's my ration, I'm afraid." He looked hard at Hollis. "You're familiar with Proetus?"

"That's the space-based, kinetic kill vehicle project, isn't it?" Hollis asked rhetorically. "I've only just begun the security review."

"Well as you probably recall, it's all pretty much the brainchild of General Graham, based on his so-called 'high frontier' concept. There are two approaches under active consideration. The first, which has been dubbed 'brilliant pebbles' by some of the wags working on it, is based on placing a multitude of small but smart satellites in orbit which would have the ability to distinguish between incoming RVs, reentry vehicles containing warheads, and decoys during the midcourse phase of their trajectories, and destroy the RVs by high speed collision.

"The second approach, and the one which is believed to have much more potential for near-term development and deployment is the space-based KKV, kinetic kill vehicle, which would carry numerous small missiles. These would be aimed and fired by an on-board computer, and each would carry a heat seeking sensor so it could intercept an ICBM or SLBM during the boost phase. Here again, it would destroy its target by a high speed collision."

Montague began pacing again. "The reason I'm going into so much detail is simply that if Operation *Maskirovka* is about neutralizing our ICBMs and SLBMs, the space-based KKV is probably the means by which they would go about it."

"I'm no scientist, but the advantages of fewer satellites, simpler technology, and destroying the missile before warhead separation and decoy dispersal would certainly seem to point to the platform rather than the 'pebbles'," Hollis observed.

"That's the way we see it," Montague concurred. His face registered mild surprise at Hollis' unexpected perception of the relative merits of the two systems. "The problem is, no one believes the Soviets have the technology to build such a system on their own. So, if they suddenly turn up with the ability to put such a system in place, they've either made some major scientific breakthroughs, which we believe is unlikely, or they've somehow tapped into our research and are using our technology." Montague stopped pacing and looked at Hollis with a worried frown, "And if that's true we've got a major security problem."

Hollis nodded, "You know better than I that the way the security program is structured, no one, except very high level DOD personnel, have access to all of the information on a given project. Also, since no contractor or research firm can work on more than a single phase of a top classification project without meeting extremely stringent security requirements, it means we've probably got a 'mole' in the department, most likely in a pretty high level position."

"That's where I come out," Montague agreed. "Except that I suppose it could be someone in a consulting capacity. General Graham's team, for example, includes about thirty research scientists, some of whom are still in academia."

"Possible," Hollis mused, "but we've paid close attention to tightening up that area so that no one should see more of the big picture than the piece he's working on."

Montague thought for a moment. "Well it's always possible that Operation *Maskirovka* may be nothing more than a disinformation program to strengthen their negotiating position on the IRBM deployment and arms control negotiations, but I don't think so."

He looked at his watch. "It's almost time for dinner. There are some other things we can go over in the morning, but this was the main thing I wanted to talk about. I think you should drop everything else when you get back to Washington, and see if you can find out whether Proetus has been compromised."

Hollis nodded and rose to leave. Then, as an afterthought, he asked, "By the way, is there a project called Peregrine?"

Montague stiffened visibly. His expression became opaque. "Yes. You should have info on it shortly. It was approved by the Joint Resources Board just last week. Why?"

"I received a memorandum concerning the project in the inter-office mail late Friday."

His surprise evident, Montague said, "What did the memorandum cover?"

"Not much," Hollis replied. "As best I could tell it was feasibility response relating to a project to upgrade the onboard computer in our ICBM and SLBM rocket boosters."

Perplexed, Montague shook his head. "Peregrine has nothing to do with that. It's based on the Patriot technology and intended to supplement Proetus. As you know, Patriot is an endo-atmospheric interceptor of short range missiles. Peregrine will be an exo-atmospheric interceptor to destroy intercontinental RVs during the terminal phase of their trajectory which slip by Proetus. Once Peregrine is deployed, each unit will be mobile and use dedicated radar to track the incoming warhead, determine the optimum launch-time for the intercept missile, launch it, and guide it on an intercept course. When it reaches the point of closest approach to the warhead, a small non-nuclear blast will disperse hundreds of depleted uranium projectiles in all directions which will destroy even a hardened RV.

"One of the reasons for the heightened security of Peregrine is the sensitivity of some of its components. The Soviet Galosh system, which is already in place around Moscow and their Yurya missile launching site, is supposed to accomplish the same thing. But, so far as we can find out, they have neither the chips nor the computer technology to make the system succeed. But, if they got the ones we plan to develop, their system could quickly be upgraded."

Hollis looked puzzled. "That's obviously not the same project that was mentioned in the memo I read."

Montague fixed him with raised eyebrows. "Do you recall the date of the memo?"

Hollis paused. "Not precisely, but I'm sure it was early April."

Montage's expression turned grim. "What did you do with the memorandum?"

"I didn't have time to check into it, so I brought it with me. Would you like to see it?"

"Yes, I certainly would," Montague replied.

Hollis' trip to his room took only a few of minutes. Montague was still pacing when he returned.

"I thought I put it in my brief case before I left the office, but it's not there. It must be with the papers I put in my safe before I left. I'll have to call Mona on Monday, and have her send a copy of the memo to you."

Before Montague could answer, Sergei announced dinner.

4

The Pentagon, Arlington, Virginia
1005 Monday, December 12, 1983—Day Four

Montague hitched a ride back to Andrews Air Force Base on a military jet late Sunday, and was back in the Pentagon at his usual 0730 hours. He was having difficulty focusing on the work which had piled up in his short absence because his thoughts kept returning to his conversation with Hollis about Peregrine. Shortly after ten the intercom on his desk buzzed.

"Mr. Hollis' secretary is on line one. She says it's urgent she speak with you."

Montague picked up the phone, punched the first button, "Good morning, Mona. What's the problem?"

"I'm sorry to bother you, Mr. Montague," Mona apologized, "but Mr. Hollis called this morning to tell me there was a memorandum concerning a project called Peregrine locked in his confidential file. He asked me to find it and hand deliver it to you, but I can't locate it."

"What about his desk?" Montague asked. "Could it be in one of the drawers?"

"I've looked everywhere, but I can't find it. I tried to get back in touch with Mr. Hollis, but he's already checked out of the hotel."

Montague kept his voice calm, "Well, don't be concerned about it. I'll take care of it."

He slowly replaced the phone in its cradle.

After a few moment's thought, Montague told Sarah to call Gary Tolliver. When Tolliver answered, he skipped the amenities, "Tolliver, you've been in charge of Peregrine since conception, haven't you?"

Tolliver, who knew the undersecretary only as a participant in meetings he had attended, responded nervously, "Yes sir. Coordinator until it was approved by JRB, and director since then."

"If my memory serves me, it was officially approved by JRB only a week ago?"

"That's correct, sir."

"Are you aware of any memoranda in any of the files, particularly with an April date, which would pertain to a feasibility query concerning a computer component for the command module of our ICBM or SLBM booster rockets?"

"I'm completely familiar with the files, sir, and I am sure no such memorandum exists. But I can go back and check if you like."

"Please do," Montague's voice had turned cold. "Call me back immediately if you find anything."

Montague slowly replaced the phone and switched on his intercom. "Sarah, ask Dawson to come to my office as quickly as possible, please."

Montague glanced at his watch. Dawson's office was at Buzzard's Point, 1900 Half Street SW, in the District. Even if he left immediately, it would still take over half an hour for him to make his way to the Pentagon through Monday morning traffic.

As director of the Defense Investigative Service, David Dawson was a long time career employee who had worked his way up to head the Service. He was quite familiar with all aspects of its work and had participated in a number of important and sensitive investigations. Some had thought he was in line for the job that was given to Hollis.

Montague leafed distractedly through a stack of correspondence while waiting for Dawson. By the time Sarah ushered Dawson into his office, he was nervously pacing the floor.

Dawson made himself comfortable in a chair near Montague's desk and Sarah went out to fetch him a black coffee.

Montague studied Dawson. He was noticeably shorter than average—stocky, but not fat, and on the dark side. He was intense, but a good listener. When he did speak, his voice was colored with a slight Boston Irish accent.

The Undersecretary, by contrast, was slightly taller than average and gave the appearance of being underweight without being noticeably thin. His complexion was light, and his sandy, graying hair was receding rapidly, emphasizing his already prominent forehead and slightly hawkish nose. His bearing was aristocratic and his manner forceful and direct. People listened when he spoke.

After Sarah had delivered Dawson's coffee, Montague closed the door. "I'll come right to the point, David. I know you inevitably felt somewhat shunted aside when I brought Hollis in, but I've never detected any resentment on your part. I think you've handled the situation very well."

Dawson actually blushed, "Thank you. My assumption has always been that you felt there was adequate reason."

"It's important that you do, because I need some help in resolving a rather touchy matter," Montague waited while Dawson took a swallow of his coffee.

"I want straight answers, and I don't want you to mince words, do you understand?"

Dawson replaced the cup in the saucer on the small table by his chair and nodded.

Montague continued, "Have you noticed any behavior by Jeff Hollis that would seem out of the ordinary, or raise any question in your mind about him?"

"I assume you're asking about his loyalty?"

"Yes."

Dawson thought several moments before answering. "Well, as you know, he's been subjected to numerous security checks because of the positions he's held, and none of them has turned up a hint of anything. The only things I'm aware of, which probably don't have any great significance, are some reports which indicate he may have accessed some files without checking them out properly, and that he's either made or authorized copies of some classified documents without logging them. It's also been reported that he has checked out some technical files which don't pertain directly to security."

"You understand he has the clearance as well as the authority to view those files?" The question was more a statement.

"Yes, I do," Dawson concurred. "I guess the question is—does he have a reason."

"What did the files he checked out relate to? Any specific project?"

"I believe one was Proetus."

"And that's not significant?" Montague wondered whether that was why Hollis had picked up so quickly on the implications KKVs on a space based platform.

Again, Dawson seemed embarrassed, "The reports are unsubstantiated, and he's not been on board all that long. It takes a while to adjust. I thought it would be better to see if any sort of pattern developed before taking a hard look."

"I think there's adequate reason now," Montague replied. "I want you to do a quick and dirty check on Hollis' activities, and let me know what you find out before my meeting with the secretary at four tomorrow afternoon."

5

Palo Alto, California
0855 Monday, December 12, 1983—Day Four

Hollis was caught by a traffic light just as he prepared to turn into the parking garage underneath the headquarters building of International Intelligence Systems, Inc., or Intertel as it had become known over the years. The building was a modest, unostentatious structure in keeping with architectural scheme of the locale, even though the firm was fairly large and did business worldwide. Company security was as unobtrusive as the building; he was completely out of sight of the street before he was stopped by a guard who checked his identification and then directed him to a visitor's parking space.

In the lobby, he made his way to the reception desk, where the lady seated behind it looked up and smiled.

"Jeff Hollis to see Mr. Crowley, please. My appointment is at nine."

"May I see your identification, Mr. Hollis." She took the leather pocket-sized folder embossed with the Defense Department seal which Hollis proffered, opened it and entered his name into the computer terminal in front of her. After a moment, she returned the folder and pressed a button on the desk. A guard appeared out of the door behind her.

"Please take Mr. Hollis to room C-6 on the third floor," she instructed.

Hollis stepped into a small conference room where he found Chuck Crowley, Intertel's vice president of security and several others waiting for him. He had met Crowley several years before, when he was still with the FBI. He didn't know him well, but he was aware of his solid reputation. He assumed the man would run a tight operation.

He was not disappointed. With introductions out of the way, Crowley moved swiftly into the meeting. "You indicated the purpose of your visit was to review security procedures relative to our work on Proetus, so the only people present are those who are involved in that project. Each will discuss the aspects of the project he is responsible for and they will be open for questions at any time."

The group was well-prepared. Each had been thoroughly briefed on what his participation would be, and those charged with making presentations moved through them expeditiously. After two hours, Crowley concluded, "Well, that's about it. Any questions? Suggestions?"

"No, I think you've covered everything," Hollis replied. "Thank you for a very comprehensive presentation."

As the participants filed out and Hollis stood to leave, Crowley spoke to him in a low voice. "If you have a few minutes, there is another matter I would like to mention to you."

"Okay, but I have a meeting in LA this afternoon," Hollis hedged.

"I'm curious about Peregrine," Crowley said.

Hollis hid his surprise. "What about it?"

"Well, after we finished installing the transmitter three weeks ago, we received instructions to return all our files and work records. Since this had never occurred before, we were concerned that something might have been amiss."

Hollis was now doubly surprised. Instructions like that were issued only after a project had been discontinued, and usually long after the work was closed out. He quelled his immediate impulse to pursue the matter since it was clear he would only aggravate Crowley's concern by exposing his ignorance of the project.

"I'm not aware of any problems," he replied. "And, since you've finished the project, there's no need to go into it now. If anything's out of place, post review will catch it." He checked his watch again, and even though he had more than enough time to make his flight, he said, "If there's nothing else, I'd better get going."

Back in the Jag, Hollis put his hands on the steering wheel and sat without turning the ignition on. Peregrine had suddenly taken on a whole new dimension. Montague had told him Peregrine was the name of an R&D project to develop a ballistic missile defense system which had been approved and named less than two weeks ago. But the memo he had found seemed to define the project as an upgrade of a rocket booster component, and was dated in April. And now Crowley had revealed that Intertel had already completed a transmitter for a project of the same name. There had to be some explanation for this beyond mere compartmentalization.

If only he had the memo it might provide some answers his quick reading of it might have missed. Then it occurred to him that there might be a way to find out more about the memo. He remembered the signature at the bottom of the memo: "Lipscomb".

Doctor Lipscomb was a professor at Stanford University who was frequently used in a consulting capacity by the Pentagon. As it happened the university's main campus was only a few miles away.

Hollis went back to the lobby and found a pay phone. He called Lipscomb's home and was fortunate to catch the professor between classes. "Doctor Lipscomb, my name is Hollis, deputy undersecretary of defense, security."

"Yes, Mr. Hollis." Lipscomb's voice was reserved. "Is there something I can do for you?"

"Yes sir. If you have a few minutes, I would like to come by and discuss a memorandum you wrote some months ago."

Lipscomb's voice sounded mildly exasperated. "You are welcome to come by, Mr. Hollis, but I have a class at one o'clock, so I will have to leave for the campus shortly after twelve."

"Thank you, Doctor. I'll be there in fifteen minutes."

On his way out of Intertel's parking garage Hollis wondered what, if anything, his meeting with Lipscomb would produce. He had never met the man, but he knew he was brilliant. He also knew that he was quite vocal in his anti-war views. Hollis smiled. He remembered having been told that the only thing worse than being subjected to one of Lipscomb's lectures on astrophysics was to sit through his diatribe against war.

He expected a certain amount of antipathy from the man, and was not disappointed.

Lipscomb's Home, Palo Alto, California
1145 Monday, December 12, 1983—Day Four

Lipscomb checked his visitor's ID, then led him into his study. "What did you wish to discuss, Mr. Hollis? Something about a memo?" His tone was one Hollis guessed he probably reserved for students he didn't think much of.

"You recently worked on a project called Peregrine." It was more a statement than a question.

"Yes, I did." Lipscomb responded. "But, I'm not sure what I can tell you about it."

"According to your project report, you indicated it was conceptually sound, and that you saw no technological barriers to implementation."

"That's correct. I was asked to review and evaluate a proposal to upgrade the in-flight command module for use with our current generation of military rocket boosters. As I am sure you know, even though the flight path is preprogrammed into the on-board computer, and the boosters contain inertial guidance systems to assure they stay on course, the need for a minor course adjustment may develop after the rocket is launched. If so, it is done on the basis of telemetry and radio transmission between the ground control officer and the command module. The module also allows the launch control officer to issue destruct orders if a rocket malfunctions or goes off course. The project involved little more than a routine enhancement of fairly standard equipment."

"That's it?" Hollis asked. "There was nothing else involved?"

"That's it." Lipscomb confirmed. "Frankly, I wondered why my opinion was even solicited."

Hollis tried to recall what he had read in his brief glance at the memo. "Didn't you add something to the effect that if the module were going to be used as a replacement, the overall size would have to be changed to meet certain specific size criteria?"

"Yes." Lipscomb nodded. "Now that you mention it. I remember thinking at the time that the comment was probably unnecessary because surely anyone engaged in developing a replacement would know the size of the component being replaced. But since the referral had used measurements which seemed to relate to a previous generation of boosters no longer in use, I felt the comment appropriate."

"Doctor, your memorandum had an April date. Is it possible that you worked on the project at a different time, and just used the wrong date?"

Lipscomb's condescending tone returned. "I am not an absent-minded professor, Mr. Hollis. If the memorandum had an April date, that's when it was written."

"I'm not questioning your veracity, Doctor. There was simply a conflict in the file which I wished to clear up." Hollis stood up. "Thank you very much for seeing me on such short notice. You've been very helpful. I'll get out of your hair."

During the short drive to the airport, Hollis debated whether he should cancel the remaining meetings and return to Washington immediately, or whether he should call Montague to report what he had found out about Peregrine.

He decided to not do either. The meetings were important, and it would be after the first of the year before they could be rescheduled. Also, what could he tell Montague other than some facts he might already be aware of, and which, if placed in their proper context, might turn out to be meaningless. Deciding that he had to know more before he could justify a change of plans, he left the Jag at airport and hurried to catch his flight to Los Angeles.

6

The Pentagon, Arlington, Virginia
2210 Tuesday, December 13, 1983—Day Five

Montague hurriedly picked up his phone when his secretary informed him that Hollis was on the line. "Paul here, Jeff. I'm glad I caught you. I was afraid you might have a dinner engagement."

Back in his room in the Bonaventure after a long day of meetings, Hollis had just poured himself a scotch and soda and was preparing to take a shower. The call surprised him. It was past seven, Pacific time, which meant past ten in Washington. "No dinner engagement. I just got in from the last meeting a few minutes ago."

"I'm sorry to be calling you this late," Montague said. "But I've been in a meeting with the secretary since the middle of the afternoon. I'm calling to find out what your plans are."

"Well, I have a meeting early tomorrow morning. Then I plan to catch the ten o'clock flight back to Dulles, and be in the office Thursday morning. I can cancel the meeting and take the red eye tonight, and be in the office tomorrow morning if necessary."

"No. I don't think that's necessary," Montague paused. "What time does your flight get into Dulles?"

"Shortly after seven."

"You're familiar with the safe house at Dumfries, just north of Quantico?" Montague asked.

"Yes."

"I'd like you to meet David Dawson there at nine. Is that all right?"

"Sure," Hollis replied. Montague's voice had a strange, indefinable edge to it. What was going on? "By the way, Paul."

"Yes?"

"I'm concerned about this so-called Peregrine memorandum. Mona told me she couldn't find the copy of the memorandum we discussed, so I asked her to call Dawson and get him to check it out, but I haven't heard anything."

"I don't think we should get into that over the phone, Jeff," Montague said harshly. "David will fill you in."

Before Hollis could continue, the line went dead.

Montague immediately dialed David Dawson.

"David, I'm sorry to be calling you at this time of night."

"No problem."

"I just got out of a meeting with the secretary. We discussed all the irregularities you brought up and decided we've no choice but to take action. Hollis will arrive at the Dumfries safe house at nine tomorrow night. He's expecting to meet you. Take Jacobs and some of his enforcement people with you, and when he gets there take him into custody. We'll hold him incommunicado until we can sort this whole thing out."

"I'll take care of it." Dawson promised.

Watergate Apartments, Washington, DC
2225 Tuesday, December 13, 1983—Day Five

The small but well-appointed top floor apartment was leased to the Carrilion Trading Company. Few outside the Soviet embassy knew the Company was a front for the KGB. Even fewer knew that its current occupant, Semyon Brovikov, was a specialist in mokrie dela, or wet affairs, operating out of Department V, the Executive Action Division of the First Chief Directorate. Brovikov had been assigned to assist the recently activated deep cover agent known as Viktor.

Brovikov was slouched heavily in a low-slung leather armchair, one thick fist cradling a tumbler half-full of Stolychnia vodka, the other a remote control for a VCR. The Russian's opaque black eyes, set beneath shaggy dark eyebrows in a heavy Slavic face, were riveted to his TV screen, and the opening credits of a rented pornographic video.

His concentration was suddenly shattered by the strident ringing of a special direct line telephone fitted with a scrambler. There was no need to wonder who was calling. Viktor was the only person outside the room who had its number. Brovikov put down the vodka, hit the pause button on the remote control, and lifted the receiver.

Viktor came right to the point, "Peregrine has been compromised. Deputy Undersecretary Hollis got hold of a memorandum which was supposed to have been destroyed. But, even though I was able to get it back, the damage was already done."

"What do you want me to do?" Brovikov asked.

"Hollis will arrive at a safe house in Dumfries tomorrow shortly before nine PM. You will make arrangements for Czrnch to meet him there, and terminate him. DIS people will arrive at nine, so Hollis must be taken care of before they get there. I will send you specific information on the safe house by courier."

Brovikov's eyes strayed to the TV screen, where a big-busted young blond female had just begun removing her clothes before the action stopped. Brovikov sighed at the inconvenience. He was just getting settled in for the night. "I could take care of it without involving Czrnch," he insisted.

"No. You will follow instructions. There must be no way his death can be traced to us."

"I understand," Brovikov replaced the phone in the cradle. He extracted a small book from an inner pocket, and after finding the page he sought, picked up the phone and dialed a number.

The conversation complete, he hit the play button on the remote control. He took a large gulp of vodka and settled back to let the erection form as the blond finished disrobing and began to stroke herself.

7

Bonaventure Hotel, Los Angeles, California
0700 Wednesday, December 14—Day Six

Hollis wiped the shaving cream off and turned the TV on as he started to dress. Roger Mudd, NBC news correspondent, was reporting: "The massive military build-up by both the Soviets and the Warsaw Pact countries has continued. Even though the Soviets have characterized the movements simply as large scale winter training exercises, NATO commanders in Western Europe have become uneasy as numerous mobile surface to air missiles and tactical nuclear weapons have been moved into Eastern Europe.

"This follows a report in Pravda of Soviet vice president Vasily Kuznetsov accusing the US leadership of 'making delirious plans for world domination' which are 'pushing mankind to the brink of disaster,' and an article in Izvestia which calls on civilians to be calm, but prepared for a crisis with the West. A high level Pentagon source has stated the Soviets are simply trying to intimidate the US into not deploying its Pershing II intermediate range missiles in Europe by frightening our NATO allies, but a highly placed French government official said he believes if the US does not remove its nuclear missiles from Europe, the Soviets will be forced to take military action..."

Hollis turned the TV off.

Is it possible that the Soviets really are preparing for a confrontation with NATO and the US? Hollis asked himself. They're obviously upset over the Pershings, but all they have to do to solve that is take their damn

SS-20s out of Eastern Europe. *They're not crazy enough to risk annihilation and the end of civilization over something like that.*

His thoughts returned to Montague's cryptic Monday night phone call. He had heard nothing further from his office or from Montague, but the silence had not altered the deep-seated unease triggered by Montague's instruction that he meet Dawson at the safe house.

Safe houses were completely off limits to all except a chosen few. One of the reasons was that a primary purpose of a safe house was to have a place where a person could be taken into custody and questioned over an extended period, and no one other than those involved would know what was happening. The practice when done without a person's permission was, of course illegal, but the person held could usually do nothing even if he were subsequently released because it would be his word against everyone else. Hollis could not believe this was planned for him, but why else would the meeting be scheduled there? He decided he couldn't take a chance.

He finished dressing and checked his airlines guide. He found there was a direct flight from LA to Atlanta, which after a layover continued to Richmond and on to New York. He booked a seat all the way to New York in the name of Charles Standard, but did not cancel his flight to Dulles. Dumfries, he recalled, was no more than 75 or 80 miles north of Richmond, just off I-95. Unless his flight ran far behind schedule, he could get off at Richmond, rent a car, drive to the safe house, and check it out well before the meeting.

Safe House, Dumfries, Virginia
1945 Wednesday, December 14—Day Six

Anatoly Czrnch was short, and his heavily muscled build made him appear to have no neck. His close-set flat black eyes, devoid of feeling, matched his expressionless face as he arrived at the safe house. Brovikov's instructions had been clear. Several DIS officers would arrive promptly at nine. Hollis would most likely get there before them. If so, he was to be terminated. If the officers arrived before Hollis, Czrnch was to depart undetected. A simple task, but not to be taken lightly. He knew Hollis' reputation.

Czrnch arrived at the safe house shortly before eight. Even though Brovikov had provided him with details about the house and its surroundings, he needed to familiarize himself with the area, and give himself time to pick the location to perform his task.

He quickly determined that the best place for ambushing Hollis was from the left side of the house, just back of where the front porch joined the house proper. It would give him an unobstructed view of anyone approaching the house—and offer the fastest and safest route to the woods behind.

Satisfied with his choice, he went back to the porch. Seating himself where there was enough light to enable him to see what he was doing, he opened the briefcase he had been carrying and began assembling the Heckler & Koch MP5SD it contained.

The weapon offered firing selections of single shot, a three-shot burst, or a full automatic setting which would cycle ammunition at 800 rounds per minute. It was equipped with a detachable barrel slightly longer than eight inches, and a retractable butt, and would accommodate the clip-on daylight telescopic sight as well as the nighttime sniper scope both of which Czrnch left in the briefcase. With the 115 grain silver-tip, 9mm parabellum ammunition Czrnch had loaded in the clip, and the sound suppresser he affixed to the end of the barrel, it was an effective weapon for an assassin.

The weapon assembled, Czrnch inserted the clip and pulled the slide back and released it to load a cartridge into the breech. He checked to make certain the safety was off, then picked up the briefcase and moved to his chosen spot at the side of the house.

Old Highway US 1, Dumfries, Virginia
2015 Wednesday, December 14—Day Six

The flight to Richmond arrived on time, and Hollis rented a Chevy Celebrity and headed north. By the time he reached the northern Dumfries exit on I-95, he was forty-five minutes ahead of schedule. His destination, now not more than three miles away, was on the outskirts of town about a quarter of a mile off old US 1, at the end of a secluded side street.

Hollis parked on a street two blocks away from the safe house and ducked into the surrounding woods. It was a clear night, but with no moon the darkness hid his movements.

Hollis approached the safe house so that he could remain in the woods but still see its front door from across the street. The lights in the first floor front room were on, but there was no car parked in the driveway or any other sign that anyone was around. He stood there, motionless, for almost a minute, his senses alert for the slightest sound or movement.

Nothing.

He pulled the 357 Magnum from the spring holster under his arm. He had carried it since his days with the FBI, and had considered giving it up when he left CIA , but somehow he never got around to it. As he began circling through the woods to approach the side of the house, he was glad he had it with him.

He emerged slowly from the woods, then froze. His ears caught a faint whisper of movement, like the rustle of clothing when someone turns. He dropped into a crouch, legs apart, weight forward.

At that precise instant he felt his face slapped by a slip-stream of bullets whining past inches over his head.

He squeezed off two shots from his Magnum and ended the encounter. Both bullets struck Czrnch in the chest and slammed him against the side of the house. His heart pumped blood from his wounds for a few seconds, then faltered and stopped. He crumpled to the ground, his features fixed in a permanent expression of astonishment.

Czrnch, the professional assassin, had made a fatal mistake. The three-shot burst had pushed the muzzle of the H&K up, and he had not had time to re-acquire his crouching target and pull the trigger again before the Magnum cut him down.

Hollis removed the weapon cradled in Czrnch's lifeless hands, and pulled the body out of the shadow into the faint light coming from the front windows. His mind seemed to flip into another dimension when he recognized Czrnch. He had seen the CIA file which listed him as one of the highest paid contract killers around, available only for exceptional assignments.

A quick body search revealed nothing except a Czech CZ-75 with a sound suppresser. Recognized as one of the finest handguns in the world, they were extremely difficult to find in the West. Hollis tucked it into his waistband in the middle of his back, and put the silencer in his pocket.

Getting up from the crouched position he had assumed, Hollis looked around. The gunfire had not appeared to attract any notice from the homes nearby. He checked his watch. In the faint light from the window, he could just make out that it was eight forty-five. Dawson would be arriving shortly, and he didn't want him to find Czrnch, until he knew what was going on. There was a small opening in the lattice work covering the crawl space beneath the house. Hollis pushed Czrnch's body through it, and then shoved the H&K MP5SD and the briefcase in behind him. Once the body was out of sight he headed back into the woods.

Hollis had just faded into the shadows when two cars turned onto the street and pulled to a stop in front of the house. Dawson and Jacobs and two others whom Hollis guessed were DIS enforcement personnel, got out of the first car. They were joined by four more men from the second car, which promptly drove off after letting out its passengers.

After a short discussion which Hollis could not hear, Dawson and Jacobs went inside the safe house while the others fanned out around the outside and disappeared into the shadows.

Their actions confirmed his worst fears. If he entered that house, he would not leave.

Hollis felt as if his entire world had been turned upside down. Until a short time ago these people had been his friends; part of his team. Now the hunter had become the hunted. His change of flight plans and the rental car would soon place him in the vicinity, and once Czrnch's body was found, the manhunt would begin in earnest. He had to go someplace where he could think. He couldn't afford to get tripped up without even knowing what was going on.

Above all, he needed a head start. But, before he could really run for cover, he needed to know where the car was that had departed the scene He moved slowly and silently through the woods back toward his car.

He drove away simply as resident with an errand to run. He was rewarded when he turned onto the road leading back to old US 1. The car that he was looking for was parked on a side street. It was facing the street he was on, obviously waiting to warn those at the safe house of his approach.

When he reached I-95 he took the ramp north toward Washington.

8

Montague's Apartment, Georgetown, Washington, DC
2034 Wednesday, December 14—Day Six

The security telephone in Montague's study had begun its third ring before he picked it up.

"Dawson here. It looks like we missed him."

"What happened?"

"He was not on the Dulles flight so we couldn't put a tail on him. After checking, it appears he took a flight from LA to New York and got off at a stopover in Richmond. We believe he rented a car at the airport under the name Charles Standard. As I say, it may not have been Hollis, but the description fits."

Montague closed his eyes in frustration.

"Anyway," Dawson continued, "we got to the safe house at nine and deployed as planned, but he never showed up."

"Is it possible he got there before you, saw what you were up to, and left?" Montague asked.

"Yes," Dawson replied. "It's a pretty good bet that's what happened, because we found something else."

"What?"

"Once we had been there long enough to judge that he was a no-show, we began to look around the place. We found the body of a contract hit man named Czrnch under the house. He was hit twice in the chest. He was armed with an H&K MP5SD, which had been recently fired. We have no idea why Czrnch was here, or whether Hollis is responsible for his death, but I think we have to assume that he was."

Montague shook his head in amazement. "Where are you now?"

"Still at the safe house."

"I think this has reached the point where we can't keep it in house any longer; it's too important," Montague concluded. "What I'd like you to do is to report your finding the body to the local authorities, and your suspicions concerning Hollis before you leave. I don't think you should disclose the weapon or the briefcase, and do not actually accuse Hollis, but tell them you were to meet him there, and that he may have arrived early in a rental car posing as Charles Standard. See if you can get them to issue an APB on him and bring in a state law enforcement team."

"I'll get right on it," Dawson responded. "Anything else?"

"Yes. Make sure the locals know that Hollis is under investigation for possible security violations. Tomorrow I'll discuss the situation with the deputy attorney general, so you can bring in the FBI."

"Does this mean DIS is out of it?" Dawson asked.

"No. Continue your efforts. If you can take him without involving any other law enforcement agencies, you are authorized to proceed as planned; take him to the safe house and hold him incommunicado for debriefing. Understood?"

"Understood."

9

I-95 South of Woodbridge, Virginia
2045 Wednesday—December 14, 1983—Day Six

Hollis had no clear destination in mind when he reached I-95, so he turned north. South would take him back to Richmond, and there was no reason to go there. But if he were a fugitive, going to his apartment or even into Washington was out. If the car were found there, his trail would be too easy to follow.

He was approaching Woodbridge, about twenty miles south of DC when he made up his mind. He took a back road to Virginia Route 234 West, and turned north onto US 15. This would take him to Leesburg, a small Virginia town 25 miles northwest of the District, and not far from Dulles airport. With several motels in the area to choose from, it would be a good place to lose himself overnight while he tried to figure out what he should do.

At the outskirts of town, Hollis spotted a restaurant with a telephone booth outside. A short distance beyond a narrow, unpaved road branched off the highway. He turned onto it. As soon as he was out of sight of the highway, he pulled over and stopped the car. Before locking and closing the door, he got his suitcase out and dropped the keys on the floor out of sight. After tying his handkerchief to the antenna, he picked up his suitcase and headed back toward Route 15. He encountered no traffic during his brief walk to the phone booth.

After a short wait, a taxi arrived and took him to a nearby motel.

Settled in his room, Hollis turned his full attention to what had happened at the safe house. Nothing made sense. Why was Czrnch there to kill him? Also, who hired him, and why? Why was Dawson there to take him into custody? Should he have stayed to meet with Dawson and explain what happened with Czrnch?

Only questions. No answers.

It was almost five A.M. before Hollis fell into a fitful sleep.

Old Coach Road, Outside Leesburg, Virginia
0645 Thursday—December 15, 1983—Day Seven

Officer Troy Hill, a recent graduate of the Virginia police academy, was the newest member of the Leesburg police force. Determined to advance quickly, he made a point of getting to work at seven, even though his tour on patrol did not begin until eight, and he had to get up at five-thirty in order to meet his self-imposed deadline.

Usually, he avoided Old Coach Road in favor of US 15, because even though the unpaved road was shorter, it meant the patrol car entrusted to his care might get splashed with mud or covered with dust, either of which would require that he wash it at the first opportunity.

But he was late, so he used the short cut to save a few minutes. He was approaching Route 15 when he saw the blue Chevy Celebrity at the side of the road, with the handkerchief tied to the antenna. Alert to any possible trouble, Officer Hill turned on his flashers and pulled off the road beside the vehicle. After making sure that it was locked and empty, he wrote out a time tag, affixed to the handle on the driver's side, and returned to his car. He made a mental note to check on it when he began his patrol.

Twenty minutes later, seated at an unused desk with a cup of coffee, Hill was going through the overnight bulletins when one caught his eye. An APB had been issued by the Dumfries police department the night before to pick up and hold for questioning one Charles Standard, a.k.a.

Matthew Hollis. It stated that Standard, or Hollis, was believed to be driving a blue rental Chevy Celebrity, Virginia license tag RTA-445.

Hill jumped up as he yelled, "Hey Sarge!"

The sergeant growled. He had just finished his shift, and he didn't like being interrupted by a new recruit.

"This APB on Standard, or Hollis. I saw the car just off 15 on Old Coach Road coming in this morning. I put a time tag on it. I wonder what Standard, or Hollis, or whatever his name is would be doing on that road."

When the sergeant responded with a faintly exasperated expression, Hill added, "There's no doubt it's the car. The plate matches."

"Jesus Christ!" the sergeant yelled. "You don't understand a Goddamned thing, do you? He abandoned the car there because he thought it'd be a while before anybody found it."

Hill started to reply, but the sergeant held his hand up for quiet while he thought it through:

"Okay...Luke's Bar-B-Que is on 15 right at Old Coach Road, and there's a pay phone just outside that restaurant. Chances are this guy used it to call a cab. There ain't too many taxis active at night around here. Get on the horn and locate the one that picked him up. When you do, find out where it took him. I'll give the lieutenant a call."

Holiday Inn, Leesburg, Virginia
0705 Thursday—December 15, 1983—Day Seven

Hollis awoke with a start. With the blinds closed, it was pitch dark in the room even though the digital clock on the bedside table told him it was well past eight.

For a moment he could not remember where he was. He stumbled into the bathroom and turned the light on. The haggard, unshaven image he saw in the mirror reflected exactly the way he felt.

When he had gotten into his room the night before, he had flicked on the TV set in time to catch a portion of the late news. What he heard concerned a high level Defense Department official who was suspected of possible security violations as well as wanted for questioning in a possible murder investigation. He missed the name, if one was given, but had no doubt he was the subject. It was not a surprise, but it did serve to confirm his suspicion that Dawson had been sent to take him into custody.

He had then spent several hours tossing and turning, rolling the events of the past several days through his mind, until he had finally fallen into an exhausted sleep.

A shower restored a sense of purpose, and after shaving, he dressed, went to the lobby, and checked out. He bought a Washington Post, picked up a coffee and returned to his room.

He set his coffee on the small table between two chairs and unfolded the newspaper. The story he was looking for was right there on the front page, complete with his photograph.

The terse account, quoting an unnamed Department of Defense spokesperson, confirmed that he was the object of a Defense Department investigation into security violations which were believed to involve espionage, and that he was suspected of having killed an unarmed man who was thought to be assisting in the investigation.

Hollis picked up the cup and took a sip of the coffee. It was cold. He made a face and set the cup down. He still had no answers, but several things seemed apparent. He had known when he took the job as head of security that, like Caesar's wife, he would be held to a higher standard than others. Knowing that, he had scrupulously adhered to all the security regulations. He was not guilty of any violation, no matter how small. Thus, either a gross misunderstanding had occurred, or someone had arranged to make him appear guilty. As unlikely as that might seem, it was supported by the fact that Czrnch's death was being labeled a murder, and he was the suspect.

But, again, why? And then it hit him. The connecting link had to be the memorandum. All that had happened started when he accidentally discovered it. Then, the second bomb exploded. If that were true, then it meant that there was a Soviet mole in a very high position—a mole who was determined to keep him from finding out anything more about the Peregrine memorandum, and determined to prevent him from revealing what he already knew.

Hollis paced the room. Somehow or other he had to get this information to Paul Montague, but to do so meant turning himself in with only suspicions to explain his actions. Remembering what had been planned for him at the safe house, he knew that if a mole had arranged it by framing him, the mole might also be in a position to sidetrack any investigation based merely on speculation.

And there was also the murder charge to contend with. What he needed was an informal one-on-one meeting with Paul. Barring that, the only way he could clear himself and expose the mole was to find out what the memorandum referred to and why it was so important for the mole to keep it hidden.

He stopped pacing and shrugged into his coat. As he closed his suitcase, he glanced out the window just in time to see three police cruisers pulling up across the street, and a fourth stopping at the front entrance of the motel.

He had stayed too long.

10

Oval Office, The White House, Washington, DC
0830 Thursday, December 15, 1983—Day Seven

President Reagan looked up and smiled as Robert McFarlane entered the oval office for his morning national security briefing.

The serene grandeur of the Oval Office still took McFarlane's breath away. This was where History was made, and McFarlane was never more acutely aware of that fact than he was this morning.

McFarlane nodded deferentially and managed a small grin, "Good morning Mr. President."

"Morning, Bud," Reagan closed and pushed aside the folder containing his daily overnight intelligence briefs. "I see no more wars have broken out since yesterday."

"No sir," McFarlane replied, stiffly. As deputy national security advisor to William Clark, he had been in many meetings with Reagan, but he had not yet been able to entirely shed that feeling of profound intimidation that many feel in the presence of a president of the United States, particularly a president with Reagan's high-wattage star quality. The problem had become acute in October, when he replaced Clark and now was required to go one-on-one with Reagan.

"But it's no better either. We're still tracking forty-five conflicts, both conventional and guerrilla. We're supplying arms to twenty, the Soviets are supplying thirteen. That's up one from last week."

Aware of McFarlane's discomfort, Reagan smiled, leaned back and locked his fingers behind his head. "Well, we can't let them gain on us, can we? Isn't there another island down there in the Caribbean that we can rescue from the Evil Empire? Say like Tobago or Barbados? The weather up here is getting chilly."

McFarlane realized the president was trying to put him at ease. "I don't think so, Mr. President, but I'll check. Anything you'd like to start with?"

Reagan cocked his head in that peculiar manner of his. "Well, how's Andropov doing? Is he still calling the shots?"

"As far as we know."

"Casey thinks he won't last long. A wounded fish in shark-infested waters, he called him. Chernenko and Ustinov are both circling in for the kill. Andropov isn't exactly a close friend of the United States, but at least I don't think he'd do something foolhardy. The others—who knows? It could be bad for us."

"I don't think the situation is any worse, Mr. President, but it sure doesn't seem to be getting any better. Their so-called training exercises have continued to expand. It's looking more and more like a full-scale mobilization. General Vessey and the joint chiefs are getting somewhat antsy about the situation. Some of the top Defense analysts are beginning to speculate that the Soviets may be planning a conventional arms attack against NATO to prevent further deployment of our Pershings and cruise missiles.

Reagan nodded and frowned. For the first time in his presence, McFarlane saw the president's relentlessly sunny, upbeat expression turn suddenly dark. He found the change in mood oddly unsettling.

"Secretary Weinberger wants me to reconsider my decision to stay at DefCon 4 when the Council meets tomorrow," the president said. "He also wants to move the carrier battle groups into a closer proximity to potential targets and deploy three ballistic missile subs ahead of schedule."

Reagan removed his hands from behind his head, and clasped them on the desk in front of him. "What do you think, Bud?"

McFarlane heaved a sigh and took a moment to gather his thoughts. "I've discussed the situation at length with Nitze, Mr. President, and we both find it difficult to believe the Soviets are preparing for any sort of confrontation. Their economy is in shambles, they're bogged down in Afghanistan, and morale in their armed forces is low. I think they're simply trying to intimidate us into not deploying any more Pershings and cruise missiles by making threatening moves at NATO. As soon as they find out we're not impressed, they'll back off. In fact, this seems borne out by a speech Minister of Defense Ustinov just made. It sounded fairly conciliatory compared to the other stuff that's been coming out of there lately."

"I hope you're right," the president mused. "Obviously, the Soviets will know if the carrier battle groups are repositioned, just as they'll know that the additional boomers have been deployed. I don't think this is the time to go head-to-head with them as if we're trying to force them to back down. If we do, we run the risk of escalating the situation into a real confrontation."

The President nodded, as if to re-emphasize his point. "I think our best bet is to not give the appearance that we are even concerned over what they are doing. The Soviets know we have guaranteed the safety of NATO members even to the point of using nuclear weapons. Surely the joint chiefs don't think the Soviets are planning a nuclear confrontation?"

"They feel it's important to be prepared for that as well as any other eventuality," McFarlane responded.

Reagan shook his head. "I don't even want to think about the possibility of a nuclear confrontation. I'll give some consideration to changing our alert status, even though I'm no more convinced it's the right thing to do now than I was before all this crap got started. But, if we're going to fight a nuclear war, God forbid, I don't think it makes a tinker's damn where the battle groups are or whether we have six more subs deployed. Anything else?"

"Yes," McFarlane replied. "Those satellites the Soviets put in orbit have been labeled by them as part of a series of communications and meteorological stations that will be launched over the next several days."

Reagan smiled sardonically. "What's their real purpose?"

"We don't know. The orbital inclination is wrong and they're too low. ComSats usually have zero inclination, and a perigee-apogee of almost thirty-six thousand kilometers, while weather sats have an inclination of eighty to eighty-five degrees and a perigee-apogee close to a thousand kilometers. These have a sixty degree inclination, and a perigee-apogee of only about four hundred kilometers. Belvoir has used a couple of our Keyholes to get some close up imagery, but what they see doesn't tell them very much. The satellites are just large cylinders closed at both ends with some antennae deployed."

Reagan raised an eyebrow and laughed. "You're talking way over my head here," he protested. "Cut to the chase."

McFarlane scolded himself. He was being overeager, trying to impress. He knew that the president was very impatient with technical details. He forced himself to abbreviate his answer: "CIA believes they are a new generation of radar ocean-reconnaissance satellites, or RORS. They're the Soviet's primary means of tracking our naval forces."

Reagan cocked his head to one side and squinted his eyes slightly. "Didn't one of those go down recently?"

"You're exactly right." McFarlane smiled. "That was about five years ago. The satellites are quite large and very heavy because they use a small nuclear generator to provide power since solar panels can't produce enough electricity to operate the radar. This results in a low orbit which tends to decay fairly rapidly. You may remember the one that went down burned up in the atmosphere, and left a trail of radioactive particles over Northern Canada." He paused, "By the way, Defense Intelligence disagrees with the CIA. It doesn't think that the satellites are RORS."

The president raised his eyebrows again. McFarlane hastened to explain. "They don't spend any time over either the far north or far south latitudes because of the shallow orbital inclination. This limits their tracking capability to the middle latitudes while maximizing their time over the US. General Shields thinks the satellites may be space-based weapons platforms."

"What kind of weapons does he think they might carry?" Reagan asked, leaning forward in his chair.

"Two possibilities," McFarlane answered. "The first is that they are launch platforms for nuclear missiles. The second is that the platforms are for weapons designed to destroy our ICBMs and SLBMs."

The president was skeptical, "Do you think either of these is likely? Do they have the technology?"

"They have the ability to put up launch platforms which would carry nuclear-armed missiles. But even though missiles launched from space could reach targets anywhere in the world in a fraction of the time it would take an ICBM to reach its target, it's unlikely that's the purpose of the platforms because it does not eliminate our first strike response capability. Even if they destroyed our ICBMs before we could launch them as well as a portion of the Strategic Air Command, we would still have our SLBMs; more than enough for deterrence."

"What about the other possibility?" Reagan asked. "A platform for weapons to destroy our ICBMs and SLBMs?"

"Well, Shields has pretty much ruled out such things as lasers, particle beams and impulse generators, but, theoretically, at least, they could be carrying kinetic kill weapons."

When Reagan raised his eyebrows again, McFarlane responded. "They are small, very high speed missiles designed to seek out and destroy an ICBM or SLAM by impact during its launch phase."

"Do you think there is any real likelihood that they have those?" Reagan made no effort to hide his skepticism. "All of the pundits over here are saying implementation of 'star wars' is years away, if ever."

"I think everyone agrees that it's a long shot. People familiar with the DS research believe its very unlikely the Soviets are significantly ahead of us. But one of our projects which has the most potential for early deployment is a space based KKVs system. We've had a team of over thirty top scientists working on it for almost a year now. They've proven the feasibility of the system, and General Graham says that it can be tested within a year, and the system could be in place a couple of years later. There are some, however, who believe that if the Soviets had access to our research they could have instituted a crash program..."

The door opened suddenly and an aide peeked in to remind the president that his meeting with the Republican Congressional leaders was running half an hour behind schedule.

Reagan nodded and motioned for the aide to shut the door again. McFarlane was abruptly reminded of how precious a president's time was. He closed his attaché case and stood up to leave.

"Does this have anything to do with that story about Hollis in the Post this morning?" Reagan asked.

"Yes, I'm afraid it does, Mr. President," McFarlane replied. "The CIA has been picking up indications for some time that our KKVS project might have been compromised. A preliminary investigation determined that Hollis had engaged in some questionable practices concerning that project, and a meeting was set up to question him about it. As the story indicated, a person was killed at the scene before our people arrived, and Hollis has disappeared.

"Ordinarily, Defense would not have released that information to the news media, but since it is absolutely imperative that we know whether he has compromised the project, and if so, how long ago, it was decided to issue an APB to get local law enforcement agencies involved. Also, the decision has been made to bring the FBI in to assist DIS in apprehending Hollis as quickly as possible."

Reagan came around to the front of his desk and walked with McFarlane to the door. "So, you're telling me there may be adequate reason to assume the satellites may be part of a KKV system?"

"Again, Mr. President, most of the experts believe it unlikely, but they can't completely rule out the possibility."

The door opened from the other side and an aide waited to usher McFarlane out.

Reagan took hold of his elbow and held him back. "I have a question for you, Bud. I want you to give me your answer by lunch time."

"Of course, Mr. President."

"Is my decision not to respond to the Soviet provocation's the right one, or should we match them move for move, to show them that they can't intimidate us?"

Suddenly the congressional delegation was filing in past McFarlane, and the president's attention shifted to them. Senator Dole cracked a joke and Reagan started to tell him a story.

The door closed and McFarlane found himself standing alone in the outer vestibule, wondering what answer he was going to give the president by lunch time.

11

Holiday Inn, Leesburg, Virginia
0753 Thursday, December 15, 1983—Day Seven

Hollis watched the police deploy for only a moment. He knew he would have to move fast.

He changed quickly from his business suit to slacks, sweater, took his tie off, opened his collar, and fished a pair of sun glasses out of his brief case. Next, he searched through his suitcase, and made sure there was nothing in it he would need. He pulled the door shut behind him as he left the room.

Instead of going to the elevators which served the wing he was in, he went to those serving the other wing. On the way, he found an unlocked utility closet where he deposited the suitcase. He waited until several other people appeared before taking the elevator down to the lobby.

Hollis stepped out of the elevator on the far side of the lobby away from the reception and cashier desk. As the other people went into the restaurant he noticed a police lieutenant and sergeant at the desk and two policemen at the door.

He nodded to the lone bellhop in the lobby and handed him a couple of dollars. "Could you get me a taxi? I have to meet some buddies over at the Fairfax Country club."

The bellhop went out the lobby door and Hollis sat down in a chair with his back to the desk. He heard the clerk confirm that there was indeed a man in room 366 who fit the description the Lieutenant had given him.

"At least he was there," the clerk continued. "I didn't check him in and wouldn't have known he was here, except that he checked out when he came down to get a paper about an hour ago."

Agitated, the lieutenant asked, "Do you recall what he was wearing and what he did after he checked out?"

The clerk, refusing to be hurried, thought a moment before responding, "Well, as far as I can remember, he was wearing an expensive gray suit, a white shirt and a red and gray striped tie. Very good taste. He took some coffee from the complimentary wagon with him when he went back to his room. I haven't seen him since, but he could have left without my knowing it."

"Didn't you see the newspaper this morning? His picture was on the front page. You should have reported him!" The Lieutenant's tone conveyed a high level of outraged exasperation.

"I've got the six till noon shift, Lieutenant," the clerk responded with righteous indignation. "I don't have time to look at a paper 'til afternoon, and by then the only part that's not out of date is the comics."

The bellhop returned to tell Hollis that his taxi was waiting. The lieutenant waved to the policemen at the door to join him. With the door momentarily unguarded, Hollis followed the bellhop out just as the lieutenant issued his orders. "Sergeant, get on your radio and make sure everyone knows what he's wearing and that all doors are covered. Hill, you take the front door and check the ID of everybody who tries to leave. Jones, you come with me."

As the taxi moved from the motel drive into the street, Hollis chuckled. No one made any move to stop him. Undoubtedly the police on the outside had assumed he had been cleared by those on the inside.

"Where to, sir?"

"Dulles airport. please."

Hollis used a fifty-dollar bill to pay the driver, and gave him a larger than normal tip before he made his way to the Eastern ticket counter. That would make sure he remembered the fare. Then, even though the line was relatively short, and it took less than five minutes to get an open slot, he glared at the agent and shouted at him:

"I can understand why so many people hate Eastern Airlines," his voice dripped exasperation. "If you people were willing to put a few more agents at the ticket counter, customers wouldn't have to stand in line half an hour just to get a damned ticket."

Then, ignoring the Arrivals and Departures posted behind the counter, he asked, belligerently, "When's your next flight to New York?"

"Ten forty-five, sir."

"Nothing sooner?"

"No, but the shuttle leaves National every hour on the hour. The bus at the main door will get you there in time for you to catch the next one."

"That goes to La Guardia, doesn't it?"

"Yes, sir."

"Is that where the flight out of here lands?"

"No sir. It goes to Kennedy?"

"What time does it get there?"

"Eleven-fifty."

Hollis grimaced, "Well, Goddammit! You always have everything in the wrong place, but I guess I'll have to take your flight. If you're on time, which is unlikely, I'll just make my Lufthansa flight to Frankfurt."

"What name, sir?"

"M. Holland. I want first class, and I'll pay cash." He took his change together with the ticket, and headed for the Eastern concourse. Even though the ticket agent had remained calm and unperturbed throughout the ordeal, Hollis was sure that he would be remembered. Before he reached the security gate, he found a phone booth and dialed Montague's private number at the Pentagon. The phone was answered by Montague's secretary on the second ring.

"Good morning, Sara. Jeff Hollis. I need to talk to Paul right away. Is he in?"

"Yes, Mr. Hollis. Hold on, please."

As the wait stretched out, Hollis' misgivings grew. Ordinarily he would be put through immediately. Finally, he heard Montague's voice: "Jeff, where are you?"

He hung up without replying. He knew he might be reading too much into Montague's delay in getting on the phone. It didn't necessarily mean that he had traced the call and was arranging to have him picked up. There could be a legitimate reason but he was not willing to sacrifice his freedom to find out.

The only safe way to contact Montague was through an intermediary. There was only one person he knew he could trust with his life, and that was his ex-wife, Maggie.

She had divorced him, but he knew in his heart it was not because she no longer loved him. As a friend, she could call Montague without raising suspicions, and find out whether a meeting could be arranged. With that settled, Hollis headed for the main entrance to the terminal. He got outside just in time to catch the shuttle bus to National Airport. From there, he took the Metro into the District.

From the Metro, Hollis walked to the Mayflower Hotel. The large lobby, bustling with people, was a good place to temporarily lose himself. But he knew that if he were going to avoid both the law enforcement agencies trying to capture him and whoever it was who was trying to kill him he would have to take on a new identity, and he probably should have several in reserve.

This meant coming up with all the necessary papers, and, to do that, he would need a lot more cash than he now had. He knew what he had to do, but his first task was to get a message to Maggie and arrange a meeting as quickly as possible.

He headed for a phone booth, and then stopped. It seemed unlikely that she would be under surveillance, or that her office phone would be bugged, but he decided he couldn't take the chance. Instead, he called a courier service, and then found a desk where he could compose the message.

The courier had not arrived when Hollis finished the message, so he went to the phone booth and called the New York branch of Credit Suisse and asked to speak to the banking manager. When the voice came on the telephone, Hollis said, "This is a J2389Z authority for withdrawal of one hundred thousand dollars from account 403-WST-637K, immediate value funds to be transferred to Riggs National Bank, Main Office, for release to anyone presenting the alpha-numeric sequences just given you. Any questions?"

"Your instructions are understood." The voice had a faint German accent. "When Zurich confirms, the funds will be made available as requested. It should take no more than thirty minutes."

The withdrawal Hollis had arranged was from a special DOD fund established to provide top-level security officers immediate access to emergency funds. Under normal circumstances, he would encounter no problems withdrawing whatever amount he needed. But now he had no way of knowing whether his attempt to withdraw funds would trigger an alert. It was a risk, but it was the only way he could get the money he needed. He hoped the inefficiency of DOD bureaucracy would work in his favor. If he moved fast enough, maybe he could pull it off.

12

J. Edgar Hoover Building, Washington, DC
1000 Thursday, December 15, 1983—Day Seven

Dawson was ushered into the office of Frank Tellier, executive assistant director of the FBI. In addition to Tellier, the assistant directors in charge of criminal investigation and intelligence and several division heads were also present.

After introductions were over and the group was seated, Tellier began, "Gentlemen, I apologize for asking you to meet with me on such short notice. I would not have done so except I have been informed that DOD believes there has been a major security breach and has requested our involvement. They also believe the matter is of utmost urgency. David will brief us on what's involved. David?"

"Gentlemen, I'm sure you saw this morning's Post and the article about Jeff Hollis. I'm afraid the situation is worse than portrayed. We have strong reason to believe Hollis may have compromised at least two of the key SDI research projects which the Department had hoped would give us an insurmountable lead over the Soviets in defense against nuclear weapons. If he has compromised them, he may not only have succeeded in negating that advantage, he may actually have given the Soviets an advantage over us. We must know the answer to that question. That is why it is so important that we not only prevent him from leaving the country, but that we find him and take him into custody immediately."

Dawson recounted what had happened at the Dumfries safe house, including finding the body under the house. "We do not know why Czrnch was there. The man was a contract killer, so it's possible that the

Soviets have already gotten all they expect to get out of Hollis. If so, they may believe he has become more of a liability than an asset, and ordered him to be eliminated. In any event, Hollis obviously got the better of the encounter and decided not to wait around for us. We took the opportunity to make it appear to be murder so that we could get the locals involved."

After reporting what had happened at the Holiday Inn in Leesburg, and what they had learned from the Eastern ticket agent, Dawson concluded, "The trail ends at Dulles because we haven't been able to confirm whether he actually caught the flight, but it seems likely that he did. We assume he will do his utmost to get out of the country as quickly as possible."

Tellier took the floor, "This will be brief because we've got a long way to go and a short time to get there. Most of you know Hollis personally, as I do, but for those who don't, the file's pretty complete. He is not one to underestimate. He was at the top of his group when he went through Quantico, and was one of our best agents. He is very thorough, tenacious, an extremely fast study with reflexes much better than average. In short, he's a formidable opponent."

Tellier turned to the assistant director of investigations. "John. Put this at the top of our priority list, and get out a bulletin to all offices immediately. Make sure everyone understands that we want Hollis alive so a damage assessment can be made. All efforts will be directed toward apprehending him. Once he's apprehended, he is to be transferred here without delay."

The assistant director of investigations turned to one of his division heads. "Get on the horn to New York, and get them to follow up on the flight to Kennedy. I think there's a good chance he didn't take the flight, but we need to know. If he didn't take it then he may be right here in the District, so as soon as you get New York moving, get the agent in charge of the District office started, and then light a fire under the metro and park police. The longer it takes to get moving, the slimmer our chances of catching him."

13

Mayflower Hotel, Washington, DC
1035 Thursday, December 15, 1983—Day Seven

Once the courier was gone and the arrangements for the money transfer complete, Hollis found a man's haberdashery off the lobby of the Mayflower. As he entered, a clerk gave up his pastime of admiring the cleavage of the buxom blonde cashier and hurried to assist him.

Hollis chose three distinctly different outfits: a fairly conservative business suit, a more casual one, and a lightweight tweed jacket and slacks combination. The clerk was not happy with Hollis' selections. His choices not only seemed more in keeping with someone considerably older, they were not compatible with the customer's natural coloring. Also, while not baggy, they did not fit as snugly as the clerk preferred. The clerk tried to steer him to selections he thought more appropriate, but Hollis would have none of it.

After adding several shirt-slacks-sweater combinations and underwear, Hollis bought a suitcase and packed all the clothes in it.

At a drug store off the Mayflower lobby, he purchased some toiletries, several different wash-out hair tints, spirit gum, cotton balls, and a bottle of artificial tanning lotion.

The next step was to tap the emergency funds transferred to Riggs Bank.

Hollis caught a taxi to the Hay-Adams hotel and checked in. He changed his clothes in a rest room off the lobby, checked his suitcase with the doorman, then made the short walk to the Riggs.

Inside, Hollis introduced himself as Clyde Middleton and asked to see the City Banking Officer.

The receptionist told him he'd have to wait. Mr. Jamison was busy.

Hollis took a seat outside the office and discreetly surveyed the lobby. There were two men at different customer standup desks, both of whom seemed to be making little progress with what they were doing. He wondered if they were DIS or FBI.

Finally the receptionist ushered him into Jamison's office.

Jamison rose as Hollis entered, "Please come in, Mr. Middleton. I'm Robert Jamison."

Hollis saw a young banker on the move, overly solicitous, with more polish than substance. "Mr. Jamison, I know you're quite busy, so I'll not take up your time. I've been empowered to present this to you as authorization for a prearranged withdrawal."

Hollis handed Jamison a folded slip of paper on which the authorization and account alpha-numeric sequences were written. As he watched, a shadow crossed Jamison's face. The banker regained his composure quickly, but Hollis had already read the man. He'd make a lousy poker player, Hollis thought.

"Well, we've been expecting you, Mr. Middleton," Jamison said, with a forced smile. "The New York branch of Credit Suisse cleared this wire transfer a short time ago. If you'll just tell me the denominations you'd like, I'll have the cashier bring the funds to you here."

Hollis stood up and unbuttoned his jacket. Although he did not show Jamison the Magnum, the inference conveyed by his action was clear, even to the young bank executive.

"Don't waste your cashier's time, Mr. Jamison. Ask your head teller to prepare six ten thousand dollar packets of old hundred dollar bills and to bring them to you in an envelope. When he does, you give him a receipt showing the transaction as a loan to Clyde T. Middleton, proper documentation to follow. While we wait, I think you should sit over there."

Hollis pointed to a chair at a small conference table where Jamison's hands and feet would be in sight while they waited.

Jamison, now quite white-faced, complied immediately.

In a short time the packets were brought into the office by an elderly gentleman in shirtsleeves. Hollis watched intently, but Jamison didn't try to signal the teller that anything was wrong.

As they prepared to leave the office, the bank officer asked him nervously if he'd care to check the contents of the packets.

"I don't think that will be necessary, Mr. Jamison. I'm sure Riggs is a reputable bank."

He saw Jamison glance nervously back in the direction of his desk.

"Mr. Jamison, you and I will leave here together. As we walk out of the bank, you will tell your secretary that you'll be right back. Also, I know you will remember that it's very important that whoever is out there assumes we are good friends leaving together for our morning coffee."

When they were three blocks from the bank, Hollis hailed a taxi and said good-bye to the banker. He could not be positive a trap had been set for him, but if it had been, he had just blown the Middleton identity, and would have to discard it. But before he did, he would use it to obscure his real intentions.

Ray Ad Agency, Sixteenth Street, Washington, DC
1145 Thursday, December 15, 1983 – Day Seven

Maggie was roused from her thoughts when the receptionist called to tell her that a courier was on his way to her office to deliver an envelope. She had been distracted ever since she had seen Hollis' picture staring at her from the morning paper. She chided herself over the fact that she had gotten little work done all morning; she was unable to admit to herself why. After all, they were no longer married; what happened to him did not concern her. Even so, there had to be some dreadful mistake. If she knew anything about Hollis, it was that his loyalty to his country was deep and unswerving.

She signed for the envelope and reached for her purse. The messenger smiled and shook his head, "That's already been taken care of by the sender, Ma'am. He also paid extra to make sure it was delivered to you personally before eleven-thirty."

"Thank you. I'll tell the sender it arrived on time."

Maggie opened the heavy duty outer envelope the courier service used. The envelope inside bore the name and address of the Mayflower Hotel. Her heart quickened when she recognized the handwriting. She tore the letter open and skipped quickly over the lines intended to assure her that he had committed no security violations. He didn't have to tell her that. The letter continued:

I would like you to get in touch with Paul Montague and see if you can find out what's going on. I would like to meet with him and explain what I suspect, but I can't risk being taken into custody until I know what's going on and who's behind it. I know I have no right to ask you, but there is no one else I can trust. If you do decide to call Paul, and tell me what he said, I will be waiting at our favorite place.

Remember your birthday, and please come alone.

Maggie understood Hollis' request that she get in touch with Paul. Even as close as they had been, he could not do it directly without risk. But where and when did he want her to meet him? Also, he should have known that if she went she would not take anyone with her. After rereading the letter several times she tried calling Paul only to find that he would not be able to return the call until after one o'clock. She put the letter in her purse and left the office for an early lunch.

14

Enroute to Stavros' Apartment, Washington, DC
1155 Thursday, December 15, 1983—Day Seven

After retrieving his suitcase from the Hay-Adams, Hollis directed the taxi to the intersection of Fourteenth Street and Columbia Road. After making sure that no one was following him, he got out and walked four blocks south on Fourteenth Street to an aging apartment building now mostly deserted. He climbed several flights of stairs and knocked on an unmarked door. The overwhelming decay that Hollis found in the building appalled him. When he first came to Washington, the neighborhood had been solidly middle class. But now, it was strewn with garbage and obviously the lair of homeless junkies.

Stavros, the occupant of the apartment, had been in Washington for a number of years. He had first run his operation out of a tenement in the southeast section of the city. Urban redevelopment eventually caught up with him, and he had moved his operation to its current site. The move had not affected his business in forging identification documents, Stavros was one of the best. He had the cameras, the equipment, the paper, the blanks, and could produce anything from driver's licenses, social security cards with matching facsimiles of major credit cards, to acceptable passports of most major countries.

Hollis knew he was taking a chance using Stavros because the FBI, after becoming aware of his activities, made a high-level policy decision not to interfere with his operation. Instead, it left him in business so it could keep him under surveillance. Monitoring Stavros clients proved considerably more valuable to the agency than shutting him down.

Because of this, Hollis knew his arrival and departure would undoubtedly be videotaped, and even in disguise he would be recognized. The best he could hope for was to get in and out fast, and be gone before anyone had a chance to take action. In any event, he had no choice. He had to change his identity.

As he waited for an answer, recalled that Stavros was a loner who rarely left his place of business, except to get supplies he could not trust anyone to deliver. And, although many of his clients were KGB, there had never been any evidence to indicate that he was part of the organization.

Hollis knocked again. Nothing. He knocked louder, pounding on the door insistently.

Finally he heard a gruff voice from the other side. "What do you want?"

"Three packages," Hollis said.

"You've done business here before?"

"Not here. Over in Southeast."

Hollis heard the chain clanking as Stavros finally opened the door, and stared unblinkingly at him, much like a serpent prepared to strike. His thick black hair was uncombed and matted around the back of his head. His olive complexion suggested an eastern Mediterranean origin, but it would have been difficult to associate him with any particular country.

The expressionless stare continued as Hollis entered. Stavros was careful to keep him in sight and at a distance. "What type packages do you want?" he demanded.

"Three sets of driver's licenses with matching social security cards, and a couple of major credit card facsimiles for each set. And I want them right now."

"It'll cost double."

"No problem. The packages should be made up for Jason Vanderhorst, Arlington address; Ralph B. Tucker, San Francisco; and

William R. Booker, Los Angeles. I have different clothes and make-up for the ID photos."

Hollis had long ago learned that small amounts of skin and hair coloring with a little padding around the shoulders and waist could go a long way toward changing appearance. This was particularly effective when people were trying to match a face to a picture, or a person's build to a description. It took only a few minutes to complete the process, because he wanted identities which were not only quick and easy to adopt, but could be swiftly changed or discarded. A quick change in an airport rest room might mean survival. When the last picture was taken, Hollis changed back to the Middleton identity, and waited impatiently until the last document was completed.

As he handed Stavros the payment, he counted out an extra thousand dollars. "Someone will probably be here shortly to check on this. If you're still here when they come, I want you to give them the name of Clyde Middleton, and make up two other phony IDs to go with it." He picked up the packets and fixed Stavros with a penetrating stare. "These identities go with me."

Stavros eyes shifted away after a moment. "I know how to have a short memory."

"One thing you can count on," Hollis said softly. "My memory is very long."

Hollis walked north on Fourteenth Street. When he was sure he was not being followed, he caught a taxi to the bus station. In the station rest room he opened his suitcase and changed clothes. When he left the bus station, he was wearing a sweater and slacks and a deep Florida tan.

He walked the few blocks to the Jefferson Hotel and entered through a side door. Moments later, he left through the main entrance as if he had just checked out.

He took a cab north to Rockville, Maryland and got out at the Marriott Courtyard motel on Research Boulevard, but did not register. Instead, he called the closest rental car agency and had a car delivered.

It was now time to see whether Maggie had understood and would respond to his letter.

J. Edgar Hoover Building, Washington, DC
1500 Thursday, December 15, 1983—Day Seven

The video clips covering the morning Stavros surveillance were picked up, duplicated and distributed by the middle of the afternoon. It did not take long to identify Hollis. As a top priority matter, the fact that he was wanted was getting widespread attention. Tellier, who had assumed overall charge of the matter, was one of the first to be informed. He immediately called Dawson.

"David, we were right. Hollis didn't go to New York. We taped him late this morning here in DC with a surveillance team we have covering an apartment building. There's a guy by the name of Stavros operating there. He produces phony papers."

"You didn't get Hollis?" Dawson tried not to sound surprised or disappointed.

"No. The team went on duty at six this morning. They didn't know Hollis was wanted, and it's questionable whether they would have recognized him anyway. I'm calling to get your input."

"I'll be glad to help if I can," Dawson assured him.

"I think it's safe to assume that Hollis now has one or more sets of phony identification papers. If we don't know the identity or identities he can now assume, our job of taking him will obviously be more difficult. The only way we can get this information is to break our cover and have Stavros picked up for questioning. The director and I are in agreement that it's not likely we can hold him long enough or threaten him sufficiently to make him reveal the information. And once we arrest him, he'll know he's been under surveillance, and any future value he might have had will be lost. But we're prepared to go ahead and arrest him, if DOD thinks it's important enough. We assume you do."

"I agree," David responded. "I'd like to give the okay, but I think this is a decision Paul Montague will have to make. Can I call you back?"

"That's fine," Tellier agreed, "but we need to move fast."

"I'll get back to you as soon as I talk to Paul, but that may not be until late afternoon."

"All right. We'll hold off until we hear from you. In the meantime we've beefed up our efforts to contain Hollis in the District."

"One thing more," Dawson interjected, "DOD has a contingency fund set up in a Swiss bank for emergency use by our security people. Hollis had authority to withdraw funds, and this morning he arranged for one hundred thousand dollars to be transferred to Riggs. Later, a man calling himself Clyde T. Middleton withdrew sixty thousand dollars. We're pretty sure it was Hollis. The people we had on duty there missed him,"

It was now time for Tellier to hide his disappointment. "Well, the trail can't be too cold. We'll get someone on it right away."

15

Rockcreek Park, Washington, DC
1625 Thursday, December 15, 1983—Day Seven

Hollis had been sitting on a bench just off the main trail leading through the park since four o'clock. The bench was next to a small path which branched off and led to one of the outdoor picnic sites in the park. This particular site was small and hidden from view by the trees and bushes which bordered the trail.

If Maggie understood his reference to her birthday, April thirtieth, designated the time for the meeting, she would be there in five minutes. As he waited, his thoughts wandered back to shortly after he and Maggie had gotten married. He had just graduated from law school, when he received the letter that thereafter had shaped his life.

"Maggie, I've been accepted. I report to Quantico in six weeks." He could not keep the elation out of his voice as he handed Maggie the letter from the FBI.

"I'm happy that you got what you wanted, Jeff." Maggie's response was subdued. "But I still don't understand. You had so many really good offers from law firms."

"It won't be forever, Honey," Hollis assured her, "but, it's something I've got to do." He had tried to explain his feelings to Maggie without success because he had not even been able to explain them to himself. All he knew was that they had to do with the death of his father, a sergeant in the State Highway Patrol, who was killed one night when he was off duty and volunteered to come to the rescue of several other officers.

After graduating from Quantico, Hollis was assigned to the District of Columbia office. Maggie, with still a year to go to meet the requirements for the art degree she sought, had transferred to Georgetown University to accommodate his assignment.

Hollis blinked rapidly several times as his eyes misted over. This had been the happiest time of his life. They had little money, but didn't care. They enjoyed just being together. It made little difference whether they went to the Carter Barron Amphitheater for a concert, to a movie, or to a touring play at the National Theater.

He was proud just to be seen with Maggie. He would never have admitted it, but he was secretly pleased at the admiring looks her slim, attractive figure always received from men who saw her. When the movie "Ten" catapulted Bo Derek to fame, Hollis' joking reaction was that Maggie was at least a "Fourteen". He was even more pleased with her innocent unawareness of her admirers.

On Saturdays, particularly in the Spring, when Hollis was off duty he would roll over toward Maggie before they were out of bed and gently arouse her by nibbling on her ear. When that brought a contented yawn and stretch, his hand would move to her right breast which they had named "tenderly" (her left was "tightly"). It stemmed from her having asked him once with a mock pout, "Why don't you ever just hold me tenderly and tightly?" when he had slipped up behind her to cup a hand around each of her breasts. "I am." he had assured her.

On one of their strolls through Rockcreek Park, they had found picnic area off the main path. It had become their favorite place. If they got there early enough, they could usually stake it out for their own private picnic. It was secluded enough so they could enjoy just being together. The walk to the Zoo was short and they never tired of visiting it. They had spent many weekend afternoons there.

But now when he thought of Maggie the happy thoughts gave way to the painful ones of their parting and the divorce which followed. Even though Maggie had made uneasy peace with Hollis' decision to go into the FBI only because it seemed to mean so much to him, she had never understood nor agreed with it. She felt it was too dangerous and the time he was required to be away from home was difficult for her to accept. So even though they both wanted children, that had been deferred. Maggie grew more concerned when Hollis moved to CIA and began to draw assignments outside the country that kept them separated for weeks at a time.

The conversation before each trip had become routine. When he told her he was leaving she would ask, "Can you tell me where you're going this time, or how long you'll be gone?"

His answer was almost always the same, "I wish I could, Honey, but you know I can't."

She would respond somewhat wistfully, "With all the opportunities that are available to you, I can't understand why you must do this."

And, knowing it was not an adequate explanation, he would usually say, "Somebody has to."

Both felt they were suddenly seeing a light at the end of that dismal tunnel when he was told he would be moved into a high level staff job in about six months which was opening up because of a request for early retirement. Once in the job, there would be little foreign travel and none of it would involve him directly in covert activities. Maggie was elated and shortly afterwards became pregnant.

In what was supposed to be his last covert assignment, Hollis found himself in a difficult position. He was part of a five-man team sent into Afghanistan to meet clandestinely with leaders of the *Mujahideen* to make arrangements for the first delivery of Stinger missiles. The Soviets had gotten wind of the meeting, and a sudden attack by helicopter-borne troops had almost trapped the entire group. Only Hollis' foresight in anticipating the possibility had prevented a disaster, but, even so, several guerrillas and two CIA agents were killed.

When Hollis left on the mission, Maggie's pregnancy was progressing normally and she was in good spirits. Hollis promised he would return well before the baby was due so that he could be with her when it was born. Things had changed not long after Hollis left, and then something began to go wrong and Maggie had to be hospitalized.

Terrified by the thought of losing the baby and being alone, Maggie asked that Hollis be brought back to be with her, and the Agency tried. But contact was difficult and nearly three weeks passed before Hollis could be pulled out and flown home.

By that time the little red-haired girl Maggie had so wanted and planned to name Victoria for Hollis' mother, was already buried. The umbilical cord had become wrapped around the baby's neck. Unfortunately when the symptoms reached the stage where something had to be done and labor was induced, Victoria had already suffered brain damage. She had died a week later without ever coming out of her coma.

It made little difference to Maggie that the director had attended the funeral because Hollis could not be brought back in time. He should have been there. It was only his obsession with playing "cops and robbers" that had prevented it. But that was over now. He had made his last trip.

Hollis had been home less than a week and was on leave when he received a call directly from the DCI asking him to come to his office. Reluctantly, he had gone. He was told the remaining two members of the team had been taken prisoner by Afghan army troops who planned to turn them over to the Soviets. If that happened, not only would the mission fail, but the captives would be executed.

The *Mujahideen* were willing to attempt a rescue, but only if Hollis were present. He had won their respect and friendship when he was there before, but more importantly, his presence would be a token of good faith. The DCI made it clear that Hollis should make his own decision, and if he elected not to go it would not affect his future with the agency. But it was also clear to Hollis that without him a rescue attempt would probably not succeed.

Hollis was not concerned about his future with the Agency, and he could live with the disclosure of CIA involvement. But he could not leave two friends to such a terrible fate if it was at all possible to rescue them.

Maggie had not understood when he told her he had one more trip to make. Again, he could not tell her where, for how long, nor why it was so important for him to go. When she learned he was going, despite his promise that the trip that took him away when she had needed him most was to be his last, she told him, "I guess it's taken all of this to make me realize that you never will grow up. Playing cops and robbers is something most people leave behind with childhood, but now I know you can't. I love you; I guess I always will. But if you leave now, don't expect me to be waiting when or if you come back."

His trip was successful. The team members were rescued. But when he returned she had already moved out and filed for divorce.

Was the price he paid, was paying, worth it? Had he given up the one person he most loved to the false god of arrogance; to the belief that he was the indispensable man? Could someone else have done it? He had not thought so at the time. Now, he was not sure.

His thoughts were interrupted by the figure topped by auburn hair which had just come into view from around a curve on the main path. There could be no question as to who it was. His heart skipped a beat. *God! She did come! And, she's more beautiful than ever. Why did I ever let her get away?*

Thoughts tumbled over one another as she approached. It took a major effort to keep from jumping up to meet her as the emotions he had suppressed for so long fought for control.

Hollis continued to sit on the bench as Maggie approached. He wanted to give the appearance of someone enjoying an afternoon walk who had stopped for a rest. His relaxed appearance belied the anxiety which had built up inside him as he waited. He made no move to acknowledge her presence. She would recognize him well before she reached him, and, he hoped, cue to his actions. He continued to stare at the path to the picnic area. When she reached it, she turned in without glancing in his direction.

Hollis assumed that Maggie would decipher his request to "come alone" to mean that she should make sure she was not followed. But with her lack of experience, she could easily be mistaken. So, after Maggie had gone into the picnic area, he walked casually in the direction from which she had come. It took only a few minutes for him to assure himself that she had not been followed. He turned and went back to the side path.

The emotions her presence triggered were almost overpowering. He wanted to take her in his arms and kiss her passionately, but knew he could not. Instead, he took her by the shoulders and pulled her to him. As she turned her head, his arms went around her, and he said softly, "I'm glad you came."

After a moment, Maggie extricated herself and feigning aggravation said, "Well, I hope you realize that you almost lost me with that letter. Was that really necessary?" Maggie started to say something about "still playing cops and robbers", but when she saw the concern in his eyes she could not.

"The people I'm up against are playing for keeps, Maggie. I didn't want to put you in any danger. Did you really have trouble figuring it out?"

"Yes, although now I don't think I should have."

"What happened?"

"I got the letter around eleven twenty-five. The only things I knew for sure at that point was that I should call Paul and then meet you somewhere, sometime, today. I called, but was told he couldn't return the call until after one. So I left the office for an early lunch while I tried to decipher your letter. Almost as soon as I left the office I realized I was being followed. I guess it not only surprised me, but woke me up. It triggered what you meant by 'come alone'. After that it wasn't too difficult to figure out 'favorite place', but converting my birthday into a the meeting time took a little more imagination.

"Anyway, I left the office early to see if I would be followed again. I was, but this time I was ready. It took me trips through ladies' lingerie at both Hecht's and Woody's before I finally I lost them." Maggie's worried eyes searched his face, "Jeff, what on earth is going on?"

"Did you talk to Paul?"

"Yes."

"What did he say?"

Maggie looked slightly puzzled. "Paul called back shortly after one. I told him I was appalled by the article in the Post—that he knew as well as I you were not guilty of a security breach or anything else."

Hollis smiled at her indignation and murmured, "Thanks."

"Paul agreed it was hard to believe, but said the evidence all pointed toward you. I asked if he would be willing to meet with you to hear your side, but he said that he had tried to do that, but you hadn't cooperated. So he'd been forced to turn the matter over to the FBI. He was genuinely concerned, Jeff, but he said there was nothing he could do. He told me to tell you if you got in touch his advice was to give yourself up. He'd then do whatever he could to help you."

Disappointed, Hollis asked, "He didn't say anything about what the security violations were supposed to be?"

"No. I asked, but he wouldn't discuss it. He just said there was substantial evidence, all of which pointed to you." Maggie paused. "It has to be a mistake, Jeff. Why don't you give yourself up and talk to Paul?"

Hollis told Maggie everything that had happened, beginning with the discovery of the memorandum.

"I don't know what's going on, but I do know that all of this started when I found that damned memo. What I think is going on is that there is a mole in the Department, probably in a very high position, and the memorandum refers to something he is doing which no one is supposed to know about. Also, it must be pretty damned important if he's willing to have someone killed to keep it from being exposed." He shrugged. "It's the only thing that makes sense."

"Don't you think that makes it all the more important that you go to see Paul, so you can tell him what you just told me?" Maggie asked.

"It would make a lot of sense if I could meet Paul one on one before giving myself up," Jeff replied. "But, he's already ruled that out. I probably wouldn't even get a chance to see him or even know whether what I had to say would even get to him. Since the memorandum disappeared, I can't even prove that I ever saw it. But even worse, I'd have to rely on the same people who built the case against me to reverse themselves and declare they made a mistake. Without proof, they won't do that."

"What are you going to do?"

Hollis shook his head. "The only way I can clear myself is to prove there's a mole in the Department, and to find out who it is. And the only way I can do that is to find out what the Peregrine memorandum refers to, and why it's so secret."

Maggie reached over and put her hand on Hollis' arm. "Can I help?"

Hollis paused and pursed his lips. "There is one thing you can do. You remember Al Walters? He was with me in Afghanistan and took the staff position at CIA that I was slated for before I moved to Defense. He's a straight arrow, and the only one I would take a chance with. If something happens to me, get in touch with him. Tell him everything I've told you, but whatever you do, don't tell anyone else. If you do you may find yourself in the same position I'm in. I would never forgive myself if that were to happen."

"But how will I know when I should tell Al?"

"If you don't hear from me in seventy-two hours, go to his office and stay there until you see him." He paused. "I don't think I should call you directly because they've probably bugged your phone…"

"You know Jessica Blake," Maggie cut in. "Her office is next to mine. You can call her and leave a message."

"Okay. I'll tell her I'm Robert Blake, her cousin."

Maggie nodded. "I hope I'm in her office when you call." She looked into Hollis' eyes, her expression clouded with worry. "Jeff, I'm scared."

Hollis tried to reassure her. "You'll be okay."

Maggie shook her head. "I'm not scared for me, I'm scared for you."

Hollis again placed his hands on her arms. As he looked down into her eyes he said, "I'll be all right as long as I know you're safe. I'm glad you came. I've missed you."

Maggie's eyes misted over. "I've missed you, too."

Her lips brushed his. "Be careful, damn it." She turned and within seconds was out of sight.

Hollis stood there, not moving. He had not anticipated how deep his reaction would be to seeing Maggie again. He now knew that his love was as strong as ever. He cursed Peregrine under his breath. Then the thought struck him that maybe the silver lining was it would get them back together—if he could stay alive.

He gave Maggie time to get well away before he walked back to the car. With her gone he felt more alone than ever, but he had to keep moving. His first stop was at a gas station rest room where he assumed the identity of Ralph Tucker. He then drove to Baltimore's Friendship Airport arriving with barely enough time to turn the car in before boarding his flight.

16

Fourteenth Street NW, Washington, DC
1705 Thursday, December 15, 1983—Day Seven

Brovikov moved cautiously from the sidewalk to the entrance of the apartment building. Early winter darkness was approaching, and he knew the area was frequented by muggers and drug dealers. Viktor had warned him of the around-the-clock FBI surveillance, so he had dressed himself like one of the many homeless people who roamed the neighborhood.

He knocked on the door and waited. No answer. He knocked louder. Still no answer. He put his face close to the door and stared straight at the small round security peep-hole with its fish-eye lens.

"Stavros," he said, in a stage whisper. "I've come for a package."

"Get lost. I only do business for cash." The voice from the other side of the door was muffled.

"I have cash." Brovikov replied.

"I don't know you. Who sent you?"

"A friend on Rhode Island Avenue." This was the standard introduction given by KGB agents sent to Stavros for illegal identification papers.

Stavros cracked the door open a few inches and peered out. When he saw that one of Brovikov's hands was not in sight, he tried to close it, but he was not quick enough.

The stocky Brovikov slammed into the door with his shoulder and knocked Stavros off his feet. The Greek rolled across the floor and reached a hand out toward the bottom drawer of a filing cabinet.

Brovikov swung his pistol out and trained it at Stavros' head. "I wouldn't do that!"

Stavros stopped in mid-roll. "I don't keep any money here."

"I'm not here for money."

Stavros slowly sat up, his eyes measuring the Russian. "What's the gun for, then?"

Brovikov showed a wolfish grin. "Because I'm here to collect some information about one of your customers."

"If you're with who you say you're with, then you know I don't keep information like that. They wouldn't use me if I did."

Brovikov laughed. "You're a pathetically bad liar, Stavros. Get up on your feet."

The Greek struggled to his feet, his eyes on Brovikov's pistol. "I can't help you," he said.

Brovikov's eyes became narrow slits. "Of course you can, you fool." With his free hand, the Russian extracted a roll of duct tape from the pockets of his shabby clothes and set it on a table by his side.

The Greek watched him, his anxiety growing. "What's that for? What are you doing?"

Brovikov pressed the pistol barrel against the bridge of Stavros' nose. "I need the information on the identification papers you prepared for the man who came in here about noontime. I need it very quickly."

Stavros now knew his only choice was to give his visitor the false information and hope that would satisfy him. If it didn't, he would try to maneuver into a position to use one of the weapons he kept hidden in the apartment. Once this bastard was disposed of, he'd move to a new address. He'd obviously been here too long already.

"Okay." Stavros grunted. He paused as if trying to remember the specifics. "I prepared drivers' licenses, social security cards and credit cards in the names of Clyde T. Middleton, James Morris and Peter Grafton."

"Descriptions?"

"He was five-ten, dark hair, ruddy complexion and a little on the heavy side. All the IDs used variations of that."

Brovikov stared at Stavros for a long moment. Stavros met the stare, trying not to break eye contact. He felt a trickle of sweat on his forehead.

Hollis had already used the Middleton disguise, Brovikov thought. And it doesn't fit this description. "I told you were a bad liar," he muttered. "Now give me the real IDs and descriptions."

"That's all I know!" Stavros insisted. "He was already disguised when he came."

Brovikov picked up the roll of duct tape.

"If we go to the filing cabinet in my workroom, I'll get the folder. You'll see I'm telling the truth."

Brovikov nodded and motioned with the pistol. "Okay. Get the file. Do it very slowly."

Brovikov followed Stavros into the workroom. He waited until the Greek reached the file cabinet and began to open the top drawer. As he did so, Brovikov moved swiftly behind him.

Stavros' right hand came out of the drawer holding a revolver. He pivoted to his right, dropping into a crouch almost in a single motion. He was incredibly fast, but before he could fire, Brovikov brought his pistol down sharply on Stavros' arm and sent his revolver crashing to the floor.

The Russian slammed the edge of his other hand into the back of Stavros' neck. The Greek fell. His hand snaked toward the revolver, but before he could reach it, Brovikov stomped his foot down on Stavros' wrist.

Brovikov recovered the revolver and stuck it in his pocket. He kicked Stavros violently in the side. The Greek moaned and pulled his knees up to his chest. Brovikov prodded his shoulder with the heel of his boot. "Lie on your stomach," he commanded.

The Russian bound Stavros' hands and feet with duct tape, then went to the filing cabinet and searched through it. He found nothing.

He approached Stavros, lying prone on the floor and kicked him again. "I guess we have to do this the hard way."

Brovikov tore another piece of duct tape from the roll and wound it several times around Stavros' head, covering his mouth.

He sat on the Greeks' back, took out a cigarette lighter, lit it, and held the flame close under the little finger of Stavros' left hand.

The Greek, trussed and gagged, flopped against the floor like a beached fish. His muffled screams were surprisingly loud.

Brovikov took the lighter away. The smell of scorched flesh tickled his nostrils.

"You still have nine good fingers left. As soon as you're ready to give me the information I need, nod your head and I'll stop."

Stavros knew he had lost, but hoped his value to the KGB might save him. He nodded his head, and the tape was jerked painfully from his face."

Brovikov wrote down the names and details of the three identities as Stavros talked. He was impressed that Stavros could recall the details of the three descriptions so vividly. He was also impressed to the lengths to which Stavros had gone to protect the identity of a client. Even now, though he was obviously in acute pain, he remained surprisingly calm, not even looking at the badly scorched finger on his left hand. It was too bad he had outlived his usefulness. Under other circumstances, Stavros could have remained valuable.

After placing the notes on Hollis' identities in a pocket, Brovikov rewound the tape back over Stavros' mouth.

The Russian searched a nearby supply shelf and found a large can of flammable solvent. He opened the can and poured the solvent liberally over and around Stavros. Stavros watched, his eyes consumed with terror. Brovikov smiled. He raised his lighter to ignite a balled-up sheet of paper, then tossed it on Stavros.

"You may have thought you had a bargaining chip because of your value to our organization," he said. "You didn't. Your cover was blown by the FBI long ago. You were dead, no matter."

Before closing the door, he took one last look at the soundless writhing body engulfed in flame.

Out on the street, Brovikov remembered to affect the drunken stagger of a bum. He managed to get almost five blocks from the apartment building before he heard the sounds of sirens responding to the fire.

Back in his Watergate apartment, Brovikov picked up the scrambler phone and dialed a number.

"I wish to report success," he told the party on the other end. "Stavros provided Hollis with three identities; Jason Vanderhorst, Ralph B. Tucker and William R. Booker.

"Addresses?"

"Vanderhorst was Arlington. Tucker, San Francisco, and Booker, Los Angeles." Each was followed with a description.

"Did Hollis make contact with his former wife?"

Brovikov answered cautiously, "My agents lost her for a short while this afternoon. She left work and went shopping. They lost her briefly, then picked her up again when she got back to her apartment."

Viktor broke in, "For how long did they lose her?"

Brovikov tried to put the best face on it. "For maybe a little more than an hour."

"An hour?" Viktor was not pleased. "She must have known she was being followed."

"They swear she didn't know."

"They are wrong, the fools. She may well have made contact with Hollis, and now knows what he knows. If so, she poses a threat to Peregrine and must be neutralized. I'll have her delivered to you at the Dumfries safe house tomorrow morning. You will hold her unharmed until you receive further instructions."

"I understand. What about Hollis?"

There was a short pause before Viktor answered. "He'll be on his way to San Francisco by now, disguised as Tucker."

"Do you wish me to send someone after him?"

"No. You will instruct Frolich to meet him at the airport and terminate him." There was a click as the connection was broken.

J. Edgar Hoover Building, Washington, DC
1915 Thursday, December 15, 1983—Day Seven

Tellier was at his desk when his secretary buzzed him on the intercom and told him that Dawson was calling.

"Frank, I'm sorry it took so long to get back to you on the Stavros matter, but I was only just able to get in touch with Paul. Anyway, he concurs with your plan to go ahead and pick up Stavros, and see what we can get. He feels that apprehending Hollis is of the utmost importance."

"Well, unfortunately," Tellier said, his voice flat. "it's just a little late."

"I don't understand." Dawson sounded perplexed. "What's wrong?"

"I take it you didn't see the news."

"No, I didn't."

"Stavros' apartment building was set on fire late this afternoon. There was one fatality. We believe it was Stavros."

"My God!" Dawson exclaimed. "I should have had the guts to say go ahead without waiting on Paul."

17

International Airport, San Francisco, California
2055 Thursday, December 15, 1983—Day Seven

Hollis had hoped to use the flight from Friendship to San Francisco to get some sleep, but even though he was tired, sleep would not come. The meeting with Maggie had left his emotions in a turmoil.

On his way to the baggage claims area at the San Francisco terminal, he felt drugged and lethargic from the long flight.

He also felt vulnerable. Instead of being able to duck quickly out the nearest exit with his carry-on luggage, he had to detour to the baggage area to pick up his suitcase containing the magnum and the CZ-75, which he had to check before catching his flight.

When he reached the baggage claims area, he stood and waited, watching the swarms of passengers clustering around the luggage carousels, craning their necks to spot their bags which finally began tumbling onto the carousel from the conveyor belt.

Five minutes passed and he still had not spotted his suitcase. Hollis fidgeted nervously, his impatience growing.

Maybe the suitcase had ended up on another flight or his handguns had somehow been discovered, he thought. He walked around to the end of the carousel to make sure it was marked for his flight. The conveyor belt was now loaded with luggage, and people were packed three and four deep around the edge, fighting for space to snatch their bags as they rode past.

Hollis scanned the bags quickly. There was his suitcase, just coming through. Feeling a flood of relief, he pushed himself to the edge of the carousel to be ready to intercept it.

A fat woman with a heavy luggage cart got in his way and he missed his bag. He watched it ride past, cursing silently.

As his eyes followed his suitcase on its circuit, he became aware that someone was watching him. He turned slowly with a casual motion until a figure in the far right corner of his peripheral vision caught his attention. There was an flash of recognition. The man's thin straight hair, parted in the middle and combed back on both sides, and his narrow, pinched face with the round steel-rimmed glasses, all stirred a nagging memory, but he could not bring it to the surface.

As their eyes met, the man turned and disappeared through an exit door just as Hollis remembered where he had seen the face. It was in a CIA dossier he had occasion to study several years ago. His name was Josef Frolich, an East German assassin, trained by the Stasi, the East German secret police, and occasionally loaned out to the KGB for special assignments. He had disappeared from the European scene, and was thought to have illegally entered the US.

There was no doubt the man was Frolich. But what was he doing in San Francisco? Although their eyes had met for only an instant, Hollis had seen recognition which could only mean that Frolich had been waiting for him. He felt completely devastated. It could not be a coincidence. But how in the world had they been able to track him to San Francisco?

Did they get to Stavros? They must have. He had to assume they now knew all his fake identities.

Every nerve and fiber in his body became fully alert. If they were going to try to eliminate him in the terminal, he had no way to respond or protect himself until he recovered his luggage. Rather than stand still and present a stationary target, Hollis paced nervously around the perimeter of the baggage conveyer in the manner of a long suffering passenger who is afraid his luggage is lost.

He knew his safety lay in moving with the flow of people, so he allowed his bag to travel halfway around the carousel on its second circuit before he pushed swiftly through the crowd to grab it.

As several others retrieved their bags and began to move away, Hollis moved with them. He had planned on going to a rest room to arm himself, but he discarded the thought. As much as he wanted the comfort of a sidearm, it was better not to risk being trapped.

Staying with the flow of the crowd, he exited through the doors to the rental car courtesy bus stops and quickly jumped into the line at the Hertz position. He glanced around furtively, but saw no one who appeared to pose a threat.

Maybe nothing would happen until he was away from the airport. Or maybe he was just becoming a little paranoid. He might be reading too much into Frolich's presence.

The Hertz clerk got his attention, and Hollis handed him the Tucker driver's license. "I'd like a Trans Am, if you have one."

The clerk smiled and shook his head.

"Camaro?"

The clerk again shook his head.

"Well have you got anything that's fairly small, a straight stick, and some power?"

The clerk consulted a sheet in front of him on the counter. "The only thing I've got that comes close is a Grand Am. It's got the six cylinder package, but it's automatic shift."

Hollis grimaced. "If that's the best you can do, I'll take it."

Once in the car, Hollis unpacked the Magnum and stuck it in his waistband. He fastened the seat belt, slipped the gearshift into drive, and eased into the flow of traffic leaving the airport. As he did so a silver gray BMW broke into traffic to move in behind him.

As he approached Bayshore Freeway, he watched the BMW in his rear view mirror. When he entered the Bayshore Freeway, heading toward San Francisco, he accelerated and moved to the inside lane. The BMW hung on his tail. If Frolich were in the BMW and intended to take him out, then he no doubt would have a whole team in place to keep him under surveillance. Not good news. That would make the odds against him in a car chase very high, but he might still have a chance.

Hollis' thoughts drifted back to his high school days in Florence, South Carolina, and the junked '57 Chevy he had rebuilt into a drag racer. He had won a few heats at the local strip when he was challenged to an off-track race. He knew better, but had agreed rather than back down in front of his friends.

The race was set for eleven at night on a long straight stretch of paved secondary road. As it turned out, word got around not only to the local drag buffs, but to the sheriff's office as well.

When the race got underway, he and the other contender were joined by two sheriff's cruisers. Since he had already broken several laws when the pursuit began, Hollis decided to lose his pursuer. It had been close. Most early stock racers in that part of the country learned to drive while hauling moonshine and the law enforcement officers who chased them got a lot of practice. He was not proud of what he had done, but he had proved that he was good.

As Hollis approached the Bayshore Boulevard exit ramp sign, he moved up alongside a large truck in the center lane to his right. The BMW had just moved in behind him when he quickly accelerated past the truck and swerved in front of it across the two lanes of traffic onto the exit ramp.

Blocked by truck, the BMW could not follow him. It shot past the exit ramp.

Hollis allowed himself a grim smile. So far so good. But he was under no illusions that he had lost his pursuers. If Frolich had arranged a team surveillance there'd be backup cars, all in touch by radio. On the freeway they would have lagged the BMW and when it missed the turn onto the exit ramp, they would have made it. One would tail him directly, the other would trail behind as a backup. Meanwhile, the BMW would maneuver to get back in position.

Hollis turned onto Hillside Boulevard toward Daley City. When he reached the business district, he stayed well within the posted speed limit, occasionally speeding up to run a few yellow lights so any pursuer would be forced to run the red light to stay with him.

After a while, he had isolated two cars that consistently showed up somewhere behind him. What are they waiting for, he wondered. Maybe he could force the issue.

Leaving Daley City, Hollis cut over to Portolo and headed north toward Twin Peaks. This would take him through a quiet residential district and put him onto Market Street heading into the city. As traffic thinned out, Hollis tensed. His intuition told him this was the place to expect a move.

Frolich, who now had the BMW back in position as the number three car, also decided the time had come. He picked up the radio transmitter. "Car one, move past target and proceed to Twin Peaks Road. Take a left, then turn around and come back to the intersection... Wait there, but be prepared to move... Number two, move directly behind target. Before he reaches the Twin Peaks intersection, engage the left turn signal as if you're about to pass him... Car one, you respond by turning on your right turn signal... As target moves into the intersection, car one will move out of Twin Peaks Road to block him. Car two, you'll ram the left side of his car. He's armed, so be ready... Take him dead or alive. Makes no difference... Either way, you'll put him in my car... Walter will accompany me. The other three will stay to unscramble the accident with the police. Any questions?..."

Frolich waited through a short, static-filled pause. "Okay then, proceed."

When he saw one of the cars tailing him pass and disappear around a curve, Hollis was sure they were about to make their play.

With a car in front and at least one behind, their intentions seemed clear. He was outnumbered and didn't know precisely when the attempt would be made, so he could only hope his ability to move quickly and do the unexpected would be enough. As the second tail moved up close behind him, he pulled the magnum from his belt and placed it on the seat beside him.

The intersection of Portolo and Twin Peaks came into view as Hollis rounded a curve. A moment later, the left turn signal on the car behind him began blinking. It was immediately answered by the right turn signal coming from a car stopped on Twin Peaks.

Hollis waited until the car behind him began to edge out to the left as though to pass him. He immediately flicked on his left turn blinker, swerved into the left lane and slowed down.

Then, as many people do when making a turn, he slowed down even more and cranked the wheel slightly to the right as if preparing for a wide left turn.

Several things happened at once.

Hollis dropped the automatic shift lever in low and jammed the accelerator to the floor.

Frolich, bringing up the rear sensed what Hollis was about to do and screamed, "Block him," into his radio transmitter.

Car one, confused into believing Hollis intended to turn, arrived at the intersection a split second too late and only nicked the bumper of the Grand Am as it shot by.

The driver of car two guessed what Hollis was going to do. He began to maneuver around him on his left when Hollis hit the accelerator. He could have stopped Hollis except that he was blocked by car one, which he slammed into broadside.

As he sped from the intersection, Hollis heard the squeal of brakes, the screech of rubber, and the explosive collision of metal and glass. He glanced in his rearview mirror in time to see the BMW speed around the wreck.

The odds were suddenly a lot better, Hollis thought. But it wasn't over yet.

Moving slowly down Market Street toward the Embarcadero Hollis went through a string of amber lights, forcing the BMW to run through them red to stay behind him. He studied the rear-view mirror intently, reassuring himself that the BMW was the only car still pursuing him.

It was now after eleven and the warehouse area to his right was deserted. It would be ideal for what he had in mind.

Suddenly, with no warning, he turned right and accelerated. Caught off guard, the BMW fell behind. After several blocks, when it became apparent that the BMW was gaining on him, Hollis took his first high-speed corner. He approached it with the accelerator flat out, then hit the brakes and spun the steering wheel to start the rear end sliding to his right as he lined the car up with the side street to his left. He immediately stopped braking to allow the wheels to regain traction, turned the wheel to the right at the same time to stop the turn, and again stomped on the accelerator as the car came out of the skid. The Grand Am did not handle as he had hoped, but, he now knew he could make it work.

As the wild ride continued through the dark streets, it became obvious to Hollis that even though the BMW suspension allowed it to corner better than the Pontiac, the smaller, lighter car could accelerate out of the turns faster. Because of this he was gaining yardage at every turn. If nothing happened, he would soon shake the BMW the same way he had lost that deputy sheriff so many years before. It was now simply a matter of finding the right place. He came upon it so quickly he almost missed it.

Back in Darlington County, it had been a side road with a large sign adjacent to a small grove of trees. Now it was a side street with a large truck parked at the curb.

The BMW was now a full city block behind. For the last several corners, it had been coming out of one turn as Hollis was going into the next. This time, instead of cutting the steering wheel to straighten the car out as he turned the corner, Hollis continued the skid for a full hundred and eighty degrees, doused the lights and pulled in behind the truck. Seconds after he did so, the BMW, its tires squealing, slid around the corner, straightened as the driver hit the accelerator, and headed for the next intersection. Hollis did not wait for the car to reach it. He was around the truck and had turned the corner before the BMW had reached the middle of the block.

Frolich knew something was wrong almost as soon as he came out of the turn, but he could not immediately determine what it was. It could be that Hollis had turned off his lights as he made the last turn, or it could be worse. He put the BMW into a one-eighty at the intersection so he would be in a position to go either right or left or return the way he had come.

He checked both sides of the intersection as he completed the one-eighty and seeing nothing, gunned the motor to return the way he had come. His movements had been precise and there had been no wasted time, but he already knew he had lost.

Hollis left his lights off as he went around the truck, and headed back the way he had come. It was only after he made several fast turns that took him out of the warehouse district that he turned them back on.

Shortly afterwards, he merged into the traffic entering San Francisco from the Bayshore Freeway. He found his way to Market and from there took Kinnock Street up the hill in the direction of the St. Francis Hotel.

Watergate Apartments, Washington, DC
0050 Friday, December 16, 1983—Day Eight

The sound of his telephone ringing woke Brovikov from a sound sleep. The voice on the other end was faint, almost a whisper. "Frolich here," it said.

"Speak up, I can barely hear you!"

"Hollis arrived at San Francisco International this evening as Ralph Tucker."

"Did you get him?"

"He avoided our trap...He is very clever."

Brovikov muttered a string of curses in Russian. "And you're very incompetent...There is a professor at Stanford University, a Doctor Thomas Lipscomb. He lives in Palo Alto. Hollis will visit him either at his office on the campus, or his home. When he does you will terminate both of them and dispose of their bodies. Do you understand?"

"Yes," Frolich replied.

"You also understand what another failure will mean?"

"Yes," Frolich said.

"Good," Brovikov muttered, and slammed down the phone.

18

St. Francis Hotel, San Francisco, California
2215 Thursday, December 15, 1983—Day Seven

Hollis was convinced he had lost Frolich, but he knew he was not out of danger. Whoever had hired Frolich to kill him knew he was in San Francisco. By now the FBI and the police might also know. He decided that checking into a hotel, even under an assumed name, would be risky.

But he had to stay somewhere.

He pulled up to the entrance of the St. Francis Hotel, turned the ignition off and got out. When the doorman approached, Hollis said, "I'll be checking in shortly and expect to be here several days. Go ahead and park my car. I probably won't need it until I'm ready to leave. And could you also hold my luggage for me until I check in."

Hollis accepted claim checks from the doorman, and went inside. At the main desk he paused to look around. He noticed an attractive brunette sitting alone at a small table not far from the bar. She was dressed in a very subdued maroon suit with a white, pleated blouse. Her jewelry looked expensive, but not ostentatious.

Hollis stopped by her table and when she looked up he smiled. "There doesn't seem to be any room at the bar. If I promise not to bore you with long stories you don't want to hear, may I share your table?" She looked him over carefully. It was difficult to read any sign of encouragement or discouragement.

"I'll buy you a drink," he offered.

With the suddenness of having made a snap judgment, she smiled and nodded toward the empty chair.

Hollis sat down. "My name is Ralph Tucker," he said. "What are you drinking?"

"My name is Karen." She offered her hand. "Karen Brewster. And I'm drinking Glenfiddich on the rocks."

Hollis ordered two Glenfiddichs on the rocks from the waiter. "I'm impressed," he said, turning to her with an expression of feigned awe. "I thought only a few aging Scotsmen and myself had discovered the pleasure of the true single malt."

Her eyes twinkled. "My father was one of those aging Scotsmen," she replied.

Hollis laughed and raised the glass the waiter had just set in front of him to toast his companion.

Karen broke the short silence which followed. "How did you know I was alone, Mr. Tucker? Or did you?"

"Please, call me Ralph." He would have to be careful. He had almost said Jeff. "Just a calculated guess. The chair I'm sitting in was parked against the table, looking very unused. And judging from the number of cigarettes in that ash tray, you've been here more than a few minutes. If you were waiting for someone, he would have to be very late."

"Yes. Unless you name is really Martin Tomkins, it appears I've been stood up." She took a small sip of her scotch. "What business are you in, Ralph?"

"I'm an industrial security consultant. You know, security systems for factories, warehouses and stuff like that. But that's pretty dull stuff. You're bound to be more interesting. I would guess you're a model. Or an actress."

Karen averted her eyes to her drink. "I do model occasionally...Not as much as I'd like. It's a pretty cutthroat business."

"How so?"

"People expect favors."

Hollis was mystified. "Favors?"

Karen smiled at his naiveté. "Sexual favors."

"Oh."

"I'm not averse to that, under the right circumstances. I'm just a little choosy."

Hollis swallowed hard. He felt his face flush. My God, he embarrassed easily these days. He changed the subject. "What do you do when you're not modeling?"

Karen looked squarely into his eyes. "I work for a hostess firm. I show out-of-town visiting firemen, otherwise known as traveling salesmen and conventioneers around the city. I make small talk, hold their hands while they have a good San Francisco dinner at Fisherman's Wharf, and make sure they get back to their hotel in one piece. Most of them think a little sex is part of the deal, although it usually isn't. I was supposed to meet a client here tonight, a Mr. Martin Tomkins. But he appears to have changed his mind."

"I'm sorry," Hollis said.

Karen's eyes flashed a steel gray. "Well, I'm not!"

Hollis nodded. "To tell you the truth, neither am I."

They both laughed.

"Are you positive you're not Martin Tomkins?" she asked, with a conspiratorial grin.

"What the hell, let's say I am. Show me the town. Have you eaten? Somebody told me that the Blue Fox is better than Fisherman's Wharf."

"It is, but it's pretty expensive. And we'd need a reservation."

"Well, what do you suggest?"

After a long pause, Karen asked him where he was staying.

"I thought I was staying here at the St. Francis, but I got into the city late, and my secretary forgot to ask the hotel to hold my reservation for late arrival. The desk is checking with some of the other hotels, but as of right now, I'm homeless."

Karen measured Hollis with her gray eyes for a long beat, sizing him up. He sipped his scotch, pretending not to notice.

"Come home with me. If you're hungry, I'm pretty good with scrambled eggs and bacon."

Hollis was surprised at her directness. "Are you sure?"

She shrugged. It was a cute, girlish tilt of her shoulders. "No, but I like the way you laugh, Mr. Tomkins."

Hollis paid the check, retrieved his luggage and they took a cab to her apartment in a section of the city between the Presidio and Nob Hill. It was small, but tastefully decorated.

After Karen had poured two stiff Glenfiddichs on ice and the small talk about her apartment had stopped, Hollis decided to be blunt and honest. At least as honest as he could be, under the circumstances. "Look, I don't want you to think I'm here under false pretenses. I really did need a place to stay, and I came here for that reason only."

Karen looked up with mock indignation. "You're telling me, Mr. Martin, that you do not wish to make love to me, after all the trouble I went to get you here."

He smiled ruefully. "I'm divorced, but I'm still in love with my wife."

"Your ex-wife, you mean."

"Yeah. My ex-wife."

Hollis knew he was perfectly free to do as he wanted, but the few times he had tried casual sex after the divorce had all been minor disasters. And emotions which his meeting with Maggie had aroused seemed to leave little desire for a one-night stand.

Karen became thoughtful. "That's a new one," she said. "But I certainly understand." Then after a moment she continued. "What I don't understand is why your ex-wife ever let you get away. What did you do to her?"

Hollis' face became sober. He tried to come as close to the truth as he could. "The job I had at the time involved a certain amount of danger and long periods of travel and uncertainty. I don't blame her for wanting something better."

Karen regarded him with a shrewd frown. "There's more to it than that, isn't there?"

"Yes, but it's over and done with. She did what she thought was best." He forced a smile. "But what about you? Why did you turn down all those rich handsome bachelors who must have wanted to marry you?"

"As long as we're letting our hair down, I'm a product of a broken home, with a battered mother and a father who tried to molest me when I was in junior high. Since then most of men I've met are the kind that don't hang around if they can't get in your pants ten minutes after they meet you, and the rest are married. What I'm doing now is trying to get enough ahead to open a ladies' apparel boutique. I think I could make a go at it."

"I'm sure you could."

"Care for another drink?"

"Thanks, I don't think so. I'm still on Eastern Standard time, and it's way past my bedtime."

"You're welcome to sleep with me if you want to." Karen grinned impishly. "I only have one bed, and the couch is too small for you. I don't think you would be able to sleep on the floor, but if you'd like to try, I'll get you a blanket and pillow."

Hollis grinned. "I'll take my chances with you."

Hollis showered and prepared for bed, as Karen closed up the kitchenette and put everything away. When he came out of the bathroom, in the pajamas he had previously had no reason to wear, she was already under the covers. As he slid into bed, she turned the light off. Only a queen size bed, there was no way Hollis could totally avoid contact with Karen, and he quickly found out she had nothing on. As if she had read his thoughts she said, "I always sleep this way."

Almost immediately, Hollis began the tedious effort to turn onto his side facing away from Karen without disturbing her. Before he could do so, she gently reached across him to his far shoulder and gently turned him towards her. After a few long moments of letting her perfume invade his senses, she slowly unbuttoned his pajama top and pressed two full, round, firm breasts against his chest. At the same time, he became aware of her hand behind his head gently massaging the back of his neck while he felt first her breath and then the tip of her tongue on his ear lobe.

His body wanted desperately to respond, but he kept telling himself he shouldn't. *When she finds out it won't work, she'll give up and quit.* But, suddenly it wasn't working out that way. He realized she was making no demand on him, nor was there any pretense. She was asking nothing, only offering to give. And, then his pent-up up emotions suddenly released, were as if a dam had burst. He found himself on top of Karen thrusting into her with surprising passion. Later, he found it difficult to remember precisely what had happened. He only knew that for the first time since Maggie had left, he felt whole again.

Afterward, Karen leaned over him and took his face between her hands. "Don't worry," she said softly. "This doesn't mean you don't love your wife."

Karen drifted off to sleep almost immediately, but Hollis remained awake, his thoughts in turmoil.

19

Maggie's Apartment, Silver Springs, Maryland
0745 Friday, December 16, 1983—Day Eight

Maggie had tossed and turned most of the night before finally surrendering to a fitful sleep. When the alarm went off she was instantly awake and looking suspiciously at the telephone. Once she realized where the noise was coming from, she turned the alarm off and forced herself out of bed.

The meeting with Jeff and the circumstances which had brought it about had focused her attention on how she had let her inability to understand his dedication or accept the danger it posed affect their marriage. Now that she knew they might never be together again, it was clear to her that she had been wrong. Her heart told her Jeff had always understood and was simply waiting for her. But it might already be too late.

She checked her make-up one last time, picked up her hand bag, and started for the garage. On her way out, she saw a car drive up and park in front of her apartment. The car bore no markings and the driver was neatly dressed in conservative civilian clothes, but both had the indefinable aura of government issue. Her heart skipped a beat. Maybe there was news of Jeff. The driver got out, checked the address against a slip of paper, and started up the walk. Maggie intercepted him before he reached the door.

The driver, a muscular-looking male in his early twenties, smiled engagingly. "Good morning, Ma'am. I'm looking for Missus Hollis." Maggie had kept her married name after the divorce although at the time she had not been sure why. Suddenly, she was glad; she liked the sound of it.

"I'm Missus Hollis."

The driver removed a leather folder from his inside coat pocket, opened it, and held it where Maggie could see the inside. "Ma'am, my name is Baxter. I'm with the Defense Investigative Service. I was instructed to pick you up and take you to a meeting."

Maggie looked puzzled. "That's odd. I'm not aware of any meeting I'm supposed to attend."

"I was instructed to tell you, Ma'am, that the Undersecretary Montague has requested you attend, and that the meeting concerns your former husband."

"Please come in. I'll have to call my office so my boss will know I'll be late for work. You don't by any chance know how long the meeting will take, do you?"

"No Ma'am."

Maggie went back inside. Baxter followed at a discrete distance. She picked up the phone and dialed Jessica's number, crossing her fingers that Jessica would follow her usual practice of leaving home later than she should. She gave a sigh of relief when she heard Jessica's breathless, "Hello."

"Jessica, Hon, I hate to impose on you at this time in the morning, but I need a favor." Without waiting for Jessica to agree Maggie hurried on. "There is a Defense Department driver here who is to take me to a meeting with Paul Montague concerning Jeff. I don't know how long it will last. Will you let the office know I won't be there this morning? I'll call when I know more. Oh! By the way, you may get a call from your cousin Robert. I asked him to call you if he couldn't reach me. If he does call before I get there, be a dear and tell him I had to go to this meeting."

Surprised and confused, Jessica started to respond, "But, I don't have ..."

Maggie broke in, "Thanks. I'll fill you in on the details when I see you."

Baxter escorted Maggie to the car. After closing her door, he got in the front, closed his door and fastened the seat belt. Maggie watched with surprise as the door catches on both rear doors suddenly dropped down into a locked position.

"Are you afraid I might accidentally open the door?" she asked.

The driver smiled into the rear view mirror. "Just following regulations, ma'am."

The drive through the District was uneventful, and Maggie paid little attention to what was going on outside as she wondered what Paul would tell her when she reached his office. However, as they headed south on Shirley Highway after crossing the Fourteenth Street bridge, she suddenly realized they were not going to the Pentagon.

"Mr. Baxter, I assumed the meeting would either be in the city or at the Pentagon. Could you tell me where we are going?"

"Yes ma'am. I have been instructed to take you to Dumfries."

It was a moment before Maggie remembered that Dumfries was where the attempt had been made on Jeff's life. The vague misgivings she had felt about the doors now intensified. She reached out a hand and tried to pull the door lock up. It refused to budge. "I do not wish to go to Dumfries,' she said. "Either take me to Secretary Montague's office in the Pentagon or to my own office."

Baxter continued heading south. "I'm sorry, Ma'am, I have my instructions."

When they arrived at the safe house, Maggie thought about jumping from the car the instant Baxter unlocked the doors and running for it. She'd run down the street and just scream for help. Somebody would notice.

Baxter pulled up in front of the garage attached to the house, used an electronic door opener to open the garage door, drove inside, and closed the garage door behind them. Only then did he unlock the car's rear doors.

He took Maggie by the arm and escorted her across the garage. She looked around desperately for an way to escape.

A heavyset man of medium height, slightly Slavic in appearance, appeared from inside the house.

"Welcome, Missus. Hollis," he said. "My name is Semyon Brovikov. The under-secretary asked me to convey his apologies for the inconvenience, and to assure you it was necessary to bring you here for the meeting. Unfortunately, he has been delayed. If you will please follow me, I will take you to more comfortable surroundings."

As the door leading into the house closed behind her, Maggie heard the garage door open and the car which had brought her depart. Her fear and uncertainty turned to anger. "Mr. Brovikov, I don't know who you think you are, but I do not work for the Defense Department and I don't know why I have been brought here. I want to be taken back to Washington immediately. If the under-secretary wishes to see me, he can arrange a meeting with me personally. Otherwise, I'm not available."

Brovikov's arrogant smile brought back Maggie's misgivings, but he responded politely. "I'm sorry, Missus. Hollis, but my instructions are quite specific. As I am sure you know, your former husband has been implicated in a very serious national security matter. It is imperative that we find out what you might know of his activities. You will not be harmed, if that is what worries you, but you will be detained here until you can be debriefed. Please follow me."

"You have no authority to hold me against my will," she cried, even thought she knew her protest was a waste of her breath. "If you think I've committed some crime, take me before the proper authority and charge me with it. Otherwise, I'll bring false arrest and kidnapping charges against the Department when I'm released."

Brovikov led Maggie to a suite of rooms on the second floor. "*When* you are released, Missus. Hollis, you may take whatever action you think best. In the meantime, I am sure that you understand the Department has extraordinary latitude in handling matters as serious as this one."

He opened the door for Maggie. "I'm sure you will be quite comfortable here. Meals will be provided. You should find everything else you need inside."

As the door closed behind her, Maggie made a last effort. "Look! You know I'm no longer married to Mr. Hollis. I have no knowledge of what he has or has not done and I'm sure Paul understands that. There is nothing I can tell anyone that is of any value."

"That may well be true, Missus Hollis."

"Why hold me, then?"

As the lock clicked into place, Maggie heard a faint chuckle, "If one wishes to catch a fish, he must use suitable bait."

The full meaning hit Maggie with the force of a lightning bolt. If Paul had arranged for her abduction to use her to catch Jeff, it could not have been in his official capacity. And if it were not official, then it had to be part of the illegal covert activity of which Jeff had told her.

And if this were true—if Paul really had arranged it—then he must be the Soviet mole that Jeff was trying to identify.

Somehow, she had to find a way to get that information to him.

20

The White House, Washington, DC
0900 Friday December 16, 1983—Day Eight

The National Security Council is chaired by the president. Its statutory members, in addition to the president, are the vice president and the secretaries of state and defense. The chairman of the Joint Chiefs of Staff is the statutory military advisor to the Council and the director of Central Intelligence is its intelligence advisor.

The statutory function of the Council is to advise the president with respect to the integration of domestic, foreign and military policies relating to national security.

The United States Government Manual

McFarlane watched the members of the National Security Council file silently into the Cabinet Room in the West Wing: vice president George Bush was first; then Chairman of the Joints Chiefs, General Vessey; followed by Secretary of State George Shultz; Secretary of Defense Casper Weinberger; and finally, out of breath and huffing slightly, William Casey, director of the CIA.

The mood was somber and tense. No one smiled, and only vice president Bush actually said anything, offering a polite "Thank you," to George Shultz for some recent personal favor.

When everyone was properly seated, McFarlane excused himself and went down the hall to the Oval Office to fetch the president.

Reagan entered the conference room and took his place at the head of the table. He acknowledged the presence of the others with his usual half smile and a soft "Gentlemen."

A murmured chorus of "Good morning, Mr. President," greeted him. Usually Security Counsel meetings were fairly informal gatherings, but this morning the only mood that seemed appropriate to the gathered officials was a formal one.

Reagan's own demeanor was all business as well. No jokes, no stories this morning. Instead, he went right to the matter at hand. He folded his hands in front of him and turned to Secretary of Defense Weinberger. "Cap, I understand you want to upgrade our alert status, and reposition our carrier battle groups."

Weinberger cleared his throat, betraying some uncharacteristic anxiety. "Mr. President, I know you've been thoroughly briefed on everything the Soviets and the Warsaw Pact countries are doing, so there's no need to repeat it. However, I'm quite concerned about the magnitude of all that's going on. My judgment is that we should at the very least upgrade our defense status. I also believe that prudence dictates that we also reposition the carrier battle groups to put them in a position to respond to anything the Soviets might do. I further think it would be wise to deploy some of our ballistic missile subs early."

The president shifted his gaze to the chairman of the joint chiefs, "I don't mean to put you on the spot in front of your boss, John, but do you agree that those steps are necessary?"

General Vessey hedged. "Sir, based on what we know at the moment, I can't say that it is. But if the Soviets are engaged in something more than training exercises, then we're at a disadvantage. Secretary Weinberger's recommendations would give us more flexibility to meet whatever they might have in mind."

Reagan looked over at Shultz. "George?"

The secretary of state replied in his usual phlegmatic tones. "You know how I feel, Mr. President," he said. "As misguided and barbaric as the Soviets may be, I can't believe they would risk a nuclear showdown by attacking either NATO or us, and I interpret Ustinov's recent speech as direct support for that view. I think the real danger we now face is continued escalation to the point where one or the other participants believes the only option left is a pre-emptive strike. There is no question that the Soviets would immediately pick up on the repositioning and deployment. They would assume that it's simply an implied threat of force. I do not believe that is the message we want to give them at this point in time. It will be looked at by them as a provocation."

"Well, so what?" Weinberger broke in, angrily, "*They're* provoking the hell out of me."

"My point, exactly." Shultz countered. "and if they responded with still another escalation, such as putting their missiles on stand-by alert, what will you do then?"

Before Weinberger could respond, the president intervened. "I think George has a point, particularly if Ustinov really has extended an olive branch. I don't think a move to DEFCON III is warranted right now."

"Even if that were in his nature, Mr. President, I don't think he could be trusted." Weinberger sent a fleeting frown of disapproval in Shultz's direction before he continued. "Also, there is one other thing we should consider in the context of everything else that's going on. Even though we don't actually know the purpose of the satellites they're launching, it's beginning to look more and more like they're space-based weapons platforms."

Weinberger opened a thin folder on the table in front of him and pulled out a stack of computer-enhanced satellite images. "We just received these satellite photos of three sites within the Soviet Union which could be phased-array radar installations of the type used for target acquisition and designation in ballistic missile defense systems."

The secretary handed the photos to George Bush, sitting on his right, to pass around. "That fact, by itself, would not be cause for great concern even though the installations would bear watching, but with the satellites in orbits which keep them primarily over the US, they may indicate a real problem."

Reagan picked up one of the photos, glanced at it briefly, then handed it to Shultz. "How so?" he asked.

"Up until now," Weinberger continued, "there was no evidence to support the theory that the satellites are space based platforms for antiballistic missile weapons, as General Shields suggests. And the strongest argument against that theory was the fact that such a system needs ground support facilities, which we had no reason to believe existed. However, if the purpose of the three newly discovered sites is target acquisition and guidance, that would be direct support for his suspicion that the satellites are weapons platforms. If so, then both the satellites and the ground facilities are in violation of the 1972 ABM Treaty."

"Can't this be handled under the treaty?" the president asked. "Isn't there a procedure for verifying compliance?"

"Yes," General Vessey responded. "There is a so-called Standing Consultative Commission to which the parties are required to provide on a 'voluntary' basis information which either party considers necessary to assure confidence that treaty obligations are being complied with. We've tried to use it before, but we can never get the information out of the Soviets. It takes forever even when they are in compliance, so you can imagine what would happen here if they're not in compliance."

"Mr. President," Weinberger broke in. "There is also another factor which Director Casey brought to my attention just before we came over here."

The president turned to the director of Central Intelligence. Casey, who had been fidgeting impatiently in his chair, nodded. He was a gruff man with little personal charm, but he was closer to the president than any other man in the room. Reagan, the former film star, responded to the aura of secrecy, danger and romance that surrounded his director of Central Intelligence. Although obviously brilliant, Casey was not an especially articulate man, a shortcoming that he tended to make worse by speaking in a guttural whisper that was hard to hear.

"Several days ago," he said, in a low slurring voice, "we received a message from our blind Moscow contact. It says something to the effect that Operation *Maskirovka* involves the means to render our ICBMs and SLBMs useless, and it'll become effective December twenty-fourth. But the message may have been garbled. We're trying to get a confirmation, but have not succeeded."

"If that is the true import of the message, Mr. President," Weinberger said grimly, "then it would certainly confirm what General Shields suspects, which, of course, is much more serious than we had thought."

Reagan raised his eyebrows. Weinberger pressed on. "Well, if those satellites do house weapons that give the Soviets the ability to neutralize our ICBMs and SLBMs, then maybe they're planning a strike against us. And with us out of the way they could take over Europe in a heartbeat."

Shultz shook his head vehemently. "I think that's the most outlandish suggestion I've ever heard."

The president turned to Casey, "Bill, when do you think you'll get confirmation?"

The director did not answer immediately. "It's impossible to say, Mr. President. We've asked for a repeat. But since we don't know who the source of the information is, we can't approach him directly. So we don't know when or even if he will respond."

Casey coughed into his fist, cleared his throat noisily, then continued. "All we know about him is that he appears to hold a very high level government position, and information we've received from him in the past has been quite accurate. My estimate, nothing else appearing, is that we should assume the information is accurate."

There was a long silence. Everyone's eyes were turned to the president.

"Do we have the capability to destroy the satellites?" Reagan asked.

"It's possible we may be able to bring them down, Mr. President," the chairman of the joint chiefs began tentatively, "although it's a long shot. We have no proven ASAT, anti-satellite capability at this time mainly because most of the things we'd like to develop are prohibited by either the Test Ban Treaty or the ABM treaty."

Before Vessey could continue, Reagan intervened. "I don't think we have time to cover that in full this morning, but I'll need a complete briefing on our anti-satellite capabilities before the next meeting." Reagan turned to McFarlane, sitting quietly in a chair against the wall. "Bud, maybe you can set it up for next Thursday, as part of my staff briefing."

Reagan focused his gaze at the bust of George Washington in the corner of the room and drummed his fingers on the table. He turned to the secretary of defense. "Cap, I think you should go ahead and issue a special alert to your carrier battle groups, and begin to reposition them. But try to make it look like it's a normal operation, okay? Other than that, let's go with what we've got."

The meeting turned briefly to other matters, but the discussion was perfunctory. Everyone's mind still lingered on the confrontation that seemed to be building with the Soviet Union. Everyone there remembered the Cuban Missile crisis of the early sixties, and no one wanted to live through anything like it again, let alone be responsible for shaping decisions that might risk the total destruction of the United States—indeed the destruction of civilization itself.

McFarlane watched the president, trying to gauge his mood. He couldn't. If his mind was troubled by these recent developments, he showed no overt indication of it. Reagan remained as enigmatic to him as ever.

Whatever the president's thoughts, McFarlane decided, he didn't envy him his job, not for one second.

21

Karen's Apartment, San Francisco, California
0815 Friday, December 16, 1983—Day Eight

The past events, including the mostly sleepless nights finally caught up with Hollis. He awoke from a profoundly deep slumber to find it was already past eight AM, Pacific Time.

He had planned to try to see Lipscomb before his classes started. Now he would have to try to catch him either between or after classes.

Careful not to awaken Karen, he dressed, put on a pot of coffee, picked up her keys, and went to the lobby to see if a newspaper had been delivered.

After letting himself through the security door to the outside lobby, he found Karen's box. It had a newspaper in it. He returned to the kitchen. The coffee was ready, so he poured a cup, sat down, and opened the paper.

The lead article chronicled the deteriorating relations with the Soviet Union. It detailed the mounting evidence of a full-scale Russian military mobilization, then called attention to a recent speech by the Soviet minister of defense. The speech was thought to be conciliatory, provoking some analysts to speculate that the Soviets were laying the groundwork for a thaw in relations.

Mixed signals from Moscow, Hollis thought. Was it another part of Operation *Maskirovka*, or was he just becoming paranoid.

Hollis' eyes drifted down the page to another article. The search for Deputy Undersecretary of Defense Jeff Hollis, the department's top security officer, it reported, had been expanded nationwide. It was believed on "good authority" that he was planning to defect to Russia. A Defense Department spokesman was quoted as saying that Hollis was in a position to do considerable damage to the security of the United States. The FBI had placed him at the top of its ten most wanted list.

Next to the article was a recent black and white photograph of Hollis, supplied by the Department of Defense.

Hollis heard Karen enter the room behind him. "Good morning," she said, bending down over his shoulder. "You're up early."

Hollis sensed her stiffen slightly. It was too late to hide the photograph from her. He waited for her reaction.

She walked around in front of him. Her expression was noncommittal. "It's you, isn't it?"

"Yes."

He handed her the newspaper. She stood in front of him and glanced through the article. He could smell her perfume. It brought back the night just past. Suddenly the wild thought that he wanted to make love to her again passed through his mind.

Karen handed the newspaper back to him. "Is it true?"

"No."

She raised her eyebrows.

"I am Jeff Hollis. And I do, or at least did, work for the Defense Department before this started. But the rest of the article is not true. I'm not sure I know exactly what's going on, but I do know that I haven't committed any security violations. I also know there have been a couple of attempts on my life since this started."

"If that's true, you must have some idea why the FBI is after you and the attempts were made."

"I do, but it's not the sort of thing people will fall over themselves to believe."

"Try me."

Hollis dropped the paper to the carpet and laced his fingers together on his lap. "Okay. Someone sent me a memorandum I was not supposed to see. That, together with other events, has convinced me there's a spy in a high government position involved in some sort of project—not just turning information over to the Soviets, but something which could be very damaging to this country. I have no intention of leaving the country, but I can't turn myself in and run the risk that no one will believe my story. What I am trying to do is stay free long enough to find out who and what the real threat to the country is, and expose them."

Karen stood there, three feet away from him, her hands on her hips. She looked more puzzled than worried.

"What are you going to do?" Hollis asked her.

"I don't know. What should I do?"

"To protect yourself, I guess you should report me. If you intend to do so, I won't stop you."

"If I pick up the phone and call the police?"

Hollis shrugged. "I'll get as far away from here as I can before they arrive, and hope they don't catch me."

"Well, I have no intention of calling the police."

"Why not?"

Karen thought for a moment. "I have no way of knowing whether you're telling me the truth or not, so I have to rely on my ability to judge men." Then impishly, "And I've had a lot of experience with that."

Hollis was puzzled. "Does that mean you believe me or not?"

"It means that I have no reason to doubt you. And I don't want to turn you in. I want to help you, if I can."

Hollis' first reaction was to be suspicious. This was too easy. She hadn't needed much convincing. In situations like this people usually told you what they thought you wanted to hear, not what they really believed. *Was it possible that she was simply playing for time, hoping he would leave without harming her so she could then call the FBI.*

He wanted to believe her, but he had to be careful.

"Can you help me? Sure. Take an all-expenses paid vacation to Hawaii for a week. I may need a place to hole up for a few days. Here would be perfect. But I don't want you to be in danger because of me."

If she was lying, he was giving her the perfect way out. All she had to do was agree, pack her bags, and call the police from the airport.

"You're welcome to use the apartment whether I'm here or not. But I'm not going to leave. I think you're going to need me."

Hollis got up and walked over to her. With a great deal of tenderness, he pulled her to him and kissed her briefly and very softly on the lips. "Thank you."

She searched his eyes for a moment. "And I'm going to need you, too."

Hollis shook himself free of the emotions rapidly overtaking him. "Look, I've got to get out of here. I'm already running late for what I need to do. But I really do wish you would get out of town, at least for several days. The people who are after me will stop at nothing to put me out of commission, and I don't want anything to happen to you."

"I've been taking care of myself for a long time without your help." Karen retorted. "Here is my unlisted telephone number, as well as a key to the apartment. It also fits the downstairs security door. I'll be in and out all next week, but you're welcome to use the apartment any time you need it."

"As much as I would like to see you," Hollis said sincerely, "I hope I won't need to come back."

Karen followed him into the bedroom and watched as he packed. When he was ready to leave, she said, "Would you like to borrow my car, or can I call a taxi for you?"

"Thanks, but no. The last thing I want to do is leave a trail. I'll walk to a different neighborhood and call a taxi. Then, if anyone gets around to questioning the driver, there'll be no way he can associate me with this place."

Twenty minutes later, Hollis found a phone booth and called a taxi. While he waited, he placed a call to Jessica Blake's office in Washington. "Jessica, Robert Blake here, how are you?"

"I'm fine." There was a pause. "Maggie told me you might call. How are you?" When she first answered, she had sounded uncertain. Now he was sure she had recognized his voice.

"All right. No complaints. By the way, how is Maggie?"

"Well, I assume she's all right, she hasn't come in yet."

The news stunned Hollis. "She hasn't?"

"No. She called me at home this morning to ask me to tell her boss she would be late for work. She said a Defense Department driver was at her apartment to take her to a meeting with Paul Montague."

Hollis' throat tightened. He looked at his watch. It was eleven o'clock Pacific Time, which meant it was two in the afternoon in Washington. "And she's still not there?" He asked rhetorically.

"No. But she didn't know how long the meeting was supposed to last. I'll call her tonight when I get home and tell her you asked about her."

"Thanks. I'd appreciate it." The taxi drove up and Hollis said a quick good-bye.

Hollis considered going back to the St. Francis and getting the Grand Am but decided against it. Frolich had undoubtedly gotten the license number, and he may even have located it and put it under surveillance.

He told the taxi driver to take him to the closest Budget Car Rental agency.

The Ford Taurus he rented made him feel lovesick for the Grand Am, but at least he was inconspicuous.

He drove to Point Lobo on the coast and picked up Grand Boulevard heading south. After stopping at several overlooks and reassuring himself that he was not being followed, he continued south on Skyline Boulevard to the Junipero Serra Freeway. Instead of going all the way to University Heights, he turned off on Woodside and cut over to El Camino, all the while watching his rear, then continued south through Atherton to Stanford.

When Hollis reached the university campus, he went directly to the receptionist in the main administration building.

She gave him a simplified map of the campus grounds and pointed out the building where Lipscomb's office was located. He thanked her. "Do you happen to know if he's on campus?"

She smiled. "Yes, he is. Two other gentlemen were here early this morning asking directions to his office. His secretary told me he'd be in all afternoon."

Hollis thanked her again and walked back to his car. *You deserve thanks more than you know.* The visit by the other callers might be coincidental, but he didn't think so. He studied the map and then took a circuitous route to the building housing Lipscomb's office. His efforts were rewarded.

He spotted two cars, one at each end of the parking lot, positioned so that between them they could keep all doors of the building under observation. DIS or FBI, he thought. Or maybe neither. He couldn't take a chance. He'd have to get Lipscomb at his home.

As he drove back to the main entrance to the campus his thoughts returned to the telephone call to Jessica. Why would Paul want a meeting with Maggie, and why would he send a driver to pick her up if he did? What would be so important that a telephone call would not suffice? If the driver picked her up before work in the morning, why was she not back at work by two in the afternoon? *This doesn't add up; something's not right.*

Hollis was so engrossed in his thoughts that he failed to see a car pull away from the curb and fall in behind him as he left the campus.

He took a circuitous route to Lipscomb's home, but failed to pick up the car tailing him. By the time he arrived at Lipscomb's home early winter darkness had begun to descend, and Hollis was confident that no one had followed him there.

He parked around the corner from Lipscomb's house, got out with his briefcase and locked the car as if he were home for the night. He walked up the walkway to the front door. It was locked.

He found a place near the front corner of the porch where he would be mostly out of sight to someone entering the house and leaned against a pillar to await Lipscomb's arrival.

Frolich's Apartment, San Francisco, California
1752 Friday, December 16, 1983—Day Eight

Operating as an independent, Frolich had no organization. When he needed assistance, he employed the services of a private detective agencies which could be counted on to provide men who would carry out instructions without asking questions. He was currently using two teams, one to keep Intertel under surveillance and the other to keep track of Lipscomb. He had given them his unlisted telephone number and was in his apartment when the call came on his private line:

"Smith; Best Agency. We may have your man cornered."

"Where?"

"He's at Professor Lipscomb's house, apparently waiting for him."

Frolich could barely keep the excitement from his voice. "Make sure you have all the men you need to button the house up completely. Do not attempt to go inside after him, but under no circumstances is he to be allowed to leave. I'm on the way. I'll be there in forty-five minutes. If he attempts to leave, detain him at all costs. Your men should understand he is armed and very dangerous."

He hung up and left quickly in the BMW.

Lipscomb's Home, Palo Alto, California
1825 Friday, December 16, 1983—Day Eight

Hollis did not have long to wait before a car turned into Lipscomb's driveway. He watched as the professor got out, went to the mail box, collected his mail and headed for the front door. Hollis shrank back as Lipscomb unlocked the door, but as soon as the Doctor entered, he caught the door and followed him in.

Lipscomb turned to see who was behind him.

"Good evening, Professor."

Hollis noted that to Lipscomb's credit he did not lose his composure. He simply remained standing where he had stopped. "Well, Mr. Hollis! You seem to have run into some problems since we last met."

Hollis could not help smiling. "You're quite right, Doctor. And I'd like to share them with you, if you'll listen."

Lipscomb appeared uncertain. "I'm not here to harm you," Hollis continued. "I'm here because I believe our country is in danger and you are the only person I know who might be able to help me. If after listening to me you wish me to leave or you decide to call the police, I'll not stop you."

Lipscomb didn't reply.

"Could we go to your study?" Hollis asked.

In his study, a small room cluttered with countless stacks of books and folders, Lipscomb seated himself behind his desk, pondering what Hollis had said. "I'll listen only so long as I think I should," he replied. "I don't intend to become an accessory to espionage or whatever it is you may be involved in."

"I understand, Doctor, and agree. I'll be as brief as I can." Hollis removed a stack of documents from a hardback chair across from Lipscomb's desk and sat down. "You recall when I was last here it was to ask you about the memorandum you wrote about a project code-named Peregrine."

Lipscomb nodded.

"My reason for asking, which I could not tell you then, was that until I accidentally saw your memo, I was unaware a project by that name existed, even though my responsibilities require that I be not only aware, but involved in the security of all classified projects. Since then, not only has the memo disappeared, but I found out that the Joint Resources Board only approved and officially named a project Peregrine several weeks ago even though your memo was dated in April.

There have also been several attempts to kill me, and I am wanted for security violations I did not commit."

Lipscomb's expression remained inscrutable. He was listening, but did he believe what he was hearing?

"I don't actually know for certain what's going on, but it's all tied too closely together not to be connected. The only thing I can come up with is that there is a spy in a high level position in the Department who has not only framed me, but is also trying to have me killed to keep me from finding out what your memorandum relates to."

Lipscomb folded his hand in front of him on his desk and leaned forward slightly. It was still impossible for Hollis to determine what he was thinking. There was no sign of encouragement or discouragement, but at least he had made no move toward the telephone.

"That's an interesting story, Mr. Hollis, but why should I believe it?"

"Because if I were guilty of espionage and trying to leave the country, as the news stories say, I wouldn't be here."

Hollis was not in a position to see the door to the study and Lipscomb was lost in thought, so neither noticed the door as it opened.

A sudden squeak caused Hollis to turn.

He found himself staring squarely into the face of Frolich, who was pointing a Walther P-38 at his chest.

22

Lipscomb's Home, Palo Alto, California
1820 Friday, December 16, 1983—Day Eight

A deadly silence descended on the room, broken after a few seconds by a harsh command from Frolich. "Do not move, either of you." He looked at Hollis. "Remove the pistol from your shoulder holster very slowly, lay it on the floor, and kick it towards me. Then turn around and face away from me."

Frolich's unblinking snake-like eyes, emphasized by the round steel-rimmed glasses, persuaded Hollis that he had no choice but to follow orders. He pulled the Magnum out of the clip holster with his thumb and forefinger, watching Frolich carefully as he did so, and laid it on the floor. After kicking it away, he turned around, facing Lipscomb.

"Move to the door," Frolich demanded. "And keep your back to me."

Hollis moved across the room to the door. "Hold it, right where you are," Frolich said. "Doctor, you get in front of Hollis. You're both going with me."

Lipscomb, who had been standing behind his desk watching, suddenly slammed his hand into a stack of books. "I will not!" he yelled.

The books hit the floor with the suddenness of a small explosion. Frolich's head snapped around toward the sound.

It was all the opportunity Hollis needed. He whirled, grabbed Frolich's gun hand with his left hand and delivered a hard chop to the base of Frolich's skull with his right.

Frolich's knees buckled. Hollis lowered him to the floor face down, kicked the Walther away, and took off Frolich's belt and began tying his wrists with it.

"Thanks for the help, Doc. What changed your mind?"

"I think he did," Lipscomb replied nervously. "Who is he?"

"An East German assassin. He's been after me for a week. Almost got me twice. I think this time he was supposed to take out both of us."

Hollis finished tying Frolich's hands and searched his pockets. He found a key ring and a money clip. That was all. He wasn't surprised.

"What do you plan to do now?"

"Well, I came here hoping you might be able to help me find out what's going on. Maybe a good place to start would be with a copy of the memo."

"I'm sorry but I don't have a copy. I don't keep copies of classified documents after I'm done with them. Anyway, I think I told you pretty much everything I know about the project the last time you were here."

"Yes, you did." Hollis conceded. "The problem I'm having is trying to reconcile the Peregrine project in your memo with the Peregrine project which the JRB approved. They don't seem to be compatible. Before I saw you last time I was told by the head of security at Intertel that his firm had recently completed work on a project code named Peregrine which involved a specialized radio transmitter. That doesn't seem compatible with either of the others."

"I'm sorry, Mr. Hollis. I don't think I can help you. All I'm familiar with is what was in my memo."

Hollis walked over to the window and closed the blind. "If I remember correctly, your memorandum referred to a modification of a military rocket booster component?"

Lipscomb nodded.

"Why is that so important that someone is willing to kill to protect it?"

"Well, the component being modified is the command module in the on-board computer, which controls the booster. And it can only be activated by the launch officer between lift-off and burn-out because they're designed to respond only to commands preceded by a microburst launch code chosen by the launch control officer and entered into the module just before the missile is launched. Thus the module prevents the on-board computer from receiving unauthorized or accidental radio transmissions."

There was a gleam of an idea in Hollis' eyes. "Would it be possible to modify the command modules so that they would accept orders other than those issued by the launch officer?"

"Theoretically," Lipscomb agreed. "You could add a circuit to bypass the launch code restrictions so that it would act on a specific radio signal regardless of its origin."

"Then someone other than the launch officer could issue orders changing the ultimate destination of the missile warhead." It was more a question than a statement.

Lipscomb rubbed his chin thoughtfully. "Again, that's theoretically possible, but I'm not sure how practical it would be. Such course corrections would be minute at best, and accuracy would have to be based on on-site telemetry. You could probably make sure it would miss its target, but if you're talking about redirecting it to another target or making it splash down in the middle of the ocean, that's probably not do-able."

Hollis heard Frolich groan. He walked across the room, checked that Frolich's wrists were still secured, then picked up the Walther and tucked it in his belt. "Maybe they've added something to the guidance system which when activated will steer the missile to a specific point, rather than to its target."

Lipscomb scratched his head. "Again it's possible, but extremely unlikely. Each module would have to be tailored to a specific booster because of the different points from which they originate. But even assuming the command modules were modified as you suggest, how could they be substituted for those already in the boosters without the knowledge of anyone in the Defense Department?"

"If the mole we're looking for was in the right position to cause the right paperwork to be generated and sent out, contractors outside the Department receiving standard communications would have no reason to believe the project was not official. And once the modules were produced and in the pipeline, along with the standard directives for modification and replacement, no one at the supply depots or missile bases would have any reason for questioning their validity."

Lipscomb rubbed his chin while he thought. "If that's true, it should be a simple matter for us to bring the matter to the attention of the proper people in the Pentagon and get an investigation started. Surely if the module has been tampered with it could be easily verified. I'll go with you to see them if you think it will help."

Hollis experienced a deep surge of feeling for the elderly professor who hated war, but was still first and foremost a patriot. "Thanks Doc, but all we have at the moment is a theory that's so farfetched that without some hard proof I don't think we'd have a snowball's chance in hell of convincing anybody. Remember, I'm in my present predicament because I tried to get an investigation started. I'm convinced that our mole is in a high enough position to make sure that I fail. Even have me killed. If you go with me, you'll be in the same danger."

"But they can't ignore information like that, can they? Wouldn't they at least have to check it out?"

"Only if it got to the right people." Hollis explained. "And that's what I'm afraid won't happen."

For the first time, Lipscomb appeared angry and distraught. "We should be able to do something, damn it."

"We should, but we've got to collect some hard evidence first. What would you need to be able to determine what sort of modifications have been made to the modules?"

"Well, if I had the specifications and schematics used by the contractor to fabricate the modules, I could find out."

"Do you have any idea what firm produced them?"

Lipscomb thought a moment. "No. I have no idea."

Before Hollis could pursue the matter further, Lipscomb screamed, "Look out!"

Hollis turned. Frolich had managed to get his hands untied, and he was lunging at him.

23

Lipscomb's home, Palo Alto, California
1950 Friday, December 16, 1983—Day Eight

Frolich launched himself towards Hollis with the speed of a striking rattler. The belt was still attached to one wrist, but the other was free and he was holding it with intent of looping it around Hollis' neck.

Hollis slid to the side and grabbed Frolich's arm. As Frolich's momentum carried him past, Hollis gave the arm a vicious twist, dislocating Frolich's shoulder. He crashed over the desk and fell to the floor.

Hollis stood and watched as Frolich tried to force his arm back into its socket. He marveled at the man's self-control. He was obviously in great pain.

When Frolich came to the conclusion he could do nothing to help his arm, Hollis put his foot on Frolich's shoulder close to his neck, bent his arm at the elbow, gave it a sharp tug and let it slip back into place. Frolich's eyes rolled back and his face contorted in a grotesque mask, but he didn't utter a sound.

He pulled out his Magnum and ordered Frolich to his feet. "I think it's time to get him out of here, Doc."

Lipscomb, still white-faced and shaking, nodded quickly.

Hollis turned his attention back to Frolich. "Just so you understand my position. I know who you are and I'm ready and willing to kill you if necessary. I'm guessing you brought some back-up, so when we leave here you'll appear to be in control. You'll have your Walther, unloaded, and I will have my Magnum, loaded. I'll have my hands under my coat as if immobilized, but the Magnum will be pointed at you. You will dismiss anyone out there waiting for you as we go to your car. If anything goes even slightly wrong, I'll shoot you instantly."

Hollis turned back to Lipscomb, "Thanks, Doc. I appreciate the help."

He emptied the Walther, put the cartridges in his pocket and handed the empty pistol to Frolich. Next, he placed his jacket over his hands, and with Frolich at his side, left Lipscomb's study.

On the walkway outside the house someone immediately approached from behind a car parked in the front of Lipscomb's house. "Smith, sir. Is everything all right?"

Frolich stiffened slightly, but managed the right reply. "Yes. Everything is under control. You and your men may leave now."

Hollis saw the BMW parked next to his Ford rental. He grabbed his briefcase, took out a pair of handcuffs and looped them through Frolich's belt behind his back and locked them around his wrists.

He pushed Frolich into the passenger side of the BMW and climbed into the driver's seat. One of the keys he had taken from Frolich fit the ignition, but before starting the engine he checked the car registration on the steering column.

This your address?"

Frolich said nothing.

"You and I have some unfinished business, so we'll go there."

Hollis took Mill Road out of Palo Alto, and then headed north on Bayshore Freeway. He doubted anyone was tailing him, but he drove erratically until he reached Candlestick Park, just in case.

He then floored the accelerator and maneuvered to the inside lane. The BMW responded better than he had expected, and even though the traffic was moving at better than 60 miles an hour, he rapidly sliced through it, shifting lanes repeatedly.

As he approached the Third Street off-ramp, he braked heavily, shot almost sideways across a lane of oncoming traffic, and hit the exit ramp at 50 mph. The car performed extremely well. No wonder Frolich had been so hard to outmaneuver.

Off the ramp, Hollis merged with traffic on Third Street, turned left at the first intersection, made a tight U-turn, and drove back to where he could see the exit ramp. With his headlights off he parked and left the motor running. After waiting several minutes and seeing no indication of a tail, he headed for Frolich's address.

It turned out to be a small apartment building in the Marina district. He parked in a backyard garage slot and turned to Frolich. "If for some reason we should not go in there, this is your only chance to say so."

Frolich did not respond.

"You should understand that the questions are only going to get harder," Hollis added. "I know you're an independent who sells his services to the highest bidder. Your loyalties are solely to yourself. You have nothing to gain by not talking, and a lot to lose. I'll do whatever I have to get the answers I need."

Frolich grunted unhappily. "This is my apartment. It's safe to go in."

Hollis left his luggage in the car, locked it, and prodded Frolich toward the door. One of the keys he had taken from Frolich operated the bolt on the exterior security door. They entered, with Hollis staying close behind Frolich as they moved up the stairs. The CZ-75 with the sound suppresser affixed to it was now pressed against Frolich's spine.

When they reached the door to the apartment Hollis stopped Frolich. "When I open the door, you will go to the center of the room and stand there facing away from me until I tell you otherwise."

It was not likely that Frolich was attempting to lure him into the apartment as a set up, but the apartment could be booby-trapped. The door swung open and Frolich stepped slowly to the center of the room and stopped.

Hollis pushed the door open far enough to be sure no one was behind it. He stepped into a room as impersonal and tasteless as a cheap motel accommodation. It matched the personality of its occupant, he thought.

Hollis checked the couch then seated Frolich in it while he glanced quickly into the other rooms. When he was done, he pulled a chair up in front of Frolich and sat down. "Who ordered you to kill me?"

Frolich appeared to be debating with himself, but said nothing. Hollis waited a moment before continuing. "I will not repeat this again. I have nothing to lose except time, and I can't spare much of that. You can gain nothing by silence. I *will* do what I must to get answers. How I go about it is up to you. Now, who are you working for?"

The attempt against Hollis had taken much of the defiance out of Frolich. After a short inner debate, he said, "Semyon Brovikov."

"That's interesting. But he's not running the operation, is he? Who does he get his orders from?"

"I don't know."

"Did he order you to meet me at the airport last night?"

"Yes."

"You seemed to know what I'd look like even though I'd changed my appearance."

"He gave me an accurate description."

"After you lost me last night, how did you find me again?"

As Hollis' eyes bored into his, Frolich answered reluctantly. "He instructed me to put Lipscomb under surveillance. My men picked you up as you left Stanford."

Hollis' throat tightened. Whoever was running this operation, was not only a formidable opponent, but someone who knew him well and had been able to anticipate all his moves. So far he had failed only because of the ineptitude of the people working for him.

"How do you get in touch with Brovikov?"

"I have a telephone number."

"What is it?"

Frolich hesitated. "If I give it to you he'll have me killed."

"That's a problem you may be able to cope with later, provided I don't do the job for him."

Frolich stared at Hollis for several long moments, his eyes burning with a defiant rage he could not act on. "Area code two-oh-two, four-nine-two-seven-one-four-eight."

The Washington, DC area code sent a chill through Hollis. He had expected his mole to be in the Pentagon, and this seemed to confirmed it, but it still came as a brutal shock.

"Call him," he said.

He watched Frolich dial the numbers.

After several rings, someone picked up. Hollis grabbed the receiver. He could not tell that Brovikov's call forwarding service had connected him with the safe house in Dumfries.

"Listen carefully, Brovikov. This is Hollis. I know who you are, and I don't intend to fart around with you. I will not repeat what I have to say, so listen closely. I am at Frolich's apartment. Have the person you work for call me here within the next three minutes. If he does not, I'll be gone."

He hung up.

Two and a half minutes later the phone rang. He picked up the receiver. The voice that came back was disguised by a security device but still vaguely familiar. "Ah, Mr. Hollis, you are still alive."

"So it seems. Who are you?"

"Unimportant. You'll know me only as Viktor."

"It makes no difference. I just needed to confirm your existence."

"Of course." The voice held a touch of smugness.

"Let's cut the shit. Why did you send the memorandum to me?"

There was a pause, and when Viktor answered the smugness was gone. "You are perceptive. But since you guessed that I did, I'm surprised you haven't figured out why as well. Never mind. You were the only one in a position to discover what I was doing. Once the official Peregrine was approved, and you started your security review, it's possible you would have stumbled across *my* Peregrine. I couldn't risk that so I had find a way to discredit you so your death would not raise questions or be investigated."

"I know what Peregrine is, and I intend to expose it."

"I know you met with Lipscomb, and you may have guessed its purpose," the voice replied with a note of condescension. "but, because of how I made you a fugitive, nothing you say about my Peregrine will be believed. Without incontrovertible proof, no one will listen to you. And I assure you, you'll be dead long before you find any proof."

Hollis found the smug arrogance which had returned to Viktor's voice irritating as hell. "So far, you're batting zero."

Viktor's reply took on a silken quality. "That will be remedied shortly. but it really makes little difference. In a few days the need for secrecy will no longer exist." Hollis heard a short chuckle. "By the way, have you spoken with Missus. Hollis lately?"

Hollis felt the pit of his stomach turn hard and cold as ice. His mouth felt dry and he had hard time swallowing.

"What are you talking about?"

Viktor laughed. "The reason you have not is that I arranged for her to be my guest at the safe house in Dumfries."

Hollis held his breath, not trusting himself to speak.

"You remember the place," Viktor said, in a slightly sarcastic tone. "Come on by at around ten tomorrow night and I'll swap her freedom for yours."

"How do I know you have her?"

"You know damn well I have her, Hollis. You know she didn't go to work on Friday and she's not in her apartment."

Hollis knew he should not prolong the conversation further. The mole knew where he was and might already have dispatched a team of assassins.

He had no choice, anyway. He was at the end of the trail and could not abandon Maggie.

"I'll be there." he said softly.

II

24

Kuntsevo Hospital, Moscow, USSR
1000 Saturday, December 17, 1983—Day Nine

Outside, on the streets of Moscow, another dismal mid-winter day had begun. A dry, powdery snow, the product of the intense cold, had been falling steadily since midnight and had buried the city in a deep blanket of white. Plows and shovels were out in force, but a strong wind largely defeated their efforts, blowing the fluffy drifts right back into the streets as soon as they had been cleared.

Long lines of middle-aged women still formed in front of the state stores. They huddled close together under their shawls, braving the misery of the weather with classic Russian patience.

The weather was not on the minds of those gathered in Chairman Yuri Andropov's VIP suite at Kuntsevo. Here, it was almost breathlessly hot as the patient's faltering health continued to rob him of his stamina. The round pugnacious face, whose steely stares had quelled dissent in the past, had faded. In its place was a gaunt, hollow-cheeked mask, the color of gray paste. All that was left of this powerful Communist leader was the flame of determination in his now sunken eyes, dilated by drugs.

At his side was Mikhail Sergeyevich Gorbachev, member of the Politburo, minister of agriculture, and a member of the Secretariat. He was also Andropov's aide, confidant, and choice to succeed him.

And now Gorbachev was acting as the bedridden leader's political lifeline, conveying messages to and from his hospital room. Even so, he had not been part of the group that made the decision to proceed with *Maskirovka*.

After Ustinov and Chernenko were seated, Andropov spoke in a voice whose strength belied his frail appearance. He addressed Gorbachev, "Misha, I asked that you come here this morning with Kostya and Dimitri because it is time that you know precisely what is happening, and why. At the last meeting of the Politburo, you were told only the purpose of Operation Maskirovka. The details were withheld because we have reason to believe that someone in that group has been leaking information to the West. We believe we know who. He will be caught and executed soon. But until then we must be very careful."

Andropov took a couple of deep gasping breaths and then continued, "It is absolutely imperative that the Americans not find out how the plan works. If they do, they will easily defeat it. This must not happen."

Andropov paused to catch his breath again. Gorbachev leaned forward to wipe a drop of spittle from his chin. "Dimitri has been in charge of planning the operation, while Kostya has been in charge of deceiving the West as to our intentions while we make preparations. They will explain the operation to you." He lay back against the pillows to recover his strength.

"I hope this explanation is better than the last," Gorbachev muttered.

The comment brought a sharp frown from Ustinov. Neither liked the other. And, while he had never said so, he was violently opposed to Andropov's wish that Gorbachev succeed him. He was convinced a minister of agriculture who had not fought in the Great Patriotic War could not run the Party, or the Union for that matter. And, while he knew it was unlikely that the Head of the Red Army would be allowed to succeed to the post Andropov held, he was determined to make sure the Old Guard remained in power.

"*Maskirovka*, Comrade Minister, is an integrated operation covering all phases of the mobilization, transportation and deployment of our armed forces to either occupy or destroy the US while at the same time Warsaw Pact forces mobilize to deter NATO from intervening. It also covers all of the activities which will be engaged in to deceive the US and

NATO as these preparation go forward. As I indicated at the meeting, it is obvious such an operation could not succeed so long as the US nuclear retaliatory capability remains. So, we have neutralized that capability."

Gorbachev made no effort to conceal his doubt as he said, "It'll be interesting to learn how you have managed such a breakthrough."

Ustinov frowned. "As you know, all rocket boosters have a self-destruct mechanism which is activated by a radio transmission initiated by the launch officer." Ustinov's voice took on a note of self satisfaction as he concluded, "We now have the ability to initiate self-destruct orders which will activate the destruct mechanism in all US ballistic missiles."

"How can that be?" Gorbachev asked. "Don't they have built-in safeguards to prevent unauthorized access?"

"They do, indeed," Ustinov confirmed. "US rocket boosters, like ours, contain control modules designed to reject unauthorized commands. Their boosters, however, no longer contain those modules. We have managed to substitute a modified version which will act on specific radio transmissions initiated by us. It will allow us to destroy each missile right after it is launched."

Gorbachev could not hide his incredulity. "You mean to tell me that you have somehow replaced a key component in all their missile rocket boosters?"

"That is precisely what I am telling you, Comrade Minister." Ustinov made no effort to keep the smugness out of his voice. "We have an American comrade, code-named Viktor, who holds a high level position in their defense ministry. He is well-concealed because he has only recently been activated. There is no past record of espionage to give him away, and his identity is known to only three people. The position he holds has allowed him to arrange this substitution without the knowledge of the Americans."

Gorbachev struggled to grasp the enormity of what he was hearing, "How could that be? How can he substitute a vital part in hundreds of rocket boosters, and no one know it?"

"As part of their Strategic Defense Initiative, the Americans have a highly secret R&D project which they have code named Peregrine. Viktor has used that name to cover the fact that he has a separate distinct project of which they know nothing. Because of their security procedures, if anyone comes in contact with what he is doing, they believe it to be simply part of the official Peregrine project. They do not know that it is a separate project. Not only was the module built and installed under that code name, it was also used to have the specially designed transmitter needed to activate it."

"I believe that the destruct mechanism in the booster rockets is only effective in the first few minutes after lift-off," Gorbachev countered. "Their submarines can launch missiles from almost any place on earth at any time. Are you telling me that we can determine their launch times quickly enough to send radio signals in time to activate their destruct mechanisms?"

"Actually, the areas from which their submarines can launch and hit worthwhile targets are fairly limited. The range of their Poseidon missiles is only forty-five hundred kilometers, and their most advanced missile, the Trident, only travels seventy-two hundred. We have established three very powerful phased array radar stations to work in conjunction with dedicated transmitters. They are placed so that their signals will cover most areas from which a US submarine might launch a missile. One is situated on the Kola Peninsula near Murmansk and will cover all SLBMs launched in the North Atlantic and North Sea. The second is located in Azerbaijan and will cover SLBMs launched from the Indian Ocean and the Mediterranean. The third is situated on the Sakhalin Island just off the Kamchatka Peninsula and will cover all SLBMs launched in the far Pacific and the South China Sea."

Gorbachev broke in, "The Korean airliner—?"

"Yes," Ustinov confirmed. "It over-flew the island just at the time we were running the initial tests on the radar and the transmitter. It was too much of a coincidence. The Americans had undoubtedly spotted the activity at the site with their spy satellites, and we know that they monitor all of our electronic transmissions. It would have been easy for them to use the plane for that purpose, even without the knowledge of the Koreans. Had they done so, they might have guessed the purpose of the installation. We could not take the chance, so we destroyed the aircraft."

Gorbachev shook his head, his expression grim. "Those installations cover submarine launched missiles. What about their land based missiles?"

"A fourth transmitter is situated in Northern California, and it will cover either directly or through satellite link all SLBMs launched from their coastal waters, and ICBMs launched from all bases in the US.

"The system is in place and has been tested," Ustinov continued. "There is no doubt that it will work. Its only vulnerability is that if the modified modules were somehow discovered and replaced before all of our preparations were complete, the whole operation would fail. That is why it has been so secret."

"If the entire operation is based on their not finding out about the substitute command module," Gorbachev asked, "is that not incredibly risky."

"Not really, because their attention will be diverted elsewhere. In the past few days we have launched several large satellites. These launchings will continue until we have a total of twelve in orbit, eight of which will always be in sight of the US. Our official public position is that the satellites are advanced communications and weather observation platforms. The US will suspect this is not true because of the number of satellites, as well as their size and positioning.

"This, of course, is precisely what we intend because we want them to suspect that the satellites are kinetic-kill vehicles, KKVs. We, of course, have not perfected weapons for such platforms, but the US does not know this. Also, Viktor has taken steps to make them believe that we have compromised their KKV development program, and are now using their technology against them. This diversion should lead them into believing the satellites are the weapons we will use, and their efforts will be directed against them."

Gorbachev, growing more astonished by the minute, pressed his objections. "Even assuming the operation goes as planned, how can you be so sure the Americans will capitulate and allow their country to be occupied? Their president is not noted for backing down. And, we have seen them refuse to do so before; Cuba, for example. And, they have strongly opposed us in places such as Afghanistan, Nicaragua, and Angola. Also, the action Reagan took in Grenada doesn't suggest he's afraid of a confrontation."

Ustinov met the objections confidently: "With the exception of Cuba, all of the incidents you mention fit a pattern of non-nuclear confrontation with adversaries who could not possibly stand against them. None except Cuba involved the possibility of a nuclear exchange with us. But that came at a time when they knew their nuclear capability was far superior to ours. So the real lessons that taught us was not just the importance of achieving and maintaining a balance of power, but, more importantly, it demonstrated their fear of a nuclear war.

"Even though their nuclear capability far outweighed ours at that time, they were so afraid to use it and risk any retaliation that we were able to extract promises that they would not invade Cuba and would remove their missiles from Turkey in exchange for our removing our missiles from Cuba—concessions we would never have made had the situation been reversed. But their actions should not surprise anyone. What would you expect from a society so frightened of possible nuclear contamination and radioactive fallout that they allow perfectly good nuclear power plants to stand idle because it may be difficult to evacuate people from the vicinity in case of an accident?"

"But, what if they don't capitulate?" Gorbachev demanded. "They will still have their SAC bombers."

"It is quite possible that we might sustain some damage. But it is unlikely many of their aircraft or cruise missiles will get through our air defenses. Our analysis tells us that without their ICBMs and SLBMs, they would be able to inflict a maximum of two to five percent destruction on us, while our first strike would inflict over eighty-five percent destruction on US military and industrial targets."

Ustinov's eyes burned, and his voice filled with passion. "We have always been willing to make sacrifices to achieve our goals. The revolution was not achieved without sacrifice, and during the Great Patriotic War we gave up time, distance and people, while we wore the Germans down and rebuilt our war machine. We had plenty of each, and today our land mass is large enough for us to accept a small amount of nuclear contamination, if that is the only way to achieve Party security and true socialism. We do not believe that the US, if faced with annihilation, will rely on a limited retaliation to counter it, but if they do, it would be a small price to pay in order to eliminate them as a military threat once and for all time."

"But what if the US is joined by NATO in a full scale military response to your ultimatum?"

"We will be prepared at the time the ultimatum is delivered not only to launch a full scale preemptive nuclear strike against the US but a conventional arms strike against NATO from eastern Europe. The outcome is a foregone conclusion. We believe NATO will understand this and not join the US."

After a pause Ustinov looked pointedly at Andropov and then back at Gorbachev. "All contingencies are covered. I don't understand why you are so hostile to the plan, Comrade Minister."

"I am not hostile to the purpose of the plan, Comrade Marshall," Gorbachev replied sharply. "I'm concerned about its potential vulnerabilities."

"Maybe your perceptions are based on your lack of military experience," Ustinov observed.

"And maybe yours are based on the fact that you've never served anywhere except in the military," Gorbachev countered. "In any event, I would like to know what preparations are being made for occupation of the US in the event they choose to capitulate. Are you sure this is realistic? I notice that you have not been too successful with your occupation of Afghanistan."

Ustinov replied with a dark scowl. "This is quite different. If we occupy the US, it will be because we have their unconditional surrender and guarantee of cooperation before we send our occupation forces in. But even so, we will move quickly to take control of their central government and to isolate and take over all of their command, control and communications centers."

"One final question," Gorbachev said. "With all the preparations that are going on, plus the fact that they can see that we're in the process of full mobilization, isn't there a possibility that they might launch a pre-preemptive strike and catch us off guard?"

Chernenko, who had trained as a Party propagandist, broke in. "Not likely, Misha. The operation was named *Maskirovka* because it is designed to deceive the West by disguising our true purpose and intent. As you know, people tend to believe what they hope is happening, rather than what the facts might tell them. Accordingly, we have downplayed all of the military preparations by labeling them as training exercises, and by having top military people, including Dimitri here, make conciliatory speeches for western consumption. Also, our propaganda and disinformation program was designed to convince both the US and Western European news media that we have a legitimate reason to be concerned over the deployment of Pershings and cruise missiles.

"Major western media outlets together with prominent sympathizers continue to pressure the US to ignore what we are doing so that they will not aggravate the 'deepening crisis' which 'their activities' have provoked. It now seems clear that not only does the US not intend to do anything to provoke us at the moment, but by the time we are fully mobilized and they realize what is going on, it will be too late for them to reposition their conventional strategic assets to make them into an effective nuclear deterrent force.

"Make no mistake about it, Misha," Chernenko concluded, "the operation will succeed. When Anatoly delivers the ultimatum to Reagan one week from today, the US will not be prepared. They will not receive the support they expect from their allies. And, when they realize that most of their nuclear retaliatory capability is immobilized, they *will* capitulate. And once the US has been taken, Europe will also be ours."

As his visitors rose to leave, Andropov motioned Gorbachev to remain. "Misha," he asked, after Ustinov and Chernenko were gone. "You have problems with the operation?"

"Yes, Yuri." Gorbachev answered. He used the familiar only when alone with Andropov. "Even though the preparations seem thorough with everything covered, I have the feeling that we are getting into something which if not successful, will leave us with no acceptable way out. And I am not convinced it will be successful. Everything hinges on what Dimitri has referred to as Peregrine. Should it not work for some reason, by the time we find out we may already have gone so far that we will be unable to prevent the confrontation from escalating into a full scale nuclear exchange. If that happens, it will be the end of civilization as we know it."

"Ustinov has assured me that cannot happen." Andropov replied. "But, in any event it is a risk we must take. We cannot continue the arms race without bankrupting the country. Also, many of our top scientists are convinced the US will have an effective defense against ballistic missiles before we do. Either way, once the balance of power is lost, we will then be in the same position in which Peregrine has placed them. The Union will self destruct and we will become a second rate power. We must move while we have the ability to defeat them.

"I understand your concerns, Yuri." Gorbachev replied. "But I thought you agreed with me that the answer was co-existence while we moved to fully implement *glasnost* and *perestroika*. Once that was done, we agreed we could eventually surpass capitalism."

"We have tried, Misha. We have removed many of the old entrenched bureaucrats and replaced them with younger people who are not afraid of change. But in the process, we have found out that changing the *system* without destroying it will take more time than we have. There is no other way."

25

Frolich's apartment, San Francisco, California
2325 Friday, December 16—Day Eight

Hollis replaced the telephone in its cradle, his mind furiously reviewing the conversation with Viktor. Any lingering doubts about the existence of a mole as well as the importance of the Peregrine memo had been put to rest, but he was no closer to his goal. He still did not know who Viktor was, nor did he understand the significance of the memo. And time was running out.

As he started out the door, he remembered Frolich. He stopped and looked long and hard at him. "I probably should kill you, just because the world doesn't need your kind, but I suspect Viktor will do the job for me."

Frolich said nothing.

Hollis backed the BMW out of the garage into the street. He knew from experience that during the first few days of a hunt for a fugitive like himself the most intense surveillance would be concentrated on all the major international airports.

Maybe he'd do better if he flew out of Oakland instead of San Francisco. He checked the flight guide he carried in his brief case and found a flight heading east out of Oakland for Chicago at six the next morning. He headed for the Bay Bridge. No one followed, so he pulled the BMW into the airport's long term parking area, parked in a remote section and waited.

He waited in the BMW until it was almost time to board. As a last gesture to Frolich, he dropped the keys and the parking receipt in a trash receptacle as he entered the lobby and headed for the airline ticket counter.

Almost immediately he spotted a couple of FBI agents trolling the concourse. They were young and bored and probably fatigued from long hours spent looking at the thousands of faces that passed through the terminal on any given day.

Hollis would have to hope that what little disguise he had left would be enough to fool them. He purchased a ticket, checked his bag, and walked with a shuffling gate toward the departure lounge. Periodically, he held his breath to make his face redder than normal. He felt that they were watching him, but he was careful not to look back.

Hollis was amazed at how quickly the flight passed. The pilot confirmed shortly before landing that the jet stream had given them a strong boost. They would arrive a good half hour before schedule. That was a possible break.

Hollis' seat was close to the exit, so he was among the first to deplane.

He looked around the concourse. So far, no obvious evidence of surveillance. The flight's early arrival had probably caught them off guard.

He saw them just as he was exiting the baggage for the taxi boarding area.

Several uniformed airport security guards and three conservatively dressed young men were spreading out hurriedly across the main concourse, moving into position to observe the area and close the exits.

Instead of heading for the taxi boarding area, he took the connector to the next terminal. As soon as they realized he was not inside the terminal, they would expand their search outside.

Temporarily out of their sight, he took off at a fast run crossing several approach ramps, a bus boarding area, and a parking lot exit, barely missing the front grille of a Jeep Cherokee racing out of the lot.

He dashed across the parking area, jumped over several barriers, and ran until he came to the main arrivals area on the other side of the terminal.

He slowed down, caught his breath and joined the flow of passengers entering the building.

26

Safe House, Dumfries, Virginia
1130 Saturday, December 17—Day Nine

Maggie was no longer concerned about her personal safety. If they had intended to kill her they would already have done so.

But that was little consolation. Jeff had been counting on her to get the information about the memo to Walters. Not only had she failed to do that, but she had allowed herself to be taken prisoner and used as the bait to trap him.

It had quickly become obvious that she could not escape from the safe house. She was on the second floor and the windows were outfitted with security alarms.

She had been pacing around the parlor of her two-room prison for what seemed the thousandth time when the desk caught her eye. There was stationery and envelopes and she had stamps in her handbag. Maybe, just maybe, she would have an opportunity to get to a mail box.

She wrote two letters. The first, to Walters, recounted all that Jeff had told her, plus the fact that she had been picked up by a DIS driver, and was now being held prisoner. Not knowing Walter's address, and not wanting to mail it simply to the CIA, she had written a second letter to Jessica asking her to personally deliver the enclosed letter to Walters. She addressed the envelope to the advertising agency where she and Jessica worked and stuffed both letters into an envelope.

She had only just finished and tucked the envelope inside her blouse when the door opened and Brovikov strode in.

"Get anything that belongs to you, and come with me," he ordered.

Maggie collected her belongings. "Where are you taking me?"

Instead of answering her, Brovikov made a move toward her. "Come on, I haven't got all day."

Maggie bristled. "Do not touch me," she muttered, hurrying out the door ahead of him.

Brovikov followed Maggie out of the room. Downstairs, she was met by two young men who seemed clones of the driver who had brought her to the safe house.

"Mrs. Hollis, we are here to take you to the Washington National Airport," the taller of the two said to her in a politely stern voice. "From there you'll be transported to another location."

Maggie glared at him. "I'm not going. You have no right to hold me."

"Ma'am, we can take you as you are, quietly and unprotesting, or we can drug you. The choice is yours, but either way, you will go."

Realizing that if she were drugged she would have no chance to do anything with the letter, Maggie gave in.

At Washington National, the car took them directly to the general aviation terminal. Maggie was escorted through the terminal to the waiting Gulfstream, and they were quickly airborne.

It was apparent that if she was going to leave the letter in a place where it could be found and mailed, that place would have to be somewhere on the airplane. But, where? The two who had picked her up at the safe house were still with her on the Gulfstream, and they were watching her constantly.

There was only one place she could go to that would be out of their sight. She waited until the pilot began his descent, then went into the rest room and firmly locked the door.

The cramped space did not offer much hope. No matter where she left the letter it would immediately be found by her captors.

In desperation she opened the door to the built-in trash receptacle. It contained the usual throw-away plastic bag. She pulled the bag out, pinned the letter to the outside back of it and replaced it.

She was surprised when she returned to her seat that neither of her escorts went to the rest room to check it out. She found out why after the Gulfstream had landed. She was turned over to a new team. Her escorts would have plenty of time to search the rest room on their return trip.

On her way out of the Gulfstream to a waiting car, Maggie saw the sign on the airport terminal building: "Ukiah."

In the car, Maggie tried to recall whether she had ever heard the name "Ukiah" before. She couldn't remember. She knew little about California beyond Los Angeles, where she and Hollis had lived while he was assigned there. She had been to Northern California only once—the time when she had visited Paul Montague's retreat.

Out the rear window a signpost slipped by. She turned her head just in time to read what it said, *PHILO 3 MILES.*

She shrank back against the rear seat. My God, it couldn't be, but it was. They were on the road to that same retreat.

A few minutes later the car stopped in front of the stone house she remembered that Paul Montague had called his "fishing cabin."

Maggie was overcome with shock. Her suspicions about Paul had been aroused by the driver in Washington who had told her that it was Mr. Montague who had summoned her to that imaginary meeting.

But now there was little doubt. Jeff's boss, the man he trusted the most in the entire Pentagon bureaucracy, was a Soviet mole.

If only she had spelled out her suspicions in that letter she had left on the plane.

27

I-95 North of Richmond, Virginia
2114 Saturday, December 17—Day Nine

Hollis had strode back into the terminal, bringing up the rear of a large group of middle-aged travelers on a packaged tour of the Caribbean Islands.

Halfway across the concourse, he had separated from the tour and followed the signs to the US Air ticket counter.

At the counter he found a seat on a flight to Pittsburgh, leaving immediately. He reached the boarding ramp just as a flight attendant was starting to close the door to the aircraft.

In Pittsburgh, Hollis made a connecting flight to Richmond, Virginia. He rented a car there and, once again, headed for the safe house in Dumfries to keep his appointment with Viktor.

After exiting I-95 onto Virginia 234, Hollis turned right onto US 1 and went to the first street after Tripoli before turning right again. He passed a number of small frame houses on his way to the end of the dirt road, where he parked the car.

It was just past 2030. The sky was overcast, threatening snow, and the lone street light almost a block away was so weak he did not cast a shadow. Several blocks away a dog barked sporadically and he could hear sounds of a family argument from a house nearby.

The safe house was one block away at the end of a street that ran parallel to the one he had just parked on. A thick wooded area separated the two streets.

He stood motionless until his eyes became accustomed to the darkness, then took one last look around to make sure no one was watching him before slipping into the woods.

The trees were mostly pines and scrub oaks and the undergrowth was heavy. In the dark, movement was slow and difficult. Caught several times by briars and low hanging limbs, Hollis swore under his breath as the journey to the safe house dragged past a quarter of an hour.

He made a slow circuit around the house. Nothing appeared to have changed since his last visit, when Czrnch had ambushed him. He was still early and the place appeared to be empty. Could he set up an ambush, he wondered?

Remaining in the shelter of the woods as long as he could, he approached the house. Once in its shadows, he slipped around to the front.

Should he go in? Or wait out in the shadows?

He knew the security procedures pertaining to safe houses, and he could deactivate the silent alarm and enter if need be. But, as Czrnch had apparently decided, it would probably be better to ambush someone outside the house than inside. And the place Czrnch had chosen was probably the best.

He turned to slip back to the side of the house closest to the woods when he heard a click behind him.

For a fleeting moment, Hollis considered diving for the ground, rolling over and firing. But instinct told him he wouldn't make it.

The voice from the shadows behind him sounded familiar. "You will carefully lay that gun on the ground and kick it toward me and turn around."

Hollis followed the instructions, and after Brovikov picked up the Magnum, he continued, "You will enter the house through the front door, go straight through to the hall, then turn left and enter the room in front of you. The light switch will be on your right."

Once the light was on, Brovikov moved carefully around Hollis to take a seat behind a desk, the only furniture in the room other than a chair behind it was one in front of it—bolted to the floor. The interrogation room.

For the first time Hollis saw his captor. "Well, well. Semyon Brovikov, the psycho from mokrie dela. I was hoping I'd get a chance to meet you, but I was afraid the FBI would put you away before I did."

He saw the smirk spread across Brovikov's broad Slavic features. His voice conveyed the gloating pleasure he felt. "They are incompetent fools compared to the KGB."

Hollis knew of Brovikov's reputation as a bully with an oversize ego, and he tried immediately to exploit it. "There may be a few good agents in the KGB, but there's no way a pile of shit like you could be one of them. You're way too stupid. You're nothing but the roll of toilet paper they use to clean up the asshole jobs no one else has the stomach for."

Predictably, Brovikov bristled. His dark, close-set, pig-like eyes smoldered with deeply rooted brutality and malevolence. Hollis had hit the raw nerve he was aiming for.

"You'll find out who's the piece of shit, Hollis. And you'll find out the hard way. You got lucky with Czrnch. You won't have that kind of luck with me."

"With you I don't need luck. Where's Viktor?"

"He sent me to take care of you."

"That's too bad. I had hoped he was a man of his word when he said I could exchange my freedom for Maggie's. But if you're working for him, I must be wrong."

Brovikov scowled. He held the gun; he wanted Hollis to be cowering before him. He wanted him to be crawling and begging for his life before he killed him. But it wasn't working that way. It infuriated him.

"As soon as I take care of you, Hollis, I'm going to take care of that whore you were married to. I'm really looking forward to that."

Hollis felt a icy terror grip his heart, but his scornful grin stayed in place as he said, "That's the only way a shit ass like you could get any."

Brovikov ignored the taunt. "We only needed her to bait this trap for you. After you're terminated, there'll be no reason to hold her any longer. After I'm through with her I intend to kill her. I haven't decided how yet, but I have a few ideas."

Hollis' adrenaline surged as Brovikov leaned forward and smirked at him. He had to keep Brovikov talking until a way could be found to distract him. "Well, Viktor should understand that I know what Peregrine is, and that I've taken steps to make that it will be exposed whether I'm alive or not."

"You bore me, Hollis. But it makes no difference what you know. Viktor is in complete control. He can prevent any investigation of Peregrine."

"I'm really surprised you're telling me all this."

Brovikov grinned malevolently. "What difference does it make? You're not going to leave this house alive. As soon as we entered the house, a backup crew moved into place outside."

Hollis pretended to be amused. "I'd have guessed as much. Viktor obviously knows you aren't capable of taking care of me yourself."

Brovikov's ego could tolerate no more. His anger was beginning to rob him of his concentration and he started to babble. "Look, you're dead! I could have already killed you, but first I'll just handcuff you to that chair because I need some information from you. I want to know who you have talked to about Peregrine other than Lipscomb. But I hope you don't tell me right away. I want you to think about it for a while and wonder how long it will take because I'm going to enjoy hurting you. Before I'm through, you'll be begging me to finish you off."

Brovikov was trembling with passion. As he moved to get up from the desk, his gun hand wavered slightly. Hollis guessed it was the only break he was likely to get.

After entering the room he had remained standing by the door with his hand on top of his head. The light switch was still within arms reach. When the Russian's gun wavered, he faked a move to the right, hit the light switch and dove to his left.

As the light went out he was deafened by the roar of Brovikov's gun. He felt a burning sensation in his chest, just below his right armpit.

The noise Hollis made hitting the floor brought two more random shots. Both missed. He pulled out the CZ-75 tucked in his belt and fired toward the desk. Brovikov swore in surprise. Hollis fired again in the direction of the sound. This brought a slight scuffling noise from behind the desk. He fired twice more, then heard the opening and closing of a door.

He lay still for several moments waiting for some small sound that would tell him Brovikov was still there. The burning sensation under his right arm had increased and his shirt was beginning to stick to his chest.

After what seemed an eternity, he found his way to the desk and then to the door behind it.

He flicked the light switch.

He was alone.

A quick check confirmed the bullet had only creased the skin of his ribcage under his arm. It would bleed a little until bandaged, but that could wait. Hollis guessed if a back-up team were indeed waiting outside for him, Brovikov should have left the house. There would be no reason for him to remain and risk a one-on-one shoot out. But he couldn't count on it. Brovikov was not entirely sane.

Whether Brovikov was still in the house or not, Hollis knew he had to search it for Maggie, and search it fast.

He ran quickly through the four rooms downstairs. They were all empty.

He headed upstairs. At the top of the stairs he found himself in a central hallway with several doors, all of them closed.

He yanked open the first door, made a diving roll into the room and came up on his knees ready to fire.

There was no one there, and no sign of Maggie.

He repeated the process in the next two rooms. Going through the last door into the fourth room, he found himself in the parlor of a two-room suite. The door to the bedroom was open, and a small bedside lamp was lit.

He inched his way through the door. His heart beat faster as he detected a faint hint of Maggie's perfume in the air. It was elusive, but it was not his imagination. Maggie had been there. His anger seethed as realized he had been lured into another blind alley.

The wound was still bleeding, so Hollis went into the bathroom and managed to fix a temporary bandage on it. Since he had not found Brovikov in the house, he assumed the back-up team was real. The window should provide the answer. He turned the bedside lamp off so there would be no background light in the room, and parted the blinds covering one of the windows. A faint gleam of reflected light caused by a movement on the ground below caught his eye. He moved away and let the blind fall just as a burst of automatic rifle fire shredded the portion of the blind where his chest had been.

Whatever the weapon was, it was automatic, medium to large caliber, and equipped with a sound suppresser.

He was glad Maggie was not there. He could take chances getting himself out, but it would have been impossible to have gotten them both out.

He left the suit of rooms and started back downstairs.

He stopped at the top step when he heard a window break and then a heavy thud on the floor downstairs.

Tear gas, he thought. He continued down the stairs. He knew he could handle it for a while, if he had to. It was not until he reached the bottom of the stairs that he smelled the smoke and knew the house was on fire.

28

Ustinov's Dacha, Outside Moscow
0805 Sunday, December 18, 1983 Week Two

To Dimitri Ustinov, Sunday was like every other day of the week except it was usually spent at his dacha, sometimes with his family, sometimes with his mistress. Today, neither was present. It was a working day, and he was there because Operation Maskirovka was moving into its final stage.

His aide, Colonel Maxsimov, had departed after briefing him on the status of the operation, and he was now waiting impatiently for his next visitor.

The wait was not long. A black Chaika limousine with black Volga escorts in front and behind rolled up the long, aspen-lined drive.

It stopped in front of the dacha and the driver, in the uniform of a KGB captain with the Ninth Chief Directorate, which provided bodyguard service for the Communist Party elite, got out and opened the rear door for the passenger.

Viktor Chebrikov, the chairman of the KGB pulled himself slowly from the back seat and headed toward the dacha's front door.

Ustinov waited at the door to greet his guest himself. "Come in, Comrade Chairman!"

"Good morning, Comrade Marshal."

Ustinov took Chebrikov's greatcoat and hung it on a clothes tree in the foyer, then led his guest into a study furnished with expensive items imported from the west. He motioned toward a built-in wet bar. "Would you care for a vodka?"

Chebrikov looked as if he needed a vodka very badly, but he was aware of Ustinov's antipathy for those whom he thought drank too much. He reluctantly declined.

Ustinov offered the KGB chief a chair near the fireplace. After the prerequisite exchange of small talk and inquiries into each other's health and the status of family members, Ustinov moved swiftly to the point.

"Comrade Chairman, I have just been briefed on the status of Operation Maskirovka, and I am concerned about Peregrine. I don't believe Viktor is completely on top of the situation."

Chebrikov's surprise appeared genuine. "I'm not sure I understand, Comrade. The reports I've received confirm that the command modules are in place and the transmitter has been tested and is operational. Everything is ready to go next Sunday."

Ustinov nodded. "My concern is over what might happen between now and then."

"Would the Comrade Marshal be more specific?" Chebrikov asked.

"The American security officer, Hollis I believe his name is, appears to have discovered Peregrine, and even though a Liter L authorizing his termination was approved, it has not been carried out. If this man Hollis succeeds in exposing the project, *Maskirovka* will fail."

"I understand that, Comrade Marshal," Chebrikov responded, placatingly, "but Viktor has assured us he will prevent him from exposing the project."

"The only way he can do that is to terminate him," Ustinov said angrily, the pitch of his voice rising. "Why hasn't he done that? Why should I have confidence in his ability to oversee the end of Maskirovka, if he can't handle this simple task?"

"I agree, Comrade, but he has done all that was required except that. And the position he holds within their ministry of defense assures he has the power to make good on his promise."

Ustinov got up, walked to the fireplace and threw another log on the fire. "Ordinarily, I would not be concerned," he replied, his tone softening slightly, "but there is too much at stake. I'm thinking of sending my aide, Colonel Maxsimov over to take charge of the operation. I think we need someone on the scene who understands the urgency of the situation; someone who can see the big picture, and is willing to do whatever it takes to get the job done."

Concerned that a portion of his area of responsibility was about to be usurped, Chebrikov moved quickly. "If the Comrade Marshal simply wants to make sure Hollis is eliminated, I have just the man for the job."

"Go on."

"Do you recall the traitor we killed in London with the poisoned tip of an umbrella?"

Ustinov nodded.

"Lieutenant Colonel Nikolai Gvindze, did it and was out of the country before the Brits had even determined the cause of death."

"I remember the incident," Ustinov confirmed. "Who is Gvindze."

"He is deputy head of the Executive Action Department of the First Chief Directorate," Chebrikov continued. "He has wide experience in the West as well as an established cover. He'll be able to enter the US and operate freely there without raising any suspicions. I can guarantee he'll eliminate Hollis within hours after his arrival.

"On the other hand, Colonel Maxsimov is not only known to the West, but he knows all of the details of the operation. Therefore to protect him from being subjected to questioning in the event something went wrong and he was detained in the US, he will have to have diplomatic immunity. This means sending him in as a military attaché. If he goes in under that cover, he'll be placed under surveillance immediately and his movements will be restricted. It would be extremely difficult under those circumstances for him to do the job you require."

Ustinov grabbed a fire implement and poked the logs in the fireplace back to life with several ferocious jabs. Sparks flew out onto the hearth. "But I need someone who can not only eliminate Hollis, but take charge of the Peregrine site, as well." Ustinov scowled as he hung the poker back on its wrought-iron hook. "Can you not arrange the proper means for getting Maxsimov into the country in such a manner that he can do the job?"

Chebrikov was persuaded. "When do you wish him leave?"

"This afternoon."

"I will arrange to have Gvindze make all the arrangements and brief him immediately."

"Excellent, Comrade Chairman."

Ustinov studied the KBG chief for a long moment. "Have you found out anything more on the leak?" he asked.

Chebrikov nodded. He had expected the question. "We believe it's either Grishin or Romanov, but most likely Romanov. Second Chief Directorate has had both under constant surveillance without either being aware of it, but neither has made a move. So we briefed each of them separately on the purpose of the satellites."

"What?" Ustinov cried, jumping to his feet.

"Hold on," Chebrikov replied. "Neither was told the real purpose. Romanov was told the satellites were space-based platforms for kinetic kill weapons, and Grishin was told they were space-based platforms for lasers. Now, when Viktor informs us which version reaches Washington, we will know who our traitor is."

Ustinov's face broke into a malicious grin, and after a moment he walked over to the wet bar. "Would you join me in a vodka?"

Chebrikov grinned. "Of course."

Ustinov brought two tall tumblers, each filled to within half an inch of the rim. He handed one to Chebrikov.

"What shall we drink to?" Chebrikov asked.

Ustinov held up his drink. "To Colonel Maxsimov, and the success of his mission. What else?"

"To Colonel Maxsimov," Chebrikov said, raising his glass. He took a deep drink, then lowered the glass and watched with some amazement as Comrade Chairman Ustinov drained his tumbler dry in one long gulp.

29

Safe House, Dumfries, Virginia
2200 Saturday, December 17, 1983 Day Nine

Caught between the fire on the inside and determined KGB assassins on the outside, Hollis had a tough decision to make.

If he remained inside, the fire would get him. But to simply walk out and try to fight or even surrender would have the same unfortunate result. He'd end up dead. Brovikov had made that clear.

Then a possible way out occurred to him. Few of the older houses he had lived in growing up had basements. Most had only a crawl space underneath and were heated either with fireplaces, coal-burning stoves, or both.

He had already noticed that the crawl space around the bottom of this house was trimmed with decorative lattice work, primarily to keep small animals out. So from the outside, the house would appear not to have any basement at all. The casual observer would assume there was no way for someone to get underneath it without crawling under from the outside.

But these larger two-story homes were often heated by a coal-fired furnace in a partial cellar directly underneath the downstairs hall. From there the heat rises through a register into the hall, to provide the closest thing to central heating then available.

Hollis checked the downstairs hall and confirmed there was a register in the floor. He then headed toward the kitchen door. It was becoming apparent that he had very little time. The house was a tinder box and the fire was spreading quickly. He opened the door to the room where the fire had started and made sure the other doors to the hall were closed. This probably would have little effect, but it might encourage the blaze to spread upward to the roof rather than outward through the house. For his plan to succeed, he would need some diversion.

When he reached the kitchen the smoke was so thick it was difficult to see or breathe, and he could not risk turning on the lights because the windows were uncovered. They would see him from outside.

As his eyes adjusted, he found the door he was hoping to find. His stomach went a little cold as he opened it. It was only a pantry. Had he guessed wrong? Had the door to the partial cellar been eliminated when the heating system was changed from coal to oil? No. They needed a cellar space for an oil furnace, too.

He moved inside the pantry, closed the door and turned on the light. He found the answer almost at once: a trap-door in the floor at the rear of the pantry. It was hinged with a latch so that it could be locked when down and there was a hook to hold it in the up position when in use.

He said a short, heartfelt prayer of thanks to his boyhood memories, turned the pantry light off, raised the trap-door and went down the steps, letting the door down behind him.

He found himself in a partially excavated area below the center of the house with the huge hulk of a long unused stoker coal furnace. The cellar had been shored up with heavy timber, but otherwise was not separated from the crawl space under the rest of the house.

Hollis hoisted himself up into the crawl space and scrabbled hand-over hand toward the brick and mortar pillar at the northeast corner of the house, closest to the woods. There was also an opening in the lattice work there. He knew that because he had shoved Czrnch's body through it a week earlier. The crawl space was barely two feet high, and the going was slow.

By the time he reached the corner, the fire had already eaten through the roof and was lighting up the area around the house. He heard sirens in the distance. At last the fire had been reported.

Hollis pushed himself over to the opening in the lattice work. He could see clearly the yard behind the house. A man stood by the edge of the woods watching the windows intently. He was holding an assault rifle fitted with a sniper scope and sound suppresser.

Fifty feet to the man's right, Hollis spotted a similarly equipped figure, watching the side of the house. The rest of the house would be covered in similar fashion.

But if the other guards were as intent on watching the doors and windows as these were, he would have a chance.

Hollis refitted the CZ-75 with the sound suppresser he had taken from Czrnch. For what he had in mind, it might mean the difference between success and failure.

A fire truck appeared and roared up toward the house. It distracted the KGB agent nearest to Hollis. He stepped back further into the woods to keep out of sight. Hollis, completely hidden by the lattice, picked that moment to take him out. One shot, right to the head. The man crumpled down out of sight into the undergrowth like a puppet with the strings cut.

Hollis scrambled quickly over to the other side of the stone corner pillar. The guard posted there had also moved deeper into the woods. He was watching the house windows intently and failed to notice the sudden disappearance of the man on his left.

The slight cough the pistol made as Hollis took him out was lost in the pandemonium breaking out in front of the house as firemen scrambled off the truck and began unreeling hose.

Just the diversion he needed. Hollis scrambled out the opening in the lattice and dashed in a low crouch for the woods plunging through the undergrowth. Branches snapped in his face, roots tripped him, briars scratched his hands, but in less than a minute he had found his car, got it started, and was racing away from the safe house as fast as he dared travel.

Back on I-95, Hollis headed south towards Richmond. He was at a loss as to what to do next. He had escaped Viktor's trap, but he had not found Maggie and he had done nothing to solve the riddle of Peregrine.

Should he turn himself in, and hope he could make someone listen and act on his suspicions? No, he told himself. *Viktor is still holding Maggie hostage.*

As he agonized over his situation, two things occurred to him. The Soviets must be very close to implementing this Peregrine, whatever it was, and they were going to astonishing lengths to silence him, even though he hadn't the vaguest idea of what they were up to.

In other words, they seemed to think he had a good chance of ruining their plans. Maybe they were right. Maybe he ought to start thinking the way they were thinking. If he was really that big a threat, it was time he proved it. Instead of giving up, he had to redouble his efforts.

Hollis pulled into an all night gas station. After a trip to the rest room to check his wound and change his shirt and jacket, he filled the gas tank and went to a phone booth. It was eleven o'clock in California and Lipscomb answered the phone almost at once.

"Hollis here, Doc."

"Yes, Mister. Hollis."

"Are you still willing to help?"

"Yes. What do you need?"

"I've confirmed there is a Soviet mole in a high level government position, probably the Defense Department, and he's willing to go to any lengths to keep me from exposing Peregrine, even to the point of kidnapping my ex-wife and using her for bait to trap me."

He recounted briefly his conversation with Viktor, and what had happened at the safe house. "He said I don't have much time, so I guess they're just about ready to use Peregrine. If we're going to stop them we've got to do something right away. Will you go with me if I give myself up?"

"Yes." Lipscomb did not equivocate. "Does that mean you've changed your mind as to what will happen if you do?"

"No," Hollis replied, bleakly, "but I'm fresh out of possibilities. As risky as it is, it's the only thing left."

"I did a lot of thinking after you left the other night," Lipscomb said.

"I'm listening."

"You said you could not reconcile my memo with the project the Joint Resources Board Approved. Have you considered the possibility that they may be different projects with the same name?"

"God, Doc!" Hollis exclaimed after a split second of dumbfounded silence, "That's it! Two projects. Why didn't I think of that? The mole is running his own unofficial off-the-books Peregrine project."

"That's certainly the way it appears," Lipscomb conceded, "but why would he do that? Why would he use the name of another project?"

"What better place to hide a rogue project than under the umbrella of an official one? Anyone coming in contact with the code name would know it to be an official, highly classified R&D project, and not question it. Had I not accidentally discovered a memo written before the official project was named, I'd never have thought to question it myself."

"Is that possible?" Lipscomb asked, and then added, "I mean could someone actually do that, and get away with it?"

"If they were in a high enough position, and had the know-how, they could. Information on highly sensitive projects is so compartmentalized, completely innocent people could be involved, just as you were, without suspecting anything was wrong. The only requirement would be to keep the dual identity secret. And, that's why he framed me and is trying to have me killed."

"That seems to make sense," Lipscomb replied.

"But even if I'm right," Hollis said, suddenly crestfallen. "I'm not sure where it gets us."

"What do you mean?"

"You shot down my guidance control theory, remember?"

"Sure," Lipscomb answered. "But relaying course corrections isn't the only function of the command module. In the event a booster malfunctions and strays off course, it allows the launch officer to issue self-destruct orders."

"That's it!" Hollis almost shouted into the telephone. "You've done it again. If someone has the ability to activate the self-destruct mechanism in all of our rocket boosters right after lift-off merely by the transmission of a radio signal, then they have effectively neutralized all of our ICBMs, and maybe our SLBMs, and the balance of power has been destroyed. Keeping that a secret would sure as hell be worth killing for."

"Hold on a minute." Lipscomb counseled. "I may have over-simplified the situation. What I said about the radio transmission was in the context of what the command module is built to receive. If you go outside that envelope, then to achieve what you're talking about would require a major re-do of the command module."

"I don't follow you?"

"They're built to receive sequenced frequencies in micro-burst transmissions. Another safeguard. Generally, you would need a special transmitter, probably computer controlled, to send such a signal."

"I hate to say this again, Doc, but I think you just answered the last nagging question I had about this whole thing."

Hollis related his conversation with Crowley about the transmitter Intertel built under the name of Peregrine. "If we're right about there being two projects with the same name, then what this means is that the project Intertel worked on is part of the same project your memo involves. From what Crowley said it would certainly qualify, and that closes the circle. Maybe we've got enough to go on, Doc. Even a farfetched as this might seem at first glance, it would be difficult to ignore completely, particularly if you were there."

"Well, there's one more thing I thought of," Lipscomb said. "Back when the command modules were first being developed, they were pushing the technological envelope. I was heavily involved in the research and development phase, as well as choosing the contractor thought best suited to produce it. A small firm down in Huntington Beach named Pacific Electronics Corporation was chosen."

"I'm not familiar with the firm," Hollis said. "But I believe it was removed from the list of contractors approved for high classification projects not long ago by DIS because of some minor security violations."

"Well, it just seemed logical to me that they would be the best choice to produce the modified module, but I guess that would eliminate them."

"You're wrong, Doc!" Hollis said, excitement again creeping into his voice.

"I don't understand. Wouldn't that keep them from being awarded the project?"

"If it were an official project, it certainly would, but can you think of a better contractor to work on an unofficial one? I'm heading for Huntington Beach, Doc."

Hollis was just about to hang up when something occurred to him. "Wait a minute, Doc. If I do get information about the command module, you're the only person I know who can determine whether it has the override feature we think it does. If something happens to you, we've lost. The people who are after me will no doubt expect me to get in touch with you, and they'll do everything they can to prevent it. I'm sorry to tell you this, but it's imperative that you disappear from sight immediately."

Lipscomb was astonished at the thought. "I can't do that," he protested. "I've got commitments—classes, students—to worry about."

"Jesus Christ, Doc, if what you and I think may happen does happen, your classes, students and commitments will be atomized along with everything else in the country."

There was a long pause on the other end of the line. Hollis waited impatiently.

"How can I disappear?" Lipscomb said, finally. "Where can I go?"

"I have a friend in San Francisco. Her name is Karen Brewster. She has an apartment near the Presidio. Call her and tell her that I asked that she keep you out of sight until I get there, and she'll take it from there."

Hollis gave Lipscomb Karen's unlisted number. "Professor, it's extremely important that you get out of your house as quickly as possible, right now, tonight. Make sure you're not followed, and don't go back there or to the campus. Can I count on you to do that?"

"Yes. But we'll have to bring this to a head quickly. I haven't much time."

"I don't think any of us do. If all goes well, I'll see you tomorrow afternoon."

Watergate Apartments, Washington, DC
0905 Sunday, December 18, 1983 Day Ten

Brovikov stirred himself from his stuporous slumber in response to the impatient ring of his telephone. He had consumed a prodigious amount of vodka to celebrate his success in eliminating Hollis, and he did not want to be bothered, but only one person called on the phone that was ringing.

"Brovikov," he said, brusquely The sound of Victor's voice bit into his hangover like a sledgehammer. "Hollis outsmarted you again, you damned fool! There were no remains in the ashes. He escaped."

Brovikov was instantly wide awake and sober. "Goddammit! That's not possible! We stayed until the house collapsed."

"You did not tell me two of your men were killed."

"That made no difference!" Brovikov complained. "We would have seen him if he had gotten out!"

Victor replied in a voice hard and flat as polished granite. "I have had to report that you have failed again. You will go to San Francisco immediately, and put Lipscomb, PEC, and Intertel under surveillance. If Hollis contacts Lipscomb, or anyone at either PEC or Intertel, you will immediately terminate them. Frolich has also failed us and should be terminated. You have very little time left. I cannot keep a lid on this. You know what will happen to you if Hollis exposes Peregrine."

Brovikov slammed the phone into its cradle. He felt sick, on the verge of throwing up. *How could that son-of-a-bitch Hollis possibly have gotten out?* he wondered.

He grabbed an already packed suitcase and headed for the airport.

30

Municipal Airport—Ukiah, California
0530 Sunday, December 18—Day Ten

After Maggie had been escorted off the Gulfstream the night before, the two passengers who had accompanied her deplaned. The pilot and co-pilot finished the shut-down check list, and all four spent the night in a nearby motel. They were now back on board for the return flight to Washington National.

As they buckled their seat belts the taller of the two asked, "By the way, did you ever check the rest room to see if she left anything in it?"

"She didn't take anything with her, so I don't see how she could have left anything in there," the other one growled sleepily.

The taller one glared at him. "You should have checked it."

"If you think she left something, go check the Goddamned place yourself." He put his head on a pillow and closed his eyes. In a few minutes he was asleep.

The taller passenger thought about it for a while, then went back to the rest room to check. He didn't really expect to find anything, so he didn't look very hard. Basically he just wanted to cover his ass and be able to say he checked if someone asked him.

And so he didn't find anything.

National Airport—Washington, DC
1445 Sunday, December 18 – Day Ten

The Gulfstream taxied to the transient terminal where it was guided to a parking slot. The two passengers deplaned, and the pilot was preparing to leave when the ground crew chief stuck his head in.

"Anything need looking at, Cap'n?"

"Nah. Running like a dream."

"You want the usual clean up?"

"I don't think it needs it, Mac. Have 'em take care of the waste tank and check the bar and the galley, and hold the rest of the clean-up."

"Will do."

"We've got another crew taking her out later this afternoon, so run your usual pre-flight checks and get her fueled as soon as you can."

31

International Airport, San Francisco, California
1435 Sunday, December 18, 1983—Day Ten

When Brovikov arrived at the airport, he immediately rented a car and headed for Frolich's apartment. He was still smarting from Viktor's call. As much as he hated to take orders from him, he knew Viktor was right. If Hollis did succeed in exposing Peregrine there would be no place to hide. The shit and everything else would hit the fan.

Viktor might also be held accountable, but it would make no difference. He, Brovikov, would be the first to go. Hollis should have been disposed of long ago. He had better shape up fast. He'd start by getting rid of Frolich.

Frolich had spent most of Sunday finding his car. When he pulled into his apartment garage, he didn't notice the solitary figure sitting in the car down the block and across the street. When he came out of the garage, Brovikov emerged from the shadows and walked toward him, one hand out of sight behind him. Frolich understood immediately what confronted him.

"I am Brovikov," the man announced. "Let's talk. Inside."

Frolich said nothing. He kept his hands out in clear view and led the way into his apartment. He had never met Brovikov, but he knew his reputation. Once inside, he closed the door, and in response to a motion from Brovikov, sat down on the couch.

Brovikov also took a seat—and pointed a handgun at the center of Frolich's chest. "You failed. That's not allowed."

Frolich kept his wits about him. Knowing death was only a moment away, he remained composed, and his voice remained steady. "But you still want Hollis, and I may now be the only one who can get him for you."

His voice silky with distrust, Brovikov responded, "Why should I believe you won't fail again?"

"You don't have to believe anything. I assume you're here because you think Hollis is in the area—or on his way. It happens he has an accomplice here."

"And where is this 'accomplice'?"

"That's my insurance."

Brovikov stepped over to Frolich and smashed the handgun against his jaw. Frolich's head snapped back. He bent forward, wiped the blood from his mouth with the back of his hand.

"Don't play games with me, Frolich."

Frolich felt a loosened tooth with the edge of his tongue. "There's no way you'll ever beat the information out of me. When I die the information goes with me."

Brovikov struggled to contain his rage and frustration. He had been looking forward to terminating Frolich. He always looked forward to killing someone. But now he dared not risk it—at least not yet. He'd have to postpone that pleasure. Let Frolich take one more crack at Hollis. Viktor need not know. If Frolich succeeded, that was one less job Brovikov had to worry about. And as much as he would like to get Hollis himself, he recognized the difficulties—and the dangers. So he'd let Frolich try it again. Then he'd kill Frolich afterwards, whatever the outcome. And take the credit for Hollis himself.

"All right," Brovikov replied, "same arrangement as before. You have until Wednesday. If you haven't got Hollis by then, there'll be no place where you can hide."

Without another word, Brovikov left.

Frolich repaired his face and cleaned himself up. He had bought some time, but what was he going to do with it? He didn't have the faintest idea whether Hollis had an accomplice in San Francisco or not. The thought crossed his mind only because of the ease with which Hollis had disappeared after that chase in the warehouse district.

He had just finished changing his shirt when it hit him. The car that Hollis had been driving might be the lead he was looking for. He called the Hertz rental desk at the airport.

"This is Mr. Werner," he said, using a slight German accent. "I rented a Pontiac Grand Am, License number California RYL-689, from you a week or so ago. Yes?"

"Yes," the clerk answered. "How can I help you?"

"I think I may have left my glasses in the car. They are prescription. They will be difficult to replace."

"Hold on, please."

After a pause, the clerk came back on the line. "I'm sorry sir, but no glasses have been turned in."

"Please, if the car is available, may I come and examine it. The glasses may have slipped under a seat."

After another pause, the clerk said, "I'm sorry, sir, it's not available. Our records show it was checked out several days ago on a weekly rental. It won't be back until later in the week. If you will give me a telephone number where I can reach you, someone will call if the glasses turn up."

"Thank you, young man. Just call Mr. Werner at the Cliff Hotel."

Frolich hung up, waited a moment, and then dialed another number. A voice answered, "Best Detective Agency. How may I help you?"

"This is Beerman."

"Yes, Mr. Beerman."

"This is very high priority. I need to find a red current model Grand Am, California License RYL-689 as soon as possible. Check all hotel garages, public parking garages, and anything else that makes sense, and put as many men on it as you need. Understood?"

"Yes sir."

"You've got my number. Call me before eight tomorrow morning."

Frolich hung up. It was a long shot, but it was all he had. If it turned up nothing, he would have only a short head start on the KGB.

It was after ten when Frolich's phone rang. It was Best calling to tell Frolich they had located the car in the St. Francis Hotel parking garage.

Frolich drove immediately to the St. Francis. He pulled the BMW up to the main entrance, turned the ignition off and got out. The doorman approached him.

"Can I help you, sir?"

"I hope so. Were you on duty last Thursday night?"

The doorman became instantly suspicious. "Maybe. Who wants to know?"

Frolich took a one-hundred dollar bill out of his wallet and waved it in front of the man. "I'm looking to buy some information, if you're the person who has it."

The doorman surveyed Frolich for a long moment before responding. "Yeah, I was here, what do you want to know?"

"A man driving a current model maroon Grand Am came in between eleven and twelve. Do you remember him?"

"I might. I remember people better than cars. Can you describe him?"

After Frolich had described Hollis as he had looked when he arrived at the airport, the doorman nodded, "Yeah, I remember him. I probably wouldn't except that he asked me to check his luggage in, saying he was going to come back later. Even though this is kinda unusual, I ordinarily wouldn't think anything about it except that about an hour later he came out with a pretty hot-looking broad. He picked up his luggage and they hopped into a taxi. Last I saw of him."

"Did you hear the address?"

"Nah. They were already moving away. Probably went to her place."

"You ever see her before?"

"Yeah. Once in a while."

Frolich asked impatiently, "Do you know who she is?"

"No, but she's been around. She's got a real classy figure, and sort of dark-colored hair; a real number. There's a good chance that Arnie—he's the bartender in the main bar—might know something about her. He's on duty now."

Frolich handed the hundred to the doorman. "I'll be back for the car in a few minutes." He turned and walked into the main bar and took a stool.

After a short wait the bartender came over to him. "What'll it be?"

"Are you Arnie?"

"Yeah, so what?"

Frolich laid another hundred dollar bills on the bar. "I just talked to the doorman, and he said you might have some information."

"Okay, shoot."

"I'm trying to find a guy who came into your bar last Thursday night between eleven and twelve. The doorman remembered him leaving the hotel sometime after midnight with a good-looking woman with dark hair, someone he's seen here before. He thought you might know who she is."

Arnie thought for a moment. "I'm not real sure, but if it's who I think it is, I remember seeing her here that night. She wasn't sitting at the bar, but at a small table right over there. Some joker who may have fit the description of your guy sits down with her. After a couple of drinks they left."

"Does she come in often? Do you know her name?"

"Not too often, but I've talked to her once or twice at the bar while she was waiting to meet someone. Her name's Karen. I don't know her last name."

"Any idea where she lives or works?"

"She never said anything about where she lives, but I'm pretty sure she works off and on for one of those 'hostess' firms."

"Any idea which one?"

"No, but there are only two or three that a dame as classy as that would work for."

Frolich handed Arnie the hundred dollar bill.

Back in his car, he headed for his apartment and the telephone. Whoever this Karen was, he hoped she had been more than a one-night stand.

32

Huntington Beach, California
2230 Sunday, December 18, 1983—Day Ten

After Hollis had talked to Lipscomb, a plan had begun to take shape. He had driven to Atlanta and from there flown to San Diego, avoiding LAX, which he knew would be under heavy FBI surveillance.

From San Diego he had taken a commuter line to Newport Beach, rented a car, drove the short distance to Huntington Beach and checked into a motel for a few hours of much-needed sleep.

Now, back in his car, Hollis checked the city map and headed for Pacific Electronics Company, known as PEC.

The PEC complex was built in a Spanish motif, with two low, single-level buildings and an exterior stucco facade of a color and composition resembling adobe. The buildings were windowless, and the few doors which were either locked or protected by security devices did not encourage unauthorized entry.

To be as inconspicuous as possible, Hollis parked in the area already crowded with vehicles from the midnight production shift, which had just begun work.

Hollis assumed there would be a night watchman on duty, or that Viktor might have arranged for some surveillance, so he sat in the car and waited. Ten minutes later, he spotted the watchman making his rounds, checking doors and punching his time clock. Once the watchman was out of sight, Hollis decided to wait and time the interval between appearances. Exactly one-half hour passed before the watchman again put in an appearance. There was no sign of any other surveillance.

Hollis got out of his car and headed for the night shift entrance, as if he was on his way to work. When almost there, he angled off toward a covered walkway which joined the two buildings of the complex.

Moving close to the shrubbery, Hollis ducked into the walkway. The doors leading from the walkway into the buildings were locked, since they were only used during office hours.

Hollis quickly pulled himself up onto the low roof over the walkway and from there made his way onto the roof of the office building.

Once there, he crawled along the roof, peering down through the skylights. He finally chose one situated over a large room crammed with filing cabinets. Since he could not be seen from the ground, the light from the room below was more help than hindrance.

He taped and removed a pane of glass and disconnected the security device attached to the skylight latch. After a quick examination to assure himself there were no other security devices, he opened the skylight, replaced the pane he had removed, and lowered himself into the room.

Once in, he lowered the skylight back into place. He checked to make sure the latch caught, and then reaffixed the security device. He wasn't sure yet how he would leave, but if it had to be by some other route, he did not want to leave behind obvious evidence of his break-in.

Hollis quickly determined that the room was the major filing center for current PEC activities. The room contained several hundred filing cabinets, which emphasized the problem he now faced—how to find one file among the thousands which the cabinets held—that is, he told himself, assuming it was even here.

He was further dismayed when he pulled open the first drawer and examined its contents. The filing system was based on the DOD alphanumeric procurement contract designation symbol, rather than the subject of the contract. Also, given the size and complexity of the documents, it was obvious that unless he could find something which would quickly lead him to what he sought, he would run out of time.

As he wandered through the maze of cabinets looking for some pattern that might give him a starting point, he was surprised to find a section of locked cabinets set aside specifically for classified projects.

Hollis suddenly knew he was on the right track. Once a contractor lost his security clearance, all files and information relating to classified projects were required to be returned to DOD. There was now no doubt. The removal of PEC from the approved list was window dressing to help hide Peregrine. The firm had not been notified of the action, and therefore would accept an unauthorized high security project without suspicion. He was now convinced the Peregrine file was in one of those locked cabinets.

Hollis picked the lock to the first cabinet and pulled open the top drawer. Since the filing was based on the DOD procurement number, the files were in chronological order. PEC's area of expertise was very high-tech, miniaturized electronic circuitry fabrication, and the firm engaged in many small specialized jobs, which meant Hollis was faced with a large number of contracts to examine.

Adding to this problem was the fact that since he was not sure precisely what descriptive language would be used in the contract he sought, he had to move slowly and with care. To shorten the process, he picked a file dated three months earlier and began working back from it.

He was in the fourth month preceding his starting point, and beginning to wonder whether he should go back and work in the other direction when he found it.

He moved through the file rapidly, finding the schematics together with the design and production specifications. He also confirmed that the production runs covered both the Navy's Poseidon and Trident I SLBMs and the Air Force's Titan and Minuteman ICBMs. Also the last shipment date was over six weeks before, which allowed plenty of time for them to have been installed.

Hollis was manually copying information from the file confirming acceptance by the field project officer, when his concentration was suddenly interrupted by the sound of footsteps outside the room.

He looked at his watch and was surprised to find it was almost seven-thirty. It was now Monday morning, and office hours started at eight, or maybe eight-thirty.

He could not go back the way he had come, but he had to do something fast. He stopped copying and pulled the sheet out of the file, placed it, along with the schematics and specs, in his inside coat pocket, and returned the file to its drawer. He had just locked the cabinet when he heard more footsteps past the door.

He cracked the door open and looked out as several people walked past. All wore ID badges. Without one, he'd stand out like a very sore thumb.

He pulled the door open and entered the hall. As he walked, he rubbed his ear with his left hand so that his arm covered the area of his coat where an ID badge should have been. He took the first turn into a restroom, ducked into a stall and closed the door.

A few minutes later the rest room door opened. Her heard someone laugh. "Good Lord, Joe! You must have had a helluva weekend. Are you sure you want to face Allbright looking like that? You should've hung out today."

"I can't afford it." Water splashed loudly in the lavatory, "God! You should have seen her. Gorgeous! Jugs like you can't believe; each one was at least quart size. And could she fuck! She turned me every way but loose."

"Yeah! I've heard that before." He opened the door to leave. "Look, when you get your eyes open enough to see, and if you don't bleed to death, come on in. In the meantime, I'll cover for you."

When the door closed Hollis peeked out of his stall. Joe had taken his coat off and hung it up. He stood over a lavatory filled with cold water. He was gingerly holding a wet paper towel over his eyes. Hollis silently moved out of the stall to where Joe's coat was hanging and relieved it of the ID. tag.

He affixed the tag to his own jacket pocket and quickly left the rest room.

As he approached the main entrance, it was nearing eight o'clock. Some congestion was beginning to form as the people coming in were being checked and logged in by the guards. Knowing they would now have little interest in checking anyone out, he waved the badge to the closest guard as if he were an old acquaintance and said as he continued walking, "I left my briefcase in the car. I'll be right back." The guard nodded as Hollis walked out.

Hollis crossed the parking lot to his car. When he was sure he was no longer in sight of the front entrance, he dropped the badge between two cars.

Fifteen minutes later, Hollis was on I-405, headed north.

33

Frolich's Apartment, San Francisco, California
0916 Monday, December 19, 1983—Day Eleven

Frolich was not having the success he had expected in tracking Karen down. He was appalled at the number of so-called "hostess" firms he found listed in the phone book, and he quickly found out there was no easy way he could tell a reputable firm from a fly-by-night outfit. Once he started calling the firms and asking whether they had a "Karen" working for them, he quickly recognized a pattern. Either he got an answer somewhat along the line of, "Forget Karen, we've got somebody better." or was told the firm did not give out information on its employees.

He decided on a new approach. He dialed the next number, and when a voice answered he said in a slightly excited tone of voice, "Look, my name is Bill Jackson. I was in town several weeks ago at a convention, and a hostess firm arranged for a gorgeous gal named Karen to show me around town. I'm back in town for a couple of days and I was hoping I could have dinner with her and see the rest of the city, but I don't know which firm she works for or how to get in touch with her. I was hoping you might help me."

Now at least he was getting better answers: "Sorry, it couldn't have been us, we don't have anyone named Karen working for us. But, we'll be happy to arrange for someone to meet you, if you can't find her."

He was fairly far down the list of numbers when he got a different answer. The lady's voice came back with, "We do have a Karen who works for us occasionally, Mr. Jackson, but I have her card here and there is no record of her going out with someone with your name."

Frolich put a little more excitement in his voice, "The reason is, I didn't make the arrangements, the hotel did. Is she a great looking slim brunette about five-seven?"

A reluctant voice on the other end of the line said, "Yes."

"That's her. I knew I'd find her. Can you get me in touch with her."

"No, I'm afraid not. Look, I'd like to help you, but we can't give out information on our girls without their express permission."

"Can't you just give me her telephone number?"

"No. Sorry."

"Well, how about you calling her and asking her to call me."

"I can't do that either. Even if I could, it wouldn't make any difference. She called in early this week and said under no circumstance would she be available for work before next week. I will give her your message when she calls. Good-bye, Mr. Jackson." Frolich was left listening to the dial tone.

There was no address listed with the phone number, and Frolich had not expected one. Seemingly, the hostess business was done only by telephone, but matching an address to the number was a relatively simple matter for any good private eye. It took his contact at Best Agency only a short while to come up with the one he wanted.

When Frolich arrived he could well understand why the address was not listed. It was a private home in a very posh residential neighborhood in the Twin Peaks area. Apparently Mrs. Morrow—who he now knew was the woman in whose name the number was listed—ran her business out of her home. He parked and went to the door. It was opened by a well-dressed, attractive lady in her late forties or early fifties.

Frolich smiled. "Ms. Morrow?" When she nodded, he continued, "I know the business you are in, and I have a proposition which I think will interest you. May I come in?"

It had taken Micki Morrow quite some time to build her business to its present level, and over the years she had seen scams come and go, and been ripped off by some of the best. But in the process she had learned that bending with the wind was a hell of a lot better than getting broken by trying to stand against it. There was an indefinable air about this individual and a look in his eyes that suggested now was not the time to stand on principle. She moved aside. "Come in. My office is through the first door to your left."

Frolich stepped into her office. He waited until she was seated behind the small desk and then sat down.

"My name is Jackson, Ms. Morrow. I talked to you earlier about Karen."

Somehow Micki was sure his name was not Jackson. "Yes, I remember. I thought we finished that conversation." Then, with a slight trace of anger, she demanded, "How did you find me?"

Frolich smiled, extracted ten hundred-dollar bills from his wallet. "It's not difficult when you have the resources and are willing to use them."

He laid the bills down on the desk so there was no mistaking the amount. "You see, Ms. Morrow, I am serious about Karen. I believe if she gets to know me she will accept my proposal to marry, but I haven't the time to wait until a formal meeting can be arranged. I travel too much, and I have to use my time to best advantage when I can."

"Mr. Jackson, you realize that my girls trust me. If it got around that I betrayed that trust, I'd soon be out of business."

"I understand completely. She will never know that this conversation took place."

Micki moved to pick up the ten bills. As she did, she looked pointedly at Frolich, and said, "Mr. Jackson, I have an errand to run. There is a folder on top of that stack. You might find it of interest. Please do not take anything from it. You may let yourself out when you are through."

She turned and walked out of the room, suddenly realizing that her blouse was sticking to the middle of her back.

Frolich opened the file folder. On top were several glossy color prints, both portrait and swim suit, of a striking young lady with an exceptional figure. Her name was Karen Brewster and she had worked for Morrow off and on for over a year. He pulled the chronological log of assignments out of the file, and flipped through it, noting the meticulous care that had gone into maintaining it.

He came to the last entry. Karen had been scheduled to meet someone at the St. Francis the past Thursday night, but had called in to report a no-show. He had been skeptical before, but now there was no doubt. He copied her telephone number and address into the small book he carried, and smiling mirthlessly, he returned to his car.

Frolich took the coast road back to the Presidio. An hour later he was outside the apartment building where Karen lived. Even though he was certain she was the Karen he was looking for, he still did not know whether he was on a wild goose chase.

Frolich decided that he had to get inside to talk with Karen. Even if Hollis did not intend to return, he might be able to get something out of her that would point to his trail. Otherwise, he had no insurance, and it would be time for him to disappear.

He moved his BMW several blocks away, in case Hollis showed up and recognized it, then walked back to the apartment building.

At the front entrance he encountered a set of security doors. He moved down the short line of mail boxes until he came to the one with the name Karen Brewster on it and pressed the button over it.

A female voice answered, "Yes, what is it?"

"I have a message from a Mr. Hollis. He asked that I deliver it in person."

Karen, with a new eagerness in her voice, said, "Oh, please come on up. It's the first door to the right at the top of the stairs."

She pressed the button to unlock the security door. In the apartment living room Lipscomb heard Frolich's voice. It sounded familiar.

Karen checked herself in the mirror and then headed for the door.

She had just reached it when Lipscomb remembered. "No, wait!" he cried.

He was too late. She had already unbolted it and turned the knob.

Frolich quickly pushed the door open and forced his way into the room, the Walther with the sound suppresser in his right hand.

Lipscomb shook his head sadly.

"Well, Herr Doctor, we meet again!. Now quickly, both of you, lie down on your stomachs with your hands behind your head and close your eyes. Do not move until I tell you to."

Once they had complied, Frolich made a quick search of the apartment. Finding no one, he came back into the front room and told them to get up.

"Before I'm forced to take any unpleasant action, where is Hollis? And don't lie to me. You, Herr Doctor, would not be here if you did not expect him."

Lipscomb ignored Frolich and looked out a window.

Karen decided something had to be done to back Frolich off. "We don't know where he is, or even whether he plans to come back here. He merely asked me to keep Professor Lipscomb out of sight for a few days."

Frolich scowled. "Don't force me to do something unpleasant."

Karen's eyes flashed. "I'm not forcing you to do anything. But I can't tell you something I don't know."

Her eyes locked with Frolich's until he broke off contact. His own desperation was getting in the way of his determination. He'd kill them both if he had to, but there was always the possibility she was telling the truth.

"All right... We'll wait."

34

Washington National Airport, Virginia
1015 Monday, December 19 1983—Day Eleven

The Gulfstream, which had taken Maggie to Ukiah, had returned to its home base earlier in the morning and been parked inside the general aviation hanger. It was not scheduled for use until late in the week, so the pilot had ordered a complete interior clean-up.

A member of the cleaning crew stuck his head out of the lavatory and called to the woman vacuuming the seats, "Hey, Mable! There's a Goddamned letter pinned to this trash bag. Who do you think would have done a stupid thing like that?"

"I've told you not to call me Mable. Lemme see it." It was sealed, she noticed, and had an uncancelled stamp on it. "To answer your stupid question—probably somebody who wants it mailed."

"Well you can mail it right here in this fucking bag." He held out the trash bag.

"You can just get your ass back to work. I'll take care of it."

She dropped it in a letter box a short time later on her way out of the airport.

35

Oakland, California
1430 Monday, December 19, 1983—Day Eleven

Hollis drove north on I-5.

He had been so immersed in finding out what Peregrine was that he had lost sight of the larger picture. But now that he was fairly certain he knew what it was, and that there was a mole in the Department who was controlling it under the guise of the official Peregrine, he remembered the conversation with Montague about Operation Maskirovka.

Suddenly the overall picture jumped into focus. If *Maskirovka* was a Soviet operation involving the neutralization of US ballistic missiles, then the mole's Peregrine project was the means by which it would be accomplished. And even more disturbing, according to what Viktor had said, time was about to run out.

If Lipscomb could use the schematics and specs he had gotten from PEC to prove their theory, they would have to act fast to get the information to someone who would act on it. Since he could not risk calling Paul, it would have to be Al Walters, the friend who had replaced him in the CIA. Operations, assistant to the deputy director for operations, Walters should have enough clout to get an honest hearing arranged. And, if there was a way to protect Maggie in the process, he would find it

That settled, Hollis decided to make sure that Lipscomb had gone to Karen's apartment. On the outskirts of Oakland, he hit an off ramp that had signs promising gasoline, and found a station with a telephone booth.

As he pumped gas into the tank, his thoughts turned to Karen. The sensitivity and loyalty she had exhibited even though they had been together for only a short time were rare qualities. She was indeed something special; one of only a few bright spots in the whole unreal mess. He knew that if he were not so much in love with Maggie....

After paying for the gas, he went to the telephone booth.

Karen's Apartment, San Francisco, CA
1435 Monday, December 19, 1983—Day Eleven

Frolich was prepared for the call. He had moved the bedroom telephone extension as close to the bedroom door as it would reach, and the living room extension was placed where it could be seen by someone using the one in the bedroom. When the telephone rang Karen and Lipscomb followed his instructions.

Karen went to the telephone in the living room and waited while Lipscomb and Frolich went to the other extension. Lipscomb sat on the floor facing away from Frolich, while Frolich put his pistol against the back of Lipscomb's head.

He had told Karen that if Hollis called and the telephone conversation alerted him, he would kill them both. Karen had no doubt he meant it. When they were all in position, Frolich nodded to Karen and they picked up the two extensions at the same time.

It took an extreme effort by Karen to keep her voice steady, but she managed a neutral, "Hello."

She recognized the voice on the other end to be Hollis' as soon as he said, "Karen?"

Trying to sound as she assumed a secretary would, she answered, "Yes, Is this Mr. Hollis?" Karen knew how important Lipscomb was to Hollis and that she could not risk giving Hollis an overt signal that anything was wrong. Frolich was listening too closely. The most she could do would be to try to keep the conversation formal and the tone reserved rather than releasing the friendliness she assumed Hollis would be anticipating. It was all she could think of.

Hollis was immediately taken aback by her cool reception. "I'm driving up from LA," he said. "And I was wondering whether Professor Lipscomb got in touch with you."

"Yes, he did."

"Good! Is he there now?"

"Yes."

"Did he say he had talked to anyone?"

"No, he simply called and said you wanted me to hide him for several days. He's been here since early this morning."

"Any reason why I shouldn't come to the apartment?"

"No. I'm sure the professor will be relieved to see you. I think he's about had his fill of me."

"Well, I'm still a couple of hours out, so it will be a little while before I can get there. I'll buzz a couple of times when I get to the lobby so you'll know it's me."

Oakland, California
1440 Monday, December 19, 1983—Day Eleven

Hollis hung up the phone. Something was obviously wrong. Karen would never have acted so impersonal unless she was trying to warn him of something.

But of what?

Was someone there who posed a threat to them—or to him? The police? Frolich? Viktor? Or someone else?

How could anyone have made the connection with him. And even if they had, how could they have found her?

The questions crowded his mind. He went back to the car, got in and sat without starting the motor.

He had to be overlooking something. He reviewed all that had happened since he met Karen, going back to his arrival at the St. Francis.

Then it hit him. *The car*!

He had left it in the hotel garage. Only Frolich could put him with that car. He would have remembered its description and undoubtedly have even gotten the license number. Once Frolich found it in the St. Francis parking garage, locating Karen wouldn't have been too difficult for someone who knew how. He mentally kicked himself that this possibility had not occurred to him before. He had felt so sure the precautions he had taken would be enough to protect Karen.

It was now more important than ever that he not let her down.

Only the foresight to give Karen incorrect information about where he was and what he would do when he got there as soon as he suspected something was wrong, might give him a chance.

Frolich was probably in the apartment waiting for him. Although there was no assurance Frolich would not have a back-up team, it was unlikely. He was a loner, most comfortable working by himself. And if he was in fact alone, Hollis might catch him off guard. The odds did not favor success, but he could think of nothing better.

He drove to within a block of Karen's apartment and parked on a side street. He approached the building on the blind side, away from Karen's apartment.

His plan was to surprise Frolich, first by being there earlier than Frolich would anticipate; and, second, by using the key Karen had given him to bypass the security door buzzer. Frolich would expect him to call when he reached the foyer and be prepared for his arrival at the apartment.

Even if all worked to that point as planned, success would still depend on getting the door to the apartment open without being detected. Only then might he have an edge.

Once through the security door, Hollis remembered that it was possible to hear the elevator from inside Karen's apartment. So he took the stairs.

He reached Karen's door. It was far too heavy for any one to break down with his shoulder.

He wanted to use saliva as a lubricant to make it easier to insert the key in the lock with no noise, but his mouth was so dry it was not possible. He paused, got out the CZ-75 and began the tedious, nerve-wracking process of silently inserting the key.

Inside the apartment, Frolich knew it was mandatory that he eliminate Hollis. Nothing less could save his life. Hollis was on the way. It was imperative he not underestimate him this time.

Instinctively, he had become suspicious about the conversation between Hollis and Karen. He had not detected anything specific, but felt that somehow she had put Hollis on notice, otherwise why would he have made a point of saying how long it would take him to get there, and that he would "buzz a couple of times from the lobby"?

Of one thing he was sure. Hollis would not do the expected.

Frolich made sure the front door was the only way into the apartment. Seating Karen and Lipscomb off to one side where he could watch them, but they could not interfere, he then took a partially shielded position almost directly across the living room opposite the door. He was waiting in that position with the Walther ready well before Hollis' arrival.

In the hall outside, Hollis succeeded in getting the key in the lock and turning it without producing any sound. It was not until he began to turn the doorknob that the problem developed. He was turning it very slowly and carefully to release the latch, but when it was almost to the limit of the turn, the spring operated latch moved suddenly to the open position with an audible click.

Almost simultaneously he heard a movement inside the apartment and Karen's voice raised to a level which could clearly be heard thorough the door, say, "Hollis…".

Whatever she had intended to say was ended by the cough of a pistol equipped with a sound suppresser.

Hollis' shoulder jammed into the door, slamming it open. His momentum carried him into the room.

He dove and rolled, planning to come up on his knees ready to fire before Frolich could react. But midway through the roll he saw that Frolich had guessed his intention and was perfectly positioned to get a clear shot at him.

He could hope, but he knew Frolich would not miss.

Later, he was sure what happened next startled him as much as it did Frolich. With a lunge one would never have expected from an introverted intellectual, Lipscomb launched himself at the assassin.

Reflexively, Frolich pivoted to his left and fired. The bullet took Lipscomb in the middle of the chest and slammed him back onto the chair he had just left.

Frolich's instincts were fine-tuned and normally served him well. He had earned his reputation assassinating high level political figures in Europe. A mystique surrounding his name had grown. It had not been easy. The more important the contract, the more difficult the execution became. The slightest mistake or miscalculation could not only undo the most carefully laid plans, but also result in either capture or death. He had avoided both because of his dedication to long hours of practice.

This time his reflex action in response to Lipscomb's lunge, even though consistent with his years of conditioning, was wrong. In a world where life depended on split-second decision and response, he had trained to meet the most imminent threat first and then go to the next. Thus, even though his instincts had demanded he take Lipscomb first and then Hollis, he knew even as he turned that it was a mistake.

But he was committed. He dropped into a deep crouch and pivoted back to face Hollis.

But Hollis had the extra second he needed. Frolich's Walther was just coming to bear when two shots from the CZ-75 took him in the middle of his forehead.

Hollis did not check Frolich. There was no need. He knew where the bullets went. He was concerned that Frolich might not be alone.

He turned swiftly, taking in the entire room. He heard nothing, saw nothing. He moved slowly to the front door, locked it, then looked in the other rooms. Frolich had been alone.

Karen lay on the floor not far from the chair where Lipscomb had sat. It was apparent she had been seated in another chair by Lipscomb when the spring in the door lock had betrayed his presence, and she had been moving toward the door when Frolich's shot took her.

He dropped to his knees beside her. The stain on her blouse where the bullet had entered was small and low enough on the side of her chest so that it might not be fatal if he could get help.

If by some miracle she were still living, Peregrine would have to wait. Even at the risk of getting caught, there could be no other way. He raised her head to cradle it in his lap and she moaned softly.

"Karen, I'm here. You've got to hold on until I can get help."

Karen's eyelids fluttered and opened. Her once beautiful, expressive eyes were fast losing their sparkle. "You shouldn't have done it. Why?"

Her mouth moved. Hollis leaned forward.

"You were the only one who cared," she whispered.

He held her as if by physical force he could keep within her the life that was fast slipping away. Her eyes looked searchingly into his, and in a faint voice which told him he should have known, her mouth formed the words, "I love you."

The corners of her mouth moved toward the smile he had found so beautiful.

Her eyes closed.

Hollis couldn't remember when tears had last run down his cheeks. *Why didn't I kill that Goddamned son-of-a-bitch when I had the chance?*

He moved Karen's head slowly and gently from his lap. As numb as his mind was, the picture of Frolich pivoting to fire at Lipscomb was still engraved in his memory and he knew what he would find.

Frolich's shot had been accurate and Lipscomb had died instantly. As he looked at the professor the guilt was almost too much to bear. Lipscomb had known the outcome when he leaped out of the chair, yet he had done it anyway, without hesitation.

His thoughts went back to when he first visited Lipscomb at his home in Palo Alto; when each had been suspicious of the other.

It had been obvious to both that neither liked the other, yet a friendship had been born that day which nurtured by trust and respect and love of country, had resulted in one giving up his life to protect the other.

His covenant to Lipscomb would be to complete the task for which the sacrifice had been made. Peregrine and Viktor would be exposed.

Then the full impact of his dilemma hit him. Without Lipscomb, how could he expose Peregrine?

That realization hit Hollis almost as hard as the death of his friends. He had been riding a wave of optimism after his success in getting the schematics and specs. The end of the tunnel had been in sight. Exposing the mole's project would reveal the identity of Viktor and there would no longer be any reason for Maggie to be held hostage.

Now, with Lipscomb dead, he had been thrust back to where he had been that night at the safe house when the nightmare began.

An overwhelming sense of futility enveloped him. So close to success, he had failed.

Then the all-consuming rage he had felt with Karen dying in his arms rushed in to replace it. The need to expose the mole was as great as ever.

Nothing had changed but the method for getting it done.

But first, he had to get out. He would decide where to go and what to do later.

He was approaching the door when a knock sounded. Had Frolich arranged a back-up after all? The security door buzzer had not sounded. Did that mean the back-up had been inside the building, or was there another explanation?

There was no other way out. The knock sounded again, louder and more urgent. With the CZ-75 held behind him, he opened the door.

A somewhat flustered elderly lady was standing outside the door. "I'm sorry to bother you," she said. "I'm Karen's neighbor from down the hall. I heard some noise and something that sounded like some furniture falling over, and I thought maybe it had come from this apartment."

Hollis smiled as benignly as he could manage. "We heard it too, and thought it may have come from downstairs. Maybe a TV set turned up too loud."

The elderly lady apologized for having bothered him and retreated back to her apartment. Hollis knew she had not been convinced. She had expected to see Karen and when he had made no effort to get her to come to the door, her suspicions had been further aroused.

She would get help. He crossed the room and knelt beside Karen. He brushed the hair from forehead and leaned over to tenderly kiss her. He walked out of the room without looking back.

There was no one in the hall as he left the apartment and made his way out of the building. It was a short walk to the car.

He had not driven far when the sound of sirens overtook him. At the first intersection, he turned away from their sound. He did not want to see the police cars. He knew where they were going. The elderly lady had wasted no time.

Then it occurred to him. If the old lady was as sharp as she had seemed to be, he had just blown the last identity he had gotten from Stavros.

He had kept using it because even though the mole might know about it, he had no reason to believe the police did. And, in any event, it was either that or simply no disguise at all.

He pulled into a parking place and checked the mirror. The best he could do with what he had was to go back to the identity on his old drivers license from his CIA days.

It was not a good solution because the picture on the license was very close to the Jeff Hollis being sought by the FBI, but at least it was different from the face the lady had seen.

The need to hide someplace had suddenly become critical.

36

San Francisco International Airport, California
1940 Monday, December 19, 1983—Day Eleven

Colonel Arkady Maxsimov left Sheremetyevo bound for Kennedy on one of the few Soviet flights which flew that route. He held the passport of, and was made up to look like, a Russian businessman who was known to make frequent legitimate trips to the US He experienced no delay at customs and after several hours of waiting, was on a domestic flight to San Francisco.

He had received his final instructions from Ustinov and Chebrikov on the way to the airport after Gvindze had briefed him on entry procedures and his disguise. They were still fresh in his mind as he deplaned in San Francisco:

"Viktor and Brovikov have failed, and their failure has placed the operation in jeopardy. I have copies of signed Liter Ls authorizing their termination for you to read and initial. The orders will be carried out at your discretion whenever you decide they have no more usefulness. You are now in complete control of the US portion of *Maskirovka.*

"Your most important responsibility is to make sure the operation succeeds. The American Hollis may have obtained information which will reveal the nature of Peregrine. So even after you terminate him there may still be a possibility it will be exposed. Therefore, you must also concentrate your efforts on preventing the transmission site from being discovered. If the transmitter is destroyed before the ultimatum expires, *Maskirovka* will fail. Accordingly, you will maintain radio silence at the site. Unless it's an urgent emergency, you will have Viktor relay any message you want sent through the Soviet Embassy. Is that clear?"

Maxsimov had never failed before. He would not fail this time, either.

Anyone who didn't know would not have guessed that over twenty hours had elapsed since Maxsimov had left Moscow. He looked like someone who had spent the night at home in bed rather than having just traveled halfway around the world.

He had trained himself to use time to advantage, to fall asleep quickly and be refreshed after a few minutes of total relaxation. His well-developed instinct for self-preservation would not allow him to exhibit any sign of weakness, and his arrogance would not allow him to let underlings believe him to be anything less than fully alert at all times.

He was met at the gate by Brovikov, who shepherded him to the baggage area. There was no conversation until after his luggage had been retrieved and they were in the car leaving the airport.

As they headed north on Bayshore Freeway, Brovikov cautiously opened with "I assume you wish to go to the Peregrine site."

Maxsimov was not only aware of Brovikov's duties, but the reasons for his assignment to *mokrie dela* as well. Maxsimov understood the need for the department, but he looked upon Brovikov not as a professional doing his duty, but a psychopath who got too much enjoyment from his work. He responded brusquely, "Yes. On the way you can tell me of any late developments."

"I think you will be satisfied, Colonel." Brovikov attempted to reach a compromise between friendliness and respect. "Hollis has not been eliminated yet, but he has been neutralized."

Maxsimov regarded Brovikov with a distasteful frown. "How is that?"

The tone of Maxsimov's voice caused Brovikov an involuntary shudder. With great effort he kept his voice steady. "After I was sent out here to prepare for your arrival, they determined that Hollis did not die in the safe house fire as Viktor had thought. He ordered me to continue to use Frolich in the effort to eliminate Hollis, even though I was against it. I allowed Frolich to live because only he knew the identity of Hollis' accomplice in the city."

Brovikov warmed to his subject, one eye furtively gauging the effects of his words on Maxsimov. "Unfortunately, he did not advise me of his actions, so we don't know precisely what happened. As nearly as we can tell, Frolich located the accomplice and staked out the place, assuming Hollis would return. Not only was the accomplice there, but Professor Lipscomb was also there, apparently to keep out of sight while he waited for Hollis. It is probable that Hollis did get information about the command module unit, and was bringing it back for the professor to examine. But early this afternoon, there was a shoot-out at the accomplice's apartment. She was killed, and so was the professor. Frolich also died in the shoot-out."

Maxsimov interrupted Brovikov. "I thought you said Hollis was neutralized."

"Ah, but he is, Comrade. Once I learned of the shooting I contacted Viktor and advised that he immediately contact the local police and identify Hollis as the individual at the scene. Every law enforcement officer in the area is now looking for him, and he should be arrested shortly."

Unable to read Maxsimov's reaction, Brovikov added a dubious reassurance to buttress his assertions. "But even if that doesn't happen, Viktor has made sure no one in Washington will believe him, so he can do nothing with any information he may have. He has been effectively neutralized."

Maxsimov's features did not betray his conclusion that Brovikov was claiming credit not due him. "How was Hollis able to get proof of the project if you had PEC under surveillance? You'd have caught Hollis, and he would not now be free with information which might endanger Peregrine."

"I did put PEC under surveillance. Unfortunately, it was late Sunday before I could reach our rezident, and by the time he provided the necessary men and we got them in place, Hollis had already stolen the information and Lipscomb had disappeared."

"You'll have adequate time to justify your poor performance after this is over. In the meantime, you will immediately take the following action."

The rebuke stung, but fearful of what it might mean, Brovikov responded meekly, "Yes, Comrade Colonel?"

"Hollis may contact someone at International Intelligence Systems Company. You will make sure that teams of our agents cover all of the top people, and all research facilities twenty-four hours a day. You will give each agent the description of every alias Hollis has assumed. In addition, you are to place taps on the office and home phones of all of the people you place under surveillance. If Hollis contacts any of them or is spotted, I am to be notified at once. Is that clear?"

"But we have them covered already," Brovikov asserted.

With a quiet menace in his voice which Brovikov had not heard before, Maxsimov asked, "Would you prefer that I make the arrangements?"

Brovikov paled. "Of course I'll take care of it, Colonel."

The remainder of drive from San Francisco International to the Montague retreat passed in a very tense silence. Brovikov could feel the critical gaze of Maxsimov as he drove. It was as though he was mentally cataloguing every perceived fault for future reference. He didn't turn his attention away from Brovikov until they approached the wrought-iron gate which opened into the Montague retreat.

Brovikov punched in the four-number combination and Maxsimov watched as the gate slid open. "Impressive," he said.

At the house, Sergei was waiting for them. He stepped forward and opened the door. "Welcome, Comrade Colonel. We have been looking forward to your arrival."

"Thank you, Comrade Major. The site chosen for Peregrine appears to be well-chosen. You are to be congratulated for assisting in the selection and preparation."

37

Sausalito, California
1759 Monday, December 19, 1983—Day Eleven

Hollis needed a place to think, a place to decide what to do—and most of all a place where he could blend in and not be noticed.

He decided on Sausalito, a village north of San Francisco on the bay side of Marin Peninsula across the Golden Gate bridge. It was a popular art colony, but it was also out of the way. No one would notice another tourist.

He drove across the Golden Gate bridge and down to the waterfront hardly seeing where he was going, his mind still on what had happened to his friends.

He had not been there in several years, so he was not surprised to see that there had been some changes. Some of the older, larger houses had been converted into bed-and-breakfast inns. He picked one of them away from the main part of town and checked in.

In the room he turned the TV set on and then took off his jacket and shirt to check the wound. As he was applying a fresh bandage, the local news came on.

He had expected Lipscomb's death to be covered in detail, and it was. What he had not expected was the immediate association of the death with him.

A young female reporter standing outside Karen's apartment building with police cruisers parked in the background, smiled into the camera.

"Jeffrey Hollis," she was saying, "a former a Defense Department employee currently sought by the FBI as a murder suspect and probable spy, was identified today leaving the scene of the triple slaying only minutes after it occurred."

"Professor Lipscomb was a consultant to the Department of Defense," she continued. "It is believed that Hollis had been trying to get information sensitive to national security from him. It appeared that the two people with Lipscomb had been hired by the government to hide and protect him until Hollis was apprehended. Apparently Hollis found them and is suspected of killing all three. The authorities believe the killer is still in the San Francisco area. All law enforcement agencies have launched a massive effort to find him. He is armed and considered extremely dangerous."

The report ended with a description of Hollis that was much too close to his present appearance.

Hollis flicked the TV off. The lethargy and uncertainty that had plagued him since Lipscomb's death had dissipated, replaced with a cold, consuming anger. Like the master chess player, Viktor was not only very much in control, he was continuing to anticipate and counter Hollis' every move. But the game was not over. Not as long as Hollis was still alive.

The night passed slowly. Hollis barely slept, thinking about Karen and Lipscomb.

After breakfast in the inn's small dining room, he and went outside for a newspaper and returned to his room with it.

The lead story was about the Lipscomb slaying but it added nothing to the television coverage of the night before, except that it included Hollis' photograph.

There was not much he could do at this point to alter his appearance, so venturing out would be risky. But he had to do something. Time was running out. The newspaper was filled with frightening stories about Soviet military actions and the increasing crisis between Russia and the US.

The loss of Lipscomb had at first seemed to be the final blow. Without him to analyze the schematics and specifications he did not know whether he had the proof he needed, or whether it had all been for naught. His first thought was to call Walters and set up a meeting, but then he remembered what Crowley had told him about Intertel. He knew he had one more chance.

Shortly after nine, when he knew Intertel's switchboard would be open, Hollis dialed the number and asked for Crowley. He was informed Crowley would not be in his office until noon.

He waited impatiently in his room until noontime and tried again. This time, he heard the familiar voice on the phone: "Crowley here."

Hollis knew Crowley well enough to know that his dedication and loyalty to his country were as deep and abiding as his own. He would not be surprised if Crowley refused to talk to him when he found out who was calling. But he had to try.

"Chuck, this is Jeff Hollis. Please don't hang up until you hear what I have to say."

Crowley was immediately hostile. "I'll listen, but I won't be made an accessory to treason or espionage or anything illegal you may be involved in," he replied. "I'll take whatever action I believe appropriate to protect myself, and I intend to report what you tell me to the authorities."

"Fair enough," Hollis agreed. "I only ask that you hear me out first. I have done none of the things that I have been accused of. I have been framed and several attempts have been made on my life because I discovered a plot that involves the security of our country in the gravest sense. But I need your help to prove it."

"It's difficult for me to believe that you're right while everyone else is wrong," Crowley replied, skeptically.

"You'll have to make up your own mind. I ask only that you listen to what I have to tell you." He paused for a moment. "It's a long story, and it will be difficult to tell over the phone. I was hoping you would meet me somewhere so I can give you all the details and answer your questions."

"Even if I agree, what makes you think I won't arrange for the police to meet you instead of me?"

"I need only your word. After we've talked, if you do not believe me, you'll be free to do as you wish. I won't try to stop you."

"All right. Where shall I meet you?"

"I have reason to believe you and others at Intertel are being kept under surveillance by the same people who killed Lipscomb and are trying to kill me. Can you make it to Sausalito without being followed?"

"I'm sure I can."

"When you get there go to the main square on the bay front. If you don't see me right away, pick a bench and wait. I'll find you."

Hollis waited in a small restaurant where he could see the square. He did not distrust Crowley. He had said he would come alone and Hollis was sure that he would keep his word. On the other hand, it was possible he could be followed and not be aware of it.

Almost an hour passed before Crowley arrived and found an unoccupied bench. Hollis let him wait for several minutes before walking over.

"I'm staying in an inn a couple of blocks away," Hollis said, careful not to look at Crowley as he walked past. "If it's all right with you, we can talk there."

Crowley did not answer, but fell in about fifteen yards behind Hollis.

Hollis looked around carefully to see if they were being followed, but not carefully enough. He missed two men watching them from a parked car some distance away.

Once inside his room, Hollis closed the door. Crowley, keeping some distance between them, turned to face Hollis. "I want to make it clear again that I will not be made a party to any illegal acts you may have engaged in. If at any time it appears that what you are telling me would result in my becoming an accessory after the fact to criminal conduct, I will take action to protect myself. I am here only because I find it very difficult to believe that someone who has done the things you've done can be a traitor. Otherwise, I would not have come."

Crowley paused, then added, "I have one other condition. If after you've had your say, I'm not convinced that you're telling the truth, I will turn you over to the FBI."

Hollis nodded. "You are the only person I know who may be able to help me. If you cannot, I will have no choice but to turn myself in anyway, and hope what I have is enough to expose the plot before it's too late."

"If that's true, then I think it's only fair to ask that you surrender your weapon while we talk."

Hollis pulled the Magnum out of the clip holster and handed it to Crowley. Hollis considered handing over the CZ-75 hiding in his waistband as well, then decided against it. He had no intention of harming Crowley, but he was reluctant to disarm himself completely.

Hollis began with the discovery of the memo, then related the attempts on his life, Maggie's abduction, his visit to PEC and his return to San Francisco, what had happened in Karen's apartment, and finally his conclusions concerning Viktor, *Maskirovka*, and Peregrine.

"It's a hell of a story," Crowley admitted, when he had finished. "But there's only your word against the fact that every law enforcement agency in the country is trying to find you with orders to shoot to kill if necessary."

"Intertel worked on a Peregrine project before the official Peregrine project was even approved. That should be easy to prove, and certainly tends to support my theory."

"It might, but I don't intend to discuss that project with you until I know for sure."

"Lipscomb and I had planned that he would check the command module schematics and specs to see whether it has the override feature it's not supposed to have. We believed if it did, that would prove Peregrine and the mole are real. That's what makes it so ironic to accuse me of killing him; he was the only person who could clear me."

Crowley fell silent, obviously debating something with himself. He looked hard at Hollis without saying anything. Finally, he said, "I can have the schematics and specs checked."

Hope flooded through Hollis. "You can?"

"Yes, it will take a little while, but we have someone who has the technical capability. If it does have the override, we can also determine whether it's compatible with or part of the same project that Intertel worked on."

"Time's the real problem now."

After a further long moment of self debate, Crowley said, "Look, I still have grave misgivings about this, but I'm willing to hold off doing anything until we find out about the override. We'll know the answer to that sometime tomorrow morning, so I'll hold off until then. If you'll remain here, I'll get back in touch as quickly as possible. If the command module does have the override and is compatible with the transmitter, then we'll assume Peregrine is real. If it doesn't, you'll have to turn yourself in."

"Agreed, but let me make one suggestion. You must be extremely careful. Viktor must have Intertel under surveillance. If there is even a hint that you are working with me, you'll be eliminated."

Crowley bristled. "I think I can take care of myself."

Hollis did not pursue the point. "If for some reason I can't stay here," he said. "How I get in touch with you?"

Crowley thought for a moment. Then he pulled a card out of his wallet and wrote a number on it. "Call me at this number at nine tomorrow morning. If I don't answer, try again every half hour until I do. In the meantime I don't think you'll need this."

He tucked the Magnum in his waistband and left.

Study, Montague Estate, California
1410 Tuesday, December 20, 1983—Day Twelve

Sergei answered the telephone, and turned to Maxsimov, "Colonel, the San Francisco rezident wishes to speak to you."

Maxsimov took the phone. "Yes."

"Colonel, we have located Hollis," the voice on the other end informed him. "He is at an inn in the town of Sausalito, just north of the city. I have it staked out with four of my men. What are your instructions?"

Maxsimov's mind raced as he considered how he should answer. After a moment, he replied, "Do not attempt to enter the inn and do nothing to make him suspicious. I'll be back to you with specific instructions shortly. In the meantime, Hollis must not be allowed to leave. If he attempts to do so, capture him. If you can't do that, kill him immediately."

Maxsimov replaced the telephone in its cradle and turned to Sergei. "Get Viktor immediately."

"Hollis is at an inn in Sausalito," Maxsimov told Viktor. "We have it under observation. I intend to send in sufficient forces as soon as possible to make sure there is no slip-up in eliminating him."

"There may be a better way," Viktor responded, choosing his words carefully.

Maxsimov was immediately suspicious. "Explain."

"If your men simply go into the inn and assassinate Hollis and then disappear, it'll be obvious to the FBI and others that it was a KGB hit. That will tend to support what he has been saying about Peregrine. What I suggest is that you allow me to make arrangements for him to be taken or eliminated by DIS personnel and local police. Either way, he'll be neutralized."

Maxsimov was skeptical. "How do you propose to handle it?"

"I'll have the entire area sealed off by local law officers. Since this is outside the jurisdiction of San Francisco, and I doubt that the Marin County Sheriff's office has a SWAT team, I'll arrange for a CID Special Forces Team to be sent in to take him."

"How long will it take?"

"The locals could be in position in about an hour," Viktor replied. "And I should have the CID team in place within two hours."

"All right," Maxsimov agreed. "But failure will not be tolerated."

"We will not fail, Comrade, but you should make sure your men do nothing to alert Hollis. He has proven to be slippery beyond description. They should be instructed to simply keep the inn under surveillance, and not try to enter until the CID team arrives."

"That's already been taken care of," Maxsimov replied. "Now it's up to you."

38

CIA Headquarters, Langley, Virginia
1750 Tuesday, December 20, 1983—Day Twelve

Jessica had received Maggie's letter shortly after noon and she immediately began making efforts, through his secretary, to talk to Walters.

The secretary insisted on knowing what she wanted to talk to Walters about. Jessica refused to tell her. That didn't get Walters to the phone.

First, he was at lunch, and after lunch he was in a meeting of indeterminate length.

She was getting desperate, so when she tried again and Walter's secretary told her again that he was not available, Jessica gave in and asked her if she could get a message to him.

"Of course."

"Very well. Tell him, please, that I have important information about Deputy Undersecretary of Defense, Jeffrey Hollis."

The secretary took this message to Walters immediately and Walters immediately invited Jessica to come to his office as quickly as she could get there.

Walters stood up to greet Jessica as she entered his office. "Good afternoon, Ms. Blake. I apologize for the delay, but I'm sure you understand how difficult it can be to fit a meeting in on such short notice."

"Please don't apologize, Mr. Walters," Jessica responded, "I'm sorry to impose, but I had no choice."

Walters got right to the point. "Ms. Blake, you indicated that you have information about Jeff Hollis. We're vitally interested in locating him as quickly as possible."

"I cannot help you find him, Mr. Walters, because I don't know where he is."

Walters gazed at her with raised eyebrows.

"Maggie Hollis," she continued. "His former wife. She's a close friend of mine. We work together in the same advertising agency. You're probably not aware of it, but she's been missing since last Friday morning when she called to tell me she would be late for work because the undersecretary had asked her to come to a meeting about Hollis."

As Walters fidgeted she continued, "Someone called the office to say she was all right, but I'm worried that she hasn't contacted me herself. Then, today, I received this letter. In it she asks me to bring this to you as soon as I can. So here it is."

Jessica Blake handed the letter to the deputy director. Walters took it and scanned it hurriedly. Skepticism gave way instantly to intense interest. He reread the letter slowly.

When he finished he looked at Jessica. "This is difficult to believe, in light of what we've been told. This was written Saturday, but you just got it today?"

Jessica nodded.

Walters noted that the envelope bore a Virginia postmark with yesterday's date. After a moment of thought, Walters asked, "Is there anything else you can tell me, anything that's not in the letter?"

"Well, yes. There is one thing. Before she left to go to the meeting, Maggie told me that Jeff would call me periodically, pretending to be my cousin Robert Blake. The purpose was so that Maggie would know to get the information to you if Hollis failed to call within seventy-two hours. I guess Maggie wrote this letter because she couldn't carry out those instructions."

Did Hollis ever call?" Walters cut in.

"Yes. Late Tuesday morning. He was afraid my phone might be tapped by the people after him, so the conversation was brief. But I did let him know that Maggie had not returned to the office."

"Do you have any idea where he called from?"

"No. He didn't talk long and he didn't say where he was or where he was going."

"I hate to ask, but do you mind if we put a tap on your phones in case he calls again?"

"I doubt that he will, but I have no objection."

Walters stood up and reached for Jessica's hand. "Thank you very much for bringing the letter in, Ms. Blake. We'll proceed, and if we need you for anything else we'll be in touch."

As soon as Jessica had departed, Walters called deputy director for operations Jeb Warren and replayed the news to him. They agreed the matter should be taken directly to the director himself.

William Casey looked up from the document he was studying as they entered. "I understand you have some information on Hollis."

Walters briefly recounted his meeting with Jessica. "This letter appears to have been written by Hollis' former wife, and purports to give his side of the story."

Casey held out his hand. Walters handed him the letter. "I'll summarize it for you if you'd prefer."

Casey shook his head. When he read it he looked at Walters sharply. "What the hell's this Peregrine project supposed to be? I've never heard of it."

"We haven't either, but it shouldn't be too difficult to check out."

Casey stared at Walters for a couple of seconds before reaching across his desk to depress the lever on his intercom. "Sally, see if you can get Cap on the phone for me, please."

Defense Secretary Weinberger's displeasure was evident when he learned the topic of the DCI's call. The eighteen to twenty hour days that he and his top staff members had been putting in were beginning to take their toll. At the time the call came in he was involved in an update and briefing on all of the latest Soviet military moves and their probable significance. Had the call been from someone of less importance than Casey, he would not have taken it.

After listening to a brief review of the letter, Weinberger was no longer able to keep his impatience under control.

"Look, Bill, don't misunderstand. I'm not trying to brush this off, but you have to understand DIS as well as Montague have looked into this matter pretty thoroughly, and I can tell you right now it doesn't wash. We've investigated both the possibility that Hollis was framed as well as the memo he supposedly found. We've found nothing to support either claim."

Casey grumbled and chewed his lip. He hated confusion. And this was confusion with a capital C. "Well, can you tell us anything that might help us understand the situation a little better."

"First off," Weinberger responded, exasperation clouding his voice, "no one ever saw the damned memo. If it did exist, which I doubt, Hollis couldn't produce it. There is a Peregrine project but it has nothing to do with command modules in rocket boosters. It involves an exo-atmospheric missile interceptor capable of distinguishing between decoys and warheads."

Casey stroked his forehead in bemusement. "The letter says the memo was written by a Stanford University Professor, Lipscomb. Couldn't it have been verified one way or the other?"

"Well, as I said no one saw the damn memo," Weinberger snapped. "So how the hell were we supposed to know about Lipscomb? And we sure as hell can't ask him about it now."

"Cap, I don't want to belabor this, but in this letter Hollis' former wife claims she was picked up Friday by a DOD driver on the pretext of being taken to a meeting with Montague. Instead, she was taken to your Dumfries safe house, held there, then moved somewhere else. Now nobody knows where she is."

Weinberger fairly shouted back at Casey, "Are you suggesting Paul is guilty of kidnapping?"

"You know better than that, Cap," Casey remonstrated. "But, it sure as hell suggests there may be something here to look into."

"Look Bill, I don't have time to discuss it now. If you'll have the letter sent over to Paul, I'll make sure he gets DIS on it right away."

Casey was not completely satisfied, but knew that further prodding at this point would be futile. When the phone was back in its cradle he looked at both Walters and Warren. "Well, what do you think?"

"Superficially, what he said seems to make sense," Walter replied. "But for someone who knows Hollis the way I do, it's pretty hard to take. I think there's something here that either they have totally overlooked or something's been pushed under a rug. I'd sure like to get somebody in there who could take an independent look at the whole situation. I think it's important enough to be pursued farther up the line."

Casey leaned back in his chair, folded his hands behind his head, looked out the window for a few seconds, then turned back to Warren and Walters. "Don't get so involved you lose perspective," he replied. "You know as well as I do we can't go over Cap's head without a lot more than we've got here."

39

Sausalito, California
1725 Tuesday, December 20, 1983—Day Twelve

Sausalito had seemed an ideal place to hide when Hollis first thought of it. But the longer he stayed in one place the greater the odds became that he would be recognized. After Crowley left and Hollis began to seriously consider whether to stay or leave, the decision took on a sense of urgency. He realized he had placed himself in a position where he could be trapped with no ready escape route.

The town is not a cul-de-sac, although for Hollis' purposes it might as well have been. The eastern side of the town borders on the bay and the western side abuts the steep foothills of the Marin peninsula. The main access to the town is by a road which turns off US 101 just north of the Golden Gate Bridge and rejoins the highway at Marin City about five miles further north. There is only one other road to 101, which few know of, so it would be a simple matter to seal the town off by blocking the three exits. The only other way out would be by ferry, but this could be even more of a trap since they sail on precise schedules to and from specific points. It would be altogether too easy for each departing boat to be met and searched at its destination if there were reason to believe he might be on board.

Late in the afternoon Hollis approached the desk with his luggage and informed the clerk he was checking out.

"I'm sorry, sir," the clerk responded. "We don't have late check out. I'll have to charge you for the full day."

"It's quite all right. I'm sorry I have to leave, but I have a personal emergency."

Hollis paid in cash, and as he waited for the clerk to make change he was surprised that no one was in the inn's lobby except himself and the clerk. Every other time he had passed through there had been at least a few people around. As he waited and continued to look around the clerk seemed distracted. He was having trouble determining the exact change he was supposed to give Hollis.

Something was wrong.

After receiving his change, Hollis moved his luggage to the side of the table which served as the front desk.

He smiled at the clerk and turned to go back up the stairs. "I hope you don't mind if I leave these here for a moment, I just realized I forgot something."

Before the clerk had time to respond he had rounded the turn in the stairs and was out of sight. Hollis had already determined the potential escape routes. It was something he did almost without thinking wherever he went.

The inn had a fire escape, but it was on the side of the house close to the front, and using it would be almost the same as leaving through the front door. The rear of the inn was on the western edge of town, and only a small shaded courtyard separated it from the sharply rising hills marking the western boundary of the town. Hollis went out a rear window onto the top of the back porch and dropped down into the courtyard.

He disliked leaving his luggage, but it was of no consequence now. If it turned out his fears were not justified, he could retrieve it later. If it turned out he that he couldn't, it held nothing that would tell anyone anything they didn't already know.

The shadows of twilight were rapidly deepening. It was difficult to see across the courtyard. Hollis moved cautiously to the gate and looked into the alley which separated the inn from the next building.

As he suspected, a lone figure with a small two-way radio had the inn under surveillance. The other side of the inn, which bordered a main thoroughfare, was also guarded, he discovered.

The slope at the rear of the inn was much too steep to climb, so the only way out was to cross the alley to the back yard of the building beyond.

But first he would have to find a way to eliminate the guard.

Hollis waited until it was almost dark, then stepped to the gate. Its rusty hinges assured him the gate could not be opened quietly. He knelt down behind it and watched the guard pace slowly up and down the alley.

When he reached the point farthest away from him, Hollis quietly unlatched the gate and pushed it open. The rasping noise immediately caught the guard's attention. As he turned, his right hand moved to pull a handgun from under his left arm. He paused to listen, but the only sound was the swinging of the gate. He decided to investigate.

Hollis moved away from the gate down along the wall behind some bushes. He waited until the guard went through the gate, then vaulted over the wall. The slight noise he made was lost in the grating protest the hinges made as the guard pushed the gate open and walked into the courtyard.

Once inside, the guard found it much darker than he had anticipated. He re-holstered his handgun and went back out into the alley, pulling the gate shut behind him.

Hollis, crouched beside the gate outside the wall, unleashed a hard blow to the man's groin and followed it with a karate chop to the base of his skull.

Hollis dragged the guard's unconscious body back through the gate into the courtyard and relieved him of both the handgun and the radio. He pulled the gate to the courtyard closed and ducked across the alley to the shadows behind the adjacent house.

He had just reached the other side of the building when the radio crackled to life.

"Report, Number Two."

After a few moments, a different voice replied, "Number Two. OK here."

The first voice then came back with, "Report, Number Three."

When no one answered, Hollis knew he had to gamble. He pressed the talk button. "Number Three. OK here."

"What took you so long to answer, Three?"

Hollis put his hand partially over the mouthpiece. "I was checking out a noise. It was nothing."

"Well stay alert. The CID Team will be here any minute."

Hollis now knew his troubles were only beginning. He was out of the inn, but he might still be trapped. If a CID team was really on the way, then road blocks were either already in place or would be before he could get to his car and reach 101. A taxi would be no better, and the ferries were out of the question.

How the hell was he going to get out of this place? To be bottled up and prevented from leaving would neutralize him just as effectively as if he had been taken captive.

As he moved away from the inn his attention was caught by the traffic passing through a close by intersection. Maybe there was a way out after all.

He had only been to Sausalito once several years before for dinner with friends. He vaguely recalled that the restaurant they had visited was northwest of the center of town, well up on the side of the hill with a great view of the bay. His friends had taken him there because of the restaurant's reputation for excellent food. It was also a popular stop-off for the tour buses.

He remembered the buses because he had been impressed by the skill the drivers had exhibited in bringing their oversize vehicles up the hill through the maze of narrow twisting streets leading to the restaurant. Judging from the location of the inn, the restaurant had to be close by.

It was not long before Hollis spotted several tour buses in a parking lot and knew he had found it. He turned the radio off, clipped it to his belt and crossed the parking lot.

He entered the restaurant and went straight to the main bar. The name badges he spotted on the way assured him that at least a couple of tour groups were here on wine-tasting parties.

But not all of the tour members were sampling the products of Napa Valley. Some were in the bar enjoying the products of Kentucky, Tennessee and Scotland.

Hollis chose an empty stool next to a man wearing a tour badge. He appeared to be by himself. Hollis ordered a Glenlivet on the rocks. After taking a sip, he turned to the man. "Stranger to San Francisco?"

The man turned slowly and nodded. "Yeah. I'm from Dearborn."

"Really? I spent some time over at Ann Arbor some years ago taking a couple of sales management courses."

"Yeah. I graduated from there more years ago than I care to remember."

Hollis was not familiar enough with the university to risk getting into a detailed conversation. "Well, let's drink to Ann Arbor."

"Yeah. She was some gal."

Hollis laughed at the lame joke. "Let me buy you one," he said.

Hollis ordered another round, then held out his hand. "My name's Tom Carlton," by the way.

"Ted Petoskey." They shook hands.

"Here on business?"

"Nope. I own a car dealership. Won the trip by working my butt off. After we get here the old lady gets sick and can't come on the tour. So I came without her."

"Sorry to hear it."

"Yeah, so am I. She'd enjoy all this wine tasting crap. I'm only doing it because it was already paid for."

"You're with one of the tour groups?"

"I'm with a tour, but I'm not a part of it, if you know what I mean. The tour around the city was all right, but I'm not much on wine." He looked at his watch, "We'll be leaving in about five minutes or so to go back to the hotel. Got time for one more quick one, if you'd care to join me."

They continued talking while they finished the drink. Finally Ted stood up "Time to get back to the bus. Enjoyed meeting you, Tom."

"Thanks. Hope you enjoy the rest of your stay." Hollis turned back to his drink. He waited until Petoskey was on his way out the door, then he quickly put a tip on the bar, picked up his check and headed for the cashier.

Outside, he caught up with Petoskey in the parking lot. As the man turned to see who was behind him, Hollis pulled his out CZ-75 and pressed it into Petoskey's side.

"This is a gun, Petoskey, just take it easy and you won't get hurt."

Petoskey was about the same build as Hollis, a few pounds heavier, but he had grown up in a rough neighborhood.

"You son-of-a-bitch!" he growled. He took a wild swing at Hollis. Shifting quickly sideways Hollis avoided his fist, and with Petoskey completely off balance, Hollis placed a hard karate chop against the side of his neck.

As he went limp, Hollis caught him and started walking him through the parking lot.

They passed a young couple getting out of their car. Hollis shook his head at them with and grinned. "A little too much wine-tasting. He'll be all right by the time I get him back to the hotel."

They looked at Hollis quizzically, then smiled and walked off. Hollis noticed they had not locked the car. He leaned Petoskey up against the adjacent car and exchanged jacket and tie with him, making sure that he had Petoskey's tour badge.

Hollis shoved Petoskey into the rear of the unlocked car the couple had just parked, planted the guard's radio in Petoskey's hand and the guard's gun in his belt. He then took Petoskey's driver's license and credit cards and substituted those that Stavros had prepared for him in the name of Ralph Tucker.

His conscience felt a twinge when he thought what would happen when Petoskey was discovered, but he needed as much diversion as he could create.

When he got back to the parking area, all the buses were gone save one. He hurried toward it, congratulating Petoskey on his flamboyant taste in sports jackets. The tour guide, a young and bored female, recognized the jacket in the dark.

"Well, Mr. Petoskey, we were about to leave without you."

"Sorry," Hollis responded, "I was in the bar and forgot the time."

"I hope everything's okay? I noticed you didn't take part in the wine tasting."

Hollis hoped that was all she noticed. "Yeah. I hate wine."

The bus pulled out of the parking lot just as several cars with military markings, escorted by a Marin County sheriff's cruiser and a communications van, pulled into a small square a half a block from the inn Hollis had vacated.

The agent in charge of the surveillance briefed the CID team leader. All of the people staying in the inn had been evacuated, he told him, leaving only Hollis and the desk clerk inside.

The team leader immediately dispersed the team around the inn, and when he was satisfied that it was sealed off, motioned four close-combat specialists to accompany him inside.

The clerk, who had grown progressively more nervous as the episode played itself out was visibly shaken when the heavily-armed men in SWAT gear and flak jackets appeared in his lobby.

The leader approached the desk while the others moved to flanking positions where they could keep the entire room and the staircase covered. "Where is he?"

The clerk swallowing with difficulty and stammering for the first time in his life, replied, "H-H-H-His room is number f-f-f-five. It's on the s-second floor, on the r-right about half way down the hall."

Softening his demeanor slightly in an effort to calm the clerk, the leader asked, "He is in his room, isn't he?"

"Oh yes. He came down a little while ago to check out, but said he had forgotten something and went back up. That's his luggage by the table."

The team leader glanced at the stairs leading to the second floor and grinned broadly. The chase was almost over.

He turned back to the clerk. "Thanks. You've done your part. I think it would be better if you joined the others outside."

Relieved, the clerk scurried outside as the team leader motioned his team up the staircase.

The first two up the stairs took positions in the hall on the far side of the door to room five facing away from it. The other two took similar positions on the near side. Together they could keep the doors to all of the other guest rooms on the floor covered without the possibility of catching each other in a crossfire in the event Hollis came out of one of them.

When they were in position, the leader motioned them to pull on their gas masks. Then, standing slightly to the side, he fired a short burst through the door lock with his MP5SD3. As the door swung open, he lobbed a tear-gas canister into the room.

"Come out Hollis," he yelled. "We have the place completely covered."

No response.

The team leader signaled a man on each side of the door to cover the entire hall and the other two to follow him. Together, they made a diving roll into the room, both coming up simultaneously facing opposite sides and the back of the room.

The leader was momentarily stunned to find no one there. A quick check revealed there was no way out of the room except the door or the windows which were securely locked.

"Goddamn it all to hell!"

Throwing caution aside, the team searched the remaining guest rooms and the area in the back of the inn more swiftly than their training would ordinarily have permitted.

Finally, out in the dark courtyard they found the unconscious guard.

The team leader moved quickly back to the command post in the communications van parked across the street from the inn. Both the sheriff and the deputy inside were startled by his abrupt entrance.

"Sheriff, get your deputy there on the horn and bring in as many officers as you can from whatever source. Hollis got out of the inn, but he's got to be somewhere in the town. We need to cover all ferry routes, saturate the town center and move our search out from there house to house. I want back-up road blocks on the roads leading out of town. Also, call the roadblocks already established and alert them that he's loose. Every vehicle that leaves this place must be emptied and searched. Everyone must be identified before being allowed to proceed. Any questions?"

The stunned sheriff shook his head. He turned to the deputy seated at the radio and said, "Jerry, call HQ, give them the message. Tell them to follow up on a priority basis. If you can't raise the troopers at the three road blocks leading into 101, make sure HQ relays the instructions to them."

Being the last to board the bus, Hollis found the only seat available was near the rear. He took it with mixed feelings. It was possible he might need to get off the bus in a hurry, but he had no choice. The bus began the journey back to San Francisco maneuvering down the hillside through the narrow twisting streets. They were approaching the bay front when Hollis spotted a number of vehicles with blue lights flashing.

The inn was completely cordoned off. He had gotten out of there just in time, but he was not in the clear yet.

From the bay front the bus turned south toward San Francisco. After passing Fort Baker the driver began the tortuous uphill journey which would take them back to US 101 and the Golden Gate bridge.

As they neared the hilltop and the intersection with US 101, Hollis was beginning to think that he had been wrong.

But as they rounded the last curve, they were confronted with a line of stopped cars leading to the blue lights of two patrol cruisers blocking the road.

Even though traffic was light and the line of cars in front of the bus waiting to be cleared through the roadblock was short, a chorus of good-natured complaints over the holdup broke out among the bus passengers almost at once.

Hollis scarcely heard it as the tension inside him built. The next few minutes could bring the end.

The bus inched forward as the cars were checked and released.

When the bus finally reached the road block, the driver opened the door and turned on the interior lights. A trooper stepped on board.

The tour guide looked at him anxiously. "What's the trouble, officer?"

"Nothing to be concerned about, Miss." The trooper looked down the line of seats at the passengers. "We're just on the lookout for someone. Is this a regular tour?"

"Yes," the woman responded. "We've been together since just after lunch. The last event on our agenda was a wine-tasting party at Dewey's Restaurant. We're on our way back to the San Francisco now."

"Do you have all the people back on board that you started with?" The trooper continued to look searchingly at the passengers.

The guide, mindful of the desire of her charges to get back to their hotels, gave him her best killer smile. "Yes, we do, officer. I might add we don't have any extras."

After a few more moments staring at the passengers, the trooper gave up. "Thank you for the cooperation, Miss. Sorry for the inconvenience."

He backed out the door and signaled the driver to proceed. As he stepped off the bus, his partner motioned that he was going back to the cruiser to answer a radio call.

It had taken all the willpower Hollis could muster to maintain his facade of unconcerned boredom while the trooper was on the bus. It was almost as difficult to contain the sigh of relief when he turned to depart.

Hollis finally allowed that sigh to escape when the bus pulled off the bridge and into the city. He was out of the trap and still in the game.

But he could do nothing until he heard from Crowley tomorrow, and time was getting very short.

It would be a long, anxious night.

40

VGK Headquarters (Stavka), Outside Moscow, USSR.
1000 Wednesday, December 20, 1983—Day Thirteen

> *The Defense Council is the Soviet Union's highest decision-making body for all aspects of national security policy. It conveys the Party's wishes on all defense, budgetary, organizational and senior personnel matters to the military. It is composed primarily of Party leaders, and is chaired by the general secretary.*
>
> *In peacetime, the minister of defense is the only military member, and the chief of the General Staff serves as secretary. In wartime, it is expanded with additional Party and military members. The general secretary, as chairman of the Defense Council, exercises direct leadership of the Soviet Armed Forces as commander in chief of the Supreme High Command (Verkhounoye Glavnokomandovaniye or VGK) and head of its General Headquarters (Stavka).*
>
> Soviet Military Power (Sixth Edition)

The exodus of high level Party officials from Moscow to emergency facilities was well under way. The Politburo was no longer meeting in the Kremlin. Members who did not serve on the Defense Council were moved to underground facilities provided for their respective functions. Those who did serve on the Council were relocated in hardened shelters situated between Moscow and the missile bases of Teykovo and Kostroma, the wartime headquarters of the *VGK*.

General Secretary Andropov was moved from the Kuntsevo Hospital to a suite specially prepared for him in the most secure facility. Once there, he convened the Defense Council. In addition to Ustinov, he invited Vitaly Vorotnikov, chairman of the Council of Ministers; Arkady Aliyev, chairman of the State Planning Commission (*Gosplan*); as well as Marshal Ogarkov, chief of the General Staff and secretary to the Council. Also invited to attend were Chernenko, Gromyko, Gorbachev, and Chebrikov, chairman of the KGB.

It was obvious to those present that the trip from Moscow had sapped what little energy Andropov had left. His ashen face emphasized the bluish tinge of his lips. Only his eyes continued to hold the flame of his once dominant personality.

"Comrades," he began. Again, his voice was surprisingly strong, "It is time that we officially recognize what is happening and take the final steps to put us on a complete wartime footing. Accordingly, I am officially declaring this to be an official meeting of the Defense Council."

He turned his gaze to Ogarkov. "Mr. Secretary, you will so note. And you will also note that everyone here is designated a full member of the Council."

When Ogarkov finished his writing and looked up from his notepad, Andropov continued. "All of you are aware that Operation *Maskirovka* will commence on the twenty-fourth of this month with the delivery of the ultimatum to the American president...what we expect will happen is that the US will capitulate and NATO will not intervene. In that event, we will immediately move to occupy and disarm the US."

The chairman paused, letting his words sink in with everyone at the table.

"It is possible," he went on," that even though their ballistic missiles have been neutralized they may refuse to capitulate and NATO may or may not join them. We are prepared for both of these eventualities. The purpose of this meeting is to brief those of you who have not been involved on those preparations."

Andropov turned to Ustinov. "Dmitri, you may proceed with the briefing on preparations for occupation in the event of capitulation?"

"Yes, Comrade Secretary," Ustinov smiled to himself as he reviewed his plan to precipitate an early end to the grace period so he could launch a nuclear strike against the US. But, in the meantime, the charade must be maintained, he told himself. Then, looking very self-important, he cleared his throat loudly. "If the United States capitulates, the Union of Soviet Socialist Republics will move swiftly to take control of their central government and all of their military command, communications and control centers before any local resistance can develop. Earlier this week, we dispatched ten An-124s to Cuba. They carried twenty-two hundred fully equipped troops with all support equipment, including troop carriers. After the ultimatum is issued they will depart Cuba on a schedule that will allow six of them, carrying eighteen hundred troops, to arrive at Andrews Air Force Base, and four more, with six hundred troops, to arrive at Fort Richie just as the ultimatum expires."

Ustinov looked down at the table for a moment and caught his breath. He seemed suddenly overwhelmed by the momentous occasion he was part of and by the historic significance of his own words.

"Our *Voyenno-Transportnaya aviatsia* has six hundred additional aircraft available," he continued. "Each will carry, depending on type, anywhere from ninety to four hundred fifteen fully equipped troops. They will be airborne well before the ultimatum expires, and we will have five thousand elite troops together with support equipment in Washington within two hours after the ultimatum expires. They will occupy the Capitol Buildings, the White house, the Pentagon, Andrews Air Force Base and Fort Belvoir. An additional one thousand troops, with troop carriers and equipment will land at Fort Richie, Maryland to take control of their alternate military command center."

Ustinov looked around, noting with a grim satisfaction how completely he held the attention of everyone at the table.

He raised his voice slightly: "Within the next five hours we will have fifty thousand troops in the US in control of all major military centers. In addition to Washington and Fort Richie, we will be in command of NORAD Headquarters at the Cheyenne Mountain Complex, SAC Headquarters at Offutt Air Force Base, Nebraska, as well as the alternates at Barksdale and March AFBs. We will have occupied their Atlantic Fleet Headquarters at Norfolk, and their Pacific Fleet Headquarters at Honolulu, and will be in control of key military communications and switching centers at Lyons, Nebraska; Fairview, Kansas; Hillsboro, Missouri, and Lamar, Colorado. We will also occupy major ground control stations for key defense satellites as well as the ELF and VLF radio transmitters they use to broadcast orders to their submarines.

"While this advance force is in the process of totally immobilizing their civilian government and disrupting the ability of their top military command to communicate with or issue orders to military units at bases not occupied by advance forces, regular occupation troops will begin landing. Within twenty-four hours after the initial occupation the first elements of the sea lift consisting of one hundred plus vessels will arrive and disembark ten elite divisions. The occupation force will then build rapidly with two hundred more sailings during the next two weeks."

Ustinov paused and looked over at Andropov, who was holding a hand up for him to stop.

"Excuse me for interrupting, Dmitri," he said. "Are there any are comments or questions so far?" Andropov asked. No one broke the silence. The looks on the faces of the Soviet bureaucrats ranged from worried to awestruck. Everyone around the table knew that this was nothing short of a desperate, all-or-nothing gamble. If it failed, the consequences would be horrific for everyone.

"There are no questions, so Dimitri will proceed." Andropov nodded at Ustinov to continue.

"In the event that the United States does not capitulate, we will proceed as follows," Ustinov said. "All United States ballistic missiles have already been neutralized so they will not be a threat. This leaves only their so-called strategic air arm which consists of their aging, slow B-52s, their short-range F-111s, their cruise missiles and their Navy battle groups. Our primary air defense should be more than enough to handle all of that. It consists of the recently deployed MiG-29, backed up by the MiG-27, both of which carry long-range AA-10 and short range AA-11 air-to-air missiles. They also have the new look down/shoot down radar which enables them to engage low flying aircraft and cruise missiles and also gives them multiple target engagement capabilities.

"To the extent any of their aircraft or cruise missiles succeed in getting past our first line of defense, they will be met by our new MiG-31 interceptor, and our mobile SAM-10's which have been deployed throughout Eastern Europe. Also, the new SA-X-12Bs concentrated around Moscow and other industrial centers are designed to take out any aircraft or cruise missiles which get through our primary and secondary air defense systems."

Ustinov glanced down briefly at his notes, running a heavy forefinger down a prepared page of talking points until he found what he wanted.

"And of course there is NATO," he said. "We believe it's unlikely they will move to support the United States once they know their nuclear umbrella no longer exists. Opposing their forces on our Western *Teatr Voennykh Deistvii* will be fifty-three non-Soviet Warsaw Pact divisions massed along the East European front, backed up by ninety Soviet divisions, which have available to them over thirty thousand tanks, and more than thirty thousand artillery pieces, some of which have tactical nuclear capability. Even without the twenty divisions and five thousand tanks we are holding in reserve, this is more than double NATO's capacity, and the United States will not be in a position to reinforce it. Accordingly, we believe it unlikely the NATO countries will support the US."

Ustinov paused and thrust out his chin pugnaciously. "But if they do, they will be overrun," he thundered.

The silence in the room was as palpable as a cold hand over the heart. No country in history had ever dared such a massive—and risky—military coup.

Andropov broke the silence. "What about the ultimatum, Andrei?" he asked turning to Gromyko.

"The ultimatum is in the hands of ambassador Dobrynin who will deliver it to President Reagan promptly at eight o'clock, Washington time on Saturday morning. At the same time our ambassadors to all of the NATO countries will assure each government that what is happening relates strictly to the threat which the US Pershings pose to the Soviet Union, and should not affect their relations with us. We believe only the English and Germans—and maybe the Italians—will protest very loudly. And they will not press the matter when the other NATO members refuse to join them."

Andropov nodded in agreement, then turned to Chernenko. "Kostya, you have been in charge of our propaganda efforts. Are you still of the opinion that the West is confused as to our intentions, and is not prepared for what will happen?"

"As of this time, Comrade Secretary, there is no doubt that what you say is true. However, even in the face of all our disinformation and propaganda, some in their news media are beginning to question whether we are really engaged in exercises or preparing to attack NATO. Nevertheless, there have been no detectable changes in the preparedness of United States or NATO, so it's unlikely they can do anything that would significantly enhance their position between now and Saturday."

Andropov fixed his gaze on Chebrikov. "Do you have any more information on who is responsible for leaking our plans to the West?"

"Yes, Comrade Secretary, I do," The KGB chief responded. "I have just received a report from Viktor to the effect that their high level Moscow contact has assured them that the satellites are space-based KKV platforms. This information was given only to one person, so there is no longer any doubt about his identity. We have him under surveillance, and we believe we know who his contact is at the US. embassy."

"What disposition do you propose?" Andropov asked, although it seemed clear he had already decided.

"Now that we know who is revealing our plans, we can use him to a limited extent by making sure he gets information we want the Americans to have. But after Operation *Maskirovka* succeeds I believe he should be terminated."

Andropov considered the suggestion for several seconds. "I agree. In the meantime continue your surveillance, and if need be I will approve a Liter I so you can take him into custody."

"With your permission, Comrade Secretary?" Gorbachev asked. Andropov nodded.

Gorbachev turned to the KGB Chief. "Did Viktor report on the status of Peregrine, Comrade Chairman?"

Before Chebrikov could respond, Ustinov broke in angrily. "I don't understand the purpose of your question, Comrade Minister. You have already been assured the project is complete and operational."

"I asked the question because I understand the project has been compromised by an American security officer. If that is true, am I not correct in thinking that it may be in danger?"

Ustinov blustered angrily. "Viktor has assured us the security officer is not a threat to Peregrine. Nevertheless, we have sent my aide, Colonel Maxsimov to make absolutely sure that the man is eliminated and to take control of the transmitter. I assure you it is safe and will not be compromised."

Andropov signaled the meeting was over. "For your information," he added, "Even though I may not be able to join you in the situation room when the ultimatum is delivered, I have made arrangements to monitor what is happening, and to remain in communication with everyone there. I will retain control of the operation throughout."

Everyone departed except Gorbachev. When he was alone with Andropov, the chairman looked at him with a wan smile and shook his head. "Misha, you must be careful. Dimitri is not one to be trifled with. He can be a formidable enemy."

"I understand, Yuri, but I still do not believe he is being completely honest with us."

41

Montague Retreat, California
0650 Wednesday December 21, 1983—Day Thirteen

"Colonel Maxsimov, Viktor is on the phone."

Maxsimov took the telephone which Sergei handed him.

"What is it?"

"I just found out that the person we arrested last night was not Hollis."

"What the hell happened?" Maxsimov screamed.

"Hollis took the identification papers of the person we found and left his along with your guard's gun and radio. When the local police found him in the back of the car at the road block they were convinced that he was the one we were looking for so they took him into custody. It was several hours later before we could get someone there with enough clout to check out his story and get him released. Hollis was gone long before that, probably on the tour bus that the person we caught was supposed to be on."

"So you have failed again."

Recognizing the cover-your-ass game, Viktor responded in kind. "You should understand that it was one of your guards that allowed Hollis to escape from the inn. Otherwise he would have been captured."

The silence became protracted as Maxsimov, forced back to reality, considered his options.

"We now have no leads to Hollis except through Intertel," he said, finally. "And I'm sure he realizes that. It may be that we will now have to rely on your ability to 'neutralize' his efforts to expose Peregrine. But even if he exposes the command modules, under no circumstance can he be allowed to discover the location of the transmitter."

"We may be too late," Viktor replied. "Hollis has already made contact with a person named Crowley, the top security officer at Intertel. I suspect he knows the location of the transmitter. There's also the project manager who installed it, Gary Clarke. I may be able to isolate Crowley by linking him to Hollis, but it will be up to you to take care of Clarke."

"Consider it done." Maxsimov slammed the phone back down in its cradle.

42

Econo Lodge, Oakland, California
0737 Wednesday December 21, 1983—Day Thirteen

After the tour bus dropped Hollis at Petoskey's hotel, he walked to the nearest BART station and took the train to Oakland. Once there, he took a taxi to a motel near the airport and checked in.

There was no reason to believe anyone knew where he was, but he was nevertheless unable to sleep. He kept thinking back to what he had overheard on the two-way radio about the use of a CID team. It meant that a special unit of the Army's Criminal Investigations Division had been ordered to take him, even though it had no jurisdiction to do so. The teams had been formed to provide mobile, fast-action, special purpose groups to assist DIS in its Key Assets Protection Program and the Defense Sensitive Conventional Arms, Ammunition and Explosives Security Program. But their use was limited to military installations. In his case, the FBI should have been called in. The fact that it wasn't meant that Viktor was still calling the shots.

Did this mean that Dawson was the mole? Maybe, but probably not. If he had been the one to order the team out, it would only be a short time before a report of its use would reach Montague who, unless he had been involved, would be expected to require a follow-up explanation.

The "buck" stopped at the undersecretary level, and the finger of guilt was again pointing at him.

When morning finally came, Hollis had coffee and read the paper until it was time to call Crowley. Nine o'clock, nine thirty, and ten o'clock all came and went with no answer. He was growing worried when at ten-thirty Crowley finally answered.

"I guess you probably know by now I had company last night, and I'm no longer in Sausalito," Hollis said.

"Yes, I just heard that on the news. You don't think I was responsible for that, do you?"

"No. I'm pretty sure it was set up by Viktor. What I don't know is whether his agents were tapped into your phone or followed you to our meeting."

"I think I can fill you in on that. Where and when would you like to meet?"

Hollis wanted to ask about the command modules, but now was not the time. "I'm in downtown Oakland. You name it, and I'll be there."

"I'll pick you up in front of Scott's Grill, Jack London Square, at exactly eleven-fifteen."

Hollis stepped out of an alley next to Scott's precisely at the appointed time just as a car pulled over to the curb. Crowley motioned him inside. He had barely closed the door when Crowley executed an illegal U-turn and exited the square the same way he had entered.

Crowley looked grim as he drove back across the Bay Bridge. Both men checked continually in an effort to detect any sign that they were being followed.

They were halfway across town and headed for Point Lobos, when they decided they were in the clear.

"I'm sorry it took so long to answer this morning, but there were several things I had to do which couldn't wait. What happened in Sausalito?"

Hollis told him.

"What I didn't know when I talked to you yesterday was that the phones of all the top officers of Intertel, mine included, were bugged," Crowley said. "The usual sweeps that we make had not picked them up. When I got back from talking to you, I got some of my people on it, and after a pretty thorough search we found them. You were also right about the surveillance. Not only were our headquarters and manufacturing facilities covered, but all the top officers were being tailed, as well."

Hollis grinned at Crowley's outrage. "What happened?"

"The people doing the surveillance were not locals, so I called Griffin at FBI. You may know him."

Hollis shook his head.

"He rounded them up. They were KGB for God's sake. He's assigned some agents to provide temporary cover until I can make other arrangements."

"The tempo's picking up," Hollis observed. "Frolich used locals."

They arrived at Seal Rocks Overlook. Through the windshield of the car they saw the broad Pacific Ocean stretching out to the horizon. Crowley turned the car around and parked in a position where they would have a good view of any approaching vehicles. He left the engine running.

Hollis could wait no longer. "What's the verdict on Peregrine?"

"There's no question about it. The schematics and specs show that the command module has been modified to receive the precise over-ride signals which you described, and which the transmitter we developed was designed to deliver. The Soviets can trigger the self-destruct mechanism on all the ICBM and SLBM boosters which have been modified."

Hollis felt tears in his eyes. It had been a long journey, but vindication had finally arrived. He with help of Professor Lipscomb, had come up with the right answer. The so-called unofficial or Soviet Peregrine covered not only the modified command module, but the transmitter as well, even though they were handled separately. The finger of guilt was again pointing to someone in a position to manipulate Pentagon security procedures to his advantage.

Hollis noticed that Crowley was staring at him, a puzzled expression on his face.

"You just confirmed my theory about how Viktor arranged to keep his Peregrine from being discovered," Hollis said. "Do you know where the transmitter is located?"

"Yes. It's on grounds the of a large estate near Ukiah, between Cold Spring Mountain and Hendy Woods State Park, just south of a little town called Philo."

The color drained from Hollis' face.

Crowley reached over and took his arm. "What the hell's wrong?"

"How did you get to the site?"

"By helicopter."

"Did you see a house close by?"

"Yes, I did. A large 'U' shaped stone house, with servant's quarters, a couple of tennis courts and a swimming pool."

"That house belongs to Undersecretary of Defense, Paul Montague."

"My god." Crowley released his grip. "Is he the mole, then?"

"It's not the only connection. I've been doing my best not to believe he is, but this confirms it." He paused. "But it's so goddamned unbelievable. I would have staked my life on his loyalty."

"Where do we go from here?"

Hollis thought for a moment. "I don't know precisely when or how, but this whole mess is going to come to a head very soon, maybe this weekend. We've got to get to someone in Washington who will listen long enough to understand what Peregrine is and do something about it. The problem is simply that I don't know who that someone is. It can't be anyone at DOD. I can't get through to the secretary of defense, and anyone else could be side-tracked by Paul. It's got to be someone who has the clout to go around Paul, and also take fast action."

"Don't you know someone in the FBI or CIA at a high enough level to get some attention?"

"Al Walters, who's Assistant to the deputy director for ops, might help. He and I were in Afghanistan together, and he took the position I was slated for before I left to join Paul at Defense."

"Sounds like he owes you one," Crowley observed.

"But he's not the type person to let friendship interfere with his job. What's bothering me is whether I'll be able to stay on the phone long enough to tell him what he has to know. The FBI's still after me and he'll know the number I'm calling from."

Hollis thought for a moment. "Look, your firm worked on Peregrine. Is it possible we could get the support of one of your top officers? They might have some contacts in Congress."

"I wish I could offer some encouragement, Hollis, but I can't. All they'd know about the project is that it involved a very high-tech experimental transmission system. I doubt that most of the guys you're talking about would even remember it was called Peregrine. I'd hate to try to lead them through this whole thing and expect them to accept it. They'd think I was off my rocker."

"Is there anyone at Intertel who knows what the project was as well as the precise location of the transmission site?"

"Yes. The project manager, Gary Clarke. He's the one I got to check Peregrine out for you. He's the only one other than the two of us who knows the whole story. In fact, he still has the schematics and specs."

"Good Lord!" Hollis exclaimed. "He's our ace-in-the-hole. We've got to make sure nothing happens to him." Hollis paused a moment to think. "Let's go find a pay phone. You call your FBI contact, Griffin, and ask him to put Clarke under protection. Better yet, take him into custody. Once you confirm that he'll do that, I'll call Walters."

From a pay phone outside a gas station, Crowley finally got Special Agent Griffin on the line.

"Andy, it's Crowley here, may I ask another favor?"

"Sure, go ahead." Griffin's voice sounded strangely reserved.

"Gary Clarke over at Intertel has been working on a really hush-hush project, and in view of what's happened, I'm concerned about his safety. I wonder if you could take him into protective custody, along with some files that he's holding for me. I need both protected at all costs, Andy, national security."

"I'll pick him up right now," Griffin agreed. "By the way, where are you?"

"I'm out in the field at the moment. Why?"

"Some damn cryptic note came in suggesting you might be aiding Hollis, and you should be picked up for questioning. We need to get together as soon as possible."

"I don't know what they're talking about," Crowley replied, "but I'll drop by and square it away shortly." He hung up before Griffin could respond.

Crowley started his car, and headed toward the Presidio before filling Hollis in on the conversation.

"Well, I guess Viktor now assumes you're helping me, so he's taken steps to neutralize you, too," Hollis replied, grimly. "Do you think Griffin really will pick up Clarke?"

Hollis knew the situation had now changed drastically. Griffin undoubtedly knew by now where Crowley had called from and had agents on the way. He also knew that the telephone number from which he called would be revealed to Walters as soon as the call was connected. It was not a matter of tracing a call any longer. It was now only a matter of associating the calling number with the location of the telephone.

He also knew that as soon as he identified himself Walter's secretary would be on a line to the FBI. Once they were informed, a line would be opened to the San Francisco FBI office, and with agents already dispersed throughout the area, they would home in on him as soon as his position was pinpointed. The call would have to be much shorter than he had hoped.

Hollis guessed he had no more than 45 seconds, at the outside, to get some sort of message to Walters that would give him enough information to act. This would be difficult because even though Walters undoubtedly was aware of Operation *Maskirovka*, it was unlikely that he would have any knowledge of Peregrine. Yet, what he said in those few seconds would not only have to point Walters to the transmitter, but to its significance as well.

Accusing Paul of being the mole would have to wait; it would only sidetrack them from Peregrine.

As they approached the Golden Gate bridge they spotted a telephone booth just off the main traffic thoroughfare. Hollis nodded and Crowley pulled up to it, keeping the motor running. When he identified himself, the secretary put him through immediately.

"I'm glad you called Jeff. Are you coming in?"

"Do I have time to talk, Al, or is the clock running?"

"You know the answer to that, Jeff. I have no choice."

"Then listen closely. This is extremely urgent. National security is at stake and time is running out. You're familiar with Operation *Maskirovka*?"

"Yes."

"It's real. Peregrine is the means by which they intend to neutralize our ICBMs and SLBMs. Project manager Gary Clarke, International Intelligence Systems, Inc., has information that will prove it. Special Agent Griffin, in the FBI's San Francisco office has taken him into custody and is holding him for you. But you've got to move fast, Al."

"DOD has checked out Peregrine, Jeff," Walter shouted, before Hollis could hang up. "The secretary himself says it has nothing to do with *Maskirovka*!"

Hollis shouted back: "There's a mole, possibly as high as the undersecretary, in control!" He slammed the receiver back on the hook, sprinted from the booth and jumped in the back seat of the car.

As Crowley sped away, he dropped to the floor so he could not be seen from outside the car. They had barely made it to the thoroughfare and merged into the traffic as two cars, tires squealing, turned into the street they had left.

"That was close," Crowley said.

When he was sure they were clear, he told Hollis he could get up. "How'd it go?" he asked.

Hollis shook his head. "Not well. He said they checked with Defense and were told Peregrine has nothing to do with *Maskirovka*. I couldn't take the time to go into detail, but I told him that Clarke has the information he needs. Once he gets it, he should be able to put the pieces together and arrange to have the transmission site destroyed."

"With both of us now out of it, hope is about all that's left." Crowley observed.

CIA Headquarters, Langley, Virginia
1705 Wednesday December 21, 1983—Day Thirteen

When Hollis broke the connection, Walters checked to make sure his secretary had forwarded information on the origin of the call to the FBI, even though he knew Hollis would have been gone long before they could have gotten to the phone.

He then dialed the number of the deputy director of operations. "Jeb, Hollis just called, and I think we need to get to the DCI right away."

"Hold on a second," Webster instructed. After several moments, he was back on the line. "He'll see us right now."

Walters related his conversation with Hollis to CIA Director William Casey in his office.

When he was finished, the DCI sat for several long moments, stroking his chin. Finally he looked at Webster. "What do you think?"

Webster shook his head. "Well, if this is a charade, you've got to give Hollis credit for his persistence."

"It's no charade," Walters said. "I know Hollis."

"How do you reconcile what he told you with what Cap Weinberger told me?" Casey asked.

"I can't," Walters admitted. "But I do know this. Even though Hollis may be wrong, he believes what he told me is the truth. And I'd guess the same is true with respect to the secretary of defense. He merely relayed to you what he believes to be true. But if Hollis is right about there being a mole high up in Defense, then the information the secretary has may not be correct."

"I don't think we're going to get very far on that premise," Webster mused. "Unless we can come up with a hell of a lot more than a telephone call from the prime suspect."

"You're right." the aging spy master agreed, "But, if we make any waves, we not only won't get any farther, we'll warn the mole if there is one."

"I have an idea." Walters volunteered.

After Walters spelled it out, Casey looked at Webster, who nodded in agreement.

Casey pressed an intercom button on his desk. A secretary answered. "I need to speak to the president right away," Casey said "It's urgent."

43

San Francisco, California
1540 Wednesday, December 21, 1983—Day Thirteen

Agent Griffin moved quickly after receiving Crowley's call. Within minutes, he and another agent were headed for Intertel's headquarters.

Mike Jenkins, who was driving, reflected Griffin's thoughts when he said, "I wish we knew a little bit more about what the hell's going on."

"I agree," Griffin responded. "If I didn't know Crowley so well, I'm not sure I'd have agreed to pick Clarke up without more of an explanation, particularly since Crowley's wanted for questioning. But after what happened this morning, I couldn't ignore his request."

"Yeah, for the KGB to involve its agents in that type of activity is pretty far out. What d'ya think Intertel's involved in to attract a bunch like that?"

"I don't know," Griffin replied. "But Crowley wouldn't have insisted we take Clarke into protective custody unless it was damned important."

Jenkins turned into Intertel's underground parking garage and waited while Griffin went inside to get Clarke.

Ten minutes later they emerged from the parking garage with Clarke seated up front. Jenkins pulled out into the flow of traffic and headed for the Federal Building.

Like all trained drivers, he paid as much attention to what was going on behind him as he did to what was happening in front. They were about halfway between and the Federal Building when he caught Griffin's eye in the rear view mirror.

"I think we've picked up a tail."

Griffin, sitting in back, turned around to look.

"That black Pontiac, two cars back," Jenkins said. "It's sticking with us. Shall I lose him?"

"I don't think it's necessary. We're almost there. If he follows us into the parking garage, we'll assume we have a problem."

Jenkins continued to watch the Pontiac. When he reached the drive into the Federal Building it was immediately behind him.

He started to call Griffin's attention to the fact when Griffin yelled "Look out!"

Jenkins took his eye from the rear-view mirror just in time to see a car coming out of the Federal Building suddenly swerve to its left in front of him, blocking the drive.

Cursing loudly, Jenkins slammed on the brakes. The Pontiac following them pulled in tight alongside them on the left and opened fire with an automatic weapon. Clarke, sitting on the passenger side up front, was at point blank range.

Another automatic weapon opened up from the car blocking their way.

Jenkins yelled "Hit the deck!" and pulled Clarke down behind the dashboard.

Griffin grabbed the Remington 12-gauge shotgun from its clip just below the rear of the front seats and rolled out of the door on the right side of the car. He crawled quickly to the rear and using the car as a shield, opened fire on the black Pontiac.

He fired two rounds, the buckshot taking out the left rear window and part of the windshield.

He then ducked down behind the car, dropped flat on his stomach and rolled out from behind the rear wheel and put three rounds through the windshield of the second car.

The Pontiac backed away and sped off.

Those in the second car were less fortunate. The angle had given Griffin a clear line of fire to the driver and the passenger. He had killed them both.

The entire incident was over almost before the few spectators on the street realized what was happening and began to seek cover.

Griffin looked inside the car blocking their way, saw that it was no longer posed a threat, then moved quickly back to check Jenkins and Clarke. Both had been hit.

He reached over Jenkins and grabbed the radio mike. "Control, this is Griffin, over."

"This is control, go ahead."

"I am immobile outside the Federal Building just off Turk Street. I have two down including one agent, need medical assistance immediately. Also two dead. Crowd control assistance imperative. Over."

"Message understood. Assistance on the way. Out."

Later in the afternoon the first local TV news coverage reported that two suspected terrorists had been killed in a shoot-out with the FBI, and two others, who may have been wounded, were being sought. The report also mentioned that an FBI agent had been seriously wounded.

The names of the FBI agents involved were not given, nor was the fact that a badly wounded third passenger, identity unknown, had died on the way to the hospital.

44

Montague Estate, California
1815 Thursday, December 22—Day Fourteen

Maxsimov had not reached the position he held by accepting failure. He would not permit it now. Two of his agents were dead, two were wounded, and sixteen had been taken prisoner. Even though the agents in custody undoubtedly would be freed shortly, the fact that they had been caught could reflect badly on him.

It was all Hollis' doing. The man was a devil. And he was still free. Everything—Peregrine, Maxsimov's future—would be in jeopardy until Hollis was terminated.

Viktor would pay for this. Had done his job properly Hollis would not still be causing trouble.

Sergei interrupted. "Colonel, I have Viktor for you."

Maxsimov arose and snatched up the phone. "Do you know where Hollis is?" he demanded brusquely.

"Once he left Sausalito, he could have gone anywhere. I have no way of knowing where he is."

"You have got to find him. The project remains in jeopardy until he is eliminated. I will not be responsible for your failure."

"I've tried to tell you before but you won't listen!" Viktor shouted back. "As far as the command module is concerned, even if Hollis has proof that it has been modified, he can do nothing about it!"

"How can you be so damned sure?"

"He was able to get a letter exposing Peregrine to a contact in the CIA. The contact took it to the director. The director called the secretary of defense. The secretary assured the director that a complete investigation had been undertaken, and Hollis' story was simply a smoke screen to keep us from knowing that he had compromised the US KKV program. I expect there will be no more efforts to expose Peregrine from this end, but even if there are, time is running out for Hollis. Soon it will be too late for them to do anything about the modules even if they find out about the modification. You should be more concerned over whether the transmitter is adequately protected."

"It is protected," Maxsimov replied, still seething. "Now that Clarke has been eliminated, how will they find the location? You told me he's the only one who knew where it was."

"No. Intertel's security officer, a man named Crowley, also knows. Steps have been taken to neutralize him by informing the FBI that he has joined Hollis, but so far they have not been able to take him into custody."

Maxsimov's voice again took on a note of aggravation. "If that's true, and he's working with Hollis, then Hollis will know the location of the transmitter."

"That's true," Viktor agreed. "But what can he do with the information? Even if he passes it on to someone here I can make sure no one acts on it."

"He has proven to be a very resourceful adversary. As long as he is alive, he is a threat. I cannot understand why you fail to see that."

"I agree he would be better dead. But I have made sure that even if he is alive he will not be able to do anything to endanger Peregrine at this end."

Viktor paused to think. "However, since he can't expose Peregrine, it's possible he and Crowley will try to sabotage the transmitter. I think you should make preparations to intercept him."

45

The White House, Washington DC.
0925 Thursday December 22, 1983—Day Fourteen

The president's morning staff meeting had begun promptly at nine when the vice president, accompanied by Chief of Staff Jim Baker, Ed Meese, counselor to the president, and Mike Deaver, political and press advisor, arrived at the Oval Office. The meeting moved swiftly over the agenda items, then Deaver requested the floor.

"Mr. President, the rumors are getting out of hand. The press is demanding a statement from us, and we have to make one. We have to explain what's going on with the Soviets and the Warsaw Pact countries and we have to do it today."

Reagan offered Deaver a knowing grin. He was hearing from him almost word-for-word the lecture he had already gotten from his wife Nancy earlier that morning.

"What are we going to tell them?" Reagan demanded. "That we don't know what the hell they're up to but we wish they'd knock it off?"

Deaver grinned wryly. "Well, not exactly. But you know all the crap that's coming out of Europe, France in particular, about us being responsible for the crisis, and that it's up to us to do something to defuse it. Also, since we haven't responded, some of these guys act like they're beginning to take it seriously. Speculation has even started up again over whether we would actually use US-based nuclear missiles to protect Western Europe in the event of a Soviet conventional weapons attack. Bottom line, Mr. President, you've got to issue a statement—either that or hold a short press conference."

"I don't mind doing either, but I don't want to get up before a bunch of reporters and act like nothing's going on. But I also don't want to scare them out of their pants, either."

The president looked at his watch. "Bud will be here in a couple of minutes. Let's wait and see what he has to say."

McFarlane entered the office promptly at nine-thirty, nodded to those present and took a seat in one of the chairs in the half-circle facing the desk. The half-smile with which Reagan usually greeted him was noticeably absent as he folded his hands on the desk in front of him. "We know the big picture, Bud. Give us some details."

The National Security Adviser began somberly: "Their forces on alert status are significantly larger than last week. They've continued to mobilize and call up reserves. If you look at their Western Theater of Operations by itself, there are now twenty-nine non-Soviet Warsaw Pact divisions with sixty-three Soviet divisions facing NATO forces of approximately one-third that number. There are also ten thousand Warsaw Pact tanks along with almost twenty thousand Soviet tanks in that theater. And, if you add the forces now in their Northwestern, Southwestern and Southern Theaters, together with their strategic reserves held in Russia, they have probably something like ninety more divisions and about fifteen thousand more tanks available."

The president leaned back in his chair and shook his head angrily. "Go on," he said.

"Well, beyond that, they have in excess of one hundred ships loaded either with troops, equipment, or a combination of both at sea, destination unknown. About fifty departed the Murmansk-Olenegorsk area, another twenty-five from the Black Sea, and twenty-nine from the Vladivostok, Komsomol'sk and Petropavlosk. These vessels, in total, may be carrying as many as ten to fifteen armored divisions, and the equipment to support them. Also, there are over one hundred more vessels in the process of being loaded. The ones at sea are traveling in groups or convoys, escorted by Soviet surface warships."

McFarlane shifted uncomfortably in his seat. The burden of delivering so much bad news in one sitting to the president was depressing in the extreme. For a fleeting moment he imagined that the others in the room were blaming him for the litany of horrors he was unfolding before them.

He pressed gamely on. "Over the last several days we tracked ten Soviet An-124s, which as you may recall are slightly larger than our C-5A Galaxies, to Cuba. We now know the aircraft were loaded with over a thousand paratroopers, together with equipment including armored personnel carriers. Also, there are several hundred more transport aircraft spotted at northern Soviet airfields around Skrunda, Olengorsk and Pechora which are either being loaded with equipment or have troops standing by ready to embark....In addition to forty more An-124s, they have fifty-five An-22s, which is somewhat smaller than the 124s, two hundred Il-76s, which is the equivalent of our C-141B Starlifter, and two hundred-fifty An-12s, which is about the same as our C-130 A/H Hercules. These aircraft, in combination, can transport over sixty thousand troops. There is also some indication that civilian aircraft are being diverted for troop ferrying activities."

"Jesus Christ!" Deaver interrupted, ignoring Reagan's frown. "And they say they're just engaged in some training exercises. What the hell would they do if they were preparing for war?"

When no one responded, McFarlane continued. "There are now twelve satellites in orbit, Mr. President, and there are no more on their launch pads, so there probably won't be any more. There's been no change in their appearance, but the fact that at any given time eight of them are either over or in sight of the US. seems to be further indication that they are weapons platforms. Also we have just received confirmation not only that the last message from the blind Moscow contact about Maskirovka taking effect on the twenty-fourth of this month was accurate, but the satellites are in fact, as General Shields suggested, space-based KKVs designed to transport kinetic kill weapons to destroy our ICBMs and SLBMs."

As Baker and Meese exchanged worried glances, Reagan asked. "Do we have the ability to destroy the satellites?"

McFarlane nodded. "As General Vessey indicated, Mr. President, we do not have an operational anti-satellite capability, but, theoretically, at least, there are two methods by which we may be able to destroy or bring them down."

"Go on," Reagan urged.

"We can launch nuclear-armed ICBMs or SLBMs on intercept trajectories timed to detonate at intercept. This method is in the process of being confirmed by the Army, and they have scheduled a test for June of next year, but realistically they believe the odds of success to be low. Also, even though it's theoretically possible to destroy the satellites by this method, it's not a ideal solution. The electromagnetic pulse generated by a thermonuclear blast can be disruptive not only to land based communications, but other military satellites, MILSATS, nearby which our military forces rely on for activities, such as navigation and the Navy's Aegis defense and targeting system.

"The only other means now available is the so-called Miniature Vehicle, MV, under development by the Air Force. It's a non-nuclear direct-ascent, infrared-guided, kinetic-energy intercept missile mounted on a two stage SRAM/ALTAIR booster, which is carried aloft and launched from an F-15 aircraft.

"In concept, it's simple. NORAD tracks the satellite, and predicts the orbit. After the aircraft takes off, this information is loaded into its on board computer. As launch time approaches, the information is verified and updated as necessary by NORAD. Then, shortly before launch time, the computer takes over control of the aircraft. It puts the aircraft into a steep dive to pick up speed, after which it zooms upward. When it reaches the proper altitude, with the nose pointed in the correct direction, the missile is fired. The guidance system carried by the MV does the rest."

"Has it been flight tested? Can we use it?" the president asked.

"Preliminary testing has been completed, Mr. President, so it can be used. We have three groups of six planes, one each at McCord, Griffiss, and Langley fitted out to launch the MV, and they have actually fired several, but not at legitimate targets. That's not scheduled until early next year. So, in short, we don't know how reliable it is."

"In other words, you don't know whether it works or not." Baker broke in.

"That's correct, but it's all we've got."

Meese seized the opportunity to speak. "Mr. President, I think the time for not ruffling feathers is over. We ought to stand up and be counted. They've got to be told we're not going to stand idly by while they take over the rest of Europe."

Baker and Deaver nodded agreement.

"What does Cap think?" Reagan asked.

"The secretary feels very strongly that we should move quickly to show the Soviets we are willing to meet force with force. He is prepared to recommend that we go immediately to DEFCON III, that we deploy additional tactical nuclear weapons in NATO countries, and NATO tactical air be put on semi-alert with nuclear weapons available; that we re-deploy the carrier battle groups where they will be most effective against the troop vessels and their escort as well as meeting any threat the transport aircraft may present, and that we immediately put fifty percent of SAC aircraft on airborne status, with the other fifty percent on immediate stand-by. He also wants permission to deploy whatever assets are necessary in whatever configuration it will take to destroy all of the satellites, more or less at the same time."

The president looked at his agenda for the day, shook his head and turned the page. "Cancel the staff meeting tomorrow morning and schedule an NSC meeting in its place. And tell Cap we'll take up his recommendations then. In the meantime, Mike, get to work on a news release. I think the tone ought to be firm, but not overly aggressive. I don't want an out-and-out confrontation if it can be avoided."

"There will undoubtedly be questions about what we will do in the event the Soviets move against Western Europe." Deaver guessed, looking for guidance.

"I would merely point out that we are watching the situation very closely. We have no reason to doubt the Soviet's statement that they are engaged in training exercises. And then add, very low key, that everyone knows what our commitments to our European friends and allies are, and I cannot envision a situation where we would not honor those commitments."

46

Corte Madera, California
0810 Thursday, December 22, 1983—Day Fourteen

After Hollis and Crowley raced away from the telephone booth to avoid the FBI, they had decided they needed a place to hide, and San Francisco was not it. Crowley had headed North across the Golden Gate Bridge and they had wound up in an out of the way motel north of the city.

As they prepared to leave the following morning, Hollis flipped the TV set on just in time to catch the latest news. They were stunned by how much further the crisis between the Soviet Union and the US had deteriorated in just the last 24 hours.

One of the analysts interviewed on the broadcast, a former low-level state department official during the Carter administration, blamed the crisis on the president's insistence on placing IRBMs and cruise missiles in Western Europe.

This infuriated Hollis, and he was about to say something when the news switched to update an FBI shoot-out with terrorists the day before.

The reporter described an encounter which "left the potential witness Gary Clarke dead along with two terrorists, and one severely wounded FBI agent." He speculated that since Clarke was an employee of Intertel, which engaged in significant defense work, the terrorists might have been plotting against the company.

Crowley was the first to speak. "What the hell do we do now?" he asked.

Hollis turned the TV off. He was shaken by the news but not surprised. He was beginning to expect this kind of thing. "What happened to the schematics and specs that I gave you? Didn't you say that Clarke had them?"

"That's right," Crowley confirmed, "and when I called to tell him Griffin was going to pick him up I told him to make sure that he had all of that material with him. So Griffin must have it now."

"Let's find a pay phone real quick, so you can call Griffin. We have to make sure Walters gets that information and knows what it is."

They found a phone booth at a service station near US 101. Crowley dialed Griffin's number after putting the required coins in, and waited for an answer.

"Special Agent Griffin."

"Andy, this is Crowley. Did Clarke have a package of information with him?"

Griffin demurred. "Look Chuck, I'm not in a position to talk. The heat's on. Unless you tell me that you're coming in I'll have to try to pick you up."

"Damnit, I don't have time to explain now, but you know me well enough to know that when I tell you what's involved is vital to the security of this country I know what I'm talking about. So listen closely. Al Walters is assistant to the deputy director, operations of Central Intelligence. It is imperative that he get the schematics and specs Clarke had with him, together with his write-up. It's also imperative that he be told the information came from Hollis."

"You know I can't do that. Even if I were inclined go along, what Clarke had in his possession is classified Department of Defense information, and our responsibility is to make sure that's where it goes."

"Listen, Andy," Crowley insisted. "Forget the damned bureaucratic etiquette. Just make sure Walters gets the information."

Crowley hung up.

On the assumption Griffin would have traced the call, and dispatched one or more teams to pick them up, Crowley headed back to Corte Madera, and turned south toward Almonte, before stopping at a convenience store with a phone booth outside. Hollis immediately jumped out and placed a call to Walters.

"I'm sorry, Mr. Hollis," a secretary told him, "he's not available, but he left a message in case you called."

"Yes."

"He said you must turn yourself in as soon as possible. He understands your situation, and will do everything he can to protect you while the situation is sorted out. He also said to tell you that the operation goes down on Saturday."

"Tell him I understand. And get this message back to him immediately. An FBI agent in the San Francisco office—Special Agent Griffin—has the documents that prove there is a Soviet Peregrine in addition to the official DOD Peregrine. He must get the documents from Griffin immediately or he will turn them over to the Defense Department and the mole will destroy them. Finally, tell him if he wants to see me he'll have to meet me at the transmission site. He'll know what I mean."

Hollis hung up without waiting for a reply. The conversation had been recorded so it would not be lost or forgotten. But that didn't mean his message would get to Walters.

With Hollis back in the car, Crowley headed north and cut through to Strawberry Point. "There's only one thing left to do," Hollis told him. "Somehow or other, I've got to find that transmitter and destroy it."

"You've got to be flat out of your gourd." Crowley exclaimed. "They have a security force there the size of a small city's police force—somewhere between fifty and a hundred men, and better armed. At least they did when I was there. It may be bigger now. You wouldn't have a pig's chance at a pork roast of getting close to the damn thing, much less destroying it. You'd have to go in with a small army of special forces, and even then it wouldn't be a sure thing."

"You may be right." Hollis said solemnly. "But I don't have a choice. According to Walters' message, Operation *Maskirovka* will happen on

Saturday, Christmas eve. Even if he gets my message and is able to figure it out and get the information he needs to understand what's involved and where it is, getting an operation like what you're talking about authorized and underway in the short time we've got left would be next to impossible, particularly with the mole most likely in a position to block it. The only thing left for me to do is go to the retreat and see if I can find a way to put the transmitter out of action."

Crowley shook his head in disbelief. "You're really serious aren't you?"

Hollis nodded.

"Look, you've been there," Crowley argued. "You know how rugged the terrain is. And the place they picked is right in the middle of the worst part of it, in an extremely well-camouflaged cave, surrounded by cliffs, rocks, brush, and trees. They can hold out against a large assault force almost indefinitely. You'd need air power to blast them out of there. If Walters doesn't come through with some pretty strong reinforcements, you won't have a chance."

"Nevertheless I've got to try."

Crowley paused for a moment, then in a resigned tone said, "Well, if you're crazy enough to do it, I'll go with you."

Hollis reached over, placed his hand on Crowley's shoulder. "Thanks. I was hoping you would, but I couldn't ask."

Crowley smiled weakly. "I'm sure I'll regret it, but I don't think you could find the damn thing without me."

47

The White House, Washington, DC
0945 Friday December 23, 1983—Day Fifteen

The National Security Council meeting had ended pretty much as anticipated. Weinberger's recommendations had been approved over Shultz's not very strenuous objections.

When the last agenda item had been covered, the president addressed the still-seated members of the council in a somber tone: "Gentlemen, thank you all very much for your participation. We all know where we stand, and what we've got to do. As much as I'd like to say 'have a great holiday weekend' I'm afraid that until we find out what the Soviets plan to do tomorrow, all of us will have to stay where we can be reached on a moment's notice."

As the meeting broke up, the president asked Weinberger, Shultz, Casey and Bush to stay behind.

"This will only take a few minutes, gentlemen, but it is of utmost importance."

When everyone had reseated themselves, the president turned to Casey. "Bill, will you fill everyone in on where we stand at the moment?"

"Yes, Mr. President," Casey replied. "This past Tuesday, we received a letter written by Jeff Hollis' ex-wife."

Weinberger glared at Casey with a decidedly hostile frown.

"The letter purportedly recounted a conversation she had with Hollis the preceding Thursday concerning a DOD project code named Peregrine," Casey continued. "It said that Hollis had found a memorandum concerning the project prepared by a Professor Lipscomb of Stanford University. Even though the memorandum disappeared, Hollis interviewed the Professor and became convinced that the project involved an integral component in all of our military rocket boosters, namely the command module, which is the transmission link between the ground control officer and the on board computer.

"Also, according to this letter, at least two attempts were made on Hollis' life, he was suddenly charged with security violations, and put on the FBI's most wanted list. All of which led him to believe that the project was being run by a mole in a high level DOD position who had framed him to prevent him from exposing the project"

Weinberger was having difficulty not interrupting, but he held back as the DCI continued.

"To be fair about this, I immediately called Cap to let him know we had the letter, and told him its contents. He stated that he was aware of the fact that Hollis had claimed to have found the memorandum, but the project he referred to had nothing to do with the command module. He felt it was likely that if Hollis had gone over to the other side, as the evidence indicated, he was simply trying to raise a smoke screen to obscure the fact that he had compromised our KKV program."

To clear his throat Casey took a hasty drink of water from the glass in front of him. His hand shook slightly and some of the water spilled onto the table.

"That's where the matter stood," Casey resumed, still holding the glass in his hand. "We had planned no further action, until Wednesday afternoon when Hollis called Al Walters, assistant to the deputy DCI, operations. You remember this was the slot Hollis had been approved for prior to his move to Defense, and you may also remember Walters was one of the guys who Hollis rescued in Afghanistan. Hollis didn't talk long because he knew Walters would make sure the phone call was being reported the FBI, but he did deliver a hell of a message."

Casey set the glass down carefully on the polished surface. "Basically, what he said was that *Maskirovka* is real, that there is a Soviet project by the name of Peregrine, and it is the means by which the Soviets can neutralize our ICBMs and SLBMs."

Weinberger started to break in. Casey held up a hand. "Just a couple of minutes more, Cap, and I'll be through. He also said that Gary Clarke, who was a project manager at Intertel had information that would prove he was right, and that an FBI Special Agent Griffin had taken Clarke into protective custody. He suggested Walters get the information from him."

Unable to contain his anger any longer, Weinberger almost shouted back at Casey. "And you believe that crap?" he asked, exasperated. "I told you, we made a thorough investigation of this. It was done by DIS under the direction of Paul Montague, and the results were made available to the FBI. I don't know what more we can do. And I don't like the idea of the CIA rummaging around in a matter that is strictly the business of the Department of Defense. If anything needs to be done about this, it's my responsibility to have it done—and with my people."

He turned to face Reagan directly. "Mr. President, if I don't have your complete confidence to run my department as it should be run, all you have to do is say so, and I'll resign."

"Cap, if I didn't have complete faith in you, you wouldn't be here. But there's more you haven't heard."

Weinberger folded his hands in front of him and glared at the DCI as Casey resumed. "Hollis also said he had proof there was a mole in DOD, possibly as high up as the under-secretary level."

Weinberger jumped up. "Mr. President, I'm not going to sit here and listen to someone accuse Paul Montague of being disloyal. I've known him almost all his life, and I knew his father as well. This is just too much!"

"I'm not accusing anyone of anything." The old spy master responded quietly. "I would point out, however, that you're perfectly willing to condemn someone with a long and honorable career in both the FBI and the CIA, who put his life on the line for his country, not to mention his marriage, all on evidence that may have been fabricated."

There was an awkward silence. Casey had brought the secretary of defense back to reality, and it was taking him a few moments to accept it.

"I'm sorry about the outburst," Weinberger said at last, his voice contrite. "Go ahead, Bill."

"I concede you may be right, Cap." Casey continued. "But we don't think we can take a chance. If it turns out that Hollis is right, we've got to know while there's still time to do something about it. And it's got to be done in such a manner that if there is a mole in a high level DOD position, we don't alert him."

Reagan nodded in agreement.

"Accordingly, after Hollis called," Casey went on, "I called the president and got permission to send Walters out to San Francisco to meet with Griffin and to interview Clarke. Unfortunately, Clarke was killed by KGB assassins and Griffin refused to let us see the documents he was carrying. Fortunately the FBI director at the instigation of the attorney general was able to change his mind."

"So what was the outcome?" Weinberger asked.

"Walters faxed the documents to Langley late yesterday. They had been taken from the files of a small California electronics fabricating company, named Pacific Electronics Company. They consisted of schematics, specifications and other information for an upgraded replacement command module for all of our military booster rockets. They also showed that work on the project had been completed, and the components shipped to various military bases and supply depots several months ago."

"So?" Weinberger asked, a touch of exasperation returning to his voice. "It sounds pretty routine to me."

"The files related to a project code-named Peregrine."

"That can't be." Weinberger was adamant. "Peregrine was only recently approved, and it's not in production."

"Hollis said there were two projects of that name: the official DOD project, which you're talking about, and the unofficial Soviet project which the memorandum he found related to. Anyway, we have the documents." Casey assured him.

"But, even if there is a mole, as Hollis says, he couldn't arrange for a project to receive a code name and he certainly couldn't arrange for a highly sensitive rocket booster part, such as a command module, to be produced and shipped to our supply depots without having a whole empire of spies or moles helping him. Certainly you don't think anything like that exists."

"Right now I'm not ruling anything out. But I'm not sure something like that is necessary. With all the rigid rules requiring compartmentalization of information on a need-to-know basis, it's possible that someone in the right place with the right know-how, could involve a lot of unknowing, innocent people who would have no reason to question the validity of what they were doing. Also, giving his project the same name as an official project would not only be a good way to hide it, but would also lend it an air of credibility."

Weinberger shook his head. He didn't like what he was hearing but he chose not to object. He was astute enough to recognize that Casey's arguments, however unpalatable, had an increasingly compelling logic to them.

"In any event," Casey continued, "there was also a memorandum prepared by Clarke, addressed to one C. A. Crowley, vice president, security, at Intertel stating that, as Hollis suspected, the modified module contains an override that will allow it to accept transmissions other than those issued by the launch control officer."

"My God! Weinberger exploded. "If that's true, it means the Soviets have the ability to re-target our missiles, or...." he paused as the full import of what he had heard caught up with him, "they can trigger the self-destruct mechanism in our rockets and destroy them as soon as they are launched....And that would mean Operation Maskirovka is directed against the United States."

Shultz broke in. "Are you sure you're not over-reacting. None of this has been verified. I've never been sure that the operation was anything other than a masquerade."

"We all hope you're right George," the president said. "But if Clarke's memorandum is correct, then I don't think we should discount Cap's conclusion. Is there anyway we can check that out?"

"That's being done right now, Mr. President," Casey replied. "I took the liberty of going ahead on it because of the press of time, and the fact that the people I'm using would not be known to a mole in DOD, assuming there is one." He added the last for Weinberger's benefit.

"All right," Reagan acknowledged. "Assuming Clarke is right, and those modified modules have been installed in our rocket boosters, what can be done to nullify them? Can they be disconnected, replaced or readjusted or something?"

Weinberger shook his head. "I may be wrong, but my recollection is that the rockets cannot be launched without a command module in place because, as Bill pointed out, it's the link between ground control and the on-board computer. Also, I'd be surprised if there is any way to adjust or bypass them. They're basically nothing more than very elaborate printed circuit boards, so there's no way to rewire them.

"Further, if they've already been installed, which seems likely, if we're to believe the information we have here, I don't hold out much hope that they can be replaced anytime soon. Under current procedure, the parts they replaced would have been returned to a regional supply depot for destruction."

Casey broke in: "Mr. President, there was something in Clarke's memorandum to the effect that Intertel had worked on a project also code-named Peregrine, which involved a specialized computer controlled transmitter that he believed was designed to activate the modified command module. He thought the transmitter was installed somewhere in northern California. He didn't know exactly where. But if we can find it in time, we can deactivate or destroy it."

"Bill may well be right," Weinberger said. "But I think we need to get someone involved in this who has the technical background to tell us what our options are, and how to take advantage of them, assuming we have any, and there's still time to do something."

"I agree," Reagan nodded. "Do you have someone?"

Weinberger thought a moment. "General Graham probably knows more about what's involved than anyone else. I have no reason to believe he is anything but completely loyal." He gave Casey a sideways glance.

"I have no problem with General Graham, Mr. President. But as you know, right now there are only six people who are privy to this information—the four of us plus Walters and Webster. If we're going to involve someone else I think they should be reassigned to an office at Langley, and not allowed to communicate with anyone outside this circle except under strict security constraints."

Weinberger bristled, but said nothing.

"All right," Reagan agreed. "Cap, you and Bill make the necessary arrangements. Bill, is anything being done to locate the transmitter?"

"Walters is working on it, Mr. President. So far he's reported no progress, but if it can be done, he'll do it. I'm afraid the only people who could give us the specific location are Hollis and Crowley, and we still don't know where they are. If Hollis calls in again, we've got to make sure he understands that all is forgiven and we need his help."

"I'd guess it'll be somewhat difficult to convince him of that after what he's been through." the secretary of defense observed.

"Tell him to call me," Reagan said. "I'll make sure that he'll be put through to me wherever I am. I'll convince him."

It was almost six that afternoon by the time President Reagan was finally able to leave the Oval Office and retreat to the residential quarters on the second floor.

He went to one of the small guest rooms under the North Portico which he had converted into a personal gym. He stripped down, put on his exercise suit and was about halfway through his daily routine when one of the secret service agents on duty tapped on the door and stuck his head in.

"Mr. President, Director Casey and Secretary Weinberger are holding on your secure line. They say it is urgent that they speak with you."

"Very well, Tom." Reagan wiped his face with a towel. "I'll take it in my study."

Reagan hurried across the hall and into the small study, between the master bedroom and the Yellow Oval Room, and grabbed the phone. "Yes, Bill—Cap, what is it?"

Casey led off. "Mr. President, Al Walters is holding on another line for instructions, but before that we need to give you an update."

"I'm listening."

"General Graham has examined the schematics and specs provided by Hollis, and agrees that the command modules have been modified to allow them to accept and act on an override signal, but he is skeptical as to its effectiveness. It operates only in an ultra high frequency band which requires line-of-sight transmission. Also, because it take a relatively powerful signal to activate the module, it may or may not, depending on the transmitter, respond to a satellite link, but clearly not to a signal relayed through more than one satellite.

"Graham, therefore, is of the opinion that a transmitter situated in northern California might be limited to activating command modules only in ICBMs launched from missile sites in the northwest. Clearly, it would be ineffective against SLBMs launched in the far Pacific or the north Atlantic. Other transmitters would have to be in place to handle those."

"What about those sites Belvoir came up with?"

"They are a distinct possibility, Mr. President."

Weinberger intervened. "Positioned as they are, if the command modules will accept one satellite link, then transmitters at those locations together with the one in California would pretty much blanket all positions from which a launch would ordinarily be made."

Casey again took the floor. "But that's still speculation. We don't have specs on the transmitter, and therefore we don't know its capabilities. There's some reason to believe, however, that it's more powerful than we first thought."

"Has Walters found the transmitter?"

"Not exactly, Mr. President, but he's pinned it down to the old Montague family estate up near Ukiah. The problem is that the estate encompasses about fifty square miles of very rugged terrain."

"Don't you think that's reason enough to haul Montague in and question him about it?"

"We've argued it back and forth, Mr. President, and we've come to the conclusion that we should leave him alone right now. If he is the mole, and we question him he'll deny knowing about it. Then if we let him go he'll know we've discovered his Peregrine project and will be able to take action. On the other hand if we hold him incommunicado and he's not the mole, his absence will certainly put the real mole on notice."

"So where do we stand?" Reagan asked.

"Right now, Mr. President," Casey responded, "we really don't know who's right, Hollis or our blind Moscow asset. In fact, we don't even know whether they're both right or both wrong. For example, Graham can't really evaluate Peregrine without knowing more about the location and the configuration of the transmitter, so he says that if he had to choose, he'd go with the conclusion that the Soviet MilSats are KKVs and that's what they'll use. He thinks that makes more sense than tampering with the command module, and if those newly discovered facilities are for target acquisition and ground control, it would be more dependable. Also, even though our Moscow contact told us Operation Maskirovka becomes effective tomorrow, we don't know precisely what that means."

"You still believe the operation is directed at us, and not NATO, Cap?" Reagan asked.

"Yes, Mr. President," Weinberger confirmed, "If they have the means to neutralize our ICBMs and SLBMs, or even simply to make us believe they do, they will use it to destroy us. I'm even more convinced now than I was because that's the only rationale that fits the positioning of their transport ships and aircraft. I think we should be prepared to meet that possibility by tomorrow morning.

"We've already moved the subs and aircraft into position to mount a simultaneous attack on the twelve Soviet MilSats on half hour notice. If successful, they'll all be destroyed at the same time, with no advance notice to the Soviets. Also, as you know, we were in the process of repositioning our carrier battle groups to intercept their transports. What I propose to do now is designate the transports as the secondary target, and reposition the battle groups so that the three newly discovered sites can be taken out either with cruise missile or air strikes in the shortest time possible."

"Do it," Reagan concurred.

"We also have some instructions we would like to give to Walters," Casey added.

After listening to the proposal, Reagan said, "Go ahead. I hope you're right."

The president hung up the phone and headed back toward his makeshift exercise room. But he was no longer in the mood for exercise.

On an unconscious impulse he continued on down the Center Hall toward the East Hall and the semi-circle of light made by the large Paladian window in the east wall. The hallway was deserted. He was completely alone.

He passed the doors to the Yellow Oval Room, the Treaty Room, the Lincoln Bedroom, the Queen's Bedroom, suddenly awestruck and humbled. He thought of some of the presidents in the nation's past who had paced this same floor in times of great national crisis: Lincoln, the two Roosevelts, Wilson, Truman, Eisenhower, Kennedy.

Each in his own way had risen to the occasion, had met the challenge that confronted him, and had seen the country through.

Now it was his turn.

The president stopped, looked out the window for a brief moment, then turned and headed back toward the West Sitting Hall and the family quarters.

It would be a long night, but he was ready for it.

48

US 101, North of San Francisco, California
2105 Friday, December 23, 1983—Day Fifteen

Crowley agreed to take on the task of obtaining the equipment he and Hollis would need to destroy the transmitter, because he was familiar with the terrain and the forces guarding it. He was also an ex-marine.

While Crowley did his shopping in San Francisco, Hollis waited in a small restaurant inside a bus station on the route between Novata and Petaluma in order to reduce the chances of anyone recognizing him.

As Hollis waited all the questions he had been forcing out of his consciousness now returned to feed his anxiety. *Where is Maggie? Will I ever see her again? If I hadn't involved her, she would be all right. Have I signed her death warrant by talking to Walters? What about Paul? Is he the mole? Was it Paul who had me framed, and kidnapped Maggie? Would the whole sorry mess ever be over?*

Only a little over two weeks had passed since the afternoon when he had first spotted the Peregrine memorandum in his office at the Pentagon. It seemed like two years.

The hours passed. No sign of Crowley. Hollis began to worry. There was nothing he could do but wait, so he ordered yet another cup of coffee and waited.

Six hours later he was still waiting. He was sure the manager of the restaurant was beginning to eye his presence with suspicion. It would be just his luck if the manager called the police.

Hollis was contemplating what he should do when Crowley finally returned.

Back in the car, they headed north toward Ukiah.

"Did you get what you wanted?" Hollis asked.

"Pretty much," Crowley replied. "I got a couple of M-16s fitted with Aimpoint sights for the long-range work. I had them bore-sighted in at two hundred yards, and each click will take it up or down ten yards."

"Is that the laser sight?"

"Yep. Just focus on the target, hit the button, and center the spot on what you want to hit."

"They're pretty small caliber, aren't they?"

"With the ammo I've got, they'll take out sentries at two hundred plus yards," Crowley assured him. "Also, the penetration is good, and six clips of ammo weighs only about fifteen pounds. For the close-in work, I was able to get a couple of H&K MP5K's, the cut-down version of the H&K MP5 SMG. It's only thirteen inches long, and weighs less than four pounds."

Crowley looked down at the speedometer and realized he was traveling well over the speed limit. He slowed down immediately. Getting stopped for speeding would not be a good idea just now.

"I had to cash in some chips, but I was able to get not only five pounds of plastic explosive with timers, but a dozen grenades, divided between smoke and anti-personnel."

"Sounds like you did pretty damned good," Hollis said.

"Well, it's a bare minimum. The terrain up there is pretty rough. We'll have to hoof it for better than five miles, so it's important not to be overloaded. I was also able to get what we'll need to get over the fence— a couple of Special Forces night assault uniforms, complete with flak jackets, a pair of camouflage fatigues and walkie-talkies."

"I can't think of anything you missed."

Crowley shrugged. "I missed finding about three platoons of battle-hardened Marines and a couple of Abrams tanks."

Hollis said nothing. He knew Crowley was just trying to lighten the mood by making a joke, but the odds against them were obviously no laughing matter.

"I hope they got Clarke's information to Walters," he said, after a silence. "If they did, maybe that'll clear things up and we'll get a little help."

"There's not much doubt that he got it, and it'll prove you're right on Peregrine. But there's nothing that pinpoints the location of that transmitter. The best he'll be able to do is place it somewhere in northern California, and that won't help a whole hell of a lot."

"There must be someone at Intertel who remembers the location."

Crowley thought about it. "Well, I can think of several who might be able to place it on the Montague property, but they still won't have the precise location. We follow your Pentagon regs, which means we compartmentalize everything. And since all our files and documents were returned to DOD, the information would have to be pried out of the memories of people who're trained to forget about high security projects once they're done with them. I may be the only one who actually still knows the exact location of the transmitter. Maybe we should go back to Santa Rosa so you can call Walters. I can give you the details and you can pass it on to him."

"I don't think so," Hollis replied. "If something is going down tomorrow, we're already running late. Also, for me to explain it all to them, assuming they'd even listen, I'd have to stay on the phone too long. They'd have someone here to handcuff us before I was halfway through. The risk might still be acceptable if we had any reason to believe it'd bring help in time, but it won't. You and I are all that stands between Peregrine and the country's security. Long as the odds may be, I don't think we have a choice. We've got to go ahead."

Crowley reluctantly agreed.

"It'd be great if we could just call in an air strike and level the whole place,' Hollis said. "Save everyone a hell of a lot of time and effort."

"I don't think an air strike by itself would work," Crowley said. "Unless they knew precisely where the site is and had the right type of weapons, they could drop cluster bombs and napalm around it all day without even damaging it."

"Couldn't they spot the antenna?"

"No. The system uses both a standard pole as well as a newly developed dish antenna which is very small. Both are very easy to hide. You could probably fly over them at fifty feet in a slow-moving helicopter and never see them."

"Wouldn't some near misses at least damage the transmitter?"

"I doubt it," Crowley responded. "It's computer controlled, very compact, and very well protected. A concussion won't damage it. Even a direct hit might not take it out."

"Okay, let's call off the air strike then," Hollis joked.

Crowley grinned.

Maybe I'm wrong, and we should try Walters one more time. Hollis thought. Maybe I could reach him at home, and we'd have time to talk before he reported the call. No. Nothing's changed. It's a risk we can't afford. We've got no choice but to go on.

It was after midnight when Hollis and Crowley reached Hendy Woods State Park. Neither had been in the park before, but Crowley had been able to get a California Park Service map which showed the layout of the roads and hiking trails.

Hollis spread the map out on his lap and studied it. "If you take the right fork just ahead it will take us in the direction of the estate. About three miles past the fork you'll come to a parking area for some trails that also cut off toward the estate. That'll be about as close as we can get in the Blazer."

"We don't go by any campgrounds, do we?"

"Not the way we're going," Hollis answered.

Crowley pulled off the road into the parking area and stopped. In the faint light provided by a half moon high up in the western sky, they could see the parking area was deserted. Crowley parked at the far end of the area and they began unloading their gear.

They changed into their night uniforms and pulled on a flak jacket and a backpack into which Crowley had distributed equal quantities of plastic explosive, timers and other equipment. After adjusting the straps on the M-16's and MP5's and looping two bandoleers loaded with grenades and extra ammo clips over their shoulders, they headed for the hiking trails.

The trail they chose got them off to a good start. It was mostly downhill from the knoll where the parking area was situated, well-defined, and wide enough to walk two abreast comfortably. They were able to stay on it for about a quarter of a mile before leaving, turning off to head directly for the fence which was still several hundred yards distant.

At this point Hollis began to discover what the terrain was really like. The park was old and the timber had never been harvested so the underbrush in some places was almost impenetrable. The hidden gullies, the rocky nature of the ground, and the steep slope of the hills added further to their difficulties. Traversing the distance between the trail and the fence would have been difficult in daylight. At night it was almost impossible. Over a half an hour passed before they reached the fence.

While pausing to regain his breath, Hollis listened carefully for several minutes before saying softly, "No sign of any lookouts."

"Can't really tell." Crowley responded, "But, we'll have to chance it. At the rate we're going, we won't make the site much before sun up. We need to get there before it gets light, and in position to move in just about day-break."

After leaning their weapons against the fence, they unpacked the gear Crowley had brought for scaling it. Together, they spread a sheet of heavy rubber-impregnated nylon over the top of the fence effectively covering both the razor wire and the electric cable.

"Make sure it completely covers the top part of the fence," Crowley whispered. "If they have any alarm systems, that's probably where they are."

With the nylon sheet in place, Crowley tossed the top end of a short rope ladder over the fence. The two side ropes were fastened to an insulated three-prong grapnel hook which caught in the fence on the far side.

"Go ahead," Crowley said, once the hook was firmly anchored. "I'll hold the side ropes on this side."

With Crowley holding the bottom of the ladder to keep his weight on the rope rungs from collapsing the sides against his feet, Hollis quickly made the journey over the fence. Crowley then tossed him the weapons and other equipment.

"If you'll stick the ends of the side ropes through, I'll hold them while you climb," Hollis said.

Crowley bent down and pushed the two ropes through the fence at the bottom while Hollis took hold and pulled them taut. Crowley then climbed over the fence and dropped to the ground beside Hollis.

In the faint cones of their penlights—all the illumination they dared use—neither of them noticed the small bare wire that their nylon sheet had pushed into contact with the fence.

49

Main House, Montague Retreat, California
0050 Saturday, December 24, 1983—Day Sixteen

Brovikov had no doubt who the intruders were, nor did he doubt they would be captured. It meant only one thing to him, and he had already waited too long.

He left the study and headed for the left wing of the house. This area was intended for house guests and could be closed off when not occupied. Just inside the entrance to the wing a guard was posted. "You may take a break," Brovikov said. He pointed to the locked door behind him. "I'll assume responsibility for the prisoner until further notice."

The guard acknowledged with a salute and departed toward the other end of the hall. Brovikov turned the key in the door, silently crossed the sitting room to the bedroom door and stopped, smiling in anticipation. This time he would have what he had been waiting for since he had first seen her at Dumfries.

She'd struggle, but that would make it just that much more enjoyable. He was violating his orders to do nothing to her until it was confirmed that Hollis was either dead or captured, but with the guard gone, no one would find out. Very shortly no one would care anyway. He turned the knob on the bedroom door and pushed gently. The door moved only about an inch and stopped. Brovikov cursed under his breath. What was holding it?

Stealth gave way to determination. He pushed harder and after a moment his efforts were rewarded with a very loud crash.

Maggie had not slept soundly since she had been taken to the retreat. Brovikov had visited her at least once a day to look lasciviously at her while he assured her that Hollis would soon be dead and then she would belong to him.

He had pointed out to her the guard on duty in the hall outside her room as well as the one stationed outside her windows to make it amply clear that escape was impossible.

She knew it would be only a matter of time until he would make good his threat, and she knew there would be no way she could stop him. All she could do was block the door so that if he did try to enter her bedroom he would have to wake her up in the process.

Maggie was out of bed and had the light turned on before Brovikov had the door open far enough to enter the room. By the time he was inside she was standing on the far side of the bed, fully clothed with a heavy glass ash tray in her hand.

Brovikov beamed with pleasure. "Ah! You intend to struggle. So much the better!"

"I didn't know scumbags enjoyed things like that." Maggie began edging closer to a window.

Brovikov's complexion reddened. His pig-like eyes glistened in anticipation as he moved to block her. "We'll see."

Maggie raised the ash tray and turned toward the window. "Back off pig," she warned, through clenched teeth. "Unless you want everyone to know what you're up to. One more step and I follow this ash tray through that window."

For a moment Brovikov contemplated going ahead anyway. This witch should already have been tamed. Yet she was calling his bluff. But how could she possibly know what his orders were? She couldn't. But it made no difference. He could not afford the disturbance she would create.

He managed a cruel smile. "I can wait. I'll only enjoy it more later. I came to tell you that your ex-husband will be captured within the hour. If you'd care to attend his execution, I can make the necessary arrangements."

"Get lost, you psychopath," Maggie spat back, her eyes flashing.

He made a convulsive move toward her. As Maggie turned to heave the ash tray through the window Brovikov regained control of his rage.

He had been denied the position of Department Head of the Fifth Chief Directorate which handled suppression of ideological dissidence, and shunted to the so-called Executive Branch for *mokrie dela* duties because the stupid doctors had 'wrongly' determined his 'sexual proclivities indicated psychopathic tendencies' which made him unfit for that level of responsibility. Since then he had not been given the intelligence assignments he wanted, but only the 'wet jobs' which should have been given to underlings well below his level of intellect and experience. He would show them how wrong they had been. He would not let this bitch spoil the success that was so close at hand.

"Have you ever thought about someone fucking you as you die?" he asked. His face fiery red, his voice barely under control, he pushed the words out at her through gritted teeth. "When I return that's what going to happen. I will slit your belly open and you will die with my cock inside you."

He turned and stalked out of the room.

50

Montague Retreat, California
0105 Saturday, December 24, 1983—Day Sixteen

Once both Hollis and Crowley were inside the fence they removed the nylon sheet, repacked it, and slung their back packs and bandoleers back over their shoulders.

"I've been thinking about the level of security at this place," Crowley said, as they started forward again. "It's possible there could be sensors or trip wires around. It might be better if we separate until we get to the objective. If one of us does get caught there'll still be a chance the other could get through."

"I think you're right," Hollis answered. "I'll go first. If they're expecting anyone, it's me. If they do catch me, they may drop their guard enough so that you can finish the job by yourself."

Crowley nodded. "You know how to get there. If you approach from the northeast you can stay under cover of the brush until you're almost to the large outcropping which overlooks the ravine leading to the cave. We should meet there."

"All right. Give me a ten-minute start. When I get there, I'll give you a call on the walkie-talkie. If you don't hear from me by 0530, you can assume I ran into trouble. If that happens, you do what you think is best. Okay?"

"Agreed. Good luck, and be careful. I don't want to have to take that damned thing out by myself."

Inside the fence Hollis found the going a little easier. He anticipated this because the route to his destination would take him close to the main house. There, the rocky ravines and steep slopes gave way to the rolling, timber-covered hills he had seen during the visit that now seemed an eternity ago.

When Brovikov returned to the study, he was dismayed to find Maxsimov there. This was not expected. He waited nervously while the Colonel used the intercom to call Sergei.

"Progress, Comrade Major?" Maxsimov asked.

"Our infra-red monitors have isolated one intruder at grid co-ordinates G-8 in sector eighteen, Comrade. The squad leader has been notified and is deploying to intercept. I will inform you of his success as soon as he reports."

"Very good, Comrade," Maxsimov responded. The news was good and the tension Brovikov felt began to abate.

"After the intruder is captured," Maxsimov continued, "he is to be brought here. You will continue the surveillance, and instruct the squad leaders to hold their perimeter until they receive further orders. There may be others."

Having advanced close to a quarter of a mile in less than fifteen minutes, Hollis was making better progress than he anticipated. He was now optimistic he could reach the rendezvous well before dawn.

His optimism evaporated quickly. Bright light exploded all around him.

Spotlights, three of them, zeroed in on him. A voice from behind one of them spoke. "Slowly drop your weapons and place your hands on top of your head. You are surrounded. If you try to run, you will be shot."

Hollis' instinctive reaction was to turn surprise in his favor by doing the unexpected. There were rocks and trees close enough to provide shelter if a lunging dive would allow him to successfully avoid the inevitable fusillade of bullets.

But beyond the improbability that he could reach cover unscathed, the white lights aimed directly in his face had destroyed his night vision. Even if he reached cover, he would effectively be a blind man fighting sighted adversaries. Reluctantly, he dropped his weapons and slowly placed his hands on the top of his head.

Four men approached him. All wore similar fatigue-type camouflage uniforms, but with no insignia or other markings. Three were armed with AK-47's equipped with sniper scopes. They kept them pointed at his head.

The fourth man stepped up and searched Hollis then turned and issued orders in Russian to someone outside the circle of light.

After a fifteen-minute walk, Hollis was pushed roughly into an open jeep with a driver and two armed guards. The driver bumped over a rough trail for some distance until he reached the entry road. Once on it, he drove quickly to the main house.

With the two guards flanking him, their weapons at the ready, Hollis was ushered through the front door and into the study.

The driver came to attention and saluted. "Comrade Colonel, this is the intruder. So far as we know, he was alone." He deposited Hollis' weapons and other equipment on the floor. "This is what he brought with him."

Maxsimov was sitting behind the same desk where Paul had sat during Hollis' visit. Brovikov stood behind him, holding a Walther pistol trained at Hollis' chest.

"Good work, Corporal," Maxsimov said. "Return to your squad, and notify the guards at the door that I have taken charge of the prisoner. Also tell Sergeant Rubinsky that his attention to orders will be well rewarded."

Maxsimov grinned at Hollis. "Well, well! I have been waiting impatiently to meet the one who came so close to exposing Peregrine despite the efforts of some of our best professionals."

Hollis just stared at him, still numbed by the turn of events.

"I see you brought some interesting toys along," Maxsimov said. "You didn't really think you could destroy Peregrine with those, did you?"

When Hollis did not respond, Maxsimov went on. "I'm surprised you'd try something like this all by yourself. Surely you must have known how hopeless it would be. Couldn't you get any of your old friends in Washington to buy your farfetched story?"

It was clear to Hollis that Maxsimov was attempting to get him to reveal whether he had come alone. He decided to play along. Maybe he could buy Crowley some time. "Why don't you check with Viktor? I assume he knows more about what's going on in Washington than I do. Hasn't he filled you in yet?"

"He knows," Brovikov intervened with a sneer. "He tipped us off about Clarke so we could arrange to have him eliminated." He watched for a reaction from Hollis.

"I was a little surprised he did that," Hollis said conversationally. "Other than using you, it's probably the only real mistake he's made."

"We have made no mistakes." Brovikov was now frowning. "It was necessary to remove him to prevent Walters from corroborating your story."

"Having your KGB goons kill Clarke while he was in FBI custody was better corroboration than anything he could have told them. I'm surprised Viktor didn't recognize that."

"He did. But the delay it'll cause Walters in finding out what you wanted him to know, assuming he decides to try, is more important than indirect confirmation of your story," Brovikov snorted. "After tomorrow it'll make no difference who knows what. Maskirovka will have succeeded and your so-called capitalist democracy will be no more." Suddenly becoming aware that Maxsimov was glaring at him, Brovikov shut up.

"Enough of this shit," Maxsimov ordered harshly. "You did not come alone. The walkie-talkie you brought with you confirms that. Where is Crowley?"

Hollis made no move to answer. After a long moment Maxsimov nodded to Brovikov.

A look of eager anticipation lit Brovikov's features. "You want to do it the hard way? Fine. We'll see how much pain you will allow your ex-wife to suffer before you tell us what we want to know."

Hollis' stomach turned to ice. "How do I know that you even have her?"

"Oh you'll know, all right," Brovikov replied, his voice silky. "We're going to bring her in here so you can watch."

Hollis stared hard at Brovikov. If he could find a way to make them continue to believe he was alone, Crowley might have a chance.

Finally, when Brovikov reached for the intercom, he said, "All right! I'll tell you."

He decided to stay as close to the truth as he could in order to sound convincing. "After talking to Walters, I wasn't sure whether he would help or not. I gave him Clarke's name so he could get the details he would need if help were authorized. Then Crowley and I headed here. We were just north of San Francisco when we heard on the car radio that Clarke had been killed. I let Crowley out at Santa Rosa so that he could call Walters and give him the detail that Clarke would have given him had he not been killed. Crowley, of course, knows all about Peregrine, including the rocket-booster command modules, and the transmitter, as well as its location. He was going to attempt to get Walters to organize a strike force to take out the transmitter."

"Assuming you are telling the truth," Maxsimov said. "It should make no difference. Such a mission could not be mounted without Viktor's knowledge. If it were, he could either abort or delay it."

Maxsimov paused, thought for a few moments. "But your explanation sounds quite plausible. I'll check with Viktor."

Maxsimov was reaching for the telephone when the intercom buzzed.

Sergei's voice boomed out through the speaker: "Comrade, a second intruder is now in custody. He is being brought in."

A short time later a grim-faced Crowley was ushered into the room. He met Hollis' sad gaze with a shrug and a sorrowful shake of his head.

Maxsimov rose and looked pointedly at Brovikov. "I must return to the transmitter. Execute the two prisoners immediately."

51

The White House, Washington, DC
0735 Saturday, December 24, 1983—Day Sixteen

The president had just finished breakfast when he got word that Mike Deaver needed to see him right away. Reagan sent word back that he was on the way to the Oval Office and Deaver should meet him there, along with Baker, Meese and McFarlane.

Five minutes later the president was seated at his desk when the others entered.

Deaver came in last, looking very agitated. He skipped the usual pleasantries and cut right to the chase: "Sir, Soviet ambassador Dobrynin is on his way over. He asked permission to deliver a message to you personally at eight o'clock sharp."

"That's odd," Reagan observed. "What do you think's on his mind?"

"I don't know, Deaver replied. "I took the call. He gave me no indication. He just said it was extremely important that he deliver the message directly to you."

"This doesn't sound good." Baker volunteered. "Do you think it's possible it was triggered by your news release and the Q and A?" He looked at Deaver.

"It could be," Deaver ventured, drawing a hard look from Reagan. "The press reaction was a little more violent than I anticipated. When we said we would stand by our commitments to our European allies, all hell broke loose when one of the reporters said he assumed that meant we would initiate a nuclear exchange with the Soviets to protect NATO even though we had not been attacked."

"So, what's new?" Meese asked. "That's been on the table for years."

"What's new," Reagan interjected, "is that up until now no one believed either side would be stupid enough to tempt the other. Now with everything that's going on they're not so sure. They're thinking maybe the Soviets are going to call our hand to see if we're bluffing."

"Yeah. And a lot of them are suddenly afraid we're not." Baker added.

"Mr. President," Deaver said, his voice rising slightly. "I don't think that news release or any other for that matter is going to hack it. The reporters have seen all the comings and goings of the last several days, and they strongly suspect something's going on they haven't been told about. And when they get wind of Dobrynin's visit they're going to know something's up. I think the only way to put this to rest is for you to call a televised news conference during prime time tonight. I'm sure all the networks will jump at the opportunity to cover it."

Reagan looked at his watch. "It's about time for our guest. Let's see what this is all about, and we'll decide on the conference after he leaves."

"Well, whatever the purpose is," Baker said, "I recommend you make it crystal clear to him before he leaves that we intend to take whatever action is necessary to protect ourselves."

"Is there any precedent for something like this?" Meese asked. "Maybe Dobrynin wants to defect?"

Baker and Deaver laughed nervously. McFarlane managed a smile.

Reagan gave his head that characteristic little shake. "Unfortunately there is a precedent," he reminded them. "The Japanese ambassador delivered a surprise message to FDR at eight o'clock on a Sunday morning, in December 1941, ten minutes after the Japanese attacked Pearl Harbor. The message was a declaration of war."

The others looked stunned. Reagan grinned. He didn't really think anything that serious was in the offing, but the similarity with the Pearl Harbor incident was unnerving.

The Soviet ambassador, impeccably dressed and looking no more somber than usual, was ushered into the oval office.

The Soviet ambassador bowed stiffly. "Good morning, Mr. President." He glanced at the others and acknowledged their presence with a barely audible "Gentlemen."

"What can we do for you, Mr. ambassador," Reagan asked, smiling coldly.

Dobrynin cleared his throat. He looked pale and frightened. "Mr. President, my instructions are quite specific. I must deliver this sealed message into your hands personally at eight o'clock this morning."

Dobrynin checked his watch, then opened the heavily constructed pouch bearing the Soviet diplomatic seal, breaking it in the process. He then extracted the envelope it contained, and handed it to the president.

"Once it is in your hands, I am forbidden from discussing any matter with you, or staying while you attend the message. With your permission, I will excuse myself and depart."

Open-mouthed with astonishment, the president glanced down at the envelope, then up at the ambassador.

Dobrynin bowed again and hurried out the door.

The president looked at the others only to see his own feelings mirrored in their faces. After a pause precipitated by an undefined but overwhelming sense of dread, he opened the envelope. As he read it, the color drained from his face.

"By God, Cap was right!" he exploded. "The bastards have given us an ultimatum!"

"An ultimatum?" Baker asked as though he had never heard the word before.

"Yes. This says that our ICBMs and our SLBMs have been neutralized, and we have twelve hours to either surrender and allow the country to be disarmed and occupied, or they will launch a nuclear strike to destroy our military capability."

III

52

Situation Room, The White House, Washington, DC
0846 Saturday, December 24, 1983—Day Sixteen

The District of Columbia and most of its surrounding suburbs could be destroyed by a nuclear air blast of relatively small yield. It is a foregone conclusion that if the attempt were made it would be successful. Unlike Moscow, Washington has no ballistic missile defense even though one is permitted under the 1972 ABM Treaty.

The Situation Room under the White House is a small replica of the larger one beneath the Pentagon. Although the similarity continues, it is less like the more elaborate one in the NORAD Cheyenne Mountain Complex, with its seventeen-by-seventeen-foot display screens. It is the president's command post; the point from which the Commander-in-Chief would direct a war or order the launching of a nuclear strike. It houses all of the communications links and safe-guards to assure that he will have access to current information and the ability to issue orders to meet whatever emergency may exist.

Directly over the bank of various colored telephones, arrayed in front of where the president normally sits, is a large video screen. It, as well as the white phone beneath it, labeled "SECURE," are among the most important communications links there. They provide the president with a closed circuit, on-line link and backup to the National Military Command Center, NMCC, in the Pentagon. Operated by the Joint Chiefs of Staff, it is the hub for both routine and emergency military communications. It is *also the principal message-distribution center through which the president would issue orders to initiate a nuclear strike on the Soviet Union.*

If the capital were destroyed, the command post and the president, theoretically, would survive since the Situation Room is hardened and built far enough below ground to be impregnable to anything less than a ground zero nuclear detonation. But no one really knows whether it would, and even if the president did survive, communications with the outside would most likely be lost.

Various sources

When McFarlane finished reading the ultimatum to the hastily assembled situation room staff, all hell broke loose as everyone tried to talk at once.

Suddenly, one voice rose above the others: "Jesus Christ, does that mean we're at war?"

McFarlane waited for the bedlam to ease. "Whatever it means, we've got a job to do, and we can't do it running our mouths, so settle down."

When he was sure he had everyone's attention, he continued: "I want it understood right now that under no circumstance is even a hint of what I read to you to go to anyone outside this room. Is that clear"?

A hushed, expectant silence fell as the president, flanked by Baker, Meese and Deaver entered the room. A few minutes later, Secretary of Defense Weinberger and Secretary of State Shultz arrived. Behind them, out of breath and hurrying to catch up, came DCI William Casey.

As each man entered the room, McFarlane handed him a copy of the ultimatum.

Shultz finished reading it first. His face flushed an angry red. "I don't believe it," he muttered.

"God dammit!" Weinberger shouted. "They're talking about nuclear war! Has Vessey been notified? Where's Bush?"

"The president has ordered the vice president to NORAD headquarters," McFarlane replied. "His ETA is 1115 hours, local. He's in the net, and if communications between here and NORAD are lost, he'll take command. He also has the option of shifting to Looking Glass if a nuclear strike appears imminent. General Vessey, along with the joint chiefs, has taken charge at the National Military Command Center, and has just informed us that DEFCON 1 has been set. Acknowledgments have been received, and missiles have been placed at standby launch awaiting SIOP designation."

Having listened to the exchange in silence, Casey took Weinberger aside, where no one would overhear what he said. After a brief exchange of words, he approached Reagan. "Mr. President, could I see you in private for a moment?"

The president nodded, and led the way to a small room set aside for his use only. "What is it, Bill?"

"Mr. President, we still don't know whether the Soviets are relying on the satellites or, as Hollis suggests, what they call Peregrine to neutralize our missiles, or, for that matter, whether it's all simply an elaborate masquerade. Assuming they are relying on Peregrine, there's a chance that Walters may succeed in deactivating it, but we won't know for several hours. Cap agrees that until we find out one way or the other, we should play it precisely as the mole would expect us to."

"I'm not sure I follow."

"As part of their ultimatum, the Soviets say that any attempt to bring down the satellites will be construed as an act of hostility, and they will immediately terminate the grace period and launch a nuclear strike. If Peregrine, rather than the satellites, is the means by which they can destroy our missiles, then we must assume they will do the same thing if they believe it to be in danger. Accordingly, we cannot let the mole know that we are even aware of its existence until it is either destroyed or rendered inoperative. Until then, we should act as though we believe the satellites are the only basis for their claimed ability to neutralize our missiles."

"I understand," Reagan responded. "If Cap is satisfied, that's what we'll do."

Back in the situation room, the president was joined at a small conference table by his national security adviser, those members of the National Security Council who were present, and his senior advisers.

"Gentlemen, we've got some decisions to make." He paused for a moment as though taking stock of the situation. "Even though we now know their objective, we don't know precisely where it leaves us. We don't know whether they can make good on their threat—whether they really have the means to destroy our missiles. Also, we don't know what the position of our NATO partners will be if we decide either to ignore the ultimatum, or go the other way and launch our own strike. We need answers, and we need them right now."

He addressed the secretary of state first: "George, get an eyes-only message to all NATO heads of state apprising them of the situation, and telling them we haven't yet reached a decision on what our response will be, but it's not likely we'll agree to its terms."

He turned next to his secretary of defense. "Cap, I need the judgment of your people on what our best response would be, as well as the timing, if we decide not to accept the ultimatum. I guess the alternatives include everything from a full-scale preemptive strike timed to take place immediately after the satellites are destroyed, to simply waiting for the grace period to expire to see what happens."

Deaver broke in. "Mr. President, I hate to bring this up at this point, but the press room is a goddamned mad-house. All the heavyweights from the networks are there and they know something's going on. They know who's here now, who's at the Pentagon, and they know Dobrynin was here earlier, and rumors are beginning to spread. I'm afraid if we don't tell them something soon they'll take Larry Speakes hostage."

"Well, why don't you run right down and tell them what's happening," Meese snapped. "And start a real panic."

As Deaver glared at Meese, Reagan intervened. "Hold on, you two. At some point, we may have to tell them something to the effect that the Soviets have made a proposal for ending the face-off, and we have taken it under advisement, but I don't think we should tell them anything yet. Why don't you go up and assure them that if something develops that they should know about, we'll call a press conference."

Deaver stood up. "What about the congressional leaders?" he asked.

"I think we should wait until we decide what to tell the press," Reagan replyed.

As Shultz and Weinberger moved to carry out their assignments, the president turned to the large video screen which connected the Situation Room to the Joint Chiefs in the NMCC at the Pentagon. "General, what's the latest?"

The screen showed a wide-angle panoramic view of the Command Center, where General Vessey could be seen talking to the Air Force chief of staff. As Vessey turned in response to the question, a staff member adjusted the camera so that it panned on the general.

"It's now clear that the military sea lift is destined for the US," he replied. "We estimate the vessels already at sea are carrying a minimum of ten reinforced divisions with support equipment. There are approximately one hundred additional vessels in port being loaded with troops and support equipment, which we estimate will sortie within thirty-six hours. None are equipped for amphibious operations, so we assume they're carrying occupation rather than assault troops.

"Their military transport aircraft that we've been watching, including those in Cuba, are actively engaged in preparations to airlift troops. Also, Mr. President, their entire submarine fleet is now at sea. Their Boomers appear to be dispersing to pre-designated launch areas. We're moving our Fast Boats to make sure we keep them covered. And finally, their land forces facing NATO, as well as their air defenses, are fully deployed and have been put on an immediate alert basis."

"What about the satellites?" Reagan asked.

"The shielding was jettisoned shortly after eight this morning, and Satellite Imagery was able to get some fairly detailed pictures which tend to confirm our assessment that they are KKV platforms," Vessey replied. "I think we have to assume they are real."

"Are we now in position to destroy them?"

"All of the assets are in place, Mr. President, but I'm not sanguine about the outcome. The odds against our eliminating all twelve satellites in one strike are very high."

"How many do you think can be taken out at one time, General?"

"Sir, the three groups of F-15's which are fitted out to launch the MVs are armed and manned, and have been repositioned for a maximum strike. Even so, only eight of the satellites will be in their range at any given time. Accordingly, we have positioned SSBNs at strategic locations where they can attempt to bring down the other four with low-level proximity nuclear detonations.

"Depending on when the detonations take place, the disruption which the electromagnetic pulse and debris produced by the nuclear detonations will cause with respect to our unhardened Keyhole and Com/NavSats, may be minimal or it may be catastrophic. Accordingly, an attempt to eliminate the satellites by this method could seriously impair our conventional offensive and defensive capabilities. And more important, if the Soviets do have the capability of destroying our SLBMs in the boost phase, we can't guarantee they will even reach the satellites."

"Thank you, General," Reagan responded. "I hope we don't have to resort to their use, but we may not have a choice. Please be prepared to launch a simultaneous strike on the satellites with the least advance notice possible."

The president turned to Shultz. "George, does your Soviet desk think they will back off if we destroy the satellites."

Before Shultz could answer, Deaver entered the room and caught the president's eye. When Reagan nodded, he headed toward the conference room. The president and Meese followed.

The door closed behind them. "Senator Nunn is holding, Mr. President. He asked to speak with you personally."

"Can't you put him off?"

"Not without aggravating the situation," Deaver responded. "Rumors are all over Washington that all hell's about to break loose. The media is in a panic. The speaker as well as the Senate majority and minority Leaders called to see what's going on. I was able to put them off, but Nunn insisted that he speak with you."

Remembering that without Nunn's help his defense budget would never have been passed by Congress, Reagan said, "All right. Have it piped in here."

When the phone on the table rang, Reagan picked it up.

"Hello, Sam." His voice reflected an air of levity he did not feel. "I have you on the squawk box because Mike and Ed are with me."

"Mr. President, I'll get right to the point. I've had extensive briefings on the Soviet military moves; and I, and many others on the Hill, are quite concerned about this building crisis. It appears to be escalating into an open conflict, particularly since the Soviet ambassador called on you this morning. I have not been able to contact anyone at the Pentagon, and there are some pretty nasty rumors going around. CNN and the networks are quoting various sources at the UN and elsewhere that we may be close to an all-out nuclear exchange with the Soviets. I think Congress is entitled to know what the hell's going on."

"I understand, Sam, but I don't think I should get into specifics right now…"

Senator Nunn fairly exploded. Meese and Deaver both jumped at the sudden increase in volume over the speaker-phone.

"Goddamn it, Mr. President, and pardon my language, but that is simply not acceptable. If this country is on the verge of some kind of catastrophic collision course with the Soviet Union and you are hiding that fact from the other branches of the government and the American people—"

Reagan interrupted: "Sam, there is nothing going on at the moment that I can tell you about, and I don't want to make some vague, ambiguous statement that will simply feed the rumor mill."

"Mr. President, anything you tell me in confidence is not going to feed any rumor mill and you know that."

"Yes, of course, Sam, but..."

"You do understand, Mr. President, that this country cannot go to war without the approval of Congress?"

"Yes, Sam, of course I do," Reagan answered. The president felt suddenly angry. He understood Nunn's position, but he resented the pressure from him, coming on top of everything else he was trying to cope with. "Sam," he replied, as coolly as he could, "I am commander-in-chief, I must carry out my responsibilities as I see them. As soon as I feel free to do so, I'll invite you to the White House for a personal briefing, but right now is not the time."

Nunn was not mollified. "I hope we don't have reason to regret this, Mr. President," he said, a sharp edge of pugnacity in his tone.

"So do I, Sam. So do I."

Reagan broke the connection and headed back into the Situation Room. He touched his forehead and was shocked to discover it was soaked in perspiration.

"George," he said, sitting back down and mopping his brow hastily with a handkerchief. "You were going to tell me what your Soviet desk thought."

Shultz nodded somberly. "They're of the opinion that even if we succeeded in destroying the satellites, the Soviets may have gone too far to turn back unless we can offer some sort of major compromise that would allow them to gracefully demobilize without losing face—maybe something such as unilaterally removing the Pershing IIs and cruise missiles from Western Europe. Without something like that, they don't believe we can count on them to back down as Khrushchev did."

"God-damn it!" Weinberger almost shouted. "I don't think we should submit to blackmail. They started this, not us."

Before Shultz could reply, Reagan intervened, "Any reading yet on where our NATO allies stand?"

The long work days and building tension had begun to take their toll on the secretary of state. His eyes were puffy and his face was the color of paste. "Only an indication, Mr. President." He paused until it was obvious the president was growing impatient. "We contacted our ambassador to each NATO country, gave him the message with instructions to deliver it personally to the head of government and relay the response back to us. We do not have all responses yet, but what we do have is not all positive. The UK and Germany have indicated unequivocally they will honor their treaty obligations, but that may not be the entire answer.

"All of the NATO countries received an official visit from their Soviet ambassador, apparently timed to coincide with the delivery of the ultimatum here. In each case a message was delivered assuring the head of government that the crisis which has developed was precipitated by the US, and does not involve NATO. He also assured them that the Soviet government was making every attempt to work out an honorable solution, but so far had not been successful.

"As a result, at least some NATO members, those which do not as yet have Pershings or cruise missiles, have questioned whether there would be an obligation to assist the United States in a matter strictly between it and the USSR, particularly if it had been precipitated by the US, and doesn't involve the European land mass. There's a clear indication that if we're the first to launch a strike against the Soviets, nuclear or conventional, some members—Spain, for example—would contend that NATO would be under no obligation to assist the United States.

"These are initial off-the-record reactions, not official responses. But they're disturbing. The bottom line is that we cannot take NATO assistance for granted."

"For Christ's sake!" Weinberger said. "I can't believe it. If we weren't guaranteeing their freedom, they'd already be part of the Soviet Union. This is nothing more than a classic case of divide and conquer."

The president broke in. "George, are you telling me that both Prime Minister Thatcher and Chancellor Kohl are questioning whether they should support us?"

"Not precisely, Mr. President." Shultz responded. "I talked to both of them briefly, and judging from the conversation, their reaction of disbelief was no different from that which we initially felt. Their concern was whether there was not some acceptable action we could still take that would defuse the situation."

The president took a deep breath. Again, he understood. It was natural in any crisis to expect friends to desert or turn against you. Still, it galled him that such stalwart allies should second-guess the US at such a time.

"Get back in touch with both of them," he said. "It's crucial they understand exactly what the situation is. Make it clear that our only choice is between a military response or capitulation, and that we did not precipitate the crisis. If UK and Germany understand and accept our position the others will probably follow."

Reagan turned to Weinberger. "Cap, have your people come up with any ideas on how we can determine whether they really can destroy our missiles, or whether they're bluffing?"

"General Shields is our most qualified person in this area," Weinberger replied. "I talked with him moments ago, and he suggested that if we want to find out whether the satellites really are weapons platforms, we should fire a test missile. To make the test valid, it should be armed but aimed somewhere where the detonation would not harm anyone—probably the Barents Sea. He suggests we inform the Soviets of our intention before launch, so they'll understand the purpose. If they have the capability they say they do, they should welcome the opportunity to demonstrate it. If that were to lead us to capitulate, as one might expect, the need for them to launch the nuclear strike they have threatened might then be avoided."

"What if they are bluffing about their ability to destroy it?" President Reagan asked.

Secretary of Defense Weinberger shook his head. He looked at Shultz, then at the president. None of them were young men. And these last few days were aging them fast, especially Shultz and himself. Shultz looked especially haggard, and Weinberger felt a combination of fatigue and anxiety so potent that it was all he could do to sit still and retain his composure.

The president seemed to be holding up the best. It was good thing that he was, Weinberger reflected, because no man should ever be expected to carry the burden of responsibility that now rested so heavily on this one man's shoulders.

"Well, we'll simply have to hope that by calling their bluff, they will not opt to destroy civilization."

53

Maggie's Room, Montague Estate, California
0655 Saturday, December 24, 1983—Day Sixteen

Maggie had watched Brovikov's unexpected departure with disbelief. She had understood from the beginning that he was psychopathic, but not a necrophiliac. She knew he would keep his promise when he returned, and nothing she could do would stop him. The terror that threatened to take control of her senses was only countered by her anxiety over Jeff. Brovikov had taunted her before about what he would do when Jeff was captured, but this time there had been a difference. Without understanding how or why, she sensed that Jeff needed help badly.

She knew from hours of trying that there was no way to escape. Even though she was on the ground level and there were no bars on the windows, they offered no way out. The area outside her room was well lighted at night, and she had seen at least two guards on duty every time she looked out. The door which led from her suite to the hall was even less promising. Not only was it kept locked, a guard was posted outside it, as well. Maggie first thought about trying to ambush someone as they came to bring her food, but after watching and listening every time someone came in, she abandoned the idea. The opening of the door always started and ended the same way. The guard stationed outside unlocked it and stayed well back while the door was opened and closed by the visitor as he came in. And the same routine was followed as the visitor went out. Once the windows and the door were eliminated, the possibilities were exhausted. There was no other way out.

In the face of such a hopeless situation Maggie feared that she would not be able to hold onto her composure much longer. She had to do something, anything. But what?

Suddenly the panic building inside her gave way to a faint glimmer of desperately needed hope. A recollection, not immediately registered because of the fear and revulsion she was still feeling as Brovikov stormed out of the room, floated to the surface of her thoughts.

Brovikov's anger had been so great, she recalled, that he had almost lost his self-control. Could it have made him forget?

It had to be, now that she thought about it.

Always before when Brovikov left he had followed the same routine. He would tap on the door so the guard would know he was ready to depart. This time, however, he had merely stormed out of the room and slammed the door behind him.

And she could not remember hearing the key turn in the lock. Had he relieved the guard? Considering what he had intended, it made sense.

Maggie stepped slowly to the door. She put her ear against the center panel and listened for a long time. She heard nothing. With her heart in her throat, she grasped the doorknob and twisted it slightly.

It moved!

She gasped, as much from surprise and joy.

She took her hands off the doorknob and stepped back. Brovikov might have reposted the guard. She would have to be prepared to surprise and disable anyone if she succeeded in getting out, but she had no weapon.

She looked around the sitting room and spotted the heavy silver candlestick on the table. She hefted it, and after a test swing to see whether she could handle it, she stepped back to the door, squeezing the weapon in her right fist.

Stealth would probably offer a better chance of surprise than speed, she decided. The door opened inward, so opening it wouldn't necessarily attract the attention of someone in the hall if the lights in the room were turned off.

Holding her breath, she clicked the light switch off. It made no sound. She sighed with relief and reached again for the doorknob.

She twisted the knob slowly until it stopped, then slowly, slowly, pulled the door inward. She felt almost giddy from the rush of adrenaline into her veins.

Using the door like a shield, Maggie stayed behind it as she opened it until she was able to see that there no one outside the doorway. She paused and listened. She did not think straining improved one's hearing, but she strained anyway.

She heard nothing.

With courage born of desperation, she tip-toed through the doorway. She looked cautiously in both directions, gripping the candlestick so hard that it began to slip in her now sweaty palm.

She was in a long hall with doors opening to rooms on both sides and at each end. She had no idea which door would lead her to the main part of the house.

From her previous visit with Jeff, she vaguely remembered the building was shaped like a large block "U", and that she was in one of the two sides generally used as guest quarters. The bottom of the "U" housed the family living quarters, and that was where the main entrance was located. If Brovikov was in the house, she felt sure that was where he'd be.

But which way was it?

She looked at all the doors, trying to decide, trying to stay calm. She licked her lips and swallowed to relieve the growing tightness in her throat.

The first door on the right, she decided, because it was already open.

She headed toward the door, then froze. She could hear something from other side. Heart thumping, she stood and listened. Finally she determined what it was: someone snoring.

She waited several moments, but the regularity of the heavy breathing interspersed with the staccato sound of the snores convinced her that whoever was in the room was sleeping soundly.

She inched her way forward. After a one-minute eternity, she reached the door and looked in. The room was a small kitchenette, which doubled as a pantry from which guests could be served in their rooms. Maggie recognized the sleeping occupant as one of the guards she had seen in the hall outside her room several times. She guessed the kitchenette was now being used for coffee breaks by the guards stationed at the house. No point going in there.

She glanced down the hall. She needed to pick a new door. She decided to try the one at the far end.

She reached the door, pulled it open and slipped through. She found herself in a small anteroom, facing the curtained widow panels beside an exterior door into the yard outside. She gasped involuntarily and pulled back, startled by the sudden view of a guard stationed just on the other side.

Terror then took over completely as she had realized the snoring behind her had stopped. If the guard in the kitchenette was awake her escape would be cut off.

She turned and saw him, his eyes still heavy with sleep, bracing himself against the doorjamb with both hands.

His sleepiness disappeared in an instant when he looked across the hall and saw Maggie standing there with a candlestick in her hand.

54

Study, Montague Estate, California
0705 Saturday December 24, 1983—Day Sixteen

When Brovikov received his instructions to execute Hollis and Crowley, his gimlet eyes gleamed in anticipation of the pleasure. As soon as Maxsimov left, he went to the intercom and called the security room in the servant's quarters and told Sergei to ignore the sounds of any shots he heard in the next few minutes. "We have a couple of executions to perform."

Brovikov looked back at his prisoners, searching for some reaction to their imminent death. But neither Hollis nor Crowley said anything or even changed their expressions.

Brovikov's anger increased. He turned to one of the guards. "Corporal, take the prisoners out through the main entrance. I'll follow you out. As soon as we are outside in the courtyard, you will force them to kneel and I will shoot each of them in the back of the head."

The corporal motioned with the AK-47 to the prisoners. "Place your hands on top of your head and face the door."

When Hollis and Crowley complied, the corporal and the other guard fell in behind them. "You will proceed side by side through the door and down the hall to the main entrance. We will be directly behind you. Do not make any sudden moves."

Hollis had no intention of committing suicide. But on the other hand, that issue would become moot very shortly if something were not done. He knew it was very unlikely that both Crowley and he could break free unhurt, but maybe one could if they moved together. Also, if they were going to try, it would have to be before they left the house. Once through the main entrance, there would be additional guards to contend with.

If they could take out both guards at the same time, one of them would have a chance against Brovikov. It would be a very slim chance because Brovikov would not be concerned with the safety of the guards if it became necessary to shoot. But one of them had to survive and find a way to destroy Peregrine.

Hollis was sure Crowley was thinking the same thoughts. He had to think of a way to let him know when he was going to make a move. This would be difficult. Any sudden motion would precipitate immediate retaliation, so he began to turn his head slowly toward Crowley, knowing someone would respond.

Brovikov, whose voice had now become overly harsh as the long hours of tension finally reached a head, growled at him, "Move your head anyway except back to the front and I will blow it off."

Assuming all eyes would be on him, Hollis was poised to pivot so that Crowley could key on his move.

Suddenly the door immediately behind and to his left slammed open, catching everyone in the hall by surprise.

Each responded differently. When Brovikov turned his head and saw Maggie, he knew immediately how she had escaped. He had forgot to lock the damned door. A screw-up like that could not be explained away. If he did not kill her now his future was gone.

It made no difference to him that Maggie was no more than four paces from him and was using both hands to point a very large handgun at his chest. Brovikov swung the Walther toward her. "You fucking slut!" he screamed.

Maggie had reluctantly learned to use a handgun only because Hollis had insisted on it. She had never learned to like them, but she was an able student.

As Brovikov turned, she dropped into a perfect Weaver stance and fired.

Her shot tore through Brovikov's chest well before his Walther was even in position. Brovikov watched in horror as the gun fell from fingers he no longer controlled. He crumpled slowly to the floor, eyes staring at his killer in disbelief.

Both guards had turned briefly toward the door, then their training asserted itself and they immediately turned back to their prisoners. The distraction was a mere split-second, but it was enough.

By sheer luck Hollis and Crowley were poised to move at the precise moment the door slammed open. They both turned, and with skill learned through long hours of practice, took the guards out with well-aimed blows to the back of the neck before their rifles could be raised.

Once the guards were out, Hollis quickly checked Brovikov to make sure he was dead. He looked up at Maggie. She had dropped the gun and was staring at the Russian's body, hands covering her mouth, horror-struck, on the verge of hysteria. Hollis gathered her in his arms, and pulled her head down to his shoulder. "How are my tenderly and tightly?"

Maggie's choked off her sobs and raised her head. A weak smile appeared. Hollis then took her by the shoulders and held her at arms length. "God! I'm glad to see you. I knew it would take a miracle to save us, but I never thought it would be delivered by an angel."

Crowley, who had moved to the side of the main entrance so he could see out through one of the small windows on each side of the door, ran back to them.

"Jeff! We're going to have company. The guards outside heard the shot."

Hollis handed Maggie the handgun she had just dropped. "Take this and go back in there," he told her. "You may have to do the same thing again."

Hollis nodded toward the door from which Maggie had emerged. She reluctantly took the pistol and retreated through the door.

After making sure the two unconscious guards were unarmed, Hollis and Crowley pulled them back through the same door. "Get their AK's and stay with Maggie. I'll take Brovikov into the study. When the guards come in they'll go there to find out what's happened, and we'll have 'em between us."

When both Maggie and Crowley were on the other side of the door, Hollis pulled it almost closed, picked up the Walther and hoisted Brovikov's body onto his shoulder.

In the study he had just managed to deposit Brovikov in the chair behind the desk in a position that would suggest he was sleeping when there was a loud knock.

He jumped behind the door and waited. He was sure the guards were aware of Brovikov's reputation for truculence when dealing with inferiors. There was a chance that if they got no answer they would merely resume their posts.

With more persistence than Hollis had expected, the guard in charge knocked again. "Comrade, we came to investigate the sound of a shot. Is anything wrong?"

Receiving no answer, he began to push the door open. There was a momentary pause, then a single guard came through the door and approached the desk. Hollis heard him gasp. He had noticed the blood on Brovikov's shirt.

Hollis knew there was another guard in the hall outside the door, and this put him in a vulnerable position unless Crowley acted quickly, but he had no choice.

The guard inside the room raised his weapon and began to back away from the desk. Before he could turn toward the door, Hollis shouted "Freeze!" hoping Crowley would hear him.

The guard's reaction time was good. He swung the weapon around and started firing. A burst from the Walther ended the encounter before the guard completed his turn. A fraction of a second later there was a similar blast from the hall.

After a moment Hollis heard Chuck's voice, "Jeff, you okay?"

"Yeah."

"Only two came in," Crowley continued, "so we're all right for the moment."

Hollis dashed back out into the hall. "If you can find a way to tie up our two prisoners I'll take a quick look around. Maggie, you saw some guards outside your room?"

"Yes. One at the door at the far end of the wing and at least two more outside by the swimming pool."

Hollis hurried over to the wing where Maggie had been held. The guard she had clobbered with the candlestick holder was still where she had left him. He made a mental note that he would have to be tied up and gagged before he woke up.

When he reached the outside door he heard voices and stopped. There were two guards on the other side of the door, talking to each other in Russian. He could not understand much of what they were saying, but their tone made it clear that they were alarmed about something. One turned on his walkie-talkie and began shouting into it.

Hollis hurried back to the unconscious guard, hoisted him onto his shoulder and carried him back to the study, where Crowley was just finishing tying up and gagging the other two.

"Here's the one Maggie took care of. There are three more outside that we'll have deal with. And before we head for Peregrine, we'll have to neutralize the security system."

"Do you know where the control center is?"

Hollis told Crowley of Brovikov's conversations with Sergei over the intercom. "I couldn't tell for certain, but it looked like he pressed the button to the servant's quarters. Since Sergei is also the caretaker, I'd have to guess that's where the security center is. It's a separate building about seventy-five yards north of the main house."

"What are we going to do about the guards?"

After a short discussion, they agreed on a plan and returned to the study. Hollis fished the CZ-75 out of his backpack and affixed the silencer. As Crowley picked up one of the M-16's and checked its action and ammo clip, Hollis turned to Maggie, who was not entirely over the after-effects of having killed Brovikov, and put his arms around her.

"I think it'd be best if you wait here. Chuck and I will be back in a few minutes. When we leave, lock the door and don't let anyone in, and don't answer the phone or the intercom." Hollis took her in his arms. Maggie's chin trembled slightly at the thought that she would again be alone.

"Be careful," she pleaded.

He kissed her tenderly on her forehead. "Don't worry," he whispered. "We'll be back."

Hollis waited until he heard Maggie slide the door lock into place, then he and Crowley started down the hall. He wanted more than ever before to simply go back and take Maggie in his arms and tell her how much he loved her. It would have to wait.

He and Crowley then split up. Hollis took the hall leading back to the wing and retraced his steps to the door where he had overheard the conversation between the guards, while Crowley went on to check the house's other wing.

Hollis looked at his watch. It was almost seven-thirty in the morning. They were far behind schedule and time was fast running out.

He checked his watch again when he arrived at the door where the guard was stationed. He still had a minute to wait to give Crowley time to get into place. He watched the guard through one of the small windows by the door. There was no particular pattern to his movements, but it was clear that he didn't stray far from the door.

Crowley should now be in place, Hollis thought. He waited until the guard turned his back and sauntered a few paces away. He opened the door as quickly and quietly as he could, hoping to capture the guard without alerting the other two. Before Hollis was close enough, the guard turned and saw him. There was no time for anything else, so Hollis dropped into a crouch and fired.

Hollis took the guard out before he could fire, but it had taken a second round to do it. With a superhuman effort, the guard overcame the effect of the first bullet and brought his AK-47 to bear before Hollis' second shot killed him.

Hollis was more disturbed than surprised. It was apparent they had orders to succeed or die. Since they were obviously crack assault troops, he and Crowley would have no choice from here on but to shoot first.

Only a moment after Hollis had squeezed off the second shot, his senses were shattered by automatic rifle fire directed at him from behind.

Hollis dove toward the wall. The shots were coming from within the "U" on the far side of the swimming pool. Fortunately he was partially protected by the corner of the house.

He looked up just in time to see Crowley take out the guard firing at him. This was his cue. He made a diving roll from behind the corner so that he would have a clear view of the whole area around the pool.

As he came up on his knees with the CZ-75 in position to fire, the last guard was raising his assault rifle toward Crowley. More by reflex than choice, the guard turned his attention toward Hollis as he rolled into view. Before either Hollis or the guard could shoot, Crowley shifted targets and took the guard out.

Hollis and Crowley quickly dragged the guards' bodies out of sight and retreated back inside.

"We've got to get out of here," Hollis said. "You brought the other stuff?"

Crowley nodded and grabbed the backpack and bandoleer he had left inside the door.

"It's wide open between here and the servant's quarters," Hollis said. "Let's borrow the uniforms from a couple of those guards."

Up on the second floor of the servants' quarters the operator of the security console called his boss on the intercom.

"Yes, Corporal. What is it?"

"I've heard gunfire at the house. And the guards down there do not seem to be at their posts. Should I send a detail to investigate?"

"I'll check with Brovikov," Sergei replied.

Sergei buzzed the intercom to the study several times without receiving an answer. That worried him. He went down the hall and joined the operator at the console. "There's no answer from Brovikov," he said.

Sergei knew that Brovikov's silence had a likely explanation. The bastard had been trying to stick his prick in that female prisoner ever since she got here, so that may be where he was. If so, he did not want to be the unlucky bastard who disturbed him.

"Wait a minute," Sergei said, looking at the bank of monitors. "There are the guards now. They're on the way over. Activate the door release, Corporal."

To Sergei, the explosion moments later was deafening. The noise and concussion seemed to be in the room with him. The door to the control room slammed open, admitting the two guards he had seen approaching from the house. In the confusion the blast had created inside him, he could not understand why their weapons were pointed at him. That would never do, but he could remedy that simply by sounding the alarm. Colonel Maxsimov would hear it and take care of the situation. Sergei didn't realize he had been shot until his nerveless fingers failed to reach the button, and he began to sink to the floor. The corporal, making the mistake of reaching for his weapon, followed him.

Hollis kicked the weapons away from the two downed figures, then bent down to determine if either of them was still breathing.

"I'll check the other room for survivors," Crowley said.

"I'll get Maggie," Hollis replied. "She'll be safer here."

As Hollis left, he looked at his watch. It was only eight in California, but that meant it was eleven in Washington. *We've got a long way to go,* he thought.

55

Situation Room, The White House, Washington, D. C.
1107 Saturday, December 24, 1983—Day Sixteen

Chief of Staff James Baker had listened silently to the heated debate over whether a test missile should be launched. Finally the president decided to authorize it.

Then, with the strain they were all under etched on his face, Baker finally spoke. "Mr. President, are you sure you want to take that risk? They may respond with a nuclear strike, and only then will we find out whether they're bluffing."

"We have no real choice. If they do respond with a strike, it may be that all we've done is move up by several hours what's going to happen anyway."

Before Reagan could continue, one of the staff members seated at a communications console suddenly jumped up. "My God," he cried, his voice on the edge of hysteria. "My family! I've got to get out of here!"

McFarlane nodded to the two Marine security guards at the main entrance. They moved quickly to take the staff member in custody and usher him out of the room. A nervous buzz of voices filled the room, then gradually faded. How many others were thinking the same bleak thoughts, McFarlane wondered.

The president, intently focused, continued on as if nothing had happened. "Here's my thinking. We have to at least try to find out whether they really have the ability to destroy our missiles. If they do destroy the test missile, it may tell us something we don't now know. If they're not bluffing, then there's no reason for them to respond with a full-scale nuclear strike. If they are, and they do launch a strike, they have to assume that we will respond in kind. I don't think they're bluffing, but I'm almost certain that either way they won't launch a strike. But as I said, we really have no choice. It's either this or capitulate. We have to find out."

The president walked over to the console which controlled the large viewing screen linking the NMCC at the Pentagon. After a word with the operator, General Vessey appeared on the screen. "General, how much advance notice do you need before an attempt can be made to take out the Soviet satellites?"

"Sir, the F-15's are in the air orbiting their launch area. The MV launch tracking data is being continuously fed into their on-board computers. The four SSBMs are on station, and their launch data is also being continuously updated. Once you give the order, the actual launch will take place in approximately five minutes."

"Can we abort once the process has started?"

"Yes sir, but only in the first four minutes."

"How long will these time parameters hold?"

"The aircraft currently orbiting will be refueled in air as necessary, Mr. President, so they can stay on station until the ultimatum expires; and except for those brief refueling periods, they will be available on five minutes notice. The subs, of course, can stay on station indefinitely. They'll also be available on five minutes notice."

"All right! After I notify the Soviets of our intent, I will authorize the launching of a single ICBM. I want you to choose a single warhead Minuteman at one of our sites as far away from northern California as possible, and make sure its destination is the Barents Sea—well short of the Soviet mainland and well away from any occupied areas.

"We'll give the Soviets complete information on the launch and its destination. If they make a terribly stupid miscalculation and respond with a nuclear strike, I'll expect you to respond immediately by taking out their satellites, and if I authorize it, you will launch a maximum counter strike. If they do not launch a strike, and pray God they don't, you should delay action against their satellites, but be prepared to re-initiate on short notice. Is that understood, General?"

"Understood, Mr. President."

The president turned to the chief warrant officer, Army Signal Corps, who was the top communications specialist on duty in the Situation Room. "Chief, at precisely eleven-thirty, I want to inform the Soviets by way of the computer link of a twelve noon test firing. The message should read, 'At exactly...what is the proper international time designation?"

"Greenwich time, sir. Noon here converts to seventeen-hundred, Zulu."

"All right." The president was now studying a map. "At exactly seventeen-hundred Zulu, the US will launch one, repeat, one, ICBM armed with a single nuclear warhead. The destination of the warhead will be the Barents Sea, twenty miles north of the northern tip of Novaya Zemlya, outside your territorial waters. The purpose of the launch is to determine whether you have the ability to destroy the missile—end of message. That will give them time to reply, but doesn't require them to do so."

The CWO acknowledged the president's order and moved off to carry it out.

"I'm still concerned, Mr. President," Baker said. "I know we've always relied on the concept of assured mutual destruction to prevent either the Soviets or us from starting a nuclear war. But if they do launch a nuclear strike and we respond in kind, what will we have accomplished, other than the destruction of half the world? My God, isn't there some other way?"

Reagan shook his head. "There should be, but there isn't. I've been around the barn on this one all night."

"I can't believe there isn't something..."

"What do you suggest? Should we send a message to Andropov to tell him we give up? Should we invite them in and watch two-hundred years of the best form of government yet visited upon this planet go down the drain? What else can we do?"

Baker's voice was subdued. "I don't know, Mr. President."

"I don't either, but I do know we've got to find out whether they're bluffing."

Stavka Command Center, outside Moscow, USSR
2030 Saturday, December 24, 1983—Day Sixteen

The Defense Council was taking a short recess when Ustinov's aide knocked on his door and entered. "What is it?" the Marshal asked brusquely.

"Comrade Marshal, I have a message from Colonel Maxsimov." He handed Ustinov a message board with a slip of paper attached to it.

Ustinov mouthed the words as he read the message. "Hollis captured at site. Executed."

"Son-of-a-bitch!" Ustinov spat the words out. "This was sent almost an hour ago. Why did it take so long to get here?"

"Unless it is an extreme emergency, Colonel Maxsimov was ordered to relay messages through Viktor so he would not have to break radio silence."

Ustinov rose to leave the room. "If Hollis found the site, others will follow. The grace period still has over eight more hours to run. We can't wait. I've got to find a way to force the Council to launch a strike."

In the Command Center an alarm sounded, followed by the chatter of a high-speed printer. The senior communications duty officer immediately sent orderlies to notify all members of the Defense Council.

There were other printers in the room, but that particular one was the most important. It was connected to a recently installed computer in a new secure communications link. The other end of the link was in the National Military Command Center at the Pentagon. This new link was intended to complement the so-called "hot line" telephone between Moscow and Washington. Over it could be sent specifically worded written messages of record, to eliminate any vagaries of translation that might find their way into a simultaneous interpretation of a spoken message or conversation.

Gorbachev entered the command center just as the printer ceased chattering. After a quick glance at the message, he motioned to the senior duty officer. "While I take a copy of this to the *Glavnokomadovaniye*, please inform Maxsimov at the Peregrine site. Also inform the members of the Council that I will join them as soon as my meeting with the *Glavnokomadovaniye* is finished."

The last member of the Council had just taken his seat when Gorbachev returned to the command center.

"Comrades," he began. "We have just received a message from Washington telling us that, as we expected, they have decided to launch a test missile." Turning to look at the clock, he continued, "We are advised the launch will take place at seventeen hundred hours, Zulu, which is about eighteen minutes from now. Colonel Maxsimov has been notified. I have discussed the message with the *Glavnokomadovaniye*. He requested that I get your views as to whether we should respond to the message, and, if so, how."

Chernenko, in his high-pitched voice which seemed to convey emotion his eyes did not share, asked, "Is the missile armed?"

"Yes. We are informed it will be a single warhead Minuteman."

"If Peregrine does not destroy it, where precisely will it land?"

Gorbachev nodded to the duty officer. After a moment the images on the large screen overlooking the conference table changed to depict a portion of the northern coast of Russia. On the screen to the left was the outline of northern Finland and the Kola Peninsula, and to the right were the two large islands of Novaya Zemlya bracketed by the Barents and Kara Seas. A bright red dot with a circle around it appeared north of the small island of Zhelaniya off the northern tip of the larger island of Novaya Zemlya.

"Comrade Minister," the duty officer said. "As you can see, it is set to impact north of Novaya Zemlya. The exact point is outside our territorial waters, but close enough to be observed from Mys Zhelaniyo and possibly even from Russkaya Gavan. There should be no danger to the inhabitants from the blast, since prevailing winds in that area should disperse any radioactive fallout over open sea well away from land."

"Thank you, Colonel," Gorbachev said. "Comrades, the destination clearly demonstrates that this is nothing more than a test. The Glavnokomadovaniye continues to believe there is a good chance that once they see we can destroy their missiles, they will seriously consider capitulation. Therefore, I have recommended we not respond. Our best course of action, as we originally planned, is to simply continue to observe the grace period while we wait for their answer. We are completely prepared to react should they attempt a preemptive strike."

Ustinov interrupted harshly. "I disagree," he said. His usual arrogance now became heavily authoritarian, as if he were the one in control. It was clear to all that he resented Gorbachev speaking for Andropov.

"You believe something else should be done, Comrade Minister?"

"Yes. I cannot agree that the grace period should continue for the remainder of the twelve hours. I believe that we should send the United States a message telling them that if the test missile is launched, the grace period will end exactly one-half hour later, at which time they will either capitulate or suffer destruction."

"On what do you base your sudden change of mind, Comrade?" Gorbachev parried. "We have debated the issue of time before, and agreed that if we try to push the US too far too fast, we will force them to fight. We have all agreed that a non-military solution and peaceful occupation would be much better than the destruction we would both face if they decide not to capitulate."

"Nothing will be gained by waiting." Ustinov insisted.

"I agree," Ustinov's chief of staff broke in, following the marshal's lead. "Waiting will only allow the shock of knowing their missile has been destroyed to dissipate. It would be more effective if we did not give them time to think. We should force them to make a decision immediately. Once they find out we can destroy their missiles they should be ready to capitulate."

As several heads nodded in agreement, Gorbachev quickly assumed the offensive. "Two points you should consider before making a recommendation. First, if we move precipitously to change the grace period merely because we have destroyed a single missile, the action might be misinterpreted. It may lead them to conclude that our capability does not extend to many missiles launched simultaneously. If so, that would encourage them to fight rather than capitulate.

"Second, but most important, while we have repeatedly been assured that the so-called Peregrine system works, and that it will protect us from their missiles, it has never been tested. In that sense, we are in the same position as the Americans; *we don't know whether it will destroy their missiles.* I think this is an opportunity for both them and us to find out the answer to that question before we suddenly find ourselves in the middle of a nuclear exchange that we can't call off."

The intercom beside Gorbachev crackled briefly. It was Andropov. "The decision is made," Andropov said. "The grace period will remain unchanged."

It was only with great effort that Ustinov restrained himself.

Minuteman Launch Site, Offutt AFB, North Dakota, US
1155 Saturday, December 24, 1983—Day Sixteen

DEFCON ONE. There it was. The highest state of alert. WAR! First Lieutenant Matthews couldn't believe it had actually come to pass.

He was seated at a launch console which controlled a squadron of Minuteman nuclear-armed missiles. He was intensely uncomfortable. More than uncomfortable, he was sick with anxiety. Like most sane people he did not relish the idea of launching a nuclear missile. But being a launch control officer had seemed a nice easy way to complete his active duty commitment, and he didn't believe they would ever be used anyway.

By the time he had finished his first week at Vandenberg, he was not sure. These people were serious. After a short period of indoctrination and before the fourteen weeks of intensive training began, he had been required to sign a document which proclaimed that he had no moral reservations which would prevent him from launching a missile armed with a thermonuclear warhead if ordered to do so by duly constituted authority.

That had concerned him. Not because of a lack of loyalty or an unwillingness to fight for his country. It was simply because he had never squarely faced the issue before. Could he really turn the key that would unleash destructive power many times greater than that dropped on Hiroshima? Could he be a part of killing untold thousands, maybe millions, of civilians, most of whom didn't want war anymore than he did? He honestly hadn't known.

He had signed the paper mostly because he could find no graceful way not to, and then lost sight of his reservations during the rigors of training.

He had done extremely well at Vandenberg, and his first duty assignment was at a base which was considered a choice tour. During his initial six months evaluation period he unconsciously chose to lose himself in his work rather than face his dilemma. It had paid off again. He was now considered one of the best-qualified launch control officers at the base.

But now those reservations were back again, and in the most terrifying possible form. What he had always assumed was the remotest of possibilities, more academic than realistic, had now improbably burst into life, like some monster emerging from the dark gloom of a nightmare.

The stand-by launch warning, together with a PLCB to target the sortie which would subsequently be authorized, had just been received, and he had been designated primary launch control officer. As he waited, he was fervently wishing he had asked for transportation and been sent somewhere else.

The squadron commander, there to observe the launch, broke the tense silence. "Lieutenant, you seem distracted. Any particular reason?"

"No Colonel. I guess I just really never expected any of these to be used."

The colonel was more sympathetic than he expected. "Let's pray this will be the only one," he replied. "Has the PLCB been entered?"

"Yes, sir."

"Verification?"

"Verified, sir.

At that moment an alarm sounded, followed by a voice reciting several alpha-numeric sequences. Both the lieutenant and his verification officer copied each symbol. When it ended the lieutenant said, "I have a valid message."

The launch verification officer responded. "I agree."

"Initiate check list."

"Check one on check list, insert launch keys," the verification officer replied.

After trying it first upside down, Matthews got the key to slide into the slot. "Launch key inserted."

His misgivings took a back seat to his training as he and the verification officer went through the steps of the check list. Almost before he realized it, the launch codes had been entered.

It was ten seconds to launch.

"Hands on key," he intoned.

His verification officer repeated the words.

"Key turn on my mark," he continued. "I'll watch the clock; you watch the lights."

"Three, two, one, Mark."

He watched the clock until he heard the verification officer. "Light on, light off."

He stared hard at the launch control panel. "Release key," he said.

The follow-on team turned its keys at the same instant and the lights confirmed a launch.

The bird was on its way.

Matthews was afraid he was going to vomit. All he could think of was that old movie he had seen on late night television, *Dr. Strangelove*. He remembered the last few scene showing Slim Pickins riding that atomic bomb down out of the B-52. And he was remembering in particular the haunting strains of the song Vera Ellen was singing: "We'll meet again, don't know where, don't know when...." as atomic mushrooms engulfed the world.

On a cloud of fire and smoke the Minuteman burst from its underground lair, climbed swiftly skyward and began arching to the north, toward the remote reaches of the Barents Sea.

It was a perfect launch.

Peregrine Site, Montegue Estate, California
0958 Saturday, December 24, 1983—Day Sixteen

Maxsimov was worried. The executions he had ordered had not been confirmed. He should not be forced to call Sergei for a report. He grew even more worried when he was unable to contact anyone at the security station. He was considering sending a patrol to check when the computer printer began to chatter. This could only mean one thing—a message was coming in from Moscow.

The message informed him that he had less than twenty-five minutes to destroy a United States ICBM.

Maxsimov immediately set the wheels in motion.

After the initial rush of activity to activate Peregrine, a problem seemed to develop. With the time for activation fast approaching, Maxsimov noticed a group of technicians all talking rapidly. "What's the problem?" he shouted.

The senior technician came to attention. "Comrade Colonel, we are having difficulty determining the time to activate the transmitter because we cannot compute the precise rocket booster burn time."

Maxsimov snorted, "You must have the information to compute it."

The technician looked uncomfortable. "We do not know the base from which the missile will be launched nor the precise location of its destination. The distance a warhead must travel to get to its destination will affect the angle of ascent and make a significant difference in the number of seconds of burn time. The flight of this one could be significantly shorter than any of those for which the burn time was pre-computed and programmed into the control computer."

Maxsimov felt an enormous frustration. He did not understand the technicians' problems sufficiently to give them a concrete order. He was forced to rely on their expertise. "What's your best judgment?"

"We've narrowed it to a range of between two hundred to two hundred and thirty seconds, Comrade Colonel. I recommend we use two hundred and fifteen seconds."

"We don't have time to argue. Set Peregrine to activate self-destruct two hundred seconds after lift-off. It's more important that the missile be destroyed than whether we produce the optimum illusion."

Not understanding precisely what Maxsimov meant but feeling fortunate to have escaped a major rebuke, the technician hurriedly attended to the task. The information was duly entered in the control computer and precisely two hundred seconds after lift-off of the Minuteman missile, Peregrine engaged the satellite link.

NORAD, Cheyenne Mountain, Colorado
1100 Saturday, December 24, 1983—Day Sixteen

The telemetry data on the Minuteman was displayed on two of the large screens in the NORAD Situation Room as it came in. Amid the apprehension, there was a sense of exhilaration as the Minuteman exited its silo, rapidly gained speed, and then tilted north to its destination. It was not because a missile had been launched, but because of the pride everyone there took in the perfection of its performance.

The Minuteman was quickly out of visual range, so attention shifted to the large screens which monitored the Phased Array Warning System. At the bottom of the screen the northernmost portion of the United States appeared. Above it Canada, the Arctic, and a large portion of the Soviet Union, appeared at the top. The ICBM was being tracked and its progress was being shown by a marker image on this screen.

Without warning, the image disappeared from the screen and the transmission of telemetry data ceased.

General Bedell was the first to react. "What the hell happened? Did PAWS go down?"

A senior duty officer at one of the control consoles below the screen answered him. "No, General. The system's functioning perfectly. The missile simply disappeared."

At the communications link to NMCC in the Pentagon, a light began flashing on the console. The senior communications specialist monitoring it turned to Bedell. "Sir, General Vessey is on."

Bedell picked up the white phone on the long table where most of the senior command personnel sat. "Yes, General."

"General, what the hell's going on? The Minuteman disappeared from our screen. Is there an equipment malfunction or did something happen to the bird?"

"We're at a loss to explain it, General," a shaken Bedell replied. "PAWS is functioning properly, as are all the communications and relay links. All telemetry data has been relayed to Richie for analysis. Maybe they can come up with something. All we know is that the missile's gone."

NMCC Pentagon, Arlington, Virginia
1203 Saturday, December 24, 1983—Day Sixteen

General Vessey turned to the closed-circuit video screen that was his direct link to the president. He watched as an image of the White House

Situation Room filled the screen. "Mr. President," he said. "As I'm sure you can tell from your PAWS relay screen, the Minuteman we fired is no longer being tracked."

"Have you figured out why?"

"No, sir. We don't believe it's the result of a breakdown in either the tracking radar or the relay links. The missile has simply disappeared. The only conclusion we can come to is that it was destroyed."

Stavka Command Center, Outside Moscow, USSR
2106 Saturday, December 24, 1983—Day Sixteen

As the Minuteman disappeared from the command room screen, the feelings of those watching were mixed. Ustinov was obviously smugly satisfied, while Gorbachev was attempting to maintain a neutral composure to hide the misgivings of pending disaster he continued to feel. He had privately hoped the test of Peregrine would fail. The shock might be enough to convince some of the less hawkish ideologues of the potentially disastrous course they were following. He had hoped some sanity might return while there was still time.

Even though he had told himself over and over that the end of capitalism should allow communism to flourish and reach the true potential which, so far, had been an elusive goal, he could not escape a vague undercurrent which told him it would only more strongly endow a system which had been corrupted, and was not performing as it should. All of the changes he wanted to make, and the things he wanted to fix, would be placed on indefinite hold, even if he succeeded Andropov.

Ustinov was the first to speak. "Comrades, as I assured you, Peregrine worked perfectly." He looked directly at Gorbachev. "Those of you who doubted, can now see the soundness of my plan. And now that the test has proven the system operational, I reiterate we should proceed without further delay. The grace period should be terminated and the Americans forced to decide."

"We've already had that discussion," Gorbachev responded wearily. "And the decision was made to let the grace period run its course. Nothing has changed."

"But nothing will be achieved by waiting," Ustinov insisted.

Chernenko, having lost out in his effort to succeed Brezhnev, was now convinced that no one could succeed to the position of general secretary without the backing of the leadership of the Red Army. Also aware of the growing rift between Ustinov and Gorbachev, he intervened on the side of the defense minister. "You are right, Comrade Marshall," he said, in his high-pitched voice. "The point is well taken."

"The arguments previously made against terminating the grace period are just as valid now as they were before," Gorbachev insisted. "But there is something else you should know.

He held up a torn-off sheet of computer printout. "This just came in from Viktor a few minute ago. It says, quote, American high command convinced satellites carry KKV weapons. If they do not capitulate, they will make an attempt to eliminate satellites shortly before end of grace period, unquote. I believe this supports the view that the Americans are still undecided and are actively considering capitulation. If we force their hand now, they may still go the other way."

Gorbachev turned to the intercom beside him in response to the slight sound of static, and said, "Yes, Comrade *Glavnokomadovaniye*."

Andropov's voice, weak but unyielding came back, "We will continue to abide by the terms of the ultimatum."

56

Montague Estate, Northern California
1014 Saturday, December 24, 1983—Day Sixteen

Hollis and Maggie entered the security control room. "I circled the house," Hollis said. "No sign of any more guards."

"Had I known what was here I could have saved you the trouble," Crowley replied. He beckoned to Maggie and Hollis. "Take a look at this."

The console he was standing in front of was rainbow shaped with the top slanted downward about thirty degrees off vertical toward the inside of the arc so that one person sitting at the center could easily reach all of its controls and observe all the monitors. Immediately above the rear edge of the top on the outside of the arc were three banks, each with fifteen video monitors. More impressive was the large sheet of translucent glass set above the console, with a blown-up transparency of an aerial photograph of the estate overlaid on it. There was subdued lighting behind it, which highlighted the features and grid marks of the map.

"No wonder it was so easy for them to capture us," Crowley said. "The map shows the entire estate, including the position of the main house and the access road. The grid lines on the overlay provide sector coordinates. The green and red lights around the perimeter represent sensors set to detect anyone breaching the fence, as we did. The yellow numbers mark dual-purpose video cameras, which can be used on normal setting for daylight or infra red for night observation. The number on each set of controls on the console are keyed to the numbers both on the screen and the video receivers below. The controls allow the operator to swivel a camera or change the elevation up or down."

He pointed to one of the yellow dots on the map with the number twelve beside it. "Camera number twelve is here on the map. As you can see, it overlooks the area of the access road approaching the main house." He turned one of the knobs on the console over the number twelve and pointed to the video receiver numbered twelve. "This allows the operator to pan the entire area or track a car on the access road as it approaches the main entrance of the house." After a slight pause, Crowley continued, "Well, I guess if we needed any more confirmation that Montague is the mole, we've got it."

"Not necessarily," Hollis replied.

"Why not? How could a system as elaborate as this be installed without his knowledge?"

"Sergei has had complete control of the place for over a year, and Paul made only one short visit during that time. At least, that's what he told me."

"Whatever." Crowley dropped the matter. "If you look at the transparency over the console, the point marked 'P' is where the transmitter is. The location of that point with respect to the house is exactly as I remembered from the installation."

"What do you think the distance is to point P?"

Crowley thought for a moment before answering. "It's right at four kilometers."

Hollis turned to Maggie, who had been following the explanation of the security system. "Chuck and I have to leave to destroy the transmitter, but we'll need your help."

"What can I do?"

Instead of answering, he turned to Chuck, "What's the best way to approach point P?"

Crowley moved in front of the aerial photo map and began tracing a route. "We're here right now." He pointed to the manor house. "I think the best course for us to follow is to go up the entrance road for about one and a half clicks, and then turn northwest. That way, I think we'll avoid their most heavily defended area. Once we get about here," he pointed to a spot on the photo, "we'll veer off to the west to come up on the high ground, but in a flanking position.

"When we reach this ridge, we should have a view of the antennas. If we can take them out, it'll neutralize the transmitter." Crowley paused. "What'll be difficult, of course, is that we'll have to take out any patrols we run into without making any noise. If they have any inkling that we're coming, we won't get within shouting distance of the antennas or anything else."

"This is where you come in, Maggie," Hollis told her. "We need you to sit here and monitor the estate—particularly the area between here and 'P'. I'll leave this walkie-talkie with you. If you see anything as we move along, you immediately give us a call. All you have to do is press this button and talk into the mouthpiece here. It's on a pre-set channel, so you don't have to worry about me hearing you."

Hollis and Crowley began arming themselves and checking their equipment. Maggie looked into Hollis' eyes. "Take care of yourself."

"I'll be back," Hollis said softly.

As soon as Hollis and Crowley had left, it was all Maggie could do to hold back the tears.

At the Peregrine site Maxsimov was congratulating himself. He had just received information which confirmed the system had performed precisely as planned. It should now be clear to the Americans that their nuclear deterrent no longer existed, and they had no choice but to capitulate.

His future was assured. He was lost in thoughts about his triumphant return to Moscow when he realized his senior security officer was standing at attention in front of him waiting to be recognized.

Maxsimov's head snapped up. "Yes, Captain. What is it?"

"Colonel, I am still not able to raise the security center at the main house. There is no response on any channel."

Maxsimov was irritated by the interruption. Then he remembered he had not received confirmation that Hollis and Crowley had been executed. "If Brovikov has failed again, I will personally execute the son-of-a-bitch." he said beneath his breath. Then, out loud, "You have a patrol in sector eight?"

"Yes, Colonel. They are close to the staging area for our vehicles."

"Order the squad leader to send out four men to the security office in one of the jeeps and report back immediately what they find. Also tell them to be damned careful."

After a pause, Maxsimov added, "Once that detachment is on its way move all patrols into a tighter perimeter around the security center. I want to be absolutely certain that no one can get through to even approach Peregrine."

Hollis and Crowley had just left when Maggie, who had gone back to the security console, ran out to catch them.

"Jeff!" she cried.

When Hollis reached her, she took him back inside and pointed to one of the video monitors. "A jeep with four soldiers in it came into sight briefly, and then disappeared."

Hollis made several quick adjustments to the monitor and the jeep appeared again, going away from the camera. "They're headed this way on the main road," Hollis told Crowley. "We've got to stop them."

They left Maggie and jogged across the parking area toward the entrance road.

"We've also got to make sure they don't communicate with their commander," Crowley said. "If they do we'll be up to our ears before we even get a shot at the transmitter."

About fifty yards past the first curve in the road, which hid the house from view, they stopped. Hollis hid in the brush on one side of the road while Crowley headed for the other side.

A few minutes passed.

Then two men in camouflage uniforms carrying AK-47s appeared, walking along the shoulders of the road. The other two were nowhere in sight.

Shit! Hollis thought. *They're probably in the underbrush, flanking the two in the road. But we can't let them get past us.* He assumed Crowley was thinking the same thing and that each would have to be prepared to follow the other's lead.

Hollis got out the CZ-75. After affixing the sound suppresser, he moved a little farther away from the road into a heavy cluster of bushes where he would be hidden from someone approaching.

He was rewarded moments later when a third soldier appeared.

Hollis moved to get a clear shot, but snapped a twig in the process. The figure spun around toward the sound and leveled his assault rifle. Before he could fire, Hollis hit him twice with the CZ-75. The soldier lurched backward, then folded up and collapsed to the ground.

Unslinging his M-16, Hollis moved quickly back into the cluster of bushes. He could see that the two armed men on the verge had stopped and were looking around. They had obviously heard something.

Across the road he could see Crowley watching them also. Behind Crowley the fourth soldier was quickly sneaking up on him, raising his AK-47.

There was no time for thought—or even for aiming. He swung his M-16 up to hip level, pointed it across the road and held the trigger down.

Pandemonium.

The figure behind Crowley screamed, spun around and dropped out of sight in the bushes. Crowley opened fire on the two men in the road. The one on Hollis' side of the road went down immediately, but before Hollis could shift fire to the other, the soldier fired a burst at Crowley.

Out of the corner of his eye Hollis saw Crowley drop to the ground at the same instant his bullets cut down the remaining soldier.

Hollis charged across the road just in time to see Crowley struggling to his feet with a sheepish grin on his face. "God! Was that a stupid thing to do!"

"What the hell are you talking about?" Hollis asked, almost angrily.

"Taking on two guys that far apart from a totally unprotected position."

"Are you hurt?"

"Not really," Crowley replied, looking down at the blood dripping off his left hand. "One round glanced off the side of my flack jacket, and nicked me under the arm."

"Go back and let Maggie take care of that. I'll make sure these guys are out of it. Maybe we can use their jeep."

Maggie had just finished putting a bandage on Crowley's wound when Hollis returned to the security center.

"All four are permanently out of it," he said. "One of them had a walkie-talkie, but since it was still hanging on his belt, it seems unlikely he transmitted a message."

"That's probably right," Crowley agreed. "But we'd better get moving in a hurry. Someone's going to be looking for them damned soon. They may flood the area with men."

"We can't leave Maggie here to face something like that," Hollis replied.

"Look!" Maggie broke in. "You two go and do what you have to do and don't worry about me. I can use that thing," she pointed toward the security console. "I'll be able to see anyone coming this way. If they do, I'll find a place to hide—or something."

Hollis wasn't convinced.

"Go on, Jeff. I can take care of myself!"

Hollis took her in his arms briefly, then followed Crowley toward the door. Just then a loud alarm went off on the security console.

57

Situation Room, The White House, Washington, DC
1204 Saturday, December 24, 1983—Day Sixteen

"My God, it's gone!"

The words came from the Air Force staff sergeant seated at the Situation Room monitor when the Minuteman missile disappeared.

Everyone started talking at once. Then the president turned to Vessey. "General, how long will it be before we know exactly what happened?"

"Sir, all the data was relayed real time to Richie, and General Shields is in the process of analyzing it now. The missile was destroyed, but we have no information yet as to what caused it. I hope Shields will be able to tell us something shortly, but in the meantime we have to assume it was destroyed by a KKV from one of their satellites."

"What do you recommend?"

Vessey cleared his throat loudly. It still took him several long seconds to muster the courage to say what he knew he had to say.

"Regretfully, Mr. President," he began, "regretfully, I think we have to seize the initiative and launch a pre-emptive strike. Our best judgment is that while they can take out some of our missiles, their system cannot handle a full-scale saturation strike. Therefore, to make our strike as effective as possible we could combine SIOP options 'A-1' and 'G-3' to put as many missiles in the air in the shortest time possible. I would time the strike to take place within minutes after initiating a maximum effort against the Soviet satellites. At the same time, I would order a full SAC strike, including United States and NATO forces, to take place simultaneously with the ICBM/SLBM strike. Also, all Naval forces positioned to do so should launch aircraft and cruise missiles."

There was a stunned silence in the Situation Room. What Vessey was recommending was a doomsday scenario—an all-out nuclear first strike against the Soviet Union, with all dreadful consequences that implied.

"What the hell would that accomplish?" Baker demanded angrily. "We can't destroy their launch sites before they launch a retaliatory strike."

"That's true," Vessey conceded, "but it would assure maximum damage—and that would cripple their ability to initiate a second strike."

Secretary of State Shultz broke in, shaking his head vigorously. "A full-scale nuclear response cannot be the only course of action."

Vessey became defensive. "Sir, I was an advocate of flexible response long before Presidential Directive 59 made it official policy. And let's face, We're a hell of a lot better prepared to fight and survive a conventional war than a nuclear one. But we don't have the luxury of limiting the conflict to conventional weapons when they threaten us with a nuclear strike. Even if they can take out some—or even most—of our ICBM/SLBMs, we can still knock the shit out of them."

"I agree," Weinberger interjected.

Shultz glared back. "Wait a minute. In case your memory needs jogging, you've seen the same studies I have. If the Soviets launch a full nuclear strike against us, then regardless of how much damage we may or may not be able to inflict against them, it will end civilization as we know it in this country, for hundreds of years, maybe forever." Shultz stood up, as if to help drive home the force of his conviction to the others around the table.

"The most conservative estimates predict that such a strike would immediately kill in excess of one hundred million people and another twenty-five to fifty million would suffer lethal doses of radiation poisoning. There'd be no way to care for those who might survive because most major medical facilities would have been destroyed.

Further, the radioactive fallout would render between fifty and sixty percent of the country uninhabitable for decades, if not centuries."

Shultz directed his gaze squarely at the president, who was, after all, the man he had to sway. Reagan was listening to him, looking very stone-faced.

"Over ninety percent of the country's industrial base would either be destroyed or contaminated," Shultz continued. "All of our major ports and at least seventy-five percent of the arable land in the country would no longer be usable. It'll be small comfort to us after that's happened to find out that we inflicted greater damage on them than they expected."

Stung by Shultz's lecture, Weinberger exploded. "Well, what the hell do you propose we do, give up?"

"Let me put it this way. As far as I'm concerned our so-called nuclear shield was intended to be just that, and nothing else. It was never intended to be used. It was built, and it's been expanded and improved for one purpose only—to maintain the balance of power between us and the Soviets. As long as the balance was maintained, it was a deterrent to either side starting a war. But if the Soviets have now altered that balance in their favor by rendering our ballistic missiles useless, then we no longer have an effective deterrent, *and we have lost*. If so, so be it. We should not compound that disaster by refusing to recognize it, and inviting devastation."

Before anyone could reply, Shultz, his voice full of emotion, continued, "Mr. President, I am as loyal to this country and what it stands for as any person here, but I cannot agree to a proposal which almost certainly would result in the destruction of our entire civilization. On the other hand, if we accept the ultimatum and capitulate, it would not necessarily mean the end of our way of life. It would be a temporary setback, not a permanent one. Eventually freedom and democracy—our way or life—would reassert itself.

"The Soviets might succeed in turning the clock back a few years, but they can't change the course of history. It's on our side. The constitution will live on in the hearts and minds of our people regardless of anything the Soviets do. It will only be lost if we destroy the world in our effort to save it. I can't bring myself to believe we should do anything that might precipitate a nuclear exchange no one can win. If the only way to avoid it is to capitulate, then we must do it."

"I'm not sure I disagree with you, George," the president said softly.

Reagan waited through a few moments of absolute silence, then continued. "But if what General Vessey has said is true, maybe we still have enough of a nuclear shield to be a deterrent. If we do, maybe we can still back the Soviets down."

"Even assuming you're right," Shultz replied. "That may not be the answer. Whether the Soviets will back off depends on what they *think* we can do. If they're willing to accept whatever damage they *think* we have the ability to deliver they will *not* back down. We've already had that conversation with them once."

"I understand, George, but I have to try." Reagan turned back to the monitor, "General Vessey. make preparations to carry out your plan as quickly as possible. As soon as they're complete I'll get on the hot line to Andropov."

Secretary Weinberger broke in. "Mr. President, before you call Andropov, shouldn't we find out whether Shields has come up with something?"

"You're absolutely right, Cap." Reagan turned to the senior communications officer. "Tom, see if you can get General Shields on the screen."

The view on the screen shifted from the NMCC to the alternate command center at Fort Richie, and after a few seconds the image of General Shields filled the room. "Mr. President?"

"Have you come up with anything yet on how the missile was destroyed, General?"

"I think so, Mr. President. We're not sure yet precisely how it was done, but we know the Soviet satellites had nothing to do with it."

The president reacted with surprise. "You are? Why?"

"Based on the time between missile launch and destruction, no satellite was close enough."

"I don't follow you."

"The Minuteman was in flight only two hundred seconds, Mr. President. Based on the maximum speed their type solid fuel missiles can travel, and the distance a KKV would be required to travel from the closest satellite, it would have been necessary to have launched the KKV fifteen seconds before missile lift-off for it to have reached the ICBM at the time it disappeared."

McFarlane jumped in. "What about laser or high frequency emissions?"

"We were monitoring for both, but detected neither."

The President voiced the question everyone was thinking. "If the satellites had nothing to do with the destruction, what did?"

"There's only one other possibility, Mr. President. The self-destruct mechanism in the rocket booster was somehow activated."

The president and Casey exchanged glances while an incredulous McFarlane asked, "A malfunction?"

"We haven't been able to completely rule that out, sir, but the odds are against it. The device is too simple, too straight-forward. We haven't had a malfunction in years. Nor do we believe it was triggered accidentally. There are too many safeguards to prevent it."

"Is there any way to confirm that it was not a malfunction?" Reagan asked.

"The only sure way would be to fire another test missile, Mr. President."

"We've already had one bite of that apple, General. If I were in the Soviet's position, I would say one is enough. So where does it leave us?"

There was a lengthy pause. Looking very much as if he would prefer not to answer, Shields finally spoke. "Mr. President, if the Soviets have developed a method of triggering the self-destruct mechanism in our missile rocket boosters, we're in more trouble than we thought. All the talk about KKV's and whether they have the technology for advanced guidance control and so on would be just so much rhetoric. They'd be able to destroy our missiles—no matter how many we launched or where we launched them from—merely by sending out a radio signal."

McFarlane was astonished by Shields' statement. "Good Lord, General. You can't be serious. There's no way they can do that. There are over ten thousand inhibit codes available to launch officers, and no one knows which one will be entered at any launch site until ten seconds before launch. Even if the Soviets had the codes there would be no way they could use them. There's not enough time for them to cycle through them in two hundred seconds."

"I agree sir," Shields conceded. "But if they had the ability to override the inhibit codes they could trigger the mechanism with a micro-burst transmission on a frequency of their own choosing."

"But how the hell could they override the inhibit code?" McFarlane demanded. "To do that they'd have to have modified the command module that controls the onboard computer."

Vessey, still on the conference line, broke in. For the first time there were traces of uncertainty in his voice. "Mr. President, I was just reminded by the Air Force chief of staff that less than six weeks ago we completed an up-grade program which involved replacing the command module throughout our entire arsenal of missile boosters, both land and sea-based. Con, can you determine whether the override you suspect really exists?"

"We're checking it out now, General. If we're right, the problem we'll face is whether we can do anything about it in time."

"What's the prognosis, General?" the president asked, maintaining a calm he did not feel.

Shields sighed. "The odds are very much against us, Mr. President."

58

Security Control Room, Montague Estate
1310 Saturday, December 24, 1983—Day Sixteen

Crowley was first to reach the security console. "It's the front gate," he said, looking at the label under the flashing light.

Hollis, on a quick hunch, flipped the switch by the flashing light. It activated not only the gate speaker and microphone, but a hidden video camera as well. He spoke into the mike: "Yes?"

The speaker crackled back with a response. "This is the county sheriff. I have a report that you're harboring some undesirable aliens up there. I have a search warrant. You'll have to open up and let me in."

The image in the gate video monitor showed a county sheriff's cruiser at the gate console but there was no doubt who was leaning out the rear window to speak into the microphone. For a moment Hollis was speechless.

"Al! Al Walters!" he almost shouted.

"Jeff? Is that you?"

"You bet your sweet ass it is. And we're up to our ears in some very undesirable aliens."

"What's your situation?"

"We've commandeered the security center, but they'll be coming after us any minute now. I hope you brought some help with you."

"We did. What do you want us to do?"

"What do you have with you?" Crowley asked.

"One-twenty special forces marines in armored personnel carriers, waiting just out of sight, with choppers and reserves standing by at Ukiah airport."

"When I open the gate," Hollis replied. "just follow the paved road. We'll be at the end of it, waiting for you."

Crowley intervened. "I think it would be better if you left the marine detachment where it is for the time being—just in case you're observed by the Soviets on the way in."

"Will do," Walters acknowledged.

A few minutes later Walters, together with a marine lieutenant colonel, and a first lieutenant, arrived in the sheriff's cruiser.

"God!" Hollis exclaimed, as he grabbed Walters outstretched had, and embraced him with his other arm. "It seems like a miracle that you're here."

"It just about is," Walters said grimly, returning Hollis' embrace. "I thought for a while we were going to have to declare war on the Department of Defense, but the DCI outflanked 'em in the end."

Walters hurriedly introduced Hollis and Crowley to Colonel Whitaker. "Time is of the essence," he said. "At eight this morning, east coast time, the Soviet ambassador delivered an ultimatum to the president demanding he capitulate to Soviet occupation within twelve hours, or the Soviets would launch a nuclear strike. The ultimatum also states that any hostile move by us during the grace period, which incudes an attack on Peregrine, will terminate it and result in an immediate strike.

"Since I didn't know the precise location of the transmitter, I could not run the risk of simply ordering an air strike to cover the area. So, I decided that a small special forces group might succeed in finding and taking out the transmitter before the people operating it could warn Moscow. I brought what we thought would do the job. We now have exactly," he glanced at his watch, "three hours and forty minutes to neutralize Peregrine. Can we do it?"

Hollis looked bleak. "I don't know. Chuck believes they have a large force defending the site—at least fifty to a hundred men. And it's in pretty rugged terrain. He'll have a better feel for what we need to do than me."

"Colonel, if you'll follow me, please."

Crowley led the way into the security control room where he stopped in front of the large aerial photograph and pointed out their current location and its relationship to that of 'Point P.'

"Point P is the Peregrine site. It's a good thing that you did not order an air strike. It would not have succeeded. The transmitter and related equipment is situated in a shallow cave right at the foot of this ridge." He fingered a specific spot on the photograph. Although the antennae are on the top of the ridge, right about here, they're well protected and camouflaged. The mouth of the cave is shielded by this parallel ridge, so their defensive forces are probably deployed at each end of the ravine between the two ridges, as well as along the tops of both ridges."

Colonel Whitaker looked up from the field maps he had been marking. "I have two Sikorsky CH-53Ds standing by at Ukiah airport to ferry in reserves if needed. I also have two flights of two Whiskeys each standing by. Each is set up with sixteen 5-inch Zuni rockets, eight Hellfire anti-armor missiles which can be laser designated, and seventy-six 2.75-inch fire suppression rockets. They can be on the scene in less than ten minutes."

"What about mules?" Crowley asked.

"Four, back packed."

"Sir, may I suggest a plan?"

"By all means, Captain." Whitaker replied, aware of Crowley's current status as an officer in the Marine reserves.

As Crowley began outlining his plan to Whitaker and the lieutenant, Maggie joined Hollis and Walters at the security console.

"Al, we need somebody to stay here and monitor the action," Hollis said. "Maggie can show you how the system works, and she has a walkie-talkie to keep us in touch if you need it."

Walters nodded as he smiled at Maggie.

"Also," Hollis continued, "somebody has to be in position to inform Washington as soon as the transmitter is destroyed, and, judging from immediate past experience, I think you're more likely to succeed at that than me."

Walters, Crowley, Whitaker and the lieutenant strode from the room. Hollis gave Maggie a quick kiss.

"Good luck, Jeff," she whispered.

"Don't worry," he promised. "I'll see you very soon." He ran to catch up with the others.

"You sure you're up for this?" Whitaker asked him, with a solicitous frown. "It may turn into one hell of an ugly fire fight, and I don't know if you're properly trained for it."

Hollis laughed. "Don't worry about me, Colonel. I'll try to stay out of your way."

"All right," Whitaker agreed, as they got in the car. "We'll meet my forces about three-quarters of a mile up the road and disembark. We'll divide the company into two platoons. I'll take charge of Bravo One. We'll make a direct assault up the ravine on Point P. Captain Crowley, with the lieutenant's assistance, will lead Bravo Two. He'll take two of the mules and make his way to the top of the ridge across from Point P, so he can designate the antennae for us. Two of the Whiskeys—Cobras One and Two—will orbit just above the trees, far enough out so they can't be heard. The other two we'll hold in reserve. When the mules are in place, Cobra One will launch Hellfires to destroy the antennae, then both Cobras will provide fire suppression as we go in."

"I hate to sound stupid," Hollis said, "but what are Whiskeys and mules?"

Whitaker looked chagrined. "A 'whiskey' is a Bell AH-1-W Cobra helicopter. A 'mule' is the mobile laser target designator for the eight

Hellfire anti-armor missiles each Whiskey carries. Once the Whiskeys are in range, we can designate the target by a laser beam. The Whiskey's missiles can then home on the target, even though the Whiskey never comes within sight of it."

Hollis grimaced. "Sounds simple enough."

"Simple is what it should be, but it never works out that way." Whitaker's smile had no warmth in it.

They arrived at the point of debarkation as the personnel carriers were disgorging the two platoons of marines.

Hollis watched as Crowley and the lieutenant took charge of Bravo Two and began moving out.

After a short discussion with the sergeant, Colonel Whitaker nodded at Hollis. "Okay, Sergeant. Let's move it."

Bringing up the rear, Hollis observed that the marines were experiencing almost as much trouble with the terrain as he and Crowley had, only now there was the added hazard of stumbling into an ambush.

Half a kilometer short of their destination, they heard the sound of gunfire.

The radio crackled to life. "Bravo one, this is Bravo Two. Over." Hollis recognized the lieutenant's voice.

The marine who was back-packing the Colonel's radio, immediately handed the mike to Whitaker. "Bravo Two, this is Bravo One. Go."

"Bravo One, we are at the foot of the ridge, and have come under intense fire. Unlikely we can dislodge defenders without Cobra assistance. Over."

"Roger, Bravo Two. Shift to channel two and hold."

The marine radioman shifted channels. "Cobra Leader," Whitaker said. "This is Bravo Leader, do you read me? Over."

"Bravo Leader, this is Cobra Leader, I read you five by five. Over."

"Cobra Leader, Bravo command now consists of Bravo One and Bravo Two. I am in command of Bravo One; Captain Crowley and Lieutenant Zimmerman are in command of Bravo Two. Bravo Two needs immediate assistance. Take your orders directly from Bravo Two, I'll monitor and coordinate, if necessary. Out."

In the lead Cobra, Captain Bennett reached up to press on his throat mike. "Bravo Two, this is Cobra Leader. I am orbiting outer grid marker, point zebra two-niner. What assistance do you need? Over."

"Cobra Leader, this is Bravo Two. We are now at the foot of a ridge situated at coordinates November-one-fiver. Our target is at the top of ridge, which is defended by ground troops. Suggest you approach ridge on course three-three-zero, and lay several Zunis and a barrage of two-seven-fives on our side of the ridge as well as the top. Have no information on anti-aircraft firepower of defending force, but believe it could include SAM-7's or equivalent. We cannot, I repeat, cannot laser designate, but will mark our position with smoke. Over."

"Thank you, Bravo Two. We'll take it from here. Cobra Leader out."

Bennett picked up his mike again. "Cobra Two, this is Cobra Leader, over."

"Go ahead, Boss."

"You heard the traffic with Bravo-One and Two?"

"Roger, I copied."

"I don't think we should try to sneak in at low level to a blind target. We'll move in to about a thousand yards and then elevate until the smoke is in sight. I'll launch two Zunis at the top of the ridge, and hit the deck. You cover from about a hundred yards off my right quarter. Mark any response and take counter-action if appropriate. Any questions?"

"No questions. I'll key on you."

After a few minutes, Bennett eased the cyclic back and lowered the collective as he began to bleed off some of the forward speed. When they were almost at hover, he spoke to his gunner seated in front of him. "Mike, check and arm ordnance. I'll start elevating in five seconds. As soon as I spot the smoke, I'll stop the ascent. You fire two Zunis at the top of the ridge, and we'll break for cover. Any questions?"

"No questions, sir. Ordnance checked and armed."

As they approached the target area, Bennett pulled back slightly on the cyclic, and as the forward motion stopped, he reached down and pulled up sharply on the collective. The Whiskey, which had been just above the tree tops, now rose sharply, almost vertically, with Cobra Two matching it move for move, holding position off its left quarter at a slightly lower altitude.

They saw the smoke in front of them sooner than they expected. It was slightly to their left and two ridges beyond.

Bennett swung the Cobra nose toward the target ridge beyond the smoke. When they were pointing directly at it he lowered the collective quickly to arrest their ascent. He didn't have to tell his gunner when to fire. He felt a slight shudder as the two 5-inch rockets roared off on their journey.

An alarm light in front of Bennett started flashing urgently. It was his IR jammer. A recorded voice began to repeat rapidly, "*Missile, missile, missile!*"

Seemingly in slow motion he could see a surface-to-air missile, launched from the target ridge, headed toward his craft on a twisting tail of white exhaust.

His reactions were automatic. He hit the switch to fire chaff and flares to his right, then pushed the collective down hard to dump power and shoved the cyclic left to turn in the direction of the approaching missile, to shield his hot exhaust from the heat-seeking sensors.

"Breaking left, Cobra Two!" he yelled into his mike.

Four rockets streaked by him, headed for the SAM launch point.

The SAM exploded well above and to his right.

It was close enough so that the Cobra pitched badly from the effect of the concussion, but it had no effect on his control. As he checked his descent to a hover, he could not see whether Paneral had come through safely. He keyed his mike. "Cobra Two, you all right?"

"Right behind you, Boss."

"Good, hold your position." He pressed his mike button. "Bravo Two, Cobra Leader. Over."

"Cobra Leader, this is Bravo Two. Well done! The Zunis cleared the top of the ridge, and the support fire took out the SAM launcher. Request you put a couple dozen two-seven-fives between us and the top of the ridge. Over."

"Wilco. Cobra Leader out."

After the ridge in front of Bravo Two stopped erupting from the fire-suppression rockets which had been fired into it, Crowley nodded and the sergeant waved Bravo Two up the ridge. As he moved with the platoon, dodging the sporadic rifle fire which still came from a few defenders, he heard Bennett call Zimmerman again.

"Bravo Two, Cobra Leader. Do you have further need of us? We have fuel for another twenty minutes over target. Over."

"That's affirmative, Cobra Leader. We'll be at the top of the ridge, and have a 'mule' in place to designate the main target in less than two minutes. Will need at least four Hellfires. Imperative this target be destroyed soonest. Over."

"Understood, Bravo Two. Can you provide launch instructions? Over."

"Affirmative, Cobra Leader. Suggest you take position bearing one-five zero from my last position, and prepare to fire on my command. Also, suggest you order second flight of Cobras to join you as soon as possible. After you launch Hellfires, command will shift to Bravo One. Over."

"Wilco, Bravo Two. Cobra Leader, standing by. Out"

Hollis and Whitaker had monitored the radio transmissions as they approached the ravine between the two ridges. They were almost at the entrance when it became obvious that Crowley's judgment about the deployment of the defenders had been very accurate. Automatic fire from well-concealed defenders had already produced several casualties, and the ricocheting bullets forced them to seek cover.

Whitaker had to shout in order for Hollis to hear him over the sound of gunfire, "Once the antennae are destroyed, we'll bring in the Whiskeys to clear a path to the cave!"

Hollis nodded, then moved to his left to get a better view of the top of the ridge over the cave. He was expecting what happened next, but not prepared for it.

His eardrums seem to shatter as the first Hellfire passed not more than seventy-five yards overhead. It slammed into the target ridge, followed almost immediately by three more.

In the confined space of the mouth of the ravine, Hollis felt as though the concussion of the explosions had knocked the breath out of him.

On the ridge he saw what could only be several pieces of a dish antenna erupt into the air and then plunge into the ravine.

Crowley had done it. He unclipped the walkie-talkie from his belt, and pressed the button on the side. "Walters, this is Hollis. Over."

"Walters here. Go ahead."

"The antennas have been destroyed," Hollis said. "Believe Peregrine no longer operational."

"Roger, Jeff. Well done. I'll get on the horn to Casey right away. Out."

The cave which housed the transmitter was also Maxsimov's command center. It was fast becoming obvious that time was running out. He was discussing how much longer they could hold out with the paratroop commander, when a very agitated technician ran up to his side.

"Comrade Colonel," the technician said, gasping for breath. "the antennas, they have been destroyed."

"Well shift to the back ups!" Maxsimov screamed, as the pressure of impending disaster began to take control of his emotions. "And be quick about it!"

Maxsimov turned to the messenger beside him. "Get the communications officer here, immediately!"

An officer appeared before Maxsimov and saluted, just as the tempo of gunfire outside picked up. There were several more loud explosions near the cave entrance.

"Break radio silence and send the following message immediately, highest priority, direct to Stavka: Start—Peregrine site under attack.

Have shifted to back-up antennas and placed transmitter computer on continuous broadcast cycle—end of message. Send it at once."

Maxsimov turned back to the paratroop commander. "Put all of your reserves in the best possible places to defend the transmitter. It must continue to operate as long as possible."

59

Situation Room, The White House
1845 Saturday, December 24, 1983—Day Sixteen

All eyes were on Director Casey as he returned to the situation room. He was smiling the enigmatic half smile which sometimes softened his countenance when he relaxed. For those who were unaware of Peregrine, the tension, which had continued to build as the end of the grace period approached, was pushed almost to the breaking point.

Weinberger finally broke the silence by asking anxiously, "Is this what I hope it is?"

Casey nodded. "Mr. President, I just talked to Walters. He confirmed that the transmitter has been deactivated. The Soviets can no longer destroy our ICBMs."

There was a heavy silence. Then those who had not been told about Peregrine realized what they had heard and broke into cheers. When the noise subsided the president spoke. "You said ICBMs. What about SLBMs?"

"General Shields believes the three sites we were concerned about must hold transmitters intended to be used to destroy the SLBMs. But, since the frequencies used require line-of-sight transmission, their use is limited. We are in the process of moving our boomers out of their range, and the sites are targeted for air strikes and cruise missiles. They will be inoperable shortly after hostilities begin."

"Well, let's hope it doesn't come to that," the president said dryly. He turned to the senior duty communications officer. "Let's crank up the hot line. I think it's time we talk to Andropov."

Stavka Command Center, outside Moscow, USSR
0550 Sunday, December 25, 1983—Day Seventeen

The communications officer looked up from the board he had just been handed. "Comrade, a message has just been received from Colonel Maxsimov."

"Read it," Ustinov snapped.

"'Peregrine site under attack. Have shifted to backup antennae and placed transmitter computer on continuous cycle.'"

"What does that mean?" Gorbachev asked.

"It means that if we do not launch a full strike at once we may lose the opportunity!" Ustinov bellowed, white with rage.

He turned to General Yefimov, Commander-in-Chief, Strategic Rocket Forces. "Upgrade the status of our rocket forces to Immediate Alert—Standby to Launch," he ordered.

Gorbachev jumped up. "You have no authority to issue such an order," he shouted. "Only *Glavnokomandovaniye* can do so."

Yefimov picked up the telephone and began relaying the order to his staff. "We cannot wait on a sick old man to make a decision!" Ustinov screamed. "We must move at once!"

"But you don't know whether the transmitter is still operating. It may already have been destroyed," Gorbachev shouted back.

As General Yefimov replaced the telephone, the intercom which tied Andropov to central command, crackled to life. "You will rescind that order, and take no action until I join you."

Situation Room, The White House
1900 Saturday, December 24, 1983—Day Sixteen

In the White House Situation Room, time seemed suspended as the wait for a response on the hot line lengthened. Finally, the communications officer said, "Mr. President, the general secretary is ready."

The president took the phone. "Mr. Secretary."

After several long moments, Reagan heard Andropov's respond with a faint "Mr. President."

Although the voice was weak it still contained all of the suspicion and hostility which had been a part of every communication he had received from Andropov.

The ball was in his court, and Reagan knew if he muffed it now there would be no second chance. Articulating with a measured slowness which he believed would allow Andropov to understand most of what he said without the need for an interpreter, he began: "Mr. Secretary, I will be brief so there will be no doubt as to what I have to say. The transmitter, which you called Peregrine, is no longer operational. You can no longer destroy our ICBMs. Also your other transmitters have been targeted for destruction, and our ballistic missile submarines are moving out of their range. The balance of power has been restored. You must withdraw your ultimatum."

Under ordinary circumstances the president's interpreter would translate Russian to English or English to Russian speaking almost simultaneously with the person whose words he was translating. But now his interpretation of Andropov's reply was delivered in a halting manner as he carefully considered the meaning before he translated it to English:

"We know that the site of the transmitter is under attack, Mr. President. However, we have information to the effect that the transmitter is still operational. Since the attack on the site is a violation of the terms of the ultimatum, you must consider the remaining portion of the grace period to be canceled."

Good Lord, I can't believe I'm hearing this, Reagan told himself. "Mr. Secretary, you must know that regardless of whether the transmitter works we have the ability to inflict major damage on your country, and we are prepared to do that if we are forced to, even though it may mean the end of civilization."

"Even though you may have the power to do substantial damage to our country, Mr. President, that does not restore equilibrium." Andropov replied. "How long would it be before your Strategic Defense Initiative would give you an overwhelming superiority? There are those among us who believe that since it is simply a matter of time before your country and mine must face each other on the battlefield, it is better for us to do so while we are prepared, and have the advantage.

"We are aware of your lack of preparations for a nuclear exchange which you believed would never take place. We, however, have built defenses that will give us a much greater chance of survival than you will have. There are also those among us who believe that our government could not survive another humiliation such as we experienced when we withdrew our missiles from Cuba. Do you understand, Mr. President?"

The president thought for several moments before he replied:

"Mr. Secretary, as I have told you several times before, we have always believed our countries, even with their different forms of government, could live together peaceably, if we could only build a bridge of trust between them.

"As to our Strategic Defense Initiative, I am told that an absolute security shield against nuclear-armed ballistic missiles may be impossible. If that turns out to be true, then neither of our countries should be concerned that it will disrupt the balance of power. But even if a workable shield system is developed, history has proven the fleeting nature of military secrets, and despite anything you or I can do, it will eventually belong to the world. Only then will it truly make ICBMs and SLBMs obsolete. In the meantime, if we are sincere in our quest for peace, we should return to the bargaining table and find a way to remove all IRBMs from both Eastern and Western Europe, and reduce the numbers of ICBMs and SLBMs.

"As to the question of whether your government will face humiliation by standing down from training exercises which you, of course, have a legitimate right to conduct, I would say it depends on what you wish to tell the world. For our part, we will do our best to make sure that no one, outside of those already involved, ever finds out what actually happened."

"Mr. President," Andropov's voice was so weak it could barely be heard as he said, "You are wasting valuable time. I must have your decision within five minutes."

The hot line went dead.

60

Peregrine Site, Montegue Estate, Northern California
1600 Saturday, December 24, 1983—Day Sixteen

After the Hellfires had destroyed the antennae, Hollis made his way back to Whitaker, who was issuing instructions to Crowley and Zimmerman.

"Bravo Two, this is Bravo Leader. Have ordered reserves to be airlifted to the bottom of the ridge. They'll be designated Bravo Three. Crowley will take charge of this group and move it to the north end of the ravine. Cobras Three and Four will provide firepower as Bravo Three moves down the ravine. When I give the word, Zimmerman will take Bravo Two and move down the side of the ravine for a direct frontal assault on transmitter cave. Over."

"Bravo Leader, this is Crowley. Request you reassign Lieutenant Zimmerman to Bravo Three, and that I retain command of Bravo Two. The lieutenant is more familiar with current Cobra ground control procedures than I am. Over"

"Technically you're not on active duty, Crowley, and that's the more dangerous of the two missions," Whitaker pointed out.

"I understand, sir," Crowley acknowledged. "But I'm better qualified for that job. Request renewed, sir."

"Okay," Whitaker said. "But don't move out until I give the word."

"Wilco, Bravo Two, out."

Whitaker immediately signaled Bennett, in the chopper overhead. "Cobra Leader, I'm at the south end of the ravine. When I mark my position with smoke, line up with the ravine and launch two Hellfires and two Zunis at the bottom of the ravine, right below the point on top of the ridge which Bravo Two laser designated. After that, provide fire suppression for Bravo One as we move up the ravine. When you've finished, Bravo Two will begin the frontal assault. Out."

Bennett moved the cyclic right and pulled up on the collective. The Cobra responded immediately.

As Whitaker deployed Bravo One for the assault, Cobra One leaped into sight from behind a ridge to the right of the ravine. Moments later Cobra Two appeared to the left and took up position a hundred yards behind and slightly above Whiskey One, like some guardian angel, hovering overhead.

In what seemed almost a rerun to Bennett, just as his gunner fired the first two Zunis, his missile warning system came alive as another SAM was launched at him from a point close to the target area. The defenders had held off until the Cobras were committed and seemingly without adequate speed or room to maneuver.

Even so, the outcome was testimony to the versatility of the Cobras, and the skill of the marines that flew them.

As Cobra One fired chaff and flares and broke in the direction from which the missile was launched, Cobra Two loosed a salvo of four two-seven-fives that bracketed the point of origin. The first Cobra had dropped so rapidly and the explosion of the SAM had been so close, Hollis was sure it had not survived. He was relieved when moments after the explosion it reappeared to resume the position it had just left so it could launch two Hellfires at the spot his Zunis had just targeted. Cobra One then disappeared behind a ridge as Cobra Two quickly launched two Zunis at the same target, and then followed them with two Hellfires before it disappeared behind the opposite ridge.

Moments later, with the finesse of a dancer, Cobra One reappeared just behind the smoke marking the position of Bravo One. It released a barrage of six fire-suppression rockets at the left side of the ravine. Then, as it disappeared behind the ridge to avoid gunfire, Cobra Two jumped into view and released six more at the opposite side of the ravine. As Cobra Two disappeared behind its ridge, Cobra One bobbed into sight again to fire several rockets at the center of the ravine some fifty yards ahead of the smoke.

Taking a chance there were no additional SAM launchers at the site, Cobra One then entered the ravine, followed immediately by Cobra Two. Each Whiskey mounted a duel twenty-millimeter turret just below the gunners cockpit. Both gunners had slaved the turret to his helmet-mounted sight, and were carefully examining the terrain in front of them as they moved slowly up the ravine. As the turret followed the movements of their heads, each fired short bursts at suspected targets or returned fire to targets which had exposed themselves.

As they approached the target area, Bennett came back on the air. "Bravo Leader, Cobra Leader, we seem to be running out of ammo as well as opposition and fuel. With your permission we'll head for the barn. Cobras Three and Four should be able to remain on station for another forty-five minutes. Over."

"Cobra Leader, Bravo Leader. You and Cobra Two may return to base. Well done. Cobras Three and Four, withdraw to protected area, and stand by. Bravo Two, you will begin frontal assault immediately. Bravo Leader, out."

As the Whiskeys departed, Whitaker's Bravo One, which had been following them as they progressed up the ravine, moved forward in earnest.

Hollis, who had found a protected position between some rocks, moved out just as a round hit the rock by his face, blinding him momentarily with powdered rock. Clearing his eyes, he had to move quickly to catch up. Even though the Cobras had broken the back of the defense, the fighting was not over. Bravo One was still faced with scattered intermittent fire, even though most of the defenders in the entrance to the ravine had been killed.

Within the cave it was obvious to Maxsimov that the end was near. He called the communications officer. "Send follow-up message: 'can hold out five more minutes.'"

The communications officer rushed to the transmitter and started sending.

Bravo One was the first to reach the cave. The detail from Bravo Two which was descending from the top of the ridge, was not far behind, but was having difficulty with the steep downslope. Bravo Three was farther behind, since they could not start down the ravine until they had repositioned themselves at its far end.

As the three groups converged near the cave, the remaining defenders consolidated around the entrance. Their position would have been almost impregnable but for the damage done by the Hellfires and Zunis. Now there were too few of them left to constitute an effective defense force, but they would not give up.

Hollis was sure the transmitter was no longer operational, but he felt compelled to remove any doubt. He wanted to see it completely destroyed. The difficulties he had encountered and the miserable odds which had been stacked so much against him demanded at least that much satisfaction. When Bravo One broke through the last perimeter at the mouth of the cave, he headed directly for the interior where Crowley had told him the transmitter was situated.

He had long since discarded everything except the CZ-75, which he was holding as the cave opened up in front of him. In the split second that he lost the cover of the entrance, he found not only what he sought, but the deadly peril of a Walther SMG pointing directly at him.

As Hollis' eyes locked with Maxsimov's, both knew this was the showdown; for one of them there would be no tomorrow. The handgun Hollis held was pointing away from Maxsimov, and instinct told him he could not move fast enough to bring it to bear in time. But he also knew Maxsimov was going to fire anyway.

As Hollis pivoted to bring the CZ-75 to bear, he heard someone from behind yell "No!" It sounded like Crowley, but it was barely discernible over the gunfire.

But his motion had already started the chain of events. Before either he or Crowley could fire, a brilliant light burst within his head, then abruptly faded, replaced by an all-consuming darkness.

The burst from Crowley's M-16, which ended Maxsimov's life and killed the communications officer, had come a fraction of a second too late.

61

Stavka Command Center, outside Moscow, USSR
0605 Sunday, December 25, 1983—Day Seventeen

After Andropov informed Reagan of the time limit, the tension had risen to an incredible level as the members of the Defense Council waited for a response from the American president.

The silence was suddenly broken by the doctor who had accompanied Andropov into the center to continue the monitoring of his vital signs. His patient was slumped over, eyes closed, face pallid.

"I must return Comrade Secretary to his room at once," the doctor said. "Otherwise he may die. I cannot be responsible if he stays here."

Ustinov, quick to seize the opportunity, rose to take charge. "You may return him to his quarters immediately. As defense minister I will take charge."

Andropov stirred, and then raised his head. "I am officially appointing Minister Gorbachev to act as *Glavnokomandovaniye* until I am able to reassume the position. Do you understand, Dimitri?"

Ustinov blanched as he looked quickly around the room for support. Finding none, he returned to his seat.

As Andropov was removed from the Command Center, Gorbachev turned to the communications officer. "Have you been able to contact Colonel Maxsimov yet?"

"No, Comrade. We believe he tried to send a follow-up message, but it broke off before we could confirm."

"Then that must mean the Americans are right and the transmitter is no longer operational," Gorbachev concluded.

General Yefimov, talking to someone on a telephone, suddenly slammed the receiver against the side of his thigh. "Son-of-a-bitch!" he shouted. "I don't believe it!"

Ustinov just stood there, mouth open, as if frozen to the spot.

"What's wrong?" Gorbachev demanded.

"There's been a communications malfunction," Yefimov said, his voice shaking. "Squadron One at Teykovo Missile base did not receive the rescind order, so it is still preparing to launch five SS-11s. The base commander is unable to communicate with the squadron commander."

Gorbachev eyes widened in shock and disbelief. "Can't the base commander override and prevent the missile launch?"

Yefimov shook his head. "That feature did not exist when Teykovo was constructed, and has not yet been installed. Once the authorization to launch is received, each squadron becomes autonomous. Launch can only be called off if they receive the proper stand-down signal. All the base commander can do is monitor."

"How much time before they are launched?"

"These are first-generation missiles. It takes about fifteen minutes to transfer the liquid oxygen to the booster after the decision to launch is received."

"Isn't there some way we can prevent them from being launched?" Gorbachev pressed.

Yefimov fretted, wringing his hands like a neurotic old man. "The only way is to damage the silo doors so that they won't open. But they are very strong, and the base commander may not have the means. Other than that, we may be able to destroy the missiles after they are launched by bringing in some of the new mobile SA-X-12B's, if we have time."

"Issue the necessary orders immediately," Gorbachev told him.

"Comrade Minister," Ustinov did not use the title *Glavnokomandovaniye*, since he considered himself more qualified to be supreme commander. "We have no proof the United States has actually destroyed Peregrine. If these missiles are going to be launched in any event, we should seize upon the opportunity to launch a pre-emptive strike, and end the cancer which capitalism poses to our way of life once and for all."

Gorbachev ignored Ustinov and spoke directly to Yefimov. "General, how long now before launch?"

Yefimov asked the party on the telephone and waited a few seconds for the answer. "The oxygen transfer is almost complete. We have three minutes."

"What is the status on the silo doors and the SA-X-12B's."

"Four have been rendered inoperable, and they're working on the last one. The SA-X-12B's will not be effective, because we cannot move them close enough to the launch site in the time remaining."

Situation Room, The White House
1908 Saturday, December 24, 1983—Day Sixteen

Casey had just returned to the situation room and informed Reagan that Walters had just confirmed the actual destruction of the Peregrine transmitter. The chief warrant officer, who had been monitoring the hot line, suddenly turned to face President Reagan.

"Mr. President, Minister Gorbachev is on the line. He says it is urgent that he speak with you."

The president moved quickly to the hotline. The president's interpreter listened with mounting alarm on his face as he began to translate Gorbachev's words aloud:

"Mr. President, Secretary Andropov is ill. I have been temporarily named to take his place as commander-in-chief. I must inform you that because of a communications malfunction, several nuclear missiles were prepared for launch without authorization. We took steps to prevent a launch, but we did not completely succeed. Despite everything we could do to prevent it, one missile has been launched. There is now no way that we can stop it. It is targeted for your capital,

Washington. Our monitoring devices tell us it will reach its target twenty-eight minutes from now."

Everyone in the room had just heard that they probably had less than half an hour to live, but the intensity of their concentration and the mood of extreme crisis that they had been living with for the past hours prevented that stark message of doom from sinking in. They were all in a kind of psychic shock, able to grasp reality, but unable to react to it in a normal way.

"Tell him to hold," the president said.

Reagan then turned to Vessey on the Pentagon screen. "General, is there any way in God's world we can stop it?"

"Maybe...NORAD has just reported a missile launch from their Teykovo missile base. That probably means a single warhead SS-11. If you can get them to confirm that and tell us the number of decoys in the array and the approximate position of the warhead within the array, we may have a chance."

Stavka, Outside Moscow, USSR
0609 Sunday, December 25, 1983—Day Seventeen

As Gorbachev repeated the president's questions, Ustinov immediately jumped up. "We cannot give them that information," he shouted, "they will know how to defend against that type of missile if we do."

"General Yefimov, give me the information at once," Gorbachev ordered.

Yefimov spoke hurriedly into the phone, then listened. He looked up to find Ustinov glaring at him as he turned to Gorbachev.

"The missile is an SS-11-Mod. 2, single semi-hardened warhead, thirty-five decoy array," he said. "The warhead is at the front center of the pattern, looking at it from the target."

Of those in the room, only Ustinov knew that Yefimov had been told that the warhead was at the rear of the decoy array.

Situation Room, The White House
1911 Saturday, December 24, 1983—Day Sixteen

Gorbachev quickly passed the information on to Reagan. "Is there anything else you need, Mr. President?"

The president looked at Vessey. The general shook his head.

"No, Mr. Minister. Please hold."

Reagan turned back to Vessey. "General?"

"We have a ballistic missile sub standing by off Thule, Greenland. It was positioned to attempt interception of one of the Soviet satellites with one of its Trident missiles. We can transmit the required coordinates and other data to enable it to launch a missile to intercept the incoming warhead."

"Go! You have my authorization."

Weinberger chose this moment to intervene. "Mr. President, I do not have much faith in what General Vessey is suggesting. Trying to hit a ballistic missile in the middle of its trajectory with another missile is like trying to hit a bullet with another bullet. And even if we get lucky with a near miss, there is no hard evidence that the detonation will destroy the warhead."

"You are correct, sir," General Vessey conceded. "But as you probably recall, before SDI was approved, we were looking into a low-altitude defense system called LoADS, which was based on using nuclear-armed interceptors to destroy either incoming RV's or satellites. Even though it's never been tested, all the procedures for tracking the target and aiming the interceptor are in place. Besides, it's all we've got."

"I guess you're right, Weinberrger conceded. Then, turning to the president, he continued, "We have helicopters standing by to take you and Nancy to Camp David. You can either use the situation room there or move to the alternate command center at Richie, but for God's sake you've got to get out of here."

"You know I can't do that, Cap," Reagan said softly.

Reagan turned to McFarlane. "Is the Vice-President aboard Looking Glass?"

"Yes, Mr. President. We've been in continuous contact with him since he boarded the plane two hours ago. You can talk to him on that phone." McFarlane pointing to one of several that were arrayed before the president.

Before picking up the phone the president glanced around. "Any thoughts on what I should tell him?"

Weinberger immediately responded. "Mr. President, we still don't know whether they have withdrawn the ultimatum. I think we have to at least consider the possibility that the launching of the missile may simply be an elaborate attempt to eliminate the top command here under the guise of an accident, so the Soviets can attempt to impose the ultimatum in the ensuing confusion. Their occupation plans are still proceeding. The troops that were in Cuba are now airborne and headed this way."

The president looked at the others, and when no one volunteered anything else, he picked up the phone to talk to the vice president.

"You've heard everything, George," the president said in a quiet, calm tone. "If the sub is not successful in destroying the warhead, Washington will take a direct hit. Communications from here will probably be lost. I can't advise you other than to tell you to do what you believe is right and is best for the country. For whatever it's worth, I think Gorbachev is sincere in his effort to help us destroy the incoming missile. You will have to make up your own mind." Then, very softly, "And may God be with you."

62

Baffin Bay, off Thule, Greenland
1916 Saturday, December 24, 1983—Day Sixteen

Captain Robbins was worried. The USS Florida SSBN 728 was only the Navy's third Trident submarine. It had been delivered the preceding May, and commissioned in June. It had begun its demonstration and shakedown operation several months before with the Blue Crew, and had been turned over to his Gold Crew in September.

The training of the crew had progressed normally. A few glitches in the ship's electronics and computers had been isolated and corrected. But so far the high point of the shakedown had been the successful launching of an unarmed Trident I (C-4) missile in early October.

The captain's concern did not stem from the caliber of people who made up his crew. They were well qualified and highly motivated, as good as any he had commanded. But individuals need to get to know one another and work together before they become the close-knit crew that can turn a five hundred-sixty foot nuclear-powered submarine into the fighting machine it is built to be.

He had assumed he would have time to do that because the *Florida* was not scheduled to make a strategic deterrent patrol until home-ported in Bremerton, Washington, which would not take place until late spring. But after returning to its temporary home port of Groton, Connecticut, from a sortie into the North Atlantic, fate had made it the only submarine in position to carry out the mission it was now on.

DEFCON III had been declared only hours before, and orders awaited him to proceed to the Naval Weapons Station where the dummy missiles used for training purposes were replaced with nuclear-armed C-4s. There was a separate message for his eyes only, which commanded him to get underway when the transfer was complete, and proceed to Point X-Ray, which was defined as Lat. 76° 33'N., Long. 72° 46'W, (a quick check of the chart showed the point to be in Baffin Bay, off Thule, Greenland), to arrive no later than twelve hundred hours Zulu, December twenty-four.

He was to remain there until in receipt of further orders. There was no indication of what duties would be performed at Point X-Ray, but an indication that it was something out of the ordinary was contained in the closing statement. It informed him that two of the missiles now on board had been modified. Instead of arming themselves as they entered the earth's atmosphere at the end of the mid-course trajectory, these would arm themselves at the end of the boost phase. They were also set up so they could be manually set to detonate anytime thereafter.

Clearly, the assignment was unusual. It was also extraordinarily important. He prayed that his crew would be up to the challenge.

The reports transmitted over the ELF network, and picked up by his trailing wire antenna during the transit period to Point X-Ray, had not been encouraging. And when DEFCON I had been set by the National Command Authority (NCA) Saturday morning, and then followed by the standard "Prepare For War" message, it seemed a nuclear exchange might be only minutes away.

His suspicions seemed confirmed when shortly thereafter COMSUBLANT directed him to be prepared on five minutes notice to launch one of the two modified C-4s to intercept and destroy a Soviet satellite.

The assignment was totally unexpected. Even though Navy planners had long before recognized the potential need to utilize an SLBM in such a manner, and appropriate procedures and drills had been established, no actual tests had ever been conducted. No one had seriously expected a Trident submarine to be drafted to such a purpose, since a single launch might enable an enemy to pinpoint its location and destroy it and all its remaining missiles.

He had now been on station over eight hours, running a box pattern at a speed of twelve knots and holding a depth of two hundred feet. The size of the box only was six-by-six nautical miles since it had been determined by the need to be at its center, Point X-Ray, within five minutes of notification to prepare to launch.

This was not the type of duty the captain of a Trident submarine liked. It made him more vulnerable to discovery and attack than he would have been with unrestricted movement. Also, because he might receive orders to prepare to launch the missile at any time, he had been forced to hold the crew at missile battle stations much longer than he would have preferred.

Add to all of this the uncertainty he felt over whether they had shaken off the Victor I Class Soviet nuclear attack sub, which they had encountered as they approached Davis Strait, between the southern tip of Greenland and Baffin Island.

He guessed it was on an ambush patrol to pick up boats moving up the in-shore route toward the Iceland Channel, and hoped that he might slip in behind it unnoticed since his destination was inland of Greenland rather than to the seaward. As far as he knew, it had worked.

There was no indication the Victor had discovered their presence. His nagging doubt persisted only because his need to arrive at Point X-Ray on time had not allowed him to take all the precautions he normally would have taken to avoid the other sub.

Robbins' thoughts were interrupted by a slight noise outside the vessel. His executive officer appeared. "Captain, we just lost our trailing wire antenna," the XO informed him. "Sonar believes a small fleet of trawlers probably cut it with their screws."

"Deploy the comm buoy, Mr. Hamlett," Robbins replied. "We don't have time to stream another wire."

The comm buoy had only just been deployed when the executive officer broke in again.

"Captain, we've just received a change of orders. We are now directed to prepare a single warhead C-4 for exo-atmospheric interception of a nuclear missile. Intercept coordinates, time setting for detonation, launch time, and authorization codes will be provided in three minutes for execution after a twenty-second countdown."

Captain Robbins felt an adrenaline-charged chill flood through him. This was it. "Acknowledged, Mr. Hamlett. Same launch point?"

"Yes, Sir. We're at a corner of the box. We'll have to go to flank to get there on time."

After checking the navigation plot, the captain turned to the officer of deck. "Mr. Courtland, jettison the comm buoy, change course to one-nine-seven, and proceed at flank speed."

The OOD acknowledged and began to carry out the orders.

Robbins turned to the executive officer. "Any signs of the Victor?"

"No, Sir. Not since we went through the thermocline."

As the Florida turned to the new course, the speed increase brought with it the expected noise of cavitation.

"Well, if he's anywhere around, that racket will bring him out," Robbins observed. "At this speed we should arrive at X-Ray one minute before launch. Number four tube contains the modified missile we've prepared, so we'll use it. Have the weapons officer stand by to enter coordinates and timing. You will verify."

Robbins' thoughts turned to the task facing him. To intercept and destroy a ballistic missile by firing another missile at it from a submarine, or from any other point for that matter, was an extremely long shot.

The target would be anywhere from eight-to twelve-hundred kilometers above the earth's surface and traveling at a speed of about twenty-thousand kilometers per hour, or something over three-hundred kilometers per minute.

At that speed, an error of one second in launch time could result in the detonation taking place either above or below the target by more than ten kilometers. Also, an error of one arc second, i.e., one sixtieth of an arc minute, which in turn is one sixtieth of a degree of arc, would result in a miss of about sixty kilometers. And both errors could be magnified if the submarine were not precisely on the designated launch point at the designated launch depth when the intercept missile was launched.

Failure was very probable, Robbins knew. He wondered what the consequences would be.

Back at navigation, the Captain checked the chronometer and turned to the OOD, "You may reduce speed to one-third, Mr. Courtland. Make turns for four knots. Execute baffle clear and set course of one-nine-seven. Take her up to periscope depth and raise the VHF antenna."

Execution had just been completed when the next message was received. As the weapons officer in the Missile Control entered the coordinates and detonation timing into the number-four-tube control box, the XO verified the numbers and sequence at the launch control console. The authorization to fire was now due, with the order to begin the twenty-second countdown to come shortly thereafter.

Robbins would have preferred to be at the designated launch depth, rather than periscope depth, but since the comm buoy was gone and there was no time to rig another, the extendible VHF antenna mounted in the sail with the periscopes was the only way he could maintain communications with the TACAMO relay.

He had just finished instructing the navigation officer to continue to feed the OOD course and speed adjustments necessary to bring them to the launch point at the required time, when the duty sonar operator picked up an echo:

"Conn-Sonar. New contact, bearing one-seven-eight true. Designation Sierra-One."

Before anyone could acknowledge, the executive officer said, "Captain, transmission of launch authorization codes will begin in ten seconds."

"Very well, Mr. Hamlett."

Robbins took a place at the launch console. After both he and the XO had compared the alpha-numeric sequences with the code sheets taken from their designated red alert pouches, the executive officer, in somewhat awed tones, said, "Sir, I have authentic authorization to launch."

"I also have authentic authorization, Mr. Hamlett."

Robbins turned to the weapons officer. "You may insert your key; we will launch on my command."

The officer of the deck, who had waited patiently for the ritual to be completed, now broke in. "Captain, we have a confirmed contact, designation Sierra-One, at one-seven-nine true. We judge distance to be about fourteen thousand yards. Contact appears to be moving across our bow from left to right slowly, probable course two-nine-zero true. Sound signature indicates it to be the same Victor which we were in contact with earlier."

"Any indication that he's picked us up?"

"Can't tell, sir. But he probably did when we went to flank."

At that moment the communications officer broke in. "You will commence twenty-second countdown in three seconds, three, two, one, mark."

"Lower the antenna, and take her down to designated launch depth, Mr. Courtland," the captain barked.

As the single hand on the large dial above the launch console began to tick off the twenty seconds, all eyes were on the Captain.

"Is the launch check-off procedure complete, Mr. Hamlett?" he asked.

"Launch check-off complete, Captain," Hamlett replied.

Robbins turned to the weapons officer. "We will launch number-four missile on my command."

"Aye aye, Captain."

Again the officer of the deck broke in. "Captain, the Victor is increasing speed and his bearing is now constant. He is on an intercept course."

"Very well, Mr. Courtland."

When the launch count reached fourteen the officer of the deck, urgency unmistakably in his voice for the first time, said, "Sir, the Victor has initiated active sonar and appears to have gone into attack mode. Recommend evasive action and countermeasures."

The absence of the immediate affirmative response such a recommendation ordinarily would have received served only to heighten the tension in the confined area of the sub. Recognizing this, the Captain replied unhurriedly in a tone reflecting a degree of calm he did not feel.

"Hold course and speed, Mr. Courtland. Level off at designated launch depth."

Tension continued to build as the countdown progressed, seeming to take forever as it mingled with the ongoing reports from sonar concerning the approaching Victor.

Everyone present stared, transfixed, at the captain and weapons officer standing at the launch console.

When the count reached two, the captain said, "Prepare to launch."

Both men gripped the keys already inserted in their slots.

"Launch!" Robbins said.

Both keys turned simultaneously. There was a slight tremor, accompanied by what sounded like a muffled thump as the small rocket launch motor ignited and pushed the C-4 out of the tube. The Weapons Officer confirmed a launch and reported the hatch to number-four tube secure.

"I have the conn, Mr. Courtland," Robbins said, moving to a position behind the helmsman. "Ahead flank. Right full rudder. Steady on course zero-one-zero."

He knew the captain of the Victor would hear the sound of the missile being launched and would immediately know what had happened and assume hostilities had commenced. His immediate response would be to launch torpedoes to prevent any further missile launchings.

Speed was now critical.

As the Florida heeled to the turn and began to accelerate, the sonar operator sang out, "Con-Sonar. Sierra-One just launched a spread of four torpedoes."

"Steady on course zero-one-zero," the helmsman said.

"Very well. Slow to standard, and execute baffle clear. Twenty degrees down bubble. Level off at eight-hundred feet."

As the bow began to point downward, the Captain added, "You may execute counter measures, Mr. Courtland. He's stretching his range a bit, so the noise makers and the knuckle produced by that turn ought to take care of those babies."

The *Florida* had just leveled off at the designated depth when the OOD broke into the captain's thoughts. "Sir, we were one-hundred-five feet short of designated launch depth at time of launch."

63

Situation Room, The White House, Washington, DC
1923 Saturday, December 24, 1983—Day Sixteen

"Mr. President, the *Florida* has confirmed launch. Detonation of the intercept missile should take place three minutes and forty-four seconds from now," General Vessey intoned from the Pentagon Command Center screen in the Situation room.

"How long before we know whether it succeeded, General?" Reagan asked.

"We may not know until seconds before the warhead is due to impact, Mr. President. The intercept missile fired by the Florida has no homing capability, so we used target coordinates and time settings computed to bring it close enough to the anticipated position of the incoming warhead so that detonation of our warhead would disrupt it. But as you know, this has never been done before, and the odds are against success. When our warhead detonates, we'll be able to tell whether it took out any of the incoming objects now appearing on the PAWS display. But unless it destroys all of them, which is not likely, we won't know whether it took out the warhead or only decoys until what's left enters the earth's atmosphere. The decoys will burn up; the warhead will not."

The secretary of defense broke in. "Mr. President, I think at the very least, you should instruct the vice president that if the Soviet missile destroys Washington he should launch one targeted for Moscow."

Secretary of State Shultz immediately objected. "Mr. President, I disagree! If we are sincere in our desire to find a way out of the confrontation, then I think playing nuclear tit-for-tat is not the way to show it. It may well escalate this right back to the ultimate showdown we're trying to avoid."

Weinberger was not convinced. "Yes, but if that warhead detonates over the Pentagon you're talking about two-plus million immediate casualties, and many more later. And our failure to retaliate could lead them to believe that we will bow to any ultimatum rather than risk a nuclear exchange."

"How many millions of Soviet casualties will it take to satisfy you?" Shultz asked, heatedly.

Baker interceded. "Before we make a decision which could have catastrophic consequences, Mr. President, shouldn't we see where Gorbachev stands? We're too close to bringing sanity back to the world to risk it all simply to retaliate."

Before Reagan could answer, General Vessey, still on the Command Center screen, interrupted. "Mr. President, we expect detonation of Florida's missile in ten seconds. Countdown to start at five."

At the sound of "Five," all eyes turned to the PAWS relay screen in the Situation Room. Breathing seemed to stop as the words followed one another: "Four, three, two, one, mark, minus one, detonation, about one and one-half seconds late."

The president looked at the Command Center screen and said, "General?"

"Word just coming in from NORAD, Mr. President." Vessey paused, and then continued, "The delay in detonation did not prevent the C-4 from destroying some of the incoming objects. NORAD confirms that half of the objects no longer appear on the PAWS screen. Unfortunately, due to the delay in detonation, the objects which were destroyed were to the rear of the array rather than the front where the warhead is supposed to be. If the information they gave us was correct, it would seem our intercept may not have been successful."

"How long before we will know?"

"Six minutes and fifty-six seconds, sir."

Turning to the duty communications officer, the president ordered, "Open the line to Gorbachev."

After several moments, the communications officer turned to Reagan. "Minister Gorbachev is on the line, Sir."

"Mr. Gorbachev," the president said, "I am sorry Secretary Andropov is ill, but time is running out, and we need to know your decision on the ultimatum. I'm sure you know that regardless of what this missile may do, the balance of power has been restored, and we are now assured that both countries, if not the world, will be destroyed if a nuclear strike is launched."

"Mr. President, speaking for the head of our government, who is also our supreme military commander, I can assure you that the basis for the ultimatum is no longer valid, and orders will immediately be issued to that effect. All our forces will be recalled, and the military will stand down. Can you tell me whether your efforts to destroy our missile were effective?"

"I'm sure you can tell from your own display that we were successful in destroying at least some of the objects which appeared there, but we do not know whether the warhead was among them. Therefore, we will not know for several more minutes whether Washington will be destroyed or spared."

Reagan paused for a moment. "I am sure you will understand when I say that even though the ultimatum has been withdrawn, I am under immense pressure to issue orders to retaliate by targeting Moscow in the event Washington is destroyed."

"Mr. President, I do not know what will happen if there is retaliation. All I can say is that I will do my utmost to prevent the matter from going any further. I do not wish my country to be destroyed any more than yours."

"I understand, Mr. Minister. A person who makes a decision to do otherwise must be prepared to live with it forever. If we have not destroyed the warhead, it is likely I will not be in a position to make a decision, but I am sure the vice president understands your commitment."

As Reagan turned to look at the PAWS screen, General Vessey broke in jubilantly. "Mr. President, the *Florida* succeeded. All of the remaining objects were decoys. They just burned up."

Epilogue

US. Naval Hospital, Bethesda, Maryland
0930 Thursday, December 29 1983—Day Twenty-nine

"You lost a very large amount of blood, you have not yet recovered, and it is much too soon for you to leave." The very attractive but stern lieutenant commander in a nurse's uniform had argued her point several times before with no more effect than it was having now.

Hollis smiled benignly. "If you keep me here any longer you'll spoil me, and then you won't be able to get rid of me. I'm getting out while I've got a good excuse."

He was doing his best to hide his impatience. He was ready to leave. The debriefing sessions were making his stay very tedious, even though Maggie had unlimited visiting privileges. He had been assured his wounds had not resulted in any permanent injury. Only two of the bullets Maxsimov fired at him found their mark, one piercing his shoulder just outside his flack jacket, the other creasing the side of his head. Neither did extensive damage, but the bleeding caused by the shoulder wound had been difficult to stop. Without a helicopter to ferry him to the hospital, he might not have survived.

He finished tying his shoe laces and started to get up. The lightheadedness that followed called attention unmistakably to the fact that while his body was mending rapidly, he was still weaker than he felt.

The lieutenant commander maneuvered Hollis into the wheelchair, customarily used when discharging patients, by agreeing that when they reached the main level she would let him walk into the hospital lobby.

As they left the room, they were joined by the captain who had attended Hollis after he had been flown from San Francisco to Andrews and then brought to Bethesda. Maggie and Paul were waiting in the lobby as they left the elevator. The doctor went directly to Maggie. "He's so hardheaded about getting out of here I've quit arguing with him," he said, with a grin. "But I think you should keep him quiet and bring him back here in three or four days. Unless something develops between now and then, I think we can give him a complete discharge then."

Maggie took Jeff by the arm and smiled. "Thanks for taking such good care of him, doctor. I promise I'll bring him back."

"Welcome in from the cold, Jeff." It was Paul Montague. He wanted to take the other arm to help Hollis to the waiting limousine, but he knew better. "For an ex-CIA spook you're not doing too badly," he chuckled. "That's the secretary's limo. He insisted I use it to pick you up. He'll meet us at the White House."

"Is Chuck going to be there?" he asked, as they settled into the back of the limousine.

"No," Montague replied. "The president called him personally, but he wouldn't come. He told me to tell you that Peregrine was your project, and he was glad that he was able to help."

Hollis shook his head. "Able to help? Hell, without him I would never have made it."

"I know, but he still wouldn't come."

The three passengers fell silent for a moment.

"I guess I shouldn't even ask the question, Paul, but Jeff has refused to discuss it with me," Maggie began, tentatively.

"That's all right, Maggie," Paul replied, softly. "What do you want to know?"

"I never could understand why you, of all people, were so willing to believe that Jeff was guilty."

"That's not an easy question to answer," he replied. He looked out of the window for several moments before he elaborated. "But I'll try. When

Viktor determined he had to get Jeff out of the way he sent him a copy of a memo relating to the unofficial Peregrine and then arranged for Sergei to steal it from his brief case in order to raise a question as to his credibility, so he would have an excuse to run a security check on him. The information he brought in, although mostly fabricated, was damning. We believe his intent was always to have Jeff killed, but if he discredited him first there would be little question raised about his death.

"Even though it was difficult to believe that someone with Jeff's record could be guilty of espionage, we had no choice but to take action based on what we saw. Also, since the CIA had became convinced that Operation *Maskirovka* was real and somehow involved neutralization of our nuclear first-strike capability, we concluded this could be true only if the Soviets had somehow penetrated the department, at a very high level. But, prior to Viktor implicating Jeff, we had no suspects, no leads, nothing we could take to the FBI. And not knowing who the mole might be, starting any sort of official investigation could have alerted him.

"Time was short, and we were making no progress, so the evidence against Jeff suddenly seemed like the answer. If he was guilty, so be it. If he wasn't, he had the training and background best suited not only for protecting himself, but for forcing the real mole to surface. Also, if Jeff wasn't the mole, taking the position that we believed he was might encourage the real mole to take actions which would expose him. So even though some of us personally thought and hoped Jeff was not guilty, we decided that acting as though he was might bring the matter to a head."

"I guess I can understand that," Maggie said. "I'm sure you know that for a while we both suspected you of being the mole."

Paul smiled. "Yes, I can understand why you would. Appearances can be quite deceiving, which, with hindsight, is the real mistake I made. I believed that a long-time DOD career employee with an unblemished record was above suspicion, when as it turned out, he should have been at the top of the list of suspects. He was the one with the knowledge and contacts to run an off-the-books unofficial project, as well as the know-how and resources to frame a high-level employee."

"I still don't know who Viktor is," Maggie said.

"It was Dawson," Hollis volunteered.

Maggie was surprised. She had not known Dawson well, and she had not suspected him. "Why would Dawson do such a thing?"

"We may never have all the answers, but we do know now that he was a deep-cover agent who was recruited at a very early age. We had no reason to suspect him."

"But, why couldn't you find out what Peregrine was?" Maggie asked, still troubled. "Wouldn't that have exonerated Jeff?"

"So far as anyone knew, other than Dawson," Hollis explained, "the Peregrine I was trying to track down didn't exist. I was the only one who saw the memo, and when the copy was stolen from my briefcase I had no way to prove I had even seen it. And since there was an official Peregrine project which had nothing to do with what I had discovered, everyone thought I was simply raising a smoke screen."

"Well, at least some people did," Paul said. "One bit of divine assistance we received was the delivery of your letter to Al Walters. Up until that point, both he and the DCI were unaware of Peregrine. That started the wheels turning so that when Jeff called Walters, Walters decided to talk to Casey rather than pass the info on to Dawson as protocol demanded. Had Walters called Dawson, it's unlikely we would be sitting here discussing this today.

"Dawson, who up to this point had played his cards to perfection, then made his first and only mistake. Shortly after he found out about your letter, Clarke was eliminated. That confirmed to me that Dawson was the mole even though I couldn't prove it. Fortunately, even with Clarke gone, Walters knew enough so that he and Griffin could find out from the people at Intertel what they had to know about Peregrine to put the rescue party together. And you know the rest."

Maggie shook her head. "You said Dawson *was*. What happened to him?"

Montague shrugged. "We're not exactly sure. I didn't have time to set up an adequate tail without arousing his suspicions, so after Clarke was killed, I had several of our top CID investigators positioned so that if he left Buzzards Point they would inform me. Either he was tipped off or his assignment was complete. He gave our people the slip and disappeared.

"We found out later he went to the Soviet embassy and asked for political asylum at about the time the ultimatum was delivered to the White House. We don't know specifically what happened after that. But on Monday we learned that he had suffered a heart attack and died before their medical staff could do anything to save him. They have already surrendered his remains to his next of kin, and his relatives have already had his remains cremated, so we'll never know whether he really had a heart attack or whether they used one of their exotic potions to get rid of him. After all, had he lived, he would have been an acute embarrassment to them."

Oval Office, White House, Washington, DC
1000 Thursday, December 29, 1983—Day Twenty-nine

As they were ushered into the Oval Office at the White House, Hollis found he was more impressed than he thought he would be. The President was just as unpretentious and real in person as the media image of him waving to people as he crossed the White House lawn to board a helicopter for Camp David suggested.

Hollis knew that the strain the president had been under for the last two weeks must have been unbearable, but there were no signs of any lingering after-effects. If anything, both Secretary Weinberger and DCI Casey showed more of the ravages of the crisis than did the president, who was as ebullient and charming as ever.

Reagan and the others rose as Paul ushered Maggie and Hollis into the Oval Office. After finding seats for everyone and offering coffee, the president found a chair within the circle of his guests. "May I call you Jeff?"

"Please do, Mr. President." Hollis nodded.

The president smiled and continued, "It is very important to me to tell you personally, Jeff, that our country owes you a debt of gratitude that can never be repaid. Operation *Maskirovka* and Peregrine, if successful, would have meant the end of our way of life and much of the world as we know it for generations and maybe forever. That they did not succeed is a tribute to your unswerving loyalty and perseverance under the most trying of circumstances." He paused, "It's an honor to all of us to have you here to recognize what you did for your country."

"Thank you, Mr. President. It's an honor to be here."

"Jeff," the president said, "the highest honor which I may bestow upon a civilian is the Medal of Freedom. And there is no doubt that you have earned it many times over. Unfortunately, if I did, it would become a matter of record, and the reasons would become known. This we cannot permit. Even though the world is vaguely aware of our confrontation with the Soviets, very few know of Operation *Maskirovka,* Peregrine, or the ultimatum—and as part of the agreement to stand down we promised not to divulge the information. Therefore, I can only tell you how proud and honored I am to be able to offer my heartfelt thanks for a degree of loyalty, and for actions far beyond a simple call of duty. I wish there were some reward that I could offer you."

The President stood and offered his hand to Hollis.

"Merely being invited to come here is more than adequate, Mr. President," Hollis replied, taking Reagan's hand. "I'm sure you know, however, that there are several who deserve more credit than me. Maggie, here, and Chuck Crowley-and Professor Lipscomb and Karen Brewster, who both whom lost their lives helping me. They deserve the real honor and the real gratitude."

Reagan nodded somberly. "I understand, and I hope that at some time in the future, when there is no longer a cold war or a powerful and dangerous enemy like the Soviet Union to worry about, that their contribution will become part of the historic record."

The President, feeling a little awkward sharing such deep emotions, changed the subject. "I hope your wounds are healing properly, Jeff."

"They are, Mr. President. But next time I think I'll let the Marines do it without me."

The President turned to Maggie and smiled. "I understand you're planning a trip once you get Jeff out of the doctors' clutches?"

Maggie blushed as she returned the smile. "Yes. I proposed, and Jeff accepted. We're getting married in the Pentagon Chapel this afternoon and his boss has been kind enough to give him some time off so we can take the honeymoon we missed the first time around.

"I can't tell you how happy and how fortunate I am, Mr. President. I guess I didn't realize that there are people who are frightened by democracy and will try to take it away from us unless we're willing to defend it. I know now that Jeff, like yourself, is one of those who understands and will fight to preserve it. I feel as though I've been given a second chance I didn't deserve."

With all the charm for which he was so famous, the president said, "Nonsense! From what I heard, if you hadn't bailed these two heroes out when they were being readied for execution, none of us would be here."

Hollis took Maggie's hand and pressed it in his own. "She's always been there when she was needed, Mr. President. I'm the one getting the second chance."

After all of his guests except Weinberger had left, the president said, "I wonder what Andropov's response will be to the letter I wrote on the twenty-fourth, after it was all over. I tried to make it clear to him that I was sincere in my suggestion to negotiate removal of the Pershings and cruise missiles from Europe."

"I don't know," Weinberger replied, "but I doubt there'll be any change in their position until there is a change in their government."

Weinberger stroked his chin thoughtfully. "You know, I sort of hope that Gorbachev will replace Andropov when the time comes. He seems like someone we could do business with."

"I think you're probably right. I've wondered several times whether Andropov really did become too sick to retain control."

"What do you mean?" Weinberger asked.

"Well, it's just possible he might have painted himself into a corner and passing the ball to Gorbachev was the only way he could get out."

"You could be right," Reagan nodded

The Secretary of Defense rose to leave. "Just between you and me, Mr. President, I was never quite sure what you would have done if the ultimatum had not been withdrawn."

Reagan leaned back in his chair and folded his fingers together behind his head as his eyes took on a mischievous look and his little crooked half smile appeared. "You know, if nothing else, I guess this proves we were right all along about SDI."

Weinberger paused momentarily perplexed. Then, he too smiled as he realized that was all the answer he was going to get.

Author's Note

Operation *Maskirovka* and the Peregrine memorandum are, of course, fiction, but the setting in which they were placed is history. At no time since the Cuban missile crisis were the US and the USSR closer to nuclear confrontation.

On December 26, 1983, following the events upon which the story is based, Chernenko and Ustinov, with the help of Prime Minister Tikhonov, thwarted an attempt by Andropov, to inform a central committee plenum of his desire that Gorbachev succeed him. And, when Andropov died six weeks later, on February 9, 1984, they engineered Chernenko's succession to general secretary. Thus, even though the governments of both countries took steps in early 1984 to move away from the brink of war, with the old guard hard-liners still firmly in control, the relationship between the two countries did not improve.

In late December, 1984, one year after the crisis, Ustinov died to be followed on March 10 by Chernenko. Two days later, with the backing of Gromyko, Gorbachev was named general secretary. In late April Gorbachev made KGB Chairman Chebrikov a full member of the Politburo while at the same time ousting Romanov who subsequently disappeared.

Perestroika, glasnost, the signing of the INF. Treaty, the unsuccessful attempt by the hard-liners to unseat Gorbachev, the collapse of the communist party, and the dissolution of the Soviet empire, all are now history. There is little doubt that President Reagan's insistence, in the face of Soviet intransigence, on rebuilding the military, deployment of the Pershing II intermediate range missiles in Western Europe and his introduction of the Strategic Defense Initiative brought the two nations to the brink of war. However, his real legacy to the country is not only that these same actions made the world a much safer place by providing the main catalyst for the fall of the Soviet empire, but, also, the recognition that nuclear armed ballistic missiles will become obsolete as weapons of destruction only when there is a viable defense against them.

A final note. Since the setting is so important to the story, I chose to use the names of historical figures. Insofar as research permitted, I attempted to capture the character of President Reagan, Secretary of State Shultz, Secretary of Defense Weinberger, CIA Director Casey, and National Security Adviser McFarlane. If I did not succeed, I apologize. I have nothing but the greatest admiration and respect for each, and nothing herein is intended in any way to cast aspersions on, or denigrate any of them. I think the country was indeed fortunate to have a team as well qualified as they, in place at this particular point in our history. The world will long be well served by their unwillingness to compromise principle with expediency.

About the Author

Upon graduating from Kings Point, John Dowdle entered the University of South Carolina where he earned an Bachelor of Law degree. After serving during the Korean War as a Lieutenant USNR, he attended Georgetown University School of Law where he earned a Masters Degree and his Doctorate. He was employed as a trial attorney in the Chief Counsel's office, Internal Revenue Service, Washington, DC, until he joined RJR Nabisco in Winston-Salem, NC, from which he retired as senior vice president, Financial Services.